Dear George, Dear Mary

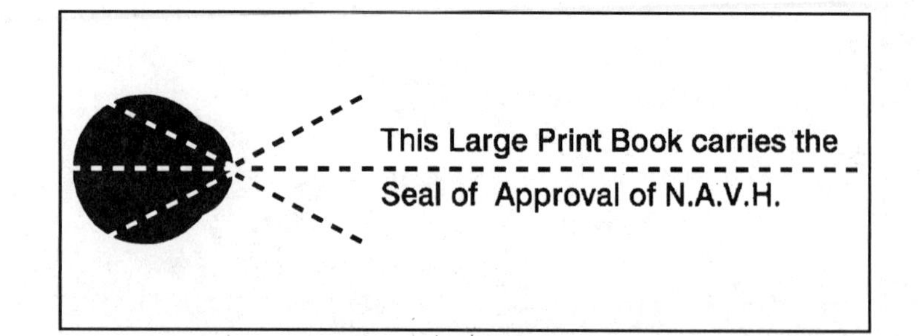
This Large Print Book carries the
Seal of Approval of N.A.V.H.

Dear George, Dear Mary

Mary Calvi

THORNDIKE PRESS
A part of Gale, a Cengage Company

Farmington Hills, Mich • San Francisco • New York • Waterville, Maine
Meriden, Conn • Mason, Ohio • Chicago

Illustration on page 13: *Philipse Manor Hall,* unknown artist "D.R." Probably New York, post-1783, ink wash on paper. Gift of La Duchesse de Talleyrand. Historic Hudson Valley, Pocantico Hills, New York (PM.65.866).

Thorndike Press, a part of Gale, a Cengage Company.

Thorndike Press® Large Print Historical Fiction.

The text of this Large Print edition is unabridged.

Other aspects of the book may vary from the original edition.

Set in 16 pt. Plantin.

LIBRARY OF CONGRESS CIP DATA ON FILE.
CATALOGUING IN PUBLICATION FOR THIS BOOK
IS AVAILABLE FROM THE LIBRARY OF CONGRESS

ISBN-13: 978-1-4328-6545-0 (hardcover alk. paper)

Published in 2019 by arrangement with Macmillan Publishing Group, LLC/St. Martin's Press

Printed in the United States of America
1 2 3 4 5 6 7 23 22 21 20 19

To my husband, my children, my family, and our hometown

CONTENTS

PART III: THE DECEPTION

PART IV: THE REPRISAL

NOTE TO THE READER

As a journalist, I search for untold stories. I never would have imagined I'd find one hidden away for centuries in my hometown. This novel has been crafted from thousands of letters, journal entries, witness accounts, publications, and other sources related to George Washington, Mary Eliza Philipse, and historical figures, known and unknown to the modern-day public, who influenced their world and the birth of a nation in the eighteenth century. Maybe history wanted their romance hidden. I do not know. What I do know is that during my research in libraries, museums, church basements, and through digital archives, document after document pieced together like a puzzle until I was awestruck by the theory it revealed. Throughout, I've used the written or spoken words of Washington and those figures whose records have been preserved. I chose to present Mary and George's story as a novel rather than nonfiction because, despite relying on historical documents, I wanted to write what captivated me most: imagining their lives and picturing the lives and habits of real flesh-and-blood young Americans in the 1700s.

A person can live or die,
no matter the breath on one's lips.

A person can be rich or poor,
no matter the pence in one's pocket.

A person can love or hate,
no matter the devotion within
one's heart.

A person can be hero or traitor, no
matter the will of one's mind.

On the 14th of February, 1756,
no matter the choice,
destiny became sealed as if
etched into metal.

Part I
The Encounter

Chapter One: Guardian's Wall

Love is said to be an involuntary passion and it is therefore contended that it cannot be resisted.

— GEORGE WASHINGTON

Yonkers-on-Hudson
February 14, 1756

Mary Eliza lay upon cold leaves whose color had washed away a season ago, wishing she could bring back the living. Dead things surrounded her; every flower bud hung shriveled. The dull winter had brought only a few flakes. Spring, when fragrance emerged from its cocoon, was her favorite time of year. That was not this time. Today nature emitted not even a scent to smell.

Wan light peeked through the dark cloud hovering above her. She'd been here at Hudson's Hook since sunrise, writing poetry in her head:

Here I lie,
As mine eyes, my heart, wait,
So close art thou and I.
Here I lie,
Where the ravens fly,
And the guardian's wall, my gate.
Here I lie,
As mine eyes, my heart, wait.

The gallop of approaching stallions echoed. She attempted to rise, but alas, guilt confined her limbs like a fetter. The horses halted. She knew who had arrived. Boots crunching across hardened grasses came next. His silly chain clinked louder as he drew closer. She expected her brother to holler. She assumed that was coming. Instead, he just stood there, glaring at her. His murmuring sounded as if impatience was boiling in a kettle.

A long silence followed. She heard another audible exhalation from him. Frederick lay down, leaving just inches between them. "Polly." He never used her birth name. "I have a great inclination to take you back by force!" Agitation combined with steam in his threat.

She added a few more inches between them.

A deep groan released from his lips. His

body shifted sideways. "This trial of my patience . . . ends now." He spoke through teeth clenched.

She didn't respond. What would she even say? Worrying thoughts had taken up much of the space in her head, for no ordinary winter's day was before them. This night, as the sun found its repose, the Philipse family would welcome the hero of the South to a grand banquet and pleasure ball with beaux dressed in princely garments and belles adorned in royal costumes. For most hosts, it would be reason for celebration. For Mary, it was reason for tumult. In the midst of such crowds, the noisomeness of hair powder lingered like a fog, bringing back the image that forever haunted her: the little boy's eyes filled with horror, filled with fear. The memory caused her to cringe.

She would rather have remained here with her disquiet fading into the season's emptiness. But with her brother about to snatch her from her stillness, she closed her eyes and repeated to herself the words she promised Papa she would say each day: You are capable of the impossible, for you have survived the unthinkable.

Slowly, she rose and retied her riding dress's silk sash into a proper bow. Throughout, she envisioned the man of honor of the evening, the most celebrated colonel of the colonies, riding more than five hundred miles to be in attendance. His name was George Washington.

The trip back to the manor was quiet, except for the clank of the chain Frederick was wearing. Then he began lecturing her. "Two hundred and twenty of the highest-ranking citizens will converge on our home, each of them viewing each of us, including you, Polly."

Mary could not even acknowledge him, not with the confusion of emotions affecting her spirit. Certainly she would want to meet the hero. She already knew more about Colonel Washington than she was comfortable talking about. He was a brave one, unlike her. But the number of guests — 220 — it sat like a weight upon her chest.

If she made the decision, she would be riding Willoughby back to the Yonkers manor. This four-wheeled, horse-drawn, covered carriage was the kind people of quality rode in, always moving at a leisurely pace to make the journey comfortable. She didn't need comfort. She needed air.

The carriage was conveying them along the dirt roads that belonged to her and Frederick and their sister Susannah. Theirs was an immense treasure of land along the Hudson River, stretching from the center of Manhattan Island to parts north in the Highlands, 390 square miles in total. As she looked upon it now, she could see only winter's barrenness instead of a season of torpid inaction when even love's embrace could not force a flower's bloom out of a dormant state.

Mary's brother waved to the elderly fellow with a pile of white hair upon his face and head who was keeping order at the bridge they needed to cross. Other travelers, including farmers with livestock and merchants with their wagons full of goods, formed a long, chaotic line. But the Philipses never needed to wait nor pay the three-pence toll, unlike every other man or animal to cross. They had inherited this, too — a toll bridge twenty-four feet in width, with a draw, the first and only link connecting the metropolis to the mainland. They called it King's Bridge. The franchise had been granted to their great-grandfather by British charter.

Frederick turned back to her and bumped upward as they crossed over the bridge's wooden planks, "As for your attendance, Polly, what is your answer?"

Mary attempted to sit up straight. "You

summon these men to our home, Frederick, and expect I should open the door to let a stranger in."

"You speak as if I've brought commoners."

"You are well aware that titles are of no consequence to me."

"Do you not realize who *you* are?"

"I am a woman who knows a good fortune does not necessitate the yearning for a husband." She tried to keep her head from bouncing up and down.

"These are accomplished men. The sheriff is a fine gentleman with a superior estate."

Mary had to cover her mouth, for the beginning of a giggle almost came from her lips. The previous attempt at a suitor left Frederick waiting alone with the sheriff for nearly an entire teatime.

"Colonel Washington is trekking from Virginia on horseback to be here!" Frederick's nostrils flared when he raised his voice to her. "Polly, you will attend!"

"Will you be wearing this accoutrement about your neck?" She pointed to the ridiculous pendant she knew he enjoyed displaying.

Frederick's eyes shifted down. "Do you not like it?" The hefty gold chain with a jeweled badge signified his role as Keeper of the Deer Forests. The ancestral office had been passed down through generations of the Philipses.

Mary only shrugged.

They arrived at Philipse Manor. The Georgian-style mansion, covered in brick and accented with ivory moldings, was the most exquisite example of refinement that could be found anywhere in the colony. It overlooked the immense Hudson River and provided a view of the Palisades' earth formation, cliffs across the water that appeared as outstretched hands reaching for the heavens. A guardian's wall is how she thought of it. She often wished she could climb to the top and embrace those who had been taken too soon.

She was glad of the weather's crispness as she exited the carriage, for she was in desperate need of cooling off. The moment Mary entered the manor, she smelled its warmth. Baking. Fresh loaves. Bread made her mouth water.

Up the grand staircase she went and entered her bedchamber that had not changed her entire life. A gilded four-poster bed with a lofty canopy sat opposite a hearth framed with blue-and-white Delft tiles. An intricately carved desk and chair paired with a massively sized bookcase climbing high to the ceiling. A tall mahogany chest took up another wall. In the closet hid a space for washing.

The morning's muted rays made the silver softly sparkle on the wall's ornate fabric covering and cast faint shadows through silk draperies over the dark wood floor. The abigails rushed over to help Mary remove her riding clothes, until she was dressed in only a laced shift. A gaze at her reflection in a mosaic-framed mirror showed a figure that looked every bit of a woman, yet acted as an awkward lassie. Poise had never been her forte. If she brought back her shoulders, that might do it, but it didn't feel quite right, as if she was pretending to be regal when she was really just Mary Eliza. Beautiful? Others had described her as such. Her sister Susannah — yes, she was definitively beautiful. Many admired her for her fair skin, her hair of light amber waves, and her feet; she had the prettiest little feet. Susannah carried herself with natural grace.

As for Mary, she was of a shy disposition when surrounded by strangers in dressy clothing. Guests weren't fond of reticence. They responded to cheerfulness, to vivaciousness. They adored the social adroitness of Susannah, who spoke of all that was in vogue.

After the lady's maids departed, Mary practiced smiling. She had to rely on the art of distraction; a dimple formed on her right cheek, providing a diversion when she had little to say. Tonight would be one of those times when she most missed her younger sister. The white plague slowly robbed Margaret of her vitality, until there was nothing left. Margaret was the free one, a madcap, the one who laughed her way through any crowd encircling Mary, taking her far from the frenzy. With Margaret now gone, Mary felt even more trepidation, imagining the crush of people who would enter the house, especially the presence of one of them. She did not like to think about him, and worked to banish him from her thoughts. At the last banquet she attended, he pointed his deformed finger at her and whispered something that nearly made her collapse: "As goes the mother, so, too, the daughter."

The sound of a horn interrupted her thinking. One long sound was followed by a pause, and proceeded by two in quicker succession. She practically leapt toward the window overlooking the river. The usual disturbance tried to make its way into her being, as it did each time she looked out over the Hudson. She needed to put that aside now. She breathed in deeply and exhaled, leaving a cloud on the pane of glass. The water was tranquil, the sole movement coming from the ship with its lofty white sails carrying it toward the family's dock. With her ear to the chilled window, she listened. The horn of the vessel sounded again — one slow, two fast. This was the signal she had waited weeks to hear. With a squint, she could see sea captain Garvan Rous at the wheel of the *Gabriel.*

Mary had little time to fuss. She was too anxious to learn the particulars. She raced to her high mahogany chest and pulled out a woolen Brunswick. She felt its heaviness when she placed it over herself. She quickly picked a ruffled cap from her collection. Slipping on her burgundy walking shoes, she rushed down the stairwell and into the kitchen. As she moved, she set her loose chestnut-brown hair under the head covering.

Mary grabbed the basket she had asked to have prepared. She counted six glass jars, five of them containing pickled ingredients: fennel, onion, white plums, lemons, and walnuts. A jar of twenty-year catsup was filled to the brim. In the center of the jars was a silver spoon. She placed above the jars a steaming loaf that was a bit too hot to the touch. The delicious aroma excited her appetite. She knocked her hip against the back door to open it and moved as quickly as possible onto the porch, pinching her cheeks with her available hand as she went. Through the boxwood-lined gardens and down the stone path she went, dashing toward the family's dock at the Hudson River's edge, arriving just as the vessel was being secured.

"A miracle, Mary!" cheered Captain Garvan as he tucked his rumpled white linen shirt into his breeches. "A miracle has happened!"

She hurried faster, while carefully keeping her shoes from slipping off the path and into the mud nearest the dock. She put the basket down on the wooden planks. "Tell me! Tell me!"

Swiftly, he moved to greet her. His days at sea were apparent from his bronzed skin and sun-weathered wavy hair. "He is alive, Mary! My son lives . . . because of *you.*" He enveloped her in an embrace that wrapped her in the essence of an ocean breeze.

Elation poured over Mary. Concern for the child had given her such worry.

"He even took a step on his own without my help." His eyes became watered. "The apothecary you sent to my home, Mary, he saved my boy's life. What you have done for me . . ."

"Your wife would have been proud of all you have accomplished with him."

"I wish she could have lived to see him. . . ." He took some time before continuing. "She would have loved his great flop of golden hair." A tear trailed down his cheek.

Mary stepped back and held his hands in hers. "He will make a fine mariner, your William Rous, just like his father and his father before him."

She made the prediction with confidence, knowing full well the fabric of which Rous men were made. It was a confidence established when she was just a child. Captain Garvan, then a lad in his teenage years, swept her right out of death's door.

That evening, one cloaked in a deep red sunset, Mary's world went dark. In the midst of a refined affair at the manor, a fright came over the little girl, causing her to run as fast as she could. She found herself outside, alone on the south porch, steps away from the smaller Neperhan River, which flowed into the Hudson. She was not by herself for long that evening. Young Elbert Peck came to ease her worry, walking out of his cottage that sat near the mansion on the property. He was the head gardener's son, a playful, freckle-cheeked boy with ginger hair always in disarray.

Elbert's head tilted. "Are you crying?"

She could not answer. Her hands covered a face full of tears.

"I will show you something. It will make you happy." Elbert started to skip in the direction of the river. "I shall get it for you by the water."

"No, Elbert. Mama says it is dangerous by the river."

But Elbert had already begun to run along the garden path.

"No. No, Elbert." Mary started after him. She cried out, "Mama says no! Mama says no!"

She reached him at the water's edge just as he picked a stem of forget-me-nots.

"They are the color of your dress." His stance became wobbly as he stretched his arm to hand the flowers to her. "They are blue." His little black shoe was covered in mud. She knew Mama wouldn't like that. No, Mama wouldn't like muddy shoes. She stood still, not moving an inch. He reached farther toward her, trying to keep his balance to give her the blossoms, but the slippery earth forced him down. His body shifted ever nearer to the ancient, unyielding river. Mary lurched forward, her shoes now sinking into the mud. Her little hand got ahold of his, and she began to cry out as his body made a splash. His green eyes turned toward the unstoppable waters behind him. Then he stared back at her.

Without words, she knew; in his eyes, she saw desperation and terror.

Despite using every ounce of her strength, she could not bring him close enough to grab hold of the long grasses that lined the bank. Her right hand held on as mightily as she could to his right hand, which still held the flowers. Her wee voice yelled out for help. A wave pulled him, plunging Elbert under the water. Refusing to let him go, she, too, went into the river.

The current moved her to and fro. She could no longer feel Elbert's hand in hers. As Mary frantically threw her head back to find breath, she caught a glimpse of Mama; Mama was coming. She looked scared.

"I am here!" Lady Joanna did not stop at the shoreline. "I am coming for you!"

Mary's heart screamed out — *It is dangerous, Mama.*

Mama's red dress with the pretty flowers spread out wide as she jumped into the water and tried to swim toward Mary. Mary could see her getting closer, calling out to her.

It was dark.

A chill overtook her body.

She was cold, so very cold.

Then all she could see was light.

As if heaven wrapped her in its embrace, Mary felt strong arms lift her from a wet grave. Cradled to a young man's chest, she could hear a voice commanding, "Breathe, child. Breathe." She remained in this angel's arms, bundled in a quilted blanket embroidered with blue flowers. Her hand held tightly to wilted forget-me-nots as pandemonium swirled around them.

She watched as they carried Mama out of the river with her pretty red dress dragging upon the ground. Papa laid her mother's body on the porch. Lantern light shone upon her pale face. Mary saw her father's hands tremble. He was crying.

Papa placed a kiss upon the forehead and closed its eyes.

Mary's anguish over the loss never ceased. Why did they perish? Why did she survive? Why didn't she immediately reach for the flowers? If only she had held on tighter to little Elbert's hand.

Though years passed, the trauma never left her. With certainty, though, she knew what she needed to do. Papa helped her find her purpose. "Protect. Save. As a beacon in the darkness, be the light," he told her. Every year on the anniversary of that fateful day, he would take her to light a tall lantern at Hudson's Hook.

Now a woman, Mary stood here near the shore. The lad who rescued her a grown man, Captain Garvan gave her a quick peck on the forehead. "I am forever in your service, my dear Mary."

"As I am in yours."

As the two spoke, the sailors transferred crates aplenty of goods and liquors from the *Gabriel* to the dock.

"They have not much time. Hasten your walk!" He pointed his men toward the cases of Madeira. His face turned back to Mary's. "This man they call a hero — I understand he arrives here this night."

Mary felt a breeze blowing from the water. "At sundown, yes." She lowered her eyes to her arms, crossed.

"He comes to see you, Mary."

She lifted a wayward curl off her face and tucked it behind her ear.

"With my own eyes I have seen it. Washington is the best chap in the regiment, riding the most splendid horse. A fitting choice." Never before had the captain offered praise for one of her potential suitors. He knew them or of them all, as gossip flowed freely on board his ship. "I believe it in your benefit to meet the major."

"Colonel." Mary corrected him. "He is now Colonel Washington."

"Seems you know of this fine fellow and his unparalleled reputation."

Yes.

She listened carefully to each detail spoken about him. His auburn hair fell below his shoulders. His face carried a square jaw, a nose that was large and straight, and penetrating eyes. Not a week earlier, her cousin Eva Van Cortlandt quoted the poet John Dryden when describing him: "a temple Sacred by birth, and built by hands divine." And Mary read Washington's journal over and over. As she stood here now, she tried to think of how many times. Ten? Fifteen? Could it be twenty times, maybe more?

To fill the moment's quiet, which lasted a heartbeat too long, she picked up the basket and placed it in Captain Garvan's hands as she told him her wish for young William: "A wind to steer the course to true happiness."

The captain responded with a wide grin. Those were his words to her on her twenty-first birthday. "And my wish for you always, Mary."

With his farewell kiss upon her cheek, Mary turned to the manor, which bustled with preparations for the affair. The nervous excitement that now filled her whole being could hardly be contained. The words "I believe it in your benefit to meet the major" replayed in her head. In equal parts, she eagerly anticipated and dreaded this night. She wished she could meet the colonel under different circumstances than a ball, which, like so many others, brought back memories of the day her world changed. It was not her decision. She should have fought her siblings on this matter; she did not, thinking it would never come to pass. Colonel Washington agreed to travel five hundred miles to see her! This surprised her completely.

As she entered the manor and walked up the back steps behind the East Hall, she heard Frederick's voice.

"Drag her out myself! I shall do it!"

Mary rolled her eyes and made sure to stay behind a wall, out of his view.

"Oh, Frederick. Every belle blooms in her own way, at her own time." Her sister spoke softly between sighs. "Tonight will be glorious."

"Just as you said about the last reception and the one before that."

"Dearest Frederick, like a jewel being polished to an utmost shine, so will our sister be. You must be patient."

"Our family's reputation is at stake. I've

invited every royal justice of the colony, the barons of New York, the Speaker of the House, the members of the Assembly, the newly installed mayor, the sheriff, the aldermen, and the lords of the manors. Susannah, we have a colonel traveling from Virginia to be here."

"She will be glad to be in Colonel Washington's presence."

"Are you certain of this?"

An empty moment in the conversation lingered.

"If it takes force, then so be it!" Frederick declared like his usual scolding self.

"Curing what ails her cannot be done with coercion. We have learned tenderness is the only path to sensibility."

Mary caught a whiff of plum pudding and knew the conversation about finding her a mate would soon come to a close. The aroma would most certainly draw Frederick's substantially sized nose to the kitchen. Thankfully, she was correct. She did not want to listen to her brother again this morning. She had had enough of his persistence and felt a tinge of irritation over the first line of the invitation, clearly written as a message to her:

While we live, let us LIVE

Your company is desired to dine with
Lord Frederick Philipse and the family of Philipse
At the Manor of Philipse
On the second month, 14th day,
Of the seventeen hundred and fifty-sixth year
Dinner to be on the table at six o'clock
Musical Entertainment at eight o'clock
Dancing to commence at nine o'clock

A group of select guests received these special invitations which included the private banquet ahead of the dancing. Expected to be welcomed in stately manner was Washington. The colonel was becoming one of only a few so highly esteemed in the military.

Hanging in an ornate frame beside the invitation on the second-floor landing of the manor was a diagram of the guests' placement. Mary walked over to it. The principal guest of the evening, Washington, would be seated at the head of the long refectory table, flanked on his right by her brother and on the left by Susannah with her true. Next to Frederick would be Mary.

She took a breath. So close.

Mary was involved with each of the stages of the elaborate event, as her brother and sister requested. For the past month, she worked with a dancing master of her own choosing for another part of the evening that made her feel ill at ease. Even after intensive instruction, she wasn't sure of her readiness. This was not due to his coaching. Dancing was an area for which the gift of natural talent was not afforded her. Whenever she pushed herself to try before at previous balls, dames around her muttered the words — "inelegant," "untaught," "unready."

Mary heard delicate footsteps climb the stairs. Her sister leaned against a banister, elegantly posed. Mary wasn't sure she knew any other way to stand.

"The time is drawing near," Susannah chimed. "Your dancing lesson commences in one hour's time, and we depart for your final fitting immediately afterward, my sister."

"What if there's a chill? The gown seems too open to be worn on a night like tonight."

"You may find a gentleman's arms to warm you, Polly. Quite a few will be attending tonight's ball and certainly one in particular."

The evening had been conjured up by Susannah. She had found love in Major Beverley Robinson. His brother, the Honorable

John Robinson, carried the title of Speaker of the Virginia House of Burgesses. It was John Robinson who was in communication via letter with Colonel Washington. Beverley and John had spent many afternoons in childish play with George while growing up as neighbors and young schoolmates in Virginia.

At Susannah's urging, an invitation to Washington was delivered directly to the colonel, inviting him to stay at the Philipse family estate. "The ball comes at a perfect time of year, Polly." Mary knew to what she was referring. " 'For this was on Saint Valentine's Day,' " said Susannah.

" 'When every bird cometh there to chose his mate.' " The sisters recited in unison a line from Geoffrey Chaucer.

"I believe I have the perfect mate for the colonel to choose."

"There will be many belles from whom the colonel may choose."

"Correct you are. Many a lady in New York has found the stories of the hero intriguing, especially as he has evaded the capture of matrimony. But there stands none so beautiful as you, Miss Polly Philipse."

"What if —"

"There are no what ifs." Susannah folded

her arms. "There will be no what ifs. Not tonight, my sister, not tonight. Now, change into your practice clothes."

Mary headed into her bedchamber. This night would be the first time the sisters would meet the gentleman whom Major Robinson often praised. The major was not alone in his opinion of the newly appointed colonel. Commanders and laymen alike spoke of George Washington as a man guided by Providence. Mary knew this from her reading of *The New-York Mercury.* Nearly every newspaper in the colonies and in London had printed the *Journal of Major George Washington.* The edition of the *Mercury* was neatly placed at perfect eye level on a shelf of her bookcase. She'd read Washington's firsthand account of his exposure to peril on the frontier, engrossed by his escapes from death. The hardships he survived through his acts of bravery were far from the comforts of polite life in New York.

For more than two years, the newspaper remained here. She would always place the publication back again on the same shelf in the same position after reading it. Mary picked it up, feeling the linen paper on her fingers. She moved toward the window's light and turned to the page that displayed his writings, in wonderment that on this night, if she found the fortitude, she would meet the man described as having the courage of a hundred men.

He began simply:

> I Was COMMISSIONED and appointed by the Honourable Robert Dinwiddie, Esq; Governor, &c of Virginia, to visit and deliver a Letter to the Commandant of the French Forces on the Ohio, and set out on the intended Journey the same Day . . .

Tension welled up inside her. She knew well the feelings that overwhelmed her at every other lavish gathering. Mary wanted to attend, but what if . . .

This time, she hoped it would be different . . . that *she* would be different.

She read on.

Chapter Two: George's Journal

. . . was I to live more retired from young Women I might in some measure eliviate my sorrows . . .

— GEORGE WASHINGTON

Fredericksburg, Virginia
October 31, 1753

Under heathery gray skies, the air holding the odor of pine, and with the sugar maples putting on a fiery display of reds, golds, and yellows, George Washington walked out of his home and into the wilderness — alone. He was used to that.

'Tis better to be alone than in bad company.

As a boy, he had written down 110 rules from a prominent book on correct behavior. George strove to incorporate each of them into his conduct. Anything he learned, he had to do on his own. Without a father in his home, 110 rules were, at least, a start.

This was the day of his intended journey

to deliver the letter to the commandant of the French forces on the Ohio. He set out on the intended journey within hours of receiving the order from the governor.

Covered in a leather match coat belted at the waist and falling past the knee, the twenty-one-year-old carried a few days' provisions on his back with necessaries for his travels, including a small tent, a sleeping blanket, dried meats, a drum canteen that he filled with a quart of water, strings of wampum, the governor's letter to the enemy, his leather journal with hand-stitching at the binding, as well as an inkwell with ink he made from blackberries and a quill from a white goose feather with a tip he cut at a precise forty-five-degree angle; he planned to keep rough minutes along the way.

His mission was clear. Ride into the fortress of the French, deliver the governor's letter, and demand surrender.

Cease. Desist. Depart.

That was, in essence, what the governor was asking George to do — singlehandedly force the French from the continent. How was this young man qualified to handle such a mission? He wasn't and he knew it. Military experience, diplomatic experience, formal education — he had none of these.

What he did have was the resolve to become a man worthy of respect, which is why he accepted this mission as a volunteer, putting aside money for a higher purpose.

One day into the mission, rain fell fast. His coat was soggy, his hair dripping. Glad of his hood, George disembarked from the ferry, which crossed the Rappahannock River. The boat pulled into the wharf, beyond which a tiny town greeted him. It was perfectly situated along the river, with establishments for a smith, a tailor, and an ordinary keeper. A coffeehouse with a stone front was first. He entered to get out of the rain. He removed his soaked hat with both hands.

"Walk in, gentle man." A round-faced woman with a ruffled cap carried a coffeepot in her right hand and a plate of biscuits in her left. He breathed deeply, inhaling flavors that reminded him of home. "Rest at your ease. Pay for what you call for and call for what you please."

He needed to inquire the whereabouts of a man he once knew well. "May I ask your assistance in finding a villager, a friend by the name of Jacobus Vanbraam?"

"Ah. You are in need of a mercenary."

"I am in need of an interpreter of the

French language, as I've been asked to deliver a letter to the commandant of the French forces."

She put down the pot. "Indeed, Jacobus is a French speaker . . . as he is a master of the blade. We shall find him." She pointed George toward seating by the fire.

George moved to a wide tree stump of a table that appeared as if it had grown right through the flooring. He sat down on one of the stools around it and began his work. He was determined to put quill to paper to map out the excursion into enemy territory. The journey would be long, he surmised, nearly one thousand miles. Part of it would be through forests he knew well, having worked as a land surveyor of these backwoods. He assessed the need for six men to assist him.

"The mercenary's in sight!" shouted the woman.

George headed to the entrance to greet his old companion, who had taught him everything he knew about fighting with a sword and who had served in the British Navy with George's older half brother, Lawrence. Clean-shaven, with long, wet, black hair neatly thrown away from the face, Jacobus steadied the saber with a curved blade attached to a scabbard at his belt as he stepped along Sophia Street with a lady in tow, the two speaking in loud-enough voices for him to hear.

"You mean to enter enemy territory," she groaned to Jacobus. Her hair and dress were damp from the rain. "And then what? Banish an army of Frenchmen with one who is barely a man?"

"Aye." Jacobus didn't even turn to her.

She slapped his arm. "Five years since you have had an exercise in arms with this boy. How can you be assured he is prepared for the roar of battle?"

"This is a mission of diplomacy, not a fight to the death." He kept his steady pace.

"Diplomacy with this enemy?" she scoffed, now in a full rage.

"You underestimate the man who has come for me."

"If he is without sword, you will see me protest this preposterous mission."

"The cutlass, the foil, the claymore, the saber — the boy mastered each under my tutelage."

"How will you safeguard him?"

"Safeguard him? Ha! The man guided by divine Providence will safeguard me." Jacobus looked toward George, whose body filled the doorway. "Drea Vanbraam, may I acquaint you with George Washington. This giant of a man was struck by lightning while still in the womb, guarded by the heavens from before his birth."

She stared long and hard at George and at his commanding height, which caused his head to reach the top of the entryway. " 'Tis true?" she asked of Jacobus.

"Have you ever known me to tell an untruth?" replied Jacobus. "The fork and knife at the table where his mother was eating fused together from the bolt."

She looked down at George's waist, from which Lawrence's sword, one uncommonly broad at the base, hung. Drea swung around to her husband. She pushed a satchel into his chest. "You have my blessing."

As the two men entered the coffeehouse, Jacobus raised his hand to reach George's shoulder. "If I remember correctly, the young lady did not survive the bolt?"

George nodded, knowing to what he was referring. He was asked to tell the story more times than he desired. On a stormy Sunday afternoon after church services, lightning struck his family's cottage. The electric bolt came through the chimney, knocking over a guest invited to supper, taking the life right out of her as she sat at the table with Mary Washington. The tragedy left his mother forever fearful of storms and worry-filled that she might never be blessed with motherhood. When her first child was born, she carried him everywhere, announcing that George Washington was protected by the Almighty.

"Truly remarkable. And pay no mind to the wife. *Une chieuse.*" Jacobus's mouth tipped into a smile as he wiped droplets from his sleeves. "And what of you? Have you selected a flower from the *jardin* or is the fortress of a military man's heart impenetrable?"

"I pass the time." He signaled to the woman with the pot.

"With the man you've become, I'm sure of it." They found seats at the stump.

"In truth, I am trying to forget a lady." A difficult task, is what he didn't say. George could still feel the silkiness of his Affa's flowing black hair in his hands.

"And where might we find this lady?"

"The lowlands."

"A beauty of the lowlands. Hard to banish from the heart, I'm sure. But fear not. We will find other such lovelies on our journey."

"That would only add fuel to fire, making me the more uneasy." That woman — Affa — had crushed his spirit. Had he been wealthier, more educated . . . Clearly, he was not enough. "Was I to live more retired from young women, I might in some measure eliviate my sorrows . . . burying passion in eternal forgetfulness."

Jacobus laughed aloud. "I guarantee you this: Before long, another passion will emerge, lifting you from such a grave of oblivion."

The round-faced woman brought brewed coffee and sweet bread to the stump. George's stomach noted their arrival, but he did not immediately partake. He thought of one of the rules he followed: *Drink not nor talk with your mouth full.*

"Lieutenant Vanbraam, my thanks for the personal respect you showed my family."

"My condolences on the distressing event that has befallen you. Your late brother was a good man. I am proud to have served with him."

"Lawrence is the reason I took up this mission." The white plague robbed George of his half brother, who had been fourteen years his senior and who had been his mentor and closest companion. With a successful mission as this, he could bring honor to Lawrence's memory and, perhaps, become a bit more like him. George and Lawrence were different. Lawrence was a product of George's father's first marriage and had received a formal education in London and vast military experience. When his father died, so went George's chances of a similar path — life among the landed gentry as his brother; there would be no moneys for that.

George spoke about what motivated him to deliver the letter of ultimatum. "Lawrence believed strongly that if the French take possession of the Ohio, they might easily invade Virginia. Our mountains are not so formidable to protect us."

"Wherever they come, they destroy. Your brother would have been glad to see you take up this mission. When the sword of war threatens, we must strike."

That afternoon, George hired his party, following another of his rules: *Associate with men of good quality if you esteem your own reputation.* He engaged a servitor, along with frontiersman Christopher Gist. If anyone could pilot them out, it would be Gist, haughty, brooding in his outward appearance, with a ruddy face covered by a full beard, the only explorer with precise knowledge of the Ohio country.

With baggage and horses, they traveled to the mouth of Turtle Creek at the Monongahela. George kept track of each detail in the land they traversed.

"Our leader's heart is fixed," Jacobus said to Gist as they trekked through marshlands, "to a beauty of the lowlands."

"I would find a woman in the highlands." Gist spoke with a slow drawl.

"Where the ladies can read and write," added Jacobus.

"Aye," replied Gist, "especially the rich ones."

George did not want to speak on the subject. He believed that if he tried such a thing again, he would receive a rejection which would only add to his agony. He halted. "Gentlemen, more pertinent matters are before us."

A scalp was staked into an elm.

Jacobus raised his eyes to it. "Such as pray they do not kill the messenger."

Positioned above the scalp was a sizable copper plate bearing France's royal arms.

"The blood is fresh. Scalping parties are near." Gist examined the clean incision from the forehead to the back of the neck. "The enemy pays thirty francs in trading goods for each scalp. The pounding of stakes has become a common sound — the French claiming the territory as theirs."

"*Vive le roi* is their call." Jacobus looked to George. "Shall we take shelter from the enemy?"

"Waiting here is very contrary to my inclinations," said George. "We must make all possible dispatch."

Mary wondered what bravery looked like in the flesh. She might learn that this night. She imagined the colonel a gallant warrior, rough-hewn, with a brawny physique, and a strong jaw that, when clenched, would display defined muscles at the sides of his face.

Washington's writings continued on to the most perilous part of the journey. In order to deliver his letter to the enemy, he had first to cross through the natives' trading post, without invitation, and get past guards staying close to their weapons, men who didn't take kindly to strangers.

Susannah would soon be calling out for her, but Mary refused to put down the newspaper. Her delicate fingers turned the page.

Day 27

The stars told George the time reached nine o'clock in the evening. The flame of a torch guided him down a dirt path. One guard in war paint walked in front of him, the other behind. He could hear chanting in the distance.

This was the natives' trading post, a place called Logstown.

Calm and composed, George convinced those at the gate to let his company through. After agreeing, guards took him alone to a narrow dwelling built among the trees. He requested a meeting with the elders to obtain permission to continue through their lands and ask for assistance in the journey.

Upon entrance, a gamy smell greeted him. Skinned hides hung across bark-covered walls. Three glowing hearths ran down the center, with gray wisps dancing to smoke holes that opened to the night sky. Seated around the second hearth were men George believed to be the chiefs of the Six Nations of Iroquois, Seneca, Onondaga, Oneida, Cayuga, Mohawk, and Tuscorona. Without a word, one of them, Chief Tanacharison, tall and strong, with a fox fur upon his head — a man whom George heard was called "Half King" — motioned for him to address the sachems.

Every action done in Company, ought to be with Some Sign of Respect, to those that are Present — rule number one. With no time to prepare, and having never given a speech of diplomatic importance, or one of any significance, he accomplished this with one word, the first:

Brothers,
I have called you together in Council, by Order of your Brother the Governor of Virginia, to acquaint you that I am sent, with all possible Dispatch, to visit, and deliver a Letter to the French Commandant, of very great Importance to your Brothers the English; and I dare say, to you their Friends and Allies.

I was desired, Brothers, by your Brother the Governor, to call upon you, the Sachems of the Nations, to inform you of it, and to ask your Advice and Assistance to proceed the nearest and best Road to the French. You see, Brothers, I have got thus far on my Journey.

His Honour likewise desired me to apply to you for some of your young Men, to conduct and provide Provisions for us on our Way; and be a Safeguard against those French Indians who have taken up the Hatchet against us. I have spoke this particularly to you, Brothers, because his Honour our Governor treats you as good Friends and Allies, and holds you in great Esteem. To confirm what I have said, I give you this String of Wampum.

Half King accepted the offering. George ended his speech there. *Let your discourse with men of business be short and comprehensive.*

Success. Provisions and passage granted. Three guides provided.

Day 46

Nearly seven weeks into the most fatiguing journey as is possible to conceive, George pushed the men onward. He could feel nothing from his fingertips. As for his toes, he knew not whether they were still connected to his feet.

They lit fires to keep warm. George made a forked stick to cook his food, hunted from the woods. He had no dish, using instead a piece of bark for a plate.

They slept on whatever natural cover they could find, right on the wilderness floor.

Then they came upon a dead end.

Before him was a creek with waters so high and rapid, any chance at rafting or fording was impossible. They were obliged to pass through this place, somehow. Only one other way was possible, Gist informed him: a swamp downstream.

George had no choice. He and his men advanced through the stench. Without the ability to see much of what was in front of him, he led the men, keeping himself upright as his horse carried him through.

The weather proved more arduous every mile the company crossed, until finally the enemy was before them. A handful of men against an army. Never before in his lifetime had George suffered such anxiety as he did in this moment. French guards swarmed them upon approach. A strikingly regal lot quickly surrounded him in the middle of the forest. The soldiers wore ornate uniforms of white coats with bright blue lapels. Frilled lace flowed from the cuffs. His focus, though, was more on the weapons they were pointing at him and his men.

Scars crossed the face of the man for whom the French soldiers cleared a path, the commandant, George surmised. *Gaze not on the marks or blemishes of others.* He had all signs of a battlefield veteran, yet he dressed as a knight, with not a wrinkle in his uniform, and he carried himself with the deportment of royalty. A black patch sat over his right eye. Through interpreter Jacobus, Captain Jacques Legardeur de Saint-Pierre demanded to know the reason for this invasion.

George stood tall and cleared his throat. His mind remained focused. *Think before you speak. Pronounce not imperfectly nor bring out your words too hastily, but orderly and distinctly.* He pulled out the letter to the enemy from the Governor, which Jacobus interpreted:

Sir,
The lands upon the River Ohio, in the western parts of the Colony of Virginia, are so notoriously known to be the property of the Crown of Great Britain that it is a matter of equal concern and surprise to me, to hear that a body of French forces are erecting fortresses and making settlements upon that river, within His Majesty's dominions.

The many and repeated complaints I have received of these acts of hostility lay me under the necessity of sending, in the name of the King, my master, the bearer hereof, George Washington, Esq., one of the Adjutants-General of the forces of this dominion, to complain to you of the encroachments thus made, and of the injuries done to the subjects of Great Britain, in violation of the law of nations, and the treaties now subsisting between the two Crowns. If these facts be true, and you think fit to justify your proceedings, I must desire you to acquaint me by whose authority and instructions you have lately marched from Canada with an armed force, and invaded the King of Great Britain's territories, in the manner complained of; that according to the purport and resolution of your answer I may act agreeably to the commission I am honored with from the King, my master.

However, sir, in obedience to my instructions, it becomes my duty to require your peaceable departure; and that you would forbear prosecuting a purpose so interruptive of the harmony and good understanding, which His Majesty is desirous to continue and cultivate with the Most Christian King.

I persuade myself you will receive and entertain Major Washington with the candor and politeness natural to your nation; and it will give me the greatest satisfaction if you return him with an answer suitable to my wishes for a very long and lasting peace between us.

I have the honor to be,
Sir,
Your very humble,
Robert Dinwiddie

Silence.

Washington watched an eye stare at him with a guarded look.

The commandant's soldiers with their heavy weaponry took a step forward now. George sensed Jacobus reach for his saber. An endless number of the enemy's men moved in closer. He could feel the cold breath of one of them at his neck.

It may have been seconds, but it felt like hours as George tried to remain as still as possible. He realized that this might have been the worst decision of his life. Who was he to step onto enemy territory and make such a demand? He was only an adjutant general! And in name only. A volunteer is all, and an ill-advised one at that. How could he have ever believed such an inexperienced person as he could negotiate a matter of such great importance? Moreover, how could the governor! The moment of clarity that struck George in that second left him scared for his life.

He watched Legardeur scan his clothing from hat to shoe; he was wearing little more than hunter's garb. He eyed George's delegation with a smirk, seemingly looking upon them as a motley sort.

"As to the summons you send me to retire, I do not think myself obliged to obey it." Legardeur's French was interpreted for George.

George moved not a muscle.

"We refuse to acquiesce," the commandant said with certainty.

The guards moved in closer. George believed this the end. He swallowed hard.

The commandant raised his hand to stop his guards' movement. "Monsieur Washington." Legardeur motioned to George to follow him into a private room and offered him a seat at a heavy table. He spoke to him through his interpreter. "You are a brave man for coming to this place."

George nodded his appreciation, although he rather would have left this place by now, for the guards again surrounded him, too close for his comfort.

The commandant put quill to paper for a response to the Colonial governor of Virginia and had his interpreter say the words aloud: "Whatever may be your instructions, mine bring me here by my general's order; and I entreat you, sir, to be assured that I shall attempt to follow them with all the exactness and determination which can be expected from a good officer. I have made it my particular care to receive Mr. Washington with a distinction suitable to your dignity, as well as his own quality and great merit, and I flatter myself, sir, that he will do me the justice to be my witness for it with you, as well as the evidences of deep respect with which . . . I have the honor to be, your very humble and very obedient servant, Jacques Legardeur de Saint-Pierre."

One guard melted gold wax. Legardeur himself sealed the paper with the mark of the French. A guard handed it to George. With the commandant's letter of refusal in hand, George and his band of men departed the enemy's fort with urgency.

The blackest night was before them, brightness coming only from the moon's light reflecting on the heavily falling snow. They did not welcome sleep this night nor for many more. Danger was too close.

Day 54

Frost reached his skin through stiff clothing. Exhaustion left George without any ability to continue. Eight days had passed since he left the commandant. This was the longest of those days. George refused any stoppage. He nearly collapsed on whatever ground was below him. He found respite seated against a naked maple. Fierce, howling winds stripped trees of their white coats. George wished for warmth. He wished for her. He imagined Affa in his embrace, the silkiness of her hair, the way its softness would feel with his hand through it.

If he were wealthier or more educated, maybe then he would be enough for her. She never responded to his letters. He forced the thought from his mind and closed his eyes to allow sleep in.

At daybreak, the company continued. For days more, they traveled. He wrote in his journal the trials of the journey:

> Our Horses were now so weak and feeble, and the Baggage heavy (as we here obliged to provide all the Necessaries that the Journey would require) that we doubted much their performing it: therefore myself and others (except for the Drivers who were obliged to ride) gave up our Horses for Packs, to assist along with the Baggage. I put myself in an Indian walking Dress, and continued with them three Days, till I found there was no Probability of their getting home in any reasonable Time. The Horses grew less able to travel every Day.
>
> Therefore as I was uneasy to get back, to make Report of my Proceedings to his Honour the Governor, I determined to

prosecute my Journey the nearest Way through the Woods, on Foot.

Accordingly, I left Mr. Vanbraam in Charge of our Baggage; with Money and Directions, to provide Necessaries from Place to Place for themselves and Horses, and to make the most convenient Dispatch in.

George chose only Gist to travel with him now. They moved quickly, completing eighteen miles in one day. Each had his reasons for a swift return. George was in a hurry to return a response to the governor.

As for Gist: "My child, George, my first, is about to be born. I have no time to waste in this godforsaken spot."

They arrived at the place others told George about. What he saw explained why it was called "Murdering Town."

Their fast pace came to a halt as they heard the sound of a stranger's feet racing in the white powder. A warrior with his face covered in paint came from behind a big standing oak, pointed a pistol at them; he fired.

Gist crouched down.

George raced to Gist's side. "Have you been shot?"

"No," he replied and began to run toward

the man behind the tree.

George hurried to the left to stop the assailant. The man was attempting to reload. George grabbed him.

"You will die today!" Gist shouted at the man.

George, with a length of rope he'd carried at his side, tied the shooter's hands behind his back. "Do not take his life, Gist. I forbid it. We shall keep him in custody. Be sure he has no other weapons." George searched the area to see if another enemy was lurking. Nearby, he discovered newly set traps and footprints. Worry set in that they could be scalped if they stayed any longer.

"Make the man build us a fire," George advised Gist. "When darkness falls, we shall let him go."

"We must get away from this place."

"We shall travel through the night. If the enemy is watching, they will believe we stayed encamped by the fire."

Hours later, they freed him and listened until he was out of earshot.

The two ran for miles through the threatening wilderness, only pausing to set their compass to lead them toward the Allegheny River, hoping to find the river frozen, which would allow them to walk over it.

Instead of an icy sheet, they found ferocious currents breaking apart whatever blocks of ice remained.

The next day was spent building a makeshift raft to cross the river. When they completed this task, they placed the raft in the water, setting their sights on the other side. It was not to be:

> before we were Half Way over, we were jammed in the Ice, in such a Manner that we expected every Moment our Raft to sink, and ourselves to perish, I put-out my setting Pole to try to stop the Raft, that the Ice might pass by; when the Rapidity of the Stream threw it with so much Violence against the Pole, that it jirked me out into ten Feet Water: But I fortunately saved myself by catching hold of one of the Raft Logs. Notwithstanding all our Efforts we could not get the Raft to either Shore; but were obliged, as we were near an Island, to quit our Raft and make to it.

A numbing chill penetrated George's body. He felt ground below his feet. They waded in the water through the dead of night, continuing to cross. George placed the knapsack above his head, tying the handles about his neck to keep the French commandant's letter secure. The struggle

left them fighting against rushing hunks of ice.

Land brushed George's hand. A small island was before them in the middle of the river. George pulled himself up onto it and assisted Gist. A great sense of relief led to a deep exhale that looked like a frozen mist in the night.

Without a raft or access to food, George believed they could be doomed. The cold turned even more severe. Gist's fingers and some of his toes became frostbitten.

Morning arrived.

George awoke to a silence emerging like a loud boom through ominous lands. His bleary eyes opened wide after seeing an unexpected occurrence of fortune. He told Gist to arise, to view the miracle before them. No longer were they in a life-or-death situation. The water had completely frozen over.

The survivors of winter's fury crossed the Allegheny on foot and headed home, battered but alive.

Mary reached the end of Colonel Washington's journal. She never put the publication down without reading every last word, as if he would not survive if she didn't finish. She knew

how he must have felt in that water, the fear of being one breath away from your last. This one moment in his life she shared with him.

She looked up, trying to imagine how far her eyes would have to rise to look into his. Carefully, she folded the newspaper and placed it on the shelf, always on the same shelf in the same position with the writing away from her. Best to keep him away from the cursed. That is how she viewed herself. She felt responsible for the deaths of a little boy, her mother, her father, her Margaret. She was the cursed one.

Chapter Three: Charming Miss Polly

. . . the passions of your sex are easier roused than allayed. Do not therefore boast too soon, nor too strongly, of your insensibility to, or resistance of its powers.

— GEORGE WASHINGTON

Yonkers-on-Hudson
February 14, 1756

The grand Banneker in the hall struck ten o'clock — time for her lesson. Mary found the dancing master already in movement on the makeshift dance floor on the second level of the manor. With finesse, Michael Tenoe, a picture of masculinity, leaped into a split in the air. When his arms extended, he reached high, appearing as if his life depended on it.

Mary never asked about the scar on his face that shone clear when angled in the light. The first time she saw it, a fright came over her. She didn't need to know. She could only imagine the trials he must have been through.

Now he greeted her. She assumed her first stance.

"In a delicate manner." His voice sounded pleasant even when correcting her. "The placing of your heel must be in gentle fashion."

She tried to perfect her posture as Tenoe directed: "Imagine a string running from the bottom of your back to the top of your head and to the ceiling."

Mary knew she was not quite balanced. "If grace could choose her dancer, I would be left at the wall."

"Free yourself." Tenoe shifted her shoulders back. "Without words, communicate what lies deep within your soul. The only limit to your possibility is the limitation you've made possible. This is your time."

Truth be told, it was also his. Mary meant to see him released from the indentured servitude out of which her family temporarily hired him, and planned to take the necessary steps to make it so. "What will you do when you're pronounced free?"

"Oh, what will I not do."

"You will make the world your dance floor."

"Each time my feet are on the floor, I am

no longer servant, but sir." He reached for her hand. "This is why I dance."

She placed her hand in his and curtsied. "Henceforth, Sir Tenoe is what I shall call you."

Like nearly everyone else, she read what was printed in an advertisement in the *New York Weekly Journal* about him:

> Michael Tenoe is my servant, and hath been for near seven years past; and all sums of money due for teaching are due and payable to me. And I do hereby forewarn all persons from paying him any money, giving him credit or dealing with him, on any account whatever, until he has discharg'd himself from all obligations due to me; which shall be publickly advertised, when accomplished.

Tenoe himself told her his story. Poor and without shelter at the age of fourteen, he sold himself to a ship's captain for passage to the New World. He confided in her the rumors that drew him across the Atlantic: bountiful feasts and limitless moneys. Those were not to be his fate, for his life dues were immediately purchased by Jones Irwin. Mary asked Tenoe to bring the contract papers with him this day.

"You will not only impress the crowd but intimidate it," Tenoe encouraged her.

The sounds of someone racing up the stairs stopped them. Eric Arthur Angevine rushed into the room.

Tenoe showed disappointment in his face. "Your expected time of arrival was a quarter of an hour ago."

Mary thought Eric Arthur the perfect choice for a dance partner. His father served as estate steward for the Philipses, loyal, efficient, and at the constant side of her brother. Eric was a working lad, helping his father, but also elected to a position at the town's church. The occupation of sexton sounded prestigious. Mary had heard Eric wanted the young females in town to know his title. While some boys turned away from girls like Saint Vitus' dance, not Eric. He gave the girls tours of the church, showing them the secret passage to the bell tower, and he always had enough coins to crowd his pockets. Mary knew, as sexton, Eric was really just the town grave digger, shoveling out an adult person's grave for eight shillings, four shillings for children. Being practically a child himself, Eric complained about that part of the job, but about shillings in his pocket he did not.

With pockets stuffed with coins, Eric took

his position apart from her on the expansive floor. They began their practice of the baroque steps of the flirtatious minuet. She became nervous as she imagined a dance with the colonel and made a failing attempt to punctuate the complex nature of the dance with the Z figure sequence of steps. Right foot. Left foot. Right again. Left toe points. Three taps. Left hands touch.

"Again." Tenoe had them join hands. Eric, with his weighty pockets, reached out his right hand to hold her left one. Coins jingled. They retreated to both touch right hands. The quick change that followed to touch left hands did not go according to Tenoe's instruction. Instead, Eric's breeches fell around his feet. His undergarment made an appearance. Tenoe howled. Mary giggled. Eric hurried to tug up his waistband. "I will never be caught with my breeches down again!"

Mary completed her lesson with glee.

Before leaving, she requested from Tenoe his contractual papers and moved to the privacy of her study to read through each detail:

This INDENTURE witnessed that Michael Tenoe doth Voluntarily put himself as servant to Jones Irwin, for and during

> the full Space, Time and Term of 10 years from the first Day of the arrival of the Ship; during which time, or term, the Master shall and will feed and supply Michael Tenoe with sufficient meat, drink, apparel, lodging and all other necessaries befitting such a servant; and at the end and expiration of the said term; Michael Tenoe is to be made Free, and receive according to the Custom of the Country. If the servant, Michael Tenoe, shall pay Jones Irwin 15 pounds British with twenty percent interest before that time, he shall be free. In Witness whereof the parties have hereunto interchangeably put their Hands and Seals.

Mary secretly tallied the amount with interest and marched to the library to make her demands. There, she informed her brother of the sum to be paid for Tenoe's services once the pleasure ball ended.

"Eighteen pounds!" Frederick shouted. "I have already settled with Mr. Irwin for a smidgeon of that amount."

"Mr. Tenoe has developed a number of new dances for the ball. I believe he deserves compensation. Besides, he is a master of dance!"

"A self-taught dancing master?" Frederick

grimaced. "It is unheard of."

She knew the total was exorbitantly higher than what should be required for one evening of work. But she also meant to see him freed. "If he is not paid properly . . . you will not see my feet upon that floor."

"Eighteen pounds for a dancing man . . . absurd! Eight is all. Not a shilling more."

"Then, Frederick, I expect a fee" — she stomped her feet — "for my attendance!"

His eyebrows lifted high. "A fee?"

She raised her hands in front of him with fingers outstretched. "Ten British pounds."

"An outrage!" His nostrils flared.

"Ten."

"Eight."

"Ten."

"I will make my decision tonight."

"Fine . . . eight. If you find the evening a success, I expect the full amount." Here she was negotiating terms for an event she wasn't even confident she would attend. If Frederick allowed her to handle her own money, this would be completed already, but Papa had written that upon his death, Frederick would remain in charge of the estate.

Susannah marched in. "We will be late." Clutching her arm, she led Mary toward the door. "Frederick, our sister has her final fitting. Now leave her be." She walked Mary out of the room, the manor, and straight into the coach awaiting them.

Mary stood atop a wooden stand inside a little yellow box of a house on a hill, a stone's throw from the manor. The cottage belonged to the Sherwoods. Rosie, with pointed spectacles hanging from her neck and a bun never quite neat atop her head, created the finest gowns in the Hudson Valley. Susannah and cousin Eva joined her for the fitting.

Throbbing started squarely between Mary's eyes and an ache moved patiently through her midsection. Did she position the newspaper on the shelf correctly with the words away from her, words always away from the cursed? She didn't have time to double-check. Clamminess on her palms was the first sign of trouble. She tried to remain calm through the pulling and tugging. She needed to take her mind off the publication and instead concentrate fully on the details of the gown or maybe on the man who would see her in it tonight. She just had to go, or at least peek out a door to see him. This was the hero of the South who charged into enemy territory with nothing more than a knapsack. Just months ago, they lauded him again for saving an army from defeat on the battlefield. This was the same person coming to her home in just a matter of hours.

She felt flushed. She took in a deep breath. What is that lingering reek overwhelming my nose? Mary wondered. At least it provided a distraction.

Susannah and their cousin, seated near Mary, kept up a bombardment of adulation. "Nature exhausted its charming stock in her creation. Every belle will stand in envy."

"Polly's beauty is beyond compare!" Her cousin added a theatrical emphasis with the flailing of her arms. Mary knew her unrelenting onslaught of flummery was nothing more than a mummery. Mary was envious of how Eva was so at ease in her own skin. She had large brown eyes, a full face, and a chuckle that was infectious. Mary called Eva her cousin, but in truth she was related via adoption; two generations earlier, Eva's grandmother had been taken in by the Philipse family. "You do look lovely," added Eva with sincerity this time, slouching comfortably in the chair.

Mary's mind would not be calmed until she got back to that shelf. Yes, she believed she placed the newspaper correctly. At least she thought so. Mary stood nervously, looking at her ref lection as she wore a shimmering gold silk dress made up of three pieces. The first was the bodice, which was corseted at the back and had an opening at the front that fell too low for Mary's comfort. She pulled it higher.

Rosie removed the needle and thread from its holding spot between her lips. "Miss Polly, we must emphasize your apple dumplin' shop, dear."

Eva broke into sounds halfway between giggling and cackling.

Mary would rather cover her full bosom than put it on display.

The skirt was conical to show off her elongated waist. The train, which could be removed for dancing, was made of a highly decorative cloth with rich embroidery in pure gold thread. The ball gown had frilling at the hem so as to allow her ivory silk shoes to show through the bottom. They were highly embellished with floral embroidery in delightful colors of blues and plums.

Rosie lowered the gown below Mary's shoulders.

"Each gentleman shall behold our charming Miss Polly with love's eye," Susannah said, continuing her near exaltation.

"A sight so amiable and lovely." Eva fluttered her eyelashes.

"Even deformity is pleasing, I suppose, if there is some good food and drink." Mary had quite enough of the encomiums.

Eva smiled. "And beauty, hideous, if there is none."

Rosie adjusted the lace at the bottom of the gown's sleeves. "Nary a thing, not even a hogshead of rum, can help a gentleman of three outs."

Mary knew exactly what she meant.

"Three outs?" inquired Susannah.

"The raucous rogues about town, men of the three outs." She lifted a middle finger. "Out of money." She raised a pointer finger. "Out of wit." And she added her thumb. "Out of manners. They're not worth a farthing of ye time."

"And what do you make of the sheriff, Rosie?" asked Eva.

"That man again," said Mary. He was the suitor who shared tea with Frederick when Mary refused to come out of her bedchamber.

"He's as divine a young fella as nature could form, plus I appreciate a belly that's fulla money."

"He's of the mind that his purse can seduce any woman to fall in love with him. He's employed every talent against the female persuasion. Each has fallen, except for one, of course." Eva stared Mary's way.

"Stay aside, ladies, from a gilly gaupus, like the man with the head that flares like a bell, Timothy Scandal, or whate'er he calls himself today." Rosie made a bell shape with her hands around her head.

"I take offense! Yes, he's a bit of an awkward fellow, but using a sobriquet is quite romantic, Rosie, and I admire his hairstyle. He's a fine writer, you know. Tell them, Polly, what the poet sent over to you." The grin on Eva's face grew larger.

"What did the scandalous one write to you this time?" Susannah appeared none too pleased.

Mary stayed quiet for a moment but relented and recited the lines he had written. " 'So desirous I felt from only a light touch . . .' "

"Oh my." Susannah huffed.

" 'Unaffected thy were, and I too much!/ How is this, that few gains move me thus, and my love reigns?' "

"Please keep going. Keep going," urged Eva.

Mary did so. " 'I grin, then sigh, I shake to and fro;/Such a fleeting moment to cause me to flutter so.' "

" 'A Touch of the Petticoat,' he entitled

it." Eva was hardly able to contain her amusement. "A touch of the petticoat."

"Did he touch your petticoat?" Susannah asked abruptly.

"Absolutely . . . not. No. No. Certainly not."

"He is a superior writer." Eva always defended the man. "I've read his elegantly styled essays with their Latin phrasing. Not many men can quote a philosopher quite like he can."

"A philosopher? Better to choose a gollumpus," Rosie muttered. "He may be clumsy, but properly fat. And if you see an owl in an ivy bush run the other way, the same goes for the nick ninny, the niffynaffy, and the nickumpoop."

"Tell us the difference, Rosie," Eva pressed her.

"The nick ninny is too simple a man. The niffynaffy is too trifling a man."

A low titter from Mary soon turned into a chorus of unrestrained merriment between her and Eva.

"And the nickumpoop is too foolish a fellow to have ever even seen his wife's . . ." She gave a cough to fill in the missing word.

Eva burst into a cachinnation.

Susannah nearly spit out her tea. She grabbed hold of her gown for the evening and left the room. Eva followed her, folded over in laughter.

Mary regained her composure, turned to Rosie, and spoke quietly. "And how is your little Lulu feeling today?"

"Praise the heavens she's out of danger. She prayed for you before her rest today. She is sleeping with the pillow doll you sent over for her."

"Oh, how precious."

"That thing woulda eaten her whole. That bloody wolf! It took the life out of her right leg." She helped Mary down from the wooden stand, walked her to the hall, and pointed to the animal head at the other end of it, hanging on the wall with her husband's initials, J.E., written in blood beneath it. "My beloved hunted that devil down."

Mary had heard the girl's screams a week prior. The sound of Willoughby's galloping caused the wolf to let go of the child's leg as it was dragging her away. The wolf turned back into the trees.

"Has she regained her strength to walk?"

"Her leg on the right drags quite a bit." Rosie dragged her own right leg to show Mary. "Don't think she'll ever be able to dance again."

"Oh, let's not even think such things. We'll be sure she receives the very best care. Why don't you bring her tonight? I'll carry her around with me if I have to."

"Your brother would run us out of the place! But I'll bring her for the costuming."

"If you care to stay, you will be my guests." Mary caught notice of Rosie's little boy, Jeffrey, peeking from the doorway. "Good day, Master Sherwood."

"Bring in some eggs, would you, son?"

Jeffrey nodded kindly.

"And be sure your father is not drinking ale before his meal?"

Only the top of Jeffrey's head could be seen around the doorway. It nodded.

The payers of compliments soon returned: Susannah and Eva in elegant gowns.

"Let the rogues move aside, for only one man stands with the stature of a king." Eva carried in both of her hands a highly ornate box tied in a glorious red satin bow.

"My true tells me Colonel Washington's height towers over that of his fellow officers." Susannah followed beside Eva.

"This is a man of commanding presence with a body hard of muscle," said Eva. "There is not a prince in any part of the world who would not appear a *valet de chambre* next to him."

"A favorite of heaven, you know," Susannah added. “A man who can never die in battle.”

“Ne’er die?” Rosie rolled a golden thread around its spool. “I’ve heard a great spirit can protect a person so not even a bullet will get ’im.”

The words “can never die” stayed with Mary. For a woman whose heart had an indifference toward the most elite of men, she wondered how she could have such admiration for one she had not ever met.

“Each of Polly’s potential suitors is of the finest quality. Half of the officers in New York stand with mouths agape as my sister rides by. Nearly all of them have asked for interviews. Frederick is quite finicky as to whom he will allow. I am in agreement. Our Polly should not be with just any man.”

For all of those desiring to be close to Mary, none received a return glance.

A bright-eyed smile flashed across Eva’s face as she handed the box to Mary. “It’s for you, Polly. Open it.”

Mary slowly lifted the lid.

Chapter Four: Miracle at Monongahela

. . . I have been protected beyond all human probability & expectation . . .
— GEORGE WASHINGTON

Princeton, New Jersey
February 14, 1756

The tailor was no beanpole. Hence, standing atop a crate, with eyes helped by round spectacles and morning's light peeking through a high window, old Gerald Vincent sized the cravat around George's neck at the rear of his millinery shop on Old Fish Street in Princeton. George and his personal secretary stood in one room. In another, a group of officers who traveled north with them awaited a transformation befitting an English gentleman.

This would be the first time George would wear a neckerchief made of fine fabric. Twice, Vincent added another inch of silk. He would have to add one more.

It was the final hour before they were to continue their journey to the New York Colony. On this day, the cavalcade would arrive before sunset, just as the banquet being given in George's honor was to begin.

Put not off your clothes in the presence of others, nor go out your chamber half dressed. Behind a privacy curtain, he removed his hunter's shirt and worn breeches. He stood bare-skinned. "Have you sent the correspondence?" George looked out with one eye.

His personal secretary, John Kirkpatrick, took a seat on a bench of worked oak nearest the hearth. "Yes, Colonel. The letter to Captain Roger Morris regarding the Braddock incident has been delivered. We await his response." The secretary began reviewing the list George had written for the tailor. "The colonel prefers the cloaks laced."

"As for the trimmings?" Vincent laid out a garment on a working table.

"Silver. Are you content with silver, Colonel?"

"I like that fashion best." George remained without a stitch of clothing.

"As for the coats, they've been faced and cuffed with scarlet, as you requested."

"My profound gratitude for your expedited service, as we are excessively hurried."

George watched as Vincent scurried away, leaving the two in private.

Keep to the fashion of your equals. His equals were no longer volunteers in the military. He was now a commander. After his brave conduct in the expedition into enemy territory to deliver the letter of ultimatum to the French, his military status rose from nothing to one level above nothing. This was followed, though, by a show of courage in the field of battle, one which almost didn't happen because he was stricken with a sickness. He had served as a major under British general Edward Braddock of His Majesty's Army. The road to get here had not been an easy one.

Today he was the newly promoted colonel of the Virginia Regiment and commander in chief of all forces of the colony.

This elevation in fashion was a necessity due to the circles in which he would find himself, especially the one beginning this night. He accepted an invitation from his childhood friend Beverley for a first visit to New York. Major Robinson became a man of great wealth and influence upon marriage. And Mrs. Robinson's sister had not yet pledged herself to another. George had heard plenty about the belle of the North.

"A ravishing beauty awaits your arrival,

Colonel. If I may be allowed to offer some advice now, since I will not be accompanying you . . . Move quickly, for others intend to batter down the virgin gates."

"I shall labor to keep alive in my breast that little spark of celestial fire called conscience." In truth, George buried his passions for women in that grave of oblivion. He was certain that might very well be the only way. The antidote, the remedy, the cure was to stay away from any one thing that brought that other woman's silky hair back into his mind.

"Ah, his love reigns with gentle sway. It is a rarity in this age, especially when a robust fortune is the consequence."

"Happiness depends more upon the internal frame of a person's own mind than on the externals in the world."

"I shall be confident in this, Colonel. After becoming acquainted with you, her heart will find warmth beyond the common degree of fondness."

Yes, George had risen to a higher rank. He was finally receiving the respect he deserved. Still, he was not convinced.

The talk of the heiress extended to the officers who would join Washington. He listened as they swooned over her; their voices came through the open door.

"A fair-faced vision who carries the scent of wildflowers," George heard Captain Robert Stewart say. Stewart was a plain, honest fellow and a brave man — he witnessed this on the battlefield.

George covered his bareness and moved closer to the doorway. He wanted to learn particulars of this beauty.

"My eyes were blessed with the sight of her," added Stewart, who had spent some time in New York.

"Does she carry a softened shape?" One junior officer motioned a woman's shape. "Parts are in proportion?"

"Sweet breath?" asked another.

"Those and one other," acknowledged Stewart. "Purity."

"Finally!" Captain George Mercer exclaimed. Mercer was of a different type than Stewart. "I've grown tired of the great imperfections we've seen along the way. The bad figures of the ladies." He shuffled with back arched and head drooping. "Many of them have a crooked shape and a very bad air." Mercer waved his hand in front of his mouth.

George quickly regretted the decision to bring Mercer. He was recommended due to his experience as a surveyor of these parts to help make the journey faster. He also had served in the Virginia Regiment before Washington took over command.

Mercer drew laughs from the group. "When she sees us dressed in regal nature" — Mercer walked with bravado to the window — "we shall introduce ourselves as captains of the finest army, as heroes."

"Think before you speak, gentlemen," Washington advised. George could take the discourteousness no longer, and beyond that, he did not favor vanity, believing it unbecoming of a gentleman. "And Captain Mercer, a man ought not to value himself of his achievements." Even on a day like this, self-admiration would not be on display, neither for himself nor for those traveling with him.

The young military officers nodded to him and remained with mouths shut as they removed their battle-worn garb to be outfitted with regimentals of scarlet superfine woolen broadcloth coats with silver lace at the arms, blue breeches, and all topped with silver-laced hats. George had ordered the garments himself. He wanted his company to look proper for the occassion. The colonel assigned five well-mounted men, in addition to two body servants, to accompany him on this trek. The servants were more vivaciously dressed. Complete livery suits in a cream color with gold accents had even been ordered.

In full costume, George approached a mirror that showed his whole body — well-groomed and elegant without being ostentatious. He adjusted the ruff led cambric about his neck. A blue coat with scarlet accents lined in gold silk fabric and adorned with two rows of ten golden buttons down the front and simple gold tassels at the shoulders was appropriate, he thought, for a night like tonight. He pulled his hair back and tied it. He placed a gold-laced hat upon his head. *To be a gentleman, act a gentleman.* Yes, this was fitting.

The body servants busily prepared a trunk next to him, removing the garb within to make room for a new, refined wardrobe. "What shall be done with your coat, Colonel?" One of them held up the garment George had worn on that doomful day. "Four clear holes right through." The servant placed his finger through each of the openings.

George hadn't noticed it before, but the gold metal seal with his family's coat of arms was missing from the coat, replaced with a bullet hole right through to where his heart would be. The tricorn hat, which they pulled from the trunk, had another two shots through it. The battle, still fresh in his mind, had been brutal. In a span of three hours, two out of every three British and Colonial officers lost their lives in the backwoods of the Monongahela. George not only managed to survive, he became a hero, a legend, a man who couldn't die.

"Protected by above." The servant raised his eyes upward in reverence, his finger still in one of the holes. "The direction of Providence."

Months Earlier
Great Crossing of the Youghiogheny, Pennsylvania

For ten days, George had been in quarantine, seized with a vile illness. The shooting pain that started around his eyes stretched its way to the back of his head. Excessive weakness made it difficult for him even to count out the prescribed small grains of fever powder. He was advised that taking one more granule of Doctor James's powder than absolutely necessary could kill a man.

The sickness confined him to a bed in a covered wagon on the side of a dirt road. His fevers were at a near-crisis level — an experience he was all too familiar with. Name a disease, and George suffered through it at one point in his life. Violent pleurisy. Diphtheria. Dysentery. Smallpox — that disease left faded pockmarks on his face. Congestive fever. Lung fever. White plague — he had watched Lawrence waste away from the same disease; the image never left his mind.

This time, bloody flux invaded George's body. The doctor forbade him to move, warning that his life would be endangered if he did so. Frustration overwhelmed him as he awaited better health.

He would have gotten here, to camp, earlier if not for his mother. She had stopped him from leaving — stopped him right at the doorway — alarmed by his decision to enlist. He could still hear her keys jangling — the ones she always wore on a large metal ring looped into the sash around her waist. He needed to convince her. There was a farm to manage, she insisted. But this was for his future. Serve king and country, certainly, and he had other reasons, selfish considerations. Learn the specifics of the British tactical battlefield maneuvers. Write each of the details into his personal journal. Secure a post of high rank. Become a man of distinction. No better opportunity would present itself than this to educate himself in the military arts. He was invited to serve as an aide-de-camp under General Braddock. These reasons contributed to his decision to join up without pay. What else was he to do? Stay on Ferry Farm forever? He sat his mother down that day to speak with her about his choice. "The God to whom you commended me, madam, when I set out upon a more perilous errand, defended me from harm, and I trust He will do so now. Do not you?"

This changed her mind. "Go, George, fulfill the high destinies which Heaven appears to have intended you for," she had told him.

The mission was not turning out as he hoped. His plan to keep a detailed journal was fading. George attended only one council of war before the weakness set in. He sent a letter to fellow aide-de-camp Captain Roger Morris, asking him to provide a copy of all of the general's orders by the first safe conveyance.

Now, a day later, a wagon arrived, driven by a scrappy lad, a couple of years his junior, with a tongue that never lay still. He walked with a spring in his step and always wore that same coonskin hat. Daniel Boone approached. He offered no salutation before his assertions began. "Sir, I must tell you . . . they believe it a joke."

"A good day to you, Boone," George said.

"Yes, good day. They reckon it a battle ill-planned in England, and ill-concerted in America. It was said and I heard it: 'We have not a single Indian on our side or the least fear of being trapped by ambush.' " Boone adjusted his hat. It had become askew. "Doomed. We are doomed. Even one of the general's own aides, not Morris, of course, believes your theory of warfare of the wilderness. He says, 'The general is in a place more adapted than any in the world to face an enemy who can fight from the woods, and yet we continue the tradition of the old in our maneuvers.' "

In his only formal council of war with the general, George laid out the maps that he had drawn of the land the enemy occupied in the backcountry, and he advised the general that these forces would find a way to conceal themselves in the brush. George knew the charts were imperfect, since they were roughly sketched for want of proper utensils, but they offered a clear indication of the dangers of the wild. Braddock marked his planned maneuvers with standard lines onto George's map with an adherence to rows of soldiers. They would never depart from the conventional linear British-style warfare. George insisted that would not suffice, keeping to his rules of civility. *Strive not with your superiors in argument, but always submit your judgment to others with modesty.*

Braddock pontificated: "The savages may have proven formidable to your raw American soldiers; however, faced with the king's troops, they will hardly make the least of effects."

The general ignored George's continued opposition.

"They will fight from the trees, General," George told him fervently. But it was to no avail. The general would not listen, even when George suggested they hurry. "If we could credit our intelligence. The French are weak at the forks but hourly expect reinforcements, which to my certain knowledge could not arrive with provisions or any supplies in time. I urge our regiment to push on with only the artillery and such other things as absolutely necessary."

Braddock scoffed at him. "We shall take our entire contingent, wagons, horses, troops, and all other supplies we see fit." His soldiers had gone on to level every molehill in their way, which decelerated the pace of troop movement. Braddock wouldn't listen to any of George's recommendations, calling him "a young hand," "a beardless boy."

It wasn't as if he was unaccustomed to that. George often heard insults directed at him — "illiterate," "unlearned," "unread."

Boone kept up his chatter. "In private, our Indian ally told us he believes the general looks upon the natives as dogs. They believe Braddock sees this country as empty of integrity and fidelity." Boone removed a scroll from his backpack. "A letter for you, sir, from Captain Morris. I'm told you should read it and offer a response to his reply if you care to." Boone stepped back to provide privacy.

Read no letters, books, or papers in company. George lifted the seal and unrolled the letter.

Dear Washington,

It is the Desire of every particular in the Family, & the Generals positive Commands to you, not to stirr, but by the Advice of the Person under whose Care you are, till you are better, which we all hope will be very soon — This I can personally assure you, that you may follow the Advice of the surgeon to whom I know you are recommended as a proper Man.

Yours &c.
Roger Morris
Monday five o'Clock in the Afternoon

George motioned for Boone to return. He would have no answer to the letter, infuriated as he was. Morris provided nothing he requested. No details of the military orders, not even the supply lists.

"And Captain Morris," Boone continued, " 'tis but assured his promotion to lieutenant colonel upon victory at Duquesne. You know the other getting what they want? That woman layered in jewels. The general's been overheard bragging about how he will take her into battle for it will be a swift victory. He's wasted months of our time as he feasts with her. Do you know what I transported to him on the evening last? Cases and cases of eatables — hams, cheeses, loaves of sugar. Sugar! Eight kegs of biscuits, sturgeon, herring, a barrel of potatoes, tubs of butter, and kegs of spirit . . . and they were set aside just for the general's table!"

George turned to Boone with astonishment at those words. *Let your judgment always be balanced. Where there is no occasion for expressing an opinion, it is best to be silent.*

"He says, Captain Stewart does, that without Washington, we cannot win."

The Day of Battle
Forks of the Ohio

George placed a hand on his brother's sword; he was glad to have it at his side. A field abloom in pristine white lay before him. The shade contrasted strikingly against a sea of brilliant red tunics worn by the British soldiers. The men were lined up in strict formation as far as the eye could see. George wore blue, not having had an opportunity to receive his uniform, since he rejoined the company only hours beforehand with a paleness in his face and a pain at his bottom that forced him to mount his horse on a couple of cushions.

Glancing one row in front, he watched a graceful woman riding a horse. Her black hair, straight and long to her waist, bounced in synchrony with the horse's gallop. She reminded him of the woman of the lowlands. That hair's length. Its shine. It was like hers — his Affa's. This woman beside the general wore a bright orange dress ornamented with pure gold bracelets about her arms. She stood out against so many red coats.

"We will strike fear in the enemy!" Braddock exclaimed. George noticed his hair, surprised a general would style it for battle. A high puff carried over his noggin from ear to ear and fell in a tail of false white curls. "Expel the French from the continent!"

For the British to take control of the Ohio country, this fort built by the French at the Forks of the Ohio would need to be captured. Here at Fort Duquesne, both the Monongahela and Allegheny Rivers came together to form the Ohio River, which was essential for trade and movement of the military.

The area appeared abandoned. The general marched the officers forth. They were lined in English tradition. The silvery lace of their uniforms glistened in the sun. With what appeared a clear path to victory on level land, despite two ravines covered with trees and high grass surrounding the final open field, the general signaled the boys to begin to play. George moved aside as the line of young fifers and drummers, just children, passed by him. The smallest of the group played the fife. The eldest carried the drum; he appeared to be beginning to show signs of manhood from the few hairs upon his face. It was he who struck the first beat.

The marching song of the British Grenadiers played.

The men began to sing.

Captain Morris, who wore a boutonniere of white clover as if on parade, was loudest of all.

Some talk of Alexander, and some of
 Hercules,
Of Hector and Lysander, and such great
 names as these,
But of all the world's great heroes, there's
 none that can compare
With a tow, row, row, row, row, row, to the
 British Grenadiers.

Those heroes of antiquity ne'er saw a
 cannon ball,
Nor knew the force of powder to slay their
 foes with all,
But our brave boys do know it, and banish
 all their fears,
With a tow, row, row, row, row, row, for the
 British Grenadiers.

When e'er we are commanded to storm the
 palisades,
Our leaders march with fuses, and we with
 hand grenades;
We throw them from the glacis about the
 enemies' ears.

Sing tow, row, row, row, row, row, for the
British Grenadiers.

Just as the last words were sung, George heard the first bullets whistle, coming from an invisible enemy among the trees. The first fire was fatal. A boy's drum fell to the ground. Blood seeped from his neck as his thin frame collapsed. The little fifer was next to fall.

A terrible carnage began. The enemy overwhelmed the soldiers with a horseshoe attack, trapping them like animals in a pen. An endless barrage came from the brush. A blur of violence faded into a cloud of chaos. The rapid discharge of musketry did not obscure the screams of injured men, dying men.

The deadly siege was exactly what George had warned against, exactly what he presaged would be the outcome of the Battle of Monongahela. His prediction of warfare in the wild was coming true.

The force of the French with their native allies aimed at the officers on horseback, and next at the officers on the ground, leaving the British force doomed. The enemy struck the first flank; every soldier was killed or wounded. Over and over again, the general ordered his men to form their proper line and march forward. Hundreds more officers advanced in British formation, an open target for the warriors firing from nature's camouflage. Before long, those officers, too, were shot and killed.

"Ye enemy! They are hidden behind the trees!" Daniel Boone shouted to George above the gunfire. "They slaughtered the men! They scalped 'em! I saw it myself."

George raced on horseback to Braddock.

"General, allow me to enter into tree fighting! We must change course." Everywhere he looked, the bodies of his comrades had fallen — were falling — all around him.

"I swear, Washington, I've a mind to run you through the body!"

"Alter the fight. Allow me to use three hundred of your men. They are in the trees, General!"

"Washington, this is my battle!"

"I implore you."

"We'll sup today in Fort Duquesne or else in hell!"

The sting of annihilation struck. A massacre unfolded before George's eyes. Morris fell to the ground. The general's lady, drenched in red, dropped from her horse. Braddock had five horses shot from under him, yet he remained in the center of the fight. A bullet struck the general in the back of his shoulder. A second shot to the breast dropped him.

With no other leader standing, George had no choice but to take control. He could have retreated; instead, he chose to reload. He could have been fearful; instead, he chose to be fearless. Leadership was thrust upon him during this dire fight. He answered the call. Refusing to let his surviving band of brothers fall, he rode in every direction, rallying the men. They took to the trees. They rushed the brush. Unlike the general, who had told the men to charge, George led the charge, with his men following.

Twice, George's horse was hit. It collapsed.

Four times, bullets pierced George's coat.

But he continued to stand. He would not go down.

Two shots struck his hat.

George's blood did not spill. He ordered cannons to fire and, with furor, grabbed his rifle, planted one hand on the muzzle, situated the other on the breach, and controlled the weapon as if it were weightless.

Gunfire directed toward him grew even more intense.

Fire after fire.

He did not fall.

He remained in the battle, sustaining not even a wound. Desperate to save the lives of the living, he continued the fight to protect his officers.

Suddenly, the bombardment from the enemy ceased.

The bullets fell silent. George was left bewildered by the quiet.

"We have General Braddock!" Captain Stewart cried out to him. Washington rushed to the general's side, hearing him murmur that he wished to be left to die with his men. Together, they placed Braddock in a tumbrel. They carried him off as he begged them to leave him there.

"The woman?" asked George of Stewart.

"Scalped and dragged off."

His focus turned to the field of clover, those white blossoms trampled and stained red. The cries of the dying pierced his heart. The stink of death surrounded him. Gloom and horror everywhere.

George saw Morris at a distance of a dozen or more yards, stumbling, seeming near collapse. He rushed to his fellow aide-de-camp and found him with hands over a bloodied face, the silver lace on his sleeve stained red. "A bullet." Morris gasped. "A bullet took my nose." He ducked under Morris's left arm and, carrying him, led him away from that meadow of death.

Four hundred and twenty-one. George, with Stewart's assistance, counted the injured lying on the ground. The two of them helped transport the wounded to a safe campsite. Each name Stewart wrote down. The last of the injured was a young boy with a small flute still across his chest, who slowly turned his desperate eyes to George when he asked his name.

"Miles Brown," he said, his voice weak. His little face resembled that of his father, a slave by the name of Billy Brown, who was in the fight and now knelt by his son's side. With George beside them, the elder Brown rose and, with rage in his voice and tears in his eyes, began to speak loudly enough for the others to hear.

"I've been given the name Billy Brown. In God's name, I tell you now. I saw the truth on that field." A great number of men turned to hear him. "Washington, he came up to the general during the fight and asked permission to take to the trees with his men." It seemed the whole camp, every wounded and the few whole, listened to his words. "The general, he screamed at him, cursed him! He said to him — and I will remember these words for the rest of my life — the general said to him, 'I've mind to run you through the body!' He swore at this man. He used these words: 'We'll sup today in Fort Duquesne or else in hell!' "

Cheers and assents erupted among the officers.

"This is the truth!" Brown yelled. "I tell you, this is the truth!" He knelt again by his young son.

From a distance, an officer's voice could be heard, reading the names of the missing and the killed on the banks of the Monongahela.

The list seemed to go on indefinitely. The force of fifteen hundred men shattered by a party of what could have been no more than a few hundred of the enemy. After the final name was read, George spoke quietly to Stewart: "The horrific scenes which showed themselves on this day are unspeakable, sickening."

"We have suffered an incomprehensible defeat." Stewart moved with him behind a large oak, away from the injured.

"The dead — the dying — the groans — lamentations — and cries along the road of the wounded for help . . . were enough to pierce the heart."

Both stood, each with a hand over his heart, face bowed.

A voice interrupted. It was Dr. James.

"Washington. The general has made a request for your presence. A bullet pierced the general's lung. We have not much time."

George walked with the doctor, passing rows upon rows of the wounded, including Captain Morris. Still bleeding about the nose, the bandaged captain jumped to his feet, appearing flabbergasted that it was Washington about to enter General Braddock's private cabin.

Morris questioned the doctor as to whether it was he the general requested.

Speak not injurious words neither in jest nor earnest scoff at none although they give occasion. George stayed silent.

The doctor gave him a firm "Nay."

In the corner of the one-room structure, light pierced through a dusty window, its rays hitting the face of the general, whose skin appeared almost grayish. "The blue," Braddock muttered in a shaky voice. "The blue saved us."

When another speaks be attentive your self and disturb not the audience if any hesitate in his words help him not nor prompt him without desired, interrupt him not, nor answer him till his speech be ended. He waited until the general finished his words.

The general turned his eyes toward George. "Who would have thought it?"

George sat on a stool next to him. Dr. James stood a few feet back.

"We shall better know how to deal with them another time." Braddock's breathing was coming short and shallow.

He nodded to the dying man. The general pointed to a small trunk near his bedside. George lifted it to him. As Braddock's shaky hands grabbed hold of it, he whispered, "For not taking your guidance, I must apologize." His fingers weakly fumbled with the latch. Inside was the commander's sash, colored in brilliant British red and stained with the general's blood, as he had worn it in the battle. "It is yours," Braddock said, as he feebly handed over the sash. "George Washington, you are the next in command."

As the only aide uninjured in the fight and the man who saved an army from utter annihilation, the raw volunteer from the Virginia woods was now commander. *Undertake not what you cannot perform but be careful to keep your promise.* Knowing this edict, George pledged his commitment to serve.

A rattling noise came from the back of the general's throat. His eyes became glassy as he stared into a distance above him. The doctor rushed over as Edward Braddock took his final breath. A blue color presenting itself upon his lips.

■ ■ ■ ■

By the light of a torch, a group of men gathered to choose the general's resting place. With a bandage covering nearly his whole face, Morris interrupted, requesting that he perform the obsequies, noting his close ties with Braddock, having signed his allegiance to the general and having traveled with him from Britain. None would have it. To the utter agitation of Morris, they turned to the new commander to determine not only the burial details but also the movement of the entire company.

The decision George made was to have Braddock buried in the middle of the high road cut for wagons. In order not to arouse any suspicion on the part of the enemy, he planned for no fanfare; not even a volley would be fired. If the enemy forces had any idea of the burial site's location, they would surely dig up the corpse and carry his scalp as a trophy.

Wrapped in two blankets, the general's body was lowered into a shallow grave. George read a devotion from the Book of Common Prayer, which Dr. James had carried with him:

Forasmuch as it hath pleased Almighty God
of his great mercy to take unto himself the
soul of our
dear brother here departed, we therefore
commit his
body to the ground, earth to earth, ashes to
ashes,
dust to dust, in sure and certain hope of the
Resurrection
to eternal life, through our Lord Jesus
Christ, who
shall change our vile body that it may be
like unto
his glorious body, according to the mighty
working,
whereby he is able to subdue all things to
himself.

"His attachments were warm," George noted upon completion of a moment of silence. "His enmities were strong, and having no disguise about him, both appeared in full force."

He signaled for the soldiers to travel on. He ordered the wagon drivers to roll over the dirt above the general's resting place and the men to march over it. He wanted to obliterate any trace of the unmarked grave, any trace of the past.

Chapter Five: Gooch's Kitchen

. . . when once the Woman has tempted us, & we have tasted the forbidden fruit, there is no such thing as checking our appetites, whatever the consequences may be.

— GEORGE WASHINGTON

Yonkers-on-Hudson
February 14, 1756

Lured by the scent of almonds, Mary's appetite was calling her to the kitchen after the return from the dressmaker's cottage. For the feast welcoming the hero and his Southern officers, Mary's brother hired an army of culinarians. From confectioners to cooks to additional dairy and scullery maids, they joined an already large staff. The Clerk of the kitchen, the ever neat and well-kempt Temperance Gooch, ruled like a crowned head; not even a drop of gravy dare land on her apron. Mary found it amusing, the disdain Temperance showed for the others her brother hired, many of whom were French. Frederick never cared much for taking sides in war, or in anything else for that matter.

Down to the kitchen Mary went, where an eruption was shaking the pots.

"A gallimaufry" — Temperance pushed aside the French cook's completed creation of *crème croquante* — "and nothing more!"

"Mademoiselle, to taste *une crème croquante,* one must pause to find *la delicatese* of each layer of flavor." This was Chef François, one of those new hires, enunciating between his curled mustache and chin beard. "This is how I create."

Mary, watching the two through the half-opened door, did not interrupt.

"Create? Imitate would be more proper a term." Temperance, Mary knew, despised the French way of cooking. "Chef d'Anjou, I shall not fill my table with such nonsense." A cook's daughter, Temperance had grown up in the manor. She began working in the kitchen when she became old enough. And now, at twenty-four years of age, she demanded certain pay for her work, to which Frederick agreed. On a day like today, Temperance would not be outprepared, especially by a French cook who was in the middle of a serenade over his pot.

"Vous insulte ma creation, Mademoiselle Gooch!" The chef walked closer to Temperance and pointed to a silver tray. "You yourself make a dessert of snowballs." His nose scrunched up, as if it had been assaulted by putrescence.

"A dish that is a creation, not an imitation," snapped Temperance. Over the balls made of boiled rice, apples, and a touch of cinnamon, she drizzled a sauce that combined butter, white wine, and nutmeg. "It is to the liking of the lady of the house."

"Mademoiselle, never has a snowflake fallen to the south" — he picked up the tray — "just as never has a snowball had a place at a banquet."

"I am aware it would not be French to show praise to a good cook," Temperance declared, storming past him. "As for your crème, it is more dull than divine."

"I am at your pleasure, Mademoiselle." He leaned near her. "As for my crème, I shall be sure to dulcify it for you."

It seemed to Mary that the chef found Temperance's superciliousness quite engaging, while Temperance nearly winced at the close proximity.

She interrupted for Temperance's sake and looked right at the dessert in François's hand. "Splendid! As we await snowfall outside, you have brought a touch of radiant frost inside."

"A day for celebration, Mademoiselle Philipse!" François happily responded, still holding the tray of snowballs.

"Miss Polly, good day." Temperance approached her with a long dish holding small sampling bowls. "Just for you, I have created an orange pudding, as well as a lemon pudding, a millet pudding, carrot pudding, quince pudding, apricot pudding, white pear and plum-apple pudding."

"The sweetness that brings me to the kitchen every time." Mary noticed Temperance's nervousness around François. Naming each pudding — it wasn't like her to do that.

"Rice pudding, custard pudding, bread pudding, chestnut pudding, prune pudding," added Temperance. For the last, she handed Mary a specially crafted blue-and-white Canton bowl containing Mary's favorite. "For our Miss Polly, the pretty almond pudding."

"They've arrived!" The heiress examined the porcelain she suggested be ordered for the special occasion from Ching-te-chen. With the family's influence, the East India Trading Company shipped with urgency the entire table set for the banquet. "And without breakage?"

"Not a one, Miss Polly."

"If you please," said François, bringing over additional samples of his own. "For you, *crème au chocolat, crème de café, crème au zeste d'orange, crème de vin du Rhin, crème croquante, crème à la fleur de vanille.*"

"*Merci beaucoup. Je suis impatiente de tous deguster.* At present, the pretty almond pudding will do my stomach just fine."

"Then all of them we shall display. A fine table it shall be!" François returned to his pot as well as to his serenade.

Temperance walked with Mary as she enjoyed the sample of pretty almond pudding.

"Your admirer's eyes remain on you," whispered Mary.

"He is impossible."

"Impossibly handsome."

"Impossibly French."

Temperance walked Mary through the many dishes that would be served during dinner, beginning with Mary's special request, the salamongundy — a salad dish of edible flowers, herbs, small onions, string beans, boiled eggs, grapes, and lemon-roasted chicken with an oil dressing beaten with vinegar, salt, and pepper.

The guests would be treated to a culinary extravaganza this night. For years, Mary helped Temperance write and rewrite recipes to attain the perfect combination of flavors. Now Mary reviewed the menu, hopeful the dishes would be to Colonel Washington's liking.

"Scotch collops, leg of lamb, rump of beef, roasted duck, and loaf of oysters," Temperance added. "The French influence for Lord Frederick will be in the *lapereaux aux truffes* and the *côtes de boeuf à la Sainte Menoux.* Your brother has asked that catsup be served as well."

"Catsup?" Mary could see that Temperance was pleased with her work. "A perfect choice. Papa, too, would have enjoyed that." The offerings were more than Mary could have imagined. This was the first time in longer than she could remember that the home was so filled with activity. Since the devastating loss of Mary's sister Margaret, her father, and, of course, her mother, the manor had never been so alive. "Everyone would have relished in this glorious feast."

Tenderly, Temperance took hold of Mary's hand. "Miss Polly, a proud night is before you." Temperance knew more than most about the Philipses, their joys and their grief.

Trying to regain her composure, trying to find her calm, her eyes began to fill. "I find it difficult to rejoice when we have been through much sorrow." Her whole being was thrust into an anxious state. She exited the kitchen. Her pace quickened as she moved into the hall. Furniture was being moved out of the foyer to make space.

Those crowds! She thought of the poking and prodding, the bumping of shoulders, the accidental and intentional brushing of a hand here, a hip there, the hollow chatter, meaningless queries, and the hall stifling from the fetor of hair powder. She knew scores of eyes would be on her on a night like tonight. The questions would be endless: Why had she not attended any recent balls or banquets? A crush of people would soon fill the room. The barrage she imagined made her feel dizzy.

Her legs grew weak. She pictured her shoes slipping through muddy ground. A chill ran through her. That night — the one when she lost her mother — plunged her spirit into a depth so deep, she had never recovered. It didn't matter that one of the guests was the hero of the South. It didn't matter that the dancing master's freedom might depend on her. Her brother's wishes were inconsequential. What occupied her thinking was the horde, her unease, and especially the disquieting presence of the man of her nightmares; just the smell of him triggered her return to the torment.

She needed to run. Hide. Get away. The same as she had done time and time again.

Pale blue.

She liked that color best.

Mary often lost track of the hours when she was in here, painting. She came to this room in the cellar when she needed to escape. It was a place to hide from the distress that often disturbed her countenance.

She delicately dried nature and gently glossed over death with the color on her paintbrush. This was madness; she knew that. Blossoms bereft of life she brought back to brightness with the stroke of her brush.

"Every flower must emerge from the darkness to bathe in the light," she remembered her mother often telling her on those mornings they gathered blooms at Hudson's Hook and tied them into a bunch with a red satin ribbon. Spring was her mother's favorite time of year. And Mary fondly recalled her younger sister with them, vivacious and exuberant, frolicking about with her bare feet on tender grasses.

Years later, Mary cut wildflowers to be placed at Margaret's bedside when the sickness took hold of her. Day after day, Mary held a handkerchief, careful to conceal her emotion, while sitting outside the door of the bedchamber, the one Mary was ordered not to enter. Every day, she would sing her sister a melody. She sang it now:

If to me as true thou art
As I am true to thee, sweetheart
We'll hear one, two, three, four, five, six
From the bells of Aberdovey.
Hear one, two, three, four, five, six
Hear one, two, three, four, five and six
From the bells of Aberdovey.

Margaret would clap along — one, two, three, four, five, six — albeit feebly. Until one day there was silence. A deafening emptiness fell upon the home.

"I remember that song." Mary hadn't heard Frederick come into the cellar room. As he spoke, he crouched to avoid garlands of dried autumn leaves she'd placed above the entry. A few leaves fell loose. "You wouldn't leave her door until you heard

Margaret clap her hands to six with you. On a night like tonight, the little rascal would have been dancing till the sun rose. What of the time she pulled the peruke right off of Lord Livingston?"

The moment came clear in her mind.

"Robert the Elder ran from the center of the room, chasing after her for it," she said.

"Right in the middle of the minuet."

"On his face was dread, with not a hair upon his head."

His rhyme about the curmudgeon always made her laugh.

Frederick placed his hands in his pockets. "You are aware, Polly, that you cannot remain hidden away forever."

She turned back to her brushstrokes. He did not understand her. How could he? How could anyone? She felt as if her soul had been shattered, and its broken shards with their jagged edges piercing her heart. Over the years, Mary attempted to carry on by building an impenetrable wall to block her emotions. Many times her brother tried to relieve her misery. And for that she was grateful. He always told her their deaths — Elbert's, Mother's, Father's, Margaret's — were not her fault. Mary knew the truth. She could have reached for the flower from Elbert. She could have stayed away from her father and from Margaret. Mary knew she was not just the cursed one; she was the one damned to stay alive.

"I know I'm not Father. I would do more for you if I knew how."

The woe that gripped her had remained for so long.

For too long.

She arose.

In the distance, the bells of St. John's Church sounded. Eric Arthur pledged he would watch for the hero's arrival. His signal to her would be one lasting chime, give it time to echo, and follow that with two more in quicker succession.

"Come, Polly, your tomorrow awaits you," said Frederick. "First, however, we may need to remove this nature from your hair."

"Mine? Wait until you see the mess you've made of yours."

The bells sounded again.

One slow followed by two fast.

Colonel George Washington had arrived.

Chapter Six: The Hero Washington

. . . I do not think vanity is a trait of my character.

— GEORGE WASHINGTON

George's horse left the dirt and moved onto the cobblestones of Albany Post Road in the town of Yonkers. The colonel rode atop a superb chestnut bay. The coaches following behind him were elegantly covered with an embroidered coat of arms on the material. The crest displayed a bird that looked like an eagle sitting atop a white shield of stars and stripes, and beneath the shield, the name George Washington was hand-stitched.

Trailing pine from a line of evergreens welcomed George to the New York Colony.

He listened to the clangs coming from the belfry of an enormous stone church. One slow followed by two fast.

"He comes. He comes." George could

hardly believe his ears, until he heard the townspeople shout his name clearly. "The hero Washington, he comes!" The hero *Washington.* He never would have expected to be recognized in such a way. Quite a site of pageantry it was. George watched what seemed to be hundreds of people lining the path to greet him.

The cheers grew louder. "The hero Washington has arrived!" Throngs of people applauded him and those riding with him, including Mercer and Stewart. Mercer seemed more interested in gazing at the belles. George reminded him of a rule he himself followed: *Play not the peacock, looking everywhere about you to see if you be well deck't.*

"He comes! The hero, he comes!" Young ladies threw flower petals before him.

A lady with pointed spectacles hanging on a chain loudly shouted from just feet away.

"The most handsome man mine eyes have ever beheld!"

"One touch of him!" exclaimed another lady with hair piled high above her head as she pushed through the crowd. "I must have just one touch!" Her actions became so intense that at one point a child in her path, a little girl with ginger hair, fell to the ground. In a panic, others hollered at the woman. George stopped the cavalcade until the child was upright. Without hesitation, the girl raced with one leg limping to embrace the woman with the pointed glasses, and cried out, "Huzza!"

Before him now lay the handsome estate of the Philipse family, surrounded by massive mills with cascading water. The powerful rushes fell to the grand Hudson River. A Georgian-style mansion by the water's edge looked even more impressive as he drew closer. It exuded wealth from its symmetrical design and classic detail. Two formal entries were accented with pilasters. Three floors high, the house had eight windows across the front and five windows at the side of the second floor. Large chimneys reached into the sky. A viewing rail sat upon the roof.

The cavalcade stopped before the path that led to the mansion. A bronze tablet, polished to perfection, caught George's attention. It was situated to the left of the walkway, engraved with the family's coat of arms, a crowned lion issuing from a coronet. Today George felt polished to perfection as well. Refined. A man of honor. It had taken him years of hard work to achieve this. New Yorkers, he thought, were a fine people indeed.

George dismounted. A kindly fellow received him. "We are honored with your arrival at the town of Yonkers-on-Hudson, Colonel Washington. Joseph Chew's the name. I shall tend to your horses. If I might further assist, please make me aware."

As he was about to answer, someone with a familiar face approached. George quickly tipped his hat to Chew before greeting Major Beverley Robinson. Fifteen years it had been since seeing his good friend.

"Colonel Washington, my congratulations on your success with command of the Virginia Regiment."

"We've certainly come a long way, friend, from throwing rocks across the Rappahannock." George could recall clearly the days they spent on the farm together, riding horses, and trying not to get into too much trouble with George's mother.

"If I remember correctly, it was only you who got them straight away to the other side of the river." Beverley pretended to toss one in the air.

"A long wait for the ferry will do that."

"It was rocks then. Today we could use silver dollars." Beverley patted his coat pocket.

"Silver dollars? Those would remain safe in my pocket."

A grinning Robinson escorted George to the dignitaries lined up to greet him. As George approached them, he followed his rule for meeting the dignified classes: *In pulling off your hat to persons of distinction, as noblemen, justices, churchmen and company, make a reverence, bowing more or less according to the custom of the better bred, and quality of the person.*

"May I introduce Colonel George Washington. A man of such strength that I've witnessed him throw . . . a silver dollar across . . . the Potomac River."

Before George were the distinguished gentlemen of the town. He could tell this from their voices, which were as sophisticated as their costume. They seemed to take Beverley's story as truth. The Potomac was twice as wide as the Rappahannock. George tried to correct him, but the major wouldn't have it and continued on with introductions to the heads of the Livingston, Jay, Van Cortlandt, and Delancey families. George took note as he approached a Delancey, who was announced as the town's sheriff. He gave George no greeting whatsoever.

Chapter Seven: The Pleasure Ball

'Tis true I profess myself a votary of love . . .

— GEORGE WASHINGTON

Mary could hear the revelry downstairs and it made her worry. What if her spirit failed her? What if she ran off in the middle of a minuet? What if the fog of hair powders enveloped her, dragged her down, and choked her? Please, Mary, no, she told herself. The last thing she wanted was to embarrass her family again. She'd done enough of that.

She shut her eyes and begged her mind to go blank as the sounds of instrumentalists playing Johann Pachelbel's Canon in D Major reached her room. She stood as still as possible while the abigails tightened her corset. She found this difficult, for she was trembling inside. With her swift transformation under way, she took in the *Chaenome-*

les speciosa. It must have been Susannah who had placed the flowering quince branches in her bedchamber. The pink blooms combined sweet and fresh and sultry in one bold fragrance.

The swoosh of her door swinging open startled her.

Dressmaker Rosie hurried into the room. "Pull it tighter!" She carried precious Lulu on her hip. "He's a vision, Miss Polly!" Rosie's bun sat even more disheveled than usual. "A vision!" She tried to catch her breath. "Colonel Washington. The chap came close 'nough for me to 'bout touch him. Almost got ahold of his big paws." She had a jolly laugh. "We saw the hero. Didn't we, darlin'?"

Lulu nodded feverishly, hanging on to her mother tightly. The little girl's hair was in crooked pigtails, one high, one low.

Rosie made her way to the gown and placed Lulu down. The child hopped on one foot to Mary and threw her arms around her, which caused Mary's hair to come loose from the waterfall braid being completed. All of this caused a scramble not just among the lady's maids but also in Mary's conflicted spirits. A vision. Mary always knew he would be. She tried to calm her nerves by taking a moment to fix the little girl's pigtails.

Rosie removed Lulu from the gown, sat her on a stool, and placed herself on the floor. Her hands adjusted the hem. "The dress gots to be below the shoulders. Shine 'em up with cream!" Rosie looked up with a large grin. "We want our angel to shimmer."

Two ladies followed the instructions, while another continued working on her hair; she placed the curling iron into the fire and twisted Mary's hair around the heated rod. Mary liked this style, for the subtle waves fell loosely from the braid that pulled her hair away from her face. A fourth lady added a red pomade to Mary's lips and a light rouge to her cheeks. Mary wondered whether she should have them add more paint to her face, or use less. How could she even know? She'd never worn any before. In the end, she decided to ask that no paint be added to her eyes.

Rosie slid back to look at her. "A vision. *You* are the vision."

She assumed Rosie was just being kind. She only hoped that, at the least, she would be presentable.

"We've not time!" Susannah sounded frantic as she rushed into the room sideways. Her sister's dress was so wide that she could not get through the door any other way. "Colonel Washington is here. He's walking into the manor!" Luxuriously dressed from crown to silk shoe, Susannah, wearing a silvery cerulean-colored gown, held out the boxed gift for Mary to open, the same one Eva presented her at the fitting at the Sherwood house.

Her cousin knew Mary well — too well. Mary lifted the lid to reveal the diadem. Made of pure gold, the half crown had hand-carved silhouettes in ivory at its points, representing women of the Philipse and Van Cortlandt families. Lady Joanna was at its center with her face carved in perfect detail. Mary felt a sense of peace knowing her mama would be with her tonight. The group carefully adjusted the decorative on her head and secured it.

"You look like a princess, my dear Polly." Susannah's face brightened. "You remind me of Princess Florine awaiting her charming."

"Miss Polly! Miss Polly!" little Lulu piped. Mary turned toward her. "You telled me that fairy's tale."

Mary reached over and gently tapped her on the top of her head. "Lulu, you remembered."

"Prince Charmin' don't care 'bout no

curses." The girl motioned a swat with her hand.

Mary adored the child. "Would you like me to read it again to you on my next visit?"

Lulu's whole face smiled, even her freckled nose.

It was one of Mary's favorite stories. The tale by Madame d'Aulnoy told of a handsome Prince Charming who had been cursed and transformed into a bluebird because of his love for a sweet-hearted princess who had been hidden away from the world. He traveled in flight for years in search of his true love.

" 'Bird, with wings of heaven's blue,' " Susannah began, reciting the tale. " 'Haste to where I wait for you.' My sister, your charming is dressed in heaven's blue."

"Please tell me he arrives not covered in feathers," Mary replied.

Susannah laughed. Lulu covered her mouth so as not to let out giggles, but a few high-pitched ones escaped.

"Come. Look at the beauty you've become." Susannah helped her sister to the mirror. The gentle rustling of gowns could be heard. "Impossible it will be for him to have eyes for anyone else than so captivating a belle."

Mary stood staring into a full-length mirror. Her reflection presented a dewy face in a glimmering dress. Her cheeks were rosy, her hair fancy, her shoulders shiny, her shoes colorful, her posture in proper position. Today she most certainly looked like Florine coming out of hiding. She knew what she really was — madness in elegant clothing.

Susannah moved her to the doorway to exit her chamber. As Mary approached the stairwell, she could hear Frederick one floor below, making one toast too many. She was well aware this was on account of her being delayed to greet the guests.

"To Colonel Washington. May you continue to show greatness against our enemy combatants."

"To the officers of the South. May you continue to commit your service for all."

"To the New York dignitaries. May your work continue to make our colony a symbol of greatness."

"For the weather —"

When he started a toast to the temperature, the guests began to sound restive, seemingly anxious to enter the dining room, where Temperance's feast awaited.

"May winter continue to remain mild and dry in our Yonkers to allow for safe and comfortable travel."

As he started one more toast, Mary hurriedly moved to the staircase. She heard a loud gasp coming from the guests. The musicians stopped playing. She took a deep breath, kept her shoulders back, and pinched the front of her dress to keep it from catching on her shoes. She placed one foot slowly below the other. She could feel a man's gaze upon her, his eyes slaying her, as if sending an arrow straight to her heart. A glimpse of him was all she could handle. He stood strong and tall, a striking figure in his azure coat with its golden accents at the shoulders. His hair, untouched by powder, was neatly pulled back, showing the strength of his features. The color of his eyes she did not see. What are the color of his eyes? she wondered. The view of him was ever so quick. She had a desire for another look, but she wouldn't dare look again.

"Ladies and gentlemen, Miss Polly Philipse," Frederick announced. She recognized that smile of his. She'd made her brother proud. The room resounded with a burst of applause. Tonight she quite liked that Frederick was introducing her. It had been years. Had it been since that affair when she was just a child? Yes. She remembered. Her brother announced her that day . . . at the banquet. Her mother told her to stay put. Why did she run? Her brother, yes, he was the one to say her name. She could remember it now. He was young then. That was before. Before the hour that changed everything.

Like a storm cloud rolling in, the odor of hair powdering — the mix of wheat flour and fine white clay — ignited an inner upheaval. She paused on the third step.

Please, Mary, don't collapse, her mind begged her.

A sea of eyes was upon her. The images that she feared most reemerged. She was afraid. The waves. The slippery earth. If she had only reached for the flower . . .

She drew quick breaths.

Not again. Not tonight. "There will be no what-ifs." She heard her sister's voice in her head.

"Protect. Save." She remembered what her father had told her. "As a beacon in the darkness. Be the light."

The bright and lively interlude of "The Arrival of the Queen of Sheba" by Handel began to play. Sir Tenoe's face — she could see the dancing master at the back of the crowd. He stood there looking proudly at her. His scar shone clear from the light of the window. At least do this for *him.* Mary focused on Tenoe's scar as she continued her descent to the grand foyer. Not a person's face turned from her, including the hero's. She could see him looking, out of the corner of her eye. She hoped her expression did not give away too much of her inner struggle. Her brother received her at the base of the stairs and walked her to the man of honor this evening.

There he was, the hero of the South before her. How handsome he looked. How brave.

"Colonel George Washington, may I introduce you to my dear sister."

"Miss Mary Eliza Philipse." The colonel used her birth name as few ever did.

Her eyes remained on his shoes. Not a speck of mud.

He placed his hand below hers, rugged to dainty. She felt him bring her hand to his lips. She raised her eyes to his.

"Your presence affords me unspeakable pleasure."

Blue.

His eyes were blue, with a hint of gray.

The feel of his lips was upon her right hand. How thankful she was that in her haste she had forgotten to slip on her lace gloves. With his warm breath on her bare skin, she decided if she could remain here in this very position for her entire life, she would be contented.

She realized she would have to respond to his greeting with words, if she could find them. She hadn't thought of a response. She knew much about him from reading his journal over and over. She could have recited every line of his writings. A plan should have been made for this moment. There was not. So, with dimpled cheek, she curtsied unhurriedly, trying to regain some type of composure.

You must say something, she thought. Her eyes shifted to the ground. If they had done justice to her state of mind, they would have revealed abounding passions. "And it is my presence to be in your pleasure, Colonel Washington."

Teeth. He had a wide mouth and his eyes smiled along with his lips. Like a prince, a charming prince. Her charming: Had he arrived? Maybe it was the sweet music, or perhaps it was his blue eyes locked on her, or maybe his strength — which gave her the feeling that he could protect her for an eternity — that made her tingly.

The two, side by side, began their walk to the dining room as the bells were rung for the banquet.

"Mary." His face, she noticed, carried a square jaw, as she had imagined. "What a charming name."

The tingle stretched from the top of her head down to her toes when he used the word *charming.*

"It is the name of my mother," he went on. "The most beautiful woman I've ever known."

She wondered if the surprise showed on her face, because she was surprised that a military commander would speak of his mother with such praise. "How fortunate I am to carry the same name."

"The sum of who I am I owe to my mother. I attribute my success in life to the moral, intellectual, and physical education I received from her."

"My mother's presence is always close to my heart," said Mary. "I hold her memory with the greatest affection." They walked a few more steps in quiet, until Mary felt the need to speak to break the momentary silence. She looked down. "My mother would have admired your shoes."

An heiress standing before him. The belle of the North. Glorious as love. George paused to take in her delightful face, her tender voice, her pleasant manner, her delicate hands, the gentleness of her dark eyes. It seemed she had no idea how lovely she was. How could it be that she carried not a hint of coquetry?

Mary Eliza Philipse.

He decided right then and there that he had never met a lady like her before. He wondered if men lost portions of their hearts to women like her. "A fair-faced vision who carries the scent of wildflowers" — Captain Stewart was correct in his assessment. She smelled as if she had been lying in a garden of lavender blooms. He enjoyed the thought of it. Her complexion, fair and smooth, glowed. Her lips carried a luster of reddish tone. Shiny waves tumbled over her round and quite shimmery shoulders. She carried a softened shape, just as his men described, which looked as if nature had formed it from a perfect mold. Her waist was so small, it seemed his fingers would touch if he wrapped his hands around it. Her gown was highly ornamented, though she needed no embellishment. Her natural grace alone was enough.

George gazed at her once more, trying not to let his eyes linger on her face for longer than appropriate. He realized he did not know of her mother's passing. His secretary, Kirkpatrick, had assured him he provided every detail — her education level, her circle of friends, her properties. Clearly, he had not learned enough.

The banquet room was masterly appointed for the occasion, decorated with deep red and blue flower bouquets and with affluence displayed in every direction he looked. The beauteous one stepped in first and motioned to a chair at the head of the table, to where his back would be to the hearth. It would not have been his choice of a seat, as he always followed his rule: *Set not yourself at the upper of the table; but if it be your due or that the master of the house will have it so, contend not, lest you should trouble the company.*

His eyes remained on her as he was seated in a fancifully carved mahogany chair with such an extreme polish that it appeared wet. Then he faced the table, which was so laden with dishes, it was impossible to see a square inch of the table covering. Set in the most orderly fashion were blue-and-white porcelain plates with gold lining the rims. Each was filled with extravagant fare. Small dishes — there must have been more than fifty of them — covered the table. The loaf of oysters grabbed his attention.

How his life had changed. Tonight he was dining with the most well-to-do family in New York, quite possibly the wealthiest family across all of the colonies. It was not long ago that dining meant using a forked stick to cook food hunted from the woods and a large chip of bark acted as his plate.

"Are you comfortable in your seating by the fire?" Beverley asked, taking his seat.

"Humbled and quite appreciative." George moved his chair closer to the table. "Happy's he that gets the berth nearest the flame."

"Have your other hosts not treated you with polite attention?" Frederick's brow furrowed as he sat down.

"My journey has been an arduous one."

"Arduous?" inquired Frederick.

"At times I had not slept above three nights or four in succession in a bed. I would lay down upon a little hay straw fodder or bearskin whichever was to be had . . ."

Frederick raised his glass of Madeira to make another toast. "Let your days ahead be filled with hospitality and friendship. To the hero of the South!"

"Hear! Hear!" The guests raised their glasses to salute him. The heiress, sitting next to Frederick, did so as well. George's thoughts turned to the feel of her smooth skin on his lips.

"Let us enjoy the banquet before us," announced Frederick.

The mix of delicious aromas whetted his

appetite. George had not eaten since the journey began at dawn. He was eager to satisfy his hunger. As he brought oysters to his tongue, one rule of civility proved challenging: *Put not another bite into your mouth till the former be swallowed. Let not your morsels be too big for the jowls.* Bite by bite, each magnificent taste finally settled his cravings. Tonight, though, he hoped hunger would be appeased not just in his stomach; it had been so long since he felt a woman's touch.

This night 'twas truly a feast for his senses.

The sounds of tinkling crystal interrupted his thinking. His glass was filled to the rim immediately after each sip. The dishes were cleared. To his astonishment, new plates of blue-and-white porcelain were set down. He'd believed dinner was completed. A suckling pig was placed at the head of the table, a dressed goose at the foot, and along the table's edges sat four roasted chickens. In the center were trays of crayfish, shrimp, and stewed dishes of hare, duck, boar, and lamb. Add to those, additional plates of pickled mackerel, mashed potatoes topped with a ragoo, partridges with truffles, and breads of many kinds. George was urged by Frederick to try the catsup.

"May we add our congratulations on your

promotion, Colonel Washington," said Frederick. "We are glad to hear of your accolades in His Majesty's Army."

"Your success and good fortune are the toasts of every table, Colonel," Beverley added. "Every officer, I hear, is willing to venture under your command."

"Be not deceived," said George. "I do not believe myself equal to such an appointment."

"Is there a place for you and your companies to feast?" Frederick took a buttered biscuit.

"The men must prepare their meals in their barracks. Each is equipped with a kettle and not much more for cooking."

The heiress appeared astonished by his comment.

"Where have they set your post?" questioned Frederick.

"In Winchester. I have been honored to form a regiment made up of sixteen companies there."

The color of rose juxtaposed against ivory as a gentle blush bloomed on the belle's cheeks.

"Where have you arrived from this day?" she asked.

He listened to how she pronounced each word, with a sweet inflection at the end of the question. "We were stopped at Laurel Hill."

"Laurel Hill?" Her radiant face tilted.

"Of New Jersey," he replied, "but not to gather laurels, except of the kind which cover the mountains." It was a pun, and not a very good one at that. Still, Mary Eliza Philipse smiled.

The dinner plates were cleared away, as was the tablecloth. A new fabric that sent up a scent of mint replaced it. Then came dessert. Trumpets led a procession. A chef wearing a toque and sporting a curled mustache entered with cooks carrying plate after plate of confections. Three dozen types of sugary eatables, maybe more, were presented for the guests to try. Tipsy cakes, pies of gooseberry, orangeado, plum, cherry, and every type of pudding made their way into the dining room.

The chef then explained in a French accent the next dish he was carrying — enticing snowballs. George ate not one but two. He made note, as well, of the numerous French-speaking attendants. It seemed the family paid no mind to the war. In addition, every race was represented in the household; a female cook entered and walked directly to the heiress, with a small bowl of pudding.

Mary Eliza Philipse gave her an appreciative look.

George watched closely as the heiress kindly smiled and whispered, "I thank you. The desserts, the feast, all divine."

"As is the company," the lady quietly responded.

The guests arose upon completion of their feast and, led by Frederick, were escorted out of the room. Mary Eliza Philipse waited in her chair. George, with belly full and spirit soaring, approached her. With a shy smile, she placed her hand inside his arm, which he had outstretched to receive her.

George's smile pierced Mary like a fork into sugar cake. Not a hint of vanity was demonstrated in his countenance.

Colonel George Washington.

She realized she had never met another man like him in all her life.

Her favorite aria from Handel's opera *Radamisto* was being performed in the music room.

"Do you play?" she asked.

"An instrument?"

She found this funny. She nodded.

"I cannot raise a single note on any one of them."

How honest of him, she thought. "And there is not a tutor in New York who would feel pride in naming me a student under his tutelage." She would be truthful as well. "Of this, I am confident."

The aria was reaching its apex. As the countertenor lingered over the words *la vendetta,* he seemed to unleash a revenge on the song itself. In overemotional fashion, a tear came to the singer's eye as he presented the chorus in a sensational manner.

"Nothing is more agreeable, and ornamental, than good music. Of what is he singing?"

"The name of it is 'Ombra Cara,' " she answered. "An enchanting woman survives death after being thrown into furious waters. She tries to escape a tyrannical ruler who desires to possess her as a city is burned to the ground in a war over her affection."

"Quite a tale."

"In the end, the strings intertwine and suddenly, her first love, her true, returns for her."

"The power of melody. It is enough to soothe even the ferocity of the wild beast."

"Love, too, can wash away the dust of the soul with just one note." What was she saying? Why would you twice use the word love? she questioned herself. It must have been the wine. Mary had already had more than a glassful while dining.

She was thankful for her cousins walking toward her. Eva carried herself in an attractive blue-green gown that outspread wide below the waist. Silk bows lined the top of it. Her hair was worn in a tuck-and-cover style, where the thin floral crown showed in the front but was wrapped with her dark hair around the back. The rest of her waves hung down. Their cousin Margaret appeared exquisite with her blond, almost white, loose curls, some placed atop her head, the others flowing down her back. Her ivory skin was as flawless as her choice of a silk gown in a pale pink fabric with hand-embroidered bleeding heart flowers throughout.

"Colonel, my cousins Miss Eva Van Cortlandt and Miss Margaret Kemble."

"Pleased to make your acquaintances," he said, after which he politely excused himself and moved toward his officers.

Eva's big eyes opened wide. She leaned toward Mary's ear. "Oh, he is lost in adoration. Unable to surrender the view that is our charming Polly."

"He still looks this way?" Mary asked without turning toward him.

"As if trapped in intoxication." Eva then

took their hands and formed a circle. "It is true, is it not, Polly, that he is a temple sacred by birth?"

"He is quite delicious, isn't he?" Mary welled up with excitement.

Eva peeked past her. "Built by hands divine."

Margaret's head tilted slightly toward him. Her ringlets followed suit. "And it doesn't appear he thinks of himself as such."

"One of the very few men of such caliber." Eva sighed.

"Polly, are you aware of how dazzling you look tonight?" Margaret gave her a broad smile.

"What I am aware of is the desperate need to take a breath. I am ever so tightly squeezed up in this gown."

The three burst into laughter as Mary separated from them and walked toward the doorway. In need of detaching her train for dancing and wanting a bit of air, she moved through the banquet room, where the dining coverings were being removed. Exquisite mahogany wood with a heavily shined surface was displayed. Silver trays of fruit were placed upon it.

Around the table, three little boys, the children of the elite, raced in a competition of sorts. "Good evening, gentlemen," Mary greeted them.

They halted, appearing frightened of a scolding, but then grinned wide. "Good evening to you, Miss Philipse," Robert and Henry Livingston, along with John Jay, announced in something like unison.

Henry broke from the group and ran over to her. "Tonight is a night to delight and not fight."

Mary reached down to hug him. "My poet Henry — that is a handsome rhyme. One day your poetry will be known around the world. I'm certain of it. And yes, boys, no fights tonight."

"Yes, Miss Philipse." They quickly recommenced their races in the parlor.

As she rounded the corner toward the powder room, she noticed the faint smell of mud. This stopped her. A forceful jerk tugged her backward. A man's arm grabbed her about the waist like a snake capturing its prey. The other arm wrapped around her neck, pressing her face against his moistened cheek. Each of his fingers, even the crooked one, was covered in metal rings.

"Your allure shakes me." The voice sounded sharp as a razor's edge. "Had you forgotten to send me an invitation, dearest Polly?"

She caught a glimpse of raven black hair

covered in hair powder; the clay dust emitted a foulness that forced her into a motionless state. Her mouth suddenly went dry. She did not scream. She could not say a word.

"Have you not read the many correspondences I have sent to you? You are the one I desire to possess, merchandise more precious than rubies, finer than gold."

She detested every word that came from the man's loathsome tongue.

"You leave me always aching for more of you. I will remain here until I hear thy word. *Yes* will be the only one I will accept."

No one would have believed it. James Jay — the physician, a member of polite society, his father, the esteemed Peter Jay. But Mary knew the real James. The signs of his rage. His erratic behavior. The twitch in his eye.

Her eyes shifted downward to see his boots, which were specked with dried mud. The heels had long gilt spurs attached to them. They made jangling sounds when he took three steps back to force her into the corner of a storage room. She was desperate for release. With his hand upon her chin, he pressed the side of her face onto his lips.

"Laissez-la partir!" A shout came from the north-side doorway.

Jay's hands held on tightly to her. "A

threat from a French cook? Go back to your kettle!"

She could feel the movement of muscles in his wet face.

A plate shattered across the floor at the doorway. It was Temperance who'd thrown it, and who now appeared with fury upon her face. François grabbed a broken piece of the porcelain up from the floor and leveled it at James Jay.

"Let her go!" Temperance shrieked.

"Je vous egorge!" François shook the shard. "I will cut you!"

"Your kind, I detest." James's obsession with the wine cup was evident from his breath. "Nothing more can you take from me and my family."

"You talk of nonsense," François said, moving closer to him.

Temperance yelled, "Let her go!"

"You, the French, you stole everything. You think we don't remember your kind's Edict of Fontainebleau, confiscating my family's land, forcing them to run from your evil country. Now you wish to take my love from me. I will not have it." James's hands wrapped around Mary's neck.

François lunged, drawing blood from James's arm.

He writhed in pain, long enough to allow

Mary to wrangle from his tight grip.

With blood dripping onto his sleeve, James looked up in a rage. "I will have my revenge!"

Frederick raced in. "What have you done?"

James raised a fist in the air, red trailing down his arm. "Your cook cut me!"

Frederick placed his body in between Mary and James. "Leave at once!" he shouted at James.

"Leave? Lord Philipse, that will never happen," countered James. "I am family, your cousin. Did you not know?"

"You will never be part of this family. You will never, never be one of us."

"Your dear little sister agreed to be mine long ago."

'Twas true, she was only a child then. Mary remembered feeling pain. He wouldn't let go. She couldn't scream. "You will be my queen, and I your king" were his words to her. She finally agreed to marry him so he would release her.

"I proposed myself a partner for life to her. And, my love, my Polly, you agreed."

"Never will you have her, James." Frederick moved Mary farther away, using his body to block her. "You have been rejected many times."

"Address me with the proper title. I am Doctor James Jay, a student of medicine."

"You shame the name of your family, you insolent drunkard, mutton-headed schemer. Poison spills from your being."

"Your family stole from mine what rightfully belongs to the family of Jay. This house, your land, the whole of your belongings — they are mine!"

"Your words excite a hateful passion. I tell you, leave now or I will bring in the guards."

James staggered toward the door. As he moved past Mary, he leaned into her. "I want all of it, including you, Polly."

She felt unsteady as the door closed behind James. A sensation took hold of her; it felt as if the room were moving, spinning about her head. She could barely hear Frederick's words. Her sight blurred.

"We will be sure to assign guards at the door," her brother's words echoed. "He will never get near her again. He will never get any of our attention ever again."

Blackness overcame her.

"Like silent poetry," announced the dancing master to the assembled in the ballroom. "Let your dance be a captivating sight as the musicians play to your ears' delight. Strong charms, each gentleman will soon impart as he makes a passage straight to each belle's heart."

"My hope is that you enjoy the evening," Beverley said to George. "I wouldn't have suggested a ball to welcome you to Philipse Manor, Colonel, if I was not aware of your prowess with the minuet."

"I shall let others lead the way." George did feel at ease on the dance floor. The minuet was one he knew well. He had experience with high society in Virginia, it was true, and he patterned his models and refined his sentiments among that colony's elite men and women. While not one of them, he spent enough time with them to understand what was needed to elevate one's position. His late half brother, Lawrence, had married Anne Fairfax. She welcomed George into her family, which was of the superior class.

Many a night she would take to the piano and encourage him to learn to dance. Anne's brother, George William Fairfax, became a dear friend, and Fairfax's wife, Sally, would serve as partner to the new dancer. On a night like tonight, George was glad of the many dances he shared with her. "A man who cannot dance is a man who cannot desire a place in polite society," she would say to him. Tonight, unlike the simple piano that played in the Fairfax house, there were a dozen instrumentalists and a dancing master.

Tonight nearly fifty couples would fill the dance floor. Moving through the crowd proved difficult, especially past the belles who seemed to be vying for his attention. George felt a woman's hand brush along his back as he stood with his officers. "A touch of him. I got a touch of him!" that woman exclaimed to her female companions. He recognized her. He noticed her hair before, off the side of the cobblestone street as he entered the town. It climbed higher now. Prodigiously powdered, the pile was white and spotted with pearls. There was even a white feather sticking out.

"We have invited fine beauties on your account, gentlemen." Beverley addressed Stewart and Mercer, who were standing by George.

"I believe one looked my way." Stewart sighed. "Which one to choose?"

"I'll take them all." Mercer winked at the females. "Oh, ladies of easy virtue, be mine. I'd like to tip the velvet of that one." He pointed to the woman with the highest pile of hair. Mercer and Stewart walked away from George and Beverley.

"Encouraging looks given for no other

purpose than to draw men to make overtures that the women may then reject," remarked Beverley. "They are pretty pictures, best kept suspended in frames."

George looked around the room, not at the coquettes, but for the heiress. She was nowhere in sight.

Mary felt cool dampness on her forehead. She opened her eyes slowly to Temperance's face, which was upside down from hers and looking at her with concern. Mary lay on the floor with a rag on her head, which was nestled into Temperance's lap.

"Cancel the pleasure ball." Frederick was speaking with urgency to the estate steward, Leonard Angevine. "Alert the dancing master and have him make the announcement."

"What shall we have him announce, Lord Philipse?" asked Angevine.

"Due to an unforeseen family matter, we must cancel — no, no, we must delay the ball due to an emergency of unexpected nature."

"Please, Frederick," Mary pleaded.

"Polly!" Frederick rushed over to her.

She took his hand in hers. "I beg you, do not. Not tonight. Not again will I be the cause of embarrassment for our family."

Mary wiped her own tears. She inhaled deeply to calm herself. She stood up, straighter than she ever had before, and looked directly at her brother. "Tonight, Frederick, we dance."

"Dancing the minuet will commence." The dancing master in his fanciful cap struck up the orchestra. "We welcome to the dance floor our hero of the South, our man of honor, Colonel George Washington."

George, knowing correct manners, bowed to him. The positioning of first of the ball was a heavy responsibility. Customarily, the best dancer was granted this position in order to lead dances throughout the evening. He knew he was certainly not the best of this group, but confident he could get by. As he awaited the announcement of his dance partner, he kept in mind another rule: *The gestures of the body must be suited to the discourse you are upon.* He knew those well, having studied not only the rules of motion but also the rules of standing: *The weight of each foot resting equally to the other and substantially separated; straight must the knees be; there must be a moderate bend at the wrist as the hands fall freely; the head must be slightly turned to the right to complete a gallant deportment.*

"And Miss Mary Eliza Philipse," announced the dancing master.

The grand doors of the ballroom opened. Mary's brother escorted the belle into the room, and she moved delicately beside him.

Appear delicate in your walk, she reminded herself as she moved through the throng of guests. This was a mocking age she lived in, and ne'er did a day pass that the other ladies did not take advantage of it.

"They've placed Polly as the first to dance with him?" She heard the angry whispers from bigheaded Bernadette Clara Belle.

Be poised, Mary reminded herself.

"One step and he will skip to his next dancer," Bernadette sneered.

Pay no mind to all the eyes watching, she kept telling herself.

"An heiress who dances with the grave digger."

Their insults on this night did not linger. She brushed past them, standing regal, refined. She wanted to be brave, strong, fearless, just like the hero in the pages of the *Journal of Major George Washington.*

"Sir Tenoe." She curtsied in a show of respect to him. He reciprocated with a bend at the waist. She knew the rules of walking: *Carry a genteel attitude. The hands shall hold the petticoat with the fingers slightly apart; there shall be no stiffness about the body, while the motion shall have a minor swing to it to avoid the appearance of stiffness, and the foot shall always move ahead of the body, the whole of your being carried with ease.*

The beaux and belles who crowded the floor parted to allow her to the center. Her charming was before her with a gallant deportment. George faced her from the middle of the floor. She had to look down for a moment. Her nerves were getting the best of her. His polished shoes. No mud. She raised her eyes to his face. Then she saw them: faded scars on George's cheeks — from sickness, she surmised. She hadn't noticed them earlier.

He was wounded, she thought. Just like me.

The two turned toward Frederick to show the outward sign of respect to the host. George bowed. Mary curtsied. She turned to George and curtsied to him; his lips curved as he bowed to her. The music commenced. His eyes fixed a stare on her. A tingle reached from the top of her head to the tips of her toes, for she knew what was coming next: her left hand was upon his right hand and his touch made her quiver as the music took them into its alluring wave, with eyes on each other, hands touching, hands releasing, stepping in close, stepping back in three-quarters time, right foot, left foot, right again, left toe points, three taps, lefts hands touch. The rhythm took her to a place far from the crowds; she even had to glance at her feet, for she sensed she could be floating.

Joyous applause followed as the instrumentalists finished the song. Broad and proud smiles emerged on the faces of her siblings.

"In honor of our Virginia officers," the dancing master trumpeted. "Strike up the Sir Roger de Coverley!"

The excitement was palpable as the crowd rushed to form two lines, gentlemen in one, ladies in the other.

As they waited for the beats to begin, Mary grabbed hold of Eva's hand, and Eva grabbed hold of Margaret's.

"Is that a quill in that woman's head?" asked Margaret as she leaned over to look at Mary.

"The ink must have landed on her face," added Eva.

Bernadette couldn't have added any more paint to her eyes, nor any more white powder to her face. Red rouge applied in large round circles covered her entire cheeks. Her eyebrows were daubed in a black color.

"It's just a feather," said Mary. "I think."

Mary stood opposite George as they formed the beginning of the lines. They would not come together for this dance. Instead, she met the gentleman from the back of the line, Sheriff Delancey, who danced his way to her. As the sheriff moved to meet her at the center of the two lines, she directed her sights to George, desiring another look into his eyes of blue with a touch of gray.

George, at the head of the gentlemen's line, met the heap of hair above a painted face at the center. The dance continued, with couples swinging at the center and adding a dos-à-dos.

Bernadette was so giddy around George, it made Mary cross.

The last couple formed an arch and the dancing couples moved through it. A roar continued in the ballroom as Tenoe carried to the center of the dance floor a chapeau bras. The dancing master presented it to Mary. She knew just what to do. The dance was called "the Magic Hat." She asked the female dancers to remove a personal article to deposit into it. Susannah added a glove; Eva, a handkerchief. Bernadette pulled that feather item from her hair and placed it into the hat. Mary noticed a bit of ink at the tip. It was a quill! Then Mary walked over to a woman who was standing by herself near the wall, Elizabeth Rutgers, a handsome woman who tragically became a widow a year prior, this being her first outing since her husband's passing. Dressed in a plain blue gown, she kindly looked at Mary and dropped in her fan. By the time each of the ladies had provided an item, the hat was filled to the top. Mary now asked the beaux to remove one article from the hat and dance with the lady to whom it belonged. Captain Stewart chose the handkerchief. He smiled as he met Eva, who reciprocated with a grin.

Mary stepped over to Frederick, who stood guard at the door, flanked by half a dozen footmen to his left and right, and offered the hat to him. His expression showed that he was not pleased to be asked to take to the dance floor. "You know the rules, brother. The dance's leader is to be obeyed, with no refusal permitted." She watched as he began to lift the fan from the hat. "Elizabeth Rutgers!" Mary was elated he did not pick the quill.

As he traipsed over to the woman, Mary noticed a bit of nature with its stem caught in the ribbon of his peruke. A dried maple leaf. Had it been on his head all night? she wondered. Since he went to see her in the cellar and said to her, "I want to see the you that used to be"? He tried for so long with her. She plucked the leaf and, not knowing where to put it, quickly tucked it below the items in the hat.

The dance exhilarated the guests, which is what Tenoe told her he expected. He urged her to allow him to try something new and attractive. This was one of the dances he suggested. "Every dancing master wishes to have the honor of promulgating that which is unique," he had told her. "If appreciated by guests, a dance becomes copied time and time again, and that is what we strive for." It seemed he was correct, as the ladies stood anxiously awaiting their item to be chosen.

Mary made sure the men turned their heads aside as their hand reached in. Mercer got a bit of ink on his when he chose Bernadette's item. George, she approached last.

Only a leaf was left. George inspected the hat thoroughly, which made her laugh. He placed it into his hand and reached out for hers as the dancing master called out the allemande. Mary tried to remember each of the steps of the Baroque dance as the orchestra played Bach's Magnificat in D Major. She relaxed as she stood near George. As the two danced, the leaf remained in his hand until it settled between their palms as they whirled about the room. Their bodies approached each other's ever so closely.

Wherever she moved, a trace of wildflowers trailed behind her, calling him to follow. It seemed there could have been no others in attendance, for the heiress occupied his attention completely. They danced the English minuet with its sink and rise steps in the form of a bourée and a half coupé. George knew this version, distinct from the other forms of this dance. He enjoyed watching redness appear on the heiress's cheeks when she circled instead of stepped. He wondered if she had any idea how prettily she moved, even when she made a misstep.

His enjoyment was ne'er interrupted. The hours passed in delight. The courante, the sarabande, the gigue, and half a score of additional minuets were danced between the two, followed by country dances. Even after the clock struck midnight, their feet remained on the floor, each dance taking them into and out of each other's touch.

"The Serpent will now be danced," announced Tenoe. "Colonel Washington, will you lead the way?"

George nodded to him. "Will you kindly follow me, Mary Eliza Philipse?"

"It would be my pleasure, Colonel." Such a gaiety appeared in her countenance.

He strolled with her to the corner of the room, gently set his hands on her bare shoulders. Her skin was smoother than he ever thought skin could be. He slowly turned her toward the wall. He lined the other women behind her, leaving space between each one. The gentlemen, formed into a loose chain, moved quickly between the ladies in a serpent's pattern until he reached Mary. A clap of Tenoe's hands had each of the men dance with the lady closest to him.

George knew the heiress must have had numerous offers from these men. He noticed Sheriff Delancey twice had the pleasure of dancing with her, but now he seemed much chagrined. George heard the displeased sheriff growl within close proximity to him as they were lined up in the chain. "Is there not a time this dancing master gives us a chance to dance with her for longer than a refrain?"

"Does the left cheek dimple?" asked a man with hair that flared out like a bell, who was standing with Delancey. "I must know the answer to a question so simple."

To this, George moved his thoughts to her dimple. Does her left cheek dimple as well as the right? he wondered.

The final dance was upon them. George asked Mary Eliza to join him for one last minuet as the instrumentalists played Vivaldi's "Spring" from *The Four Seasons* with vigor.

After being enchanted by him all evening, Mary surmised she knew what passion must feel like. His polite manner, handsome air, and cheerful demeanor — she had never seen this before in a man, or maybe had never noticed. It seemed he was ever grateful for the chance to dance with her. If only he knew how very grateful she was to dance with him, the charming prince, her charming. If the night could have gone any better, she did not know how.

She leaned into him and whispered, "Your feet have not left this dance floor." She let her hands fall upon his ever so lightly.

"I'm honored to have shared this night with you. I am hopeful I may be blessed to increase our friendship."

Mary curtsied to her hero of the South as the song came to an end.

Hurriedly, Frederick stepped toward her. "Polly, may I have your attention for a moment?" The two walked toward the doorway. "Jones Irwin is at the door. I told the guards to have him return tomorrow, but he has shown us a letter written by you that required his arrival here at this time."

"This is correct."

"Polly, it is four o'clock in the morning."

"Precisely. A payment is required of you, Frederick. I shall meet you in the library." She moved quickly out of the banquet hall, through the foyers, into the parlor, through a doorway and into the library, where she had placed the paperwork inside a closet on the north side of the room. She had been careful with the document and had made sure to have a quill at the ready on the desk.

A man of medium height with a bald, heavy head, and swollen eyelids, walked in the room alongside Frederick with a look of ire upon his shriveled face. A grimace spoiled the verbal greeting he gave Mary. As Mary placed down the papers, she spoke into Frederick's ear: "I expect the full amount."

Frederick read the contract. He cast a stern glance at her.

Mary heard a huff from Irwin before she

left them alone. She headed into the ballroom,

She passed George and kindly nodded, but at this moment she could not give him any more of her time. She asked Tenoe for his assistance in the parlor. As they neared the library together, loud voices could be heard. Angevine, who had been guarding the door, opened it to allow the dancing master to enter.

With arms crossed, Mary paced. Her finger went into the air, calculating the numbers again. She hoped she had tallied the amount correctly. She was quite anxious to see if her ruse had worked. She instructed Angevine to open the door a bit as she put her ear close to it.

"Mr. Michael Tenoe, the Philipse family has fulfilled your obligations in total," she heard Frederick announce. "This day, I can say, you are a free man."

Not a word came from Tenoe in response. A pause followed. She could hear footsteps briskly moving closer to her. The double doors swiftly opened as Sir Tenoe rushed out. He stopped in front of her. In that very spot, he fell to his knees.

"You have given me life!" Tenoe reached out for Mary's hands. "You have given me life!" Without any ability to control his emotion, Mary bent down to meet him and soon was also on her knees, embracing him. "Miss Philipse," he cried out. "I am forever in your debt!"

Teardrops flowed down his scarred cheek.

She cried, too. A healing rain to her soul.

Be the light, Mary Eliza.

Yes, Papa.

Part II
The Courtship

■ ■ ■ ■

Chapter Eight: An Heiress's Prayer

> For be assured a sensible woman can never be happy with a fool.
>
> — GEORGE WASHINGTON

The chain hanging from Mary's arm tugged a bit, leaving an indented mark upon her skin. She paid no mind to that, for she adored what it held. Connected to the silver links was a small psalmbook covered in blue velvet and smelling of dried flowers. Lady Joanna had carried it with her to services every Sunday. Few possessions did Mary treasure as much as this one. Today she let it dangle as she set herself upon the dark wood kneeling board inside St. John's Church. Although the years had passed, the memories, the moments she had shared with her mother, she kept close to her heart. Mary closed her eyes to remember her mother's lyrical voice. "Every daughter is her own kind of flower," Mama used to say.

"What kind of flower am I?" she remembered asking her.

The reverend's prayer broke her thoughts: " 'For before the harvest, as soon as the bud blossoms/And the flower becomes a ripening grape,/Then He will cut off the sprigs with pruning knives/And remove and cut away the spreading branches/They will be left together for mountain birds of prey,/ And for the beasts of the earth;/And the birds of prey will spend the summer feeding on them,/And all the beasts of the earth will spend harvest time on them.' "

Light came through the stained-glass windows, bathing the altar in a prismatic glow. Mary beheld the lofty space. The Philipse siblings built this church. Each of them offered ideas for its interior. Frederick asked that vast semicircle arches be designed at the entrance between the large wooden Ionic columns to welcome visitors. Mary suggested the chamber organ with tall pipes and huge bellows; she loved the heavenly sounds that came from it. Susannah was quite specific that carvings of angels must be holding painted flowers to help introduce the altar's grandeur.

Of course, there was the family's other house of worship, which sat twelve miles north of the manor, at the place where the

Pocantico River flowed into the Hudson. "The oldest ecclesiastical edifice in all of the New York Colony" is how Papa used to describe it. As a girl, Mary would clutch his hand tightly as he provided tours to guests. In 1697, her great-grandfather laid the pulpit with his own hands. The first Frederick's initials were engraved into it. And Mary always admired the shape of the little chapel with its gambrel roof that spread out at the bottom. The words *Si Deus Pro Nobis, Quis Contra Nos?* could be found etched inside a bell in the belfry. It meant "If God be for us, who can be against us?" Papa showed this to her to help her find strength.

Mary adored the small church. As she grew older, though, her deep devotion could not help her overcome the hollowness she felt each Lord's Day, for next to the chapel was the ground where they buried her mother, her father, and her sister Margaret. It was her brother who made the decision to build a new church, a grander one, that would allow Mary to worship free of heartache bathed in silent tears.

As she knelt this day, she opened to the back of the book, placed her hand on the pressed forget-me-not painted pale blue, and privately prayed:

Lord, I am shattered and I am frayed,
I pray what's dead inside me can breathe again,
I pray to know when my struggle will cease,
I pray to know when my spirit can rise from the ashes,
Use me, Lord, to be a beacon in the darkness,
Let me, Lord, be the light.

Mary leaned forward to gaze across the aisle past Susannah and Beverley. George was there. Even kneeling, he could almost look Frederick, standing, in the eye.

"Polly, Polly." Susannah tugged at her sleeve. "We must go. The service has concluded."

Ariose singers raised their voices in song from under the cupola. Mary closed the psalmbook and adjusted the clasp, careful to keep the delicate flowers secure.

Following Susannah and Beverley, Mary, dressed in a deep red woolen cape, made her way down the long aisle and out the front door and onto the stone path. With one hand, Mary placed the hood over her head as she stood by her sister, who was complimenting ladies on the majestic costumes they had worn to the ball. She hardly heard the words, for she felt George's eyes fixed on her. She clutched her hands inside a red feathered muff as she turned toward him. George stood at a distance, with a backdrop of the church's elegant stone facade, appearing like nobility. She peeked around, thinking he must be staring at someone else. A state of uncertainty about his intentions remained, for they had not even bid each other good night.

Susannah disturbed her moment. "I have a word to tell you. Something that I have not heard from my true, since he forbade me to utter a breath about the conversation."

"Regarding the colonel?"

"Yes, my dear Polly, about your George."

Your George. Susannah's reference ushered in that same tingle that she had experienced the night before. Just as her sister was to reveal information that Mary desperately wanted to hear, a man startled her.

"Such a radiant day is before us, Miss Polly." Sheriff Delancey's belly strained against the buttons of his tight vest.

"Mr. Delancey, a good day to you." She hoped the conversation would be short.

His chin rose a bit higher as he spoke, looking down his nose to address her. "If I may, in correction, I carry the rank of captain." He grabbed hold of one of the many medals he was wearing — there were far too many around his neck. "Upon my return from private studies abroad at Eton, then in Cambridge at my father's alma mater, as you know, Corpus Christi College, I was admitted to the esteemed Lincoln's Inn." He showed her another medal. "Following my studies of law there, the army saw fit to have me named to the prestigious position of captain." He lifted a different medal. "And, of course, the assignment of sheriff of our town was inevitable."

Mary wondered when this conversation would end.

He continued after a brief pause. "And I'm sure you are well apprised that my father has granted a charter for the creation of a fine institution. King's College is the name."

"I've read the news." She was thrilled to hear of the new institution being formed; however, she needed to turn away from him or else be fixated by his one raised eyebrow. She wondered if it was permanently lifted, or was it voluntary, like a pretentious move of some sort? Did he think it made him appear more refined?

"King's College, established to enlarge the mind, improve the understanding, polish the whole man, and qualify him to support the brightest characters in all the elevated stations of life. The first of such kind in all of New York. King George the Second has looked favorably upon our colony."

The eyebrow kept her focus.

"Do you know what is now positioned next to the educational building?"

It seemed he might go on forever.

"The finest racetrack in the entire of America." He answered his own question.

Racetrack. Yes, she had heard this.

"It is my understanding you have a fondness for horses."

"I ride a lovely horse, a fairly spirited one named Willoughby."

"A stable full of them are in my possession. They are English Thoroughbreds that I purchased, the first imported into our colony. You must get a glimpse of them, if your spirit will allow you to be among the crowds of New York City. I will have an invitation sent over to you for the inaugural Subscription Plate taking place on my track, the first horse race in the colony. I acquired a sporting taste for racing while overseas. I get such amusement from watching them run. They are fine specimens."

"Specimens?" She suddenly became miffed — both by his reference to horses and to her spirit. The Delanceys. She was sure they knew everything about her and her past.

"The finest anywhere in our New York."

Mary could take no more of his puffery or his brow. She excused herself, moved away from him, and found Susannah, who was in deep conversation with Beverley. Mary lifted her face upward; a white snowflake landed gently on the tip of her nose, like a kiss from the sky.

Susannah tapped her on the shoulder. "He's asked Beverley for an extended stay."

"He?"

"Your George will be staying another night at the manor and will then ride with us to New York for days more, and, Polly, he just asked Frederick to be granted a proposal to wait upon you. I hope you are not disagreeable to it, since I've already confirmed your agreement to such an interview. What type of tea should be served?"

Mary had not gotten past the word *proposal.* It would be the first such interview she had granted in quite some time. "I am fond of ambrosia." She could hardly even breathe.

"The food of the gods. Ambrosia and equal parts nectar. That will do. And Polly,

I suggested the interview be held this afternoon."

Chapter Nine: The Interview

> I can't say that ever in my Life I suffer'd so much Anxiety as I did in this affair.
>
> — GEORGE WASHINGTON

George waited in the west parlor inside Philipse Manor. He held his black tricorn hat in his hand as he sat alone. He was offered a seat on a hand-carved mahogany bench with a comfortable tapestry pouf. It faced the windowsill, which had a built-in long wooden bench and was also topped with a cushion. Through the opening of the sheer curtains, the sun's rays hit him in the eyes.

That anyone pictured him a suitable match for the heiress, he little anticipated. Doubt flooded his mind. Her attention to him the prior evening justly left him with a glimmer of optimism. She seemed to be fond of dancing with him, or was it just for display? This he had not ascertained. He knew for certain that Mary Eliza Philipse was beset with admiration from a great many men. This morning outside the church left him muddled, for her time was taken up by the sheriff, a man of significant wealth, who undoubtedly meant to seize her surrender.

George was costumed in the most resplendent way he knew possible: a navy and bright red coat, red breeches, white silk stockings, and black shoes with large gold buckles. He was not comfortable in these clothes. The shirt fit tolerably well, yet he would have had the wristbands made narrower, the ruffles deeper by half an inch, and the collar larger by possibly three-quarters of an inch for proper bigness. Whether it was the measurement taken or the fault of the tailor's hands in quick sewing, he did not know. Next time, he would get the measurement himself to be sure.

He followed one of his rules of civility as he checked that he had not a speck of dust on him. *Wear not your clothes foul, ripped, or dusty, but see they be brushed once every day at least and take heed that you approach not to any uncleanness.*

From the music room, a tune with sweet modulation was being played by a trio of instrumentalists. Its melody slowed into a feathery innocence.

He rose as he heard soft footsteps upon the rug. Mary Eliza Philipse arrived in an ivory gown embroidered with cherry-colored flowers throughout. At the bottom of her sleeves hung long laced accents. Around her neck, she wore a thin black velvet ribbon.

"Miss Mary Eliza Philipse. A pleasure to see you again."

"And you, Colonel Washington." Her hair was lifted demurely with a small lace veil to cover the upsweep.

"George." The vision before him nearly took his breath away. "George would be fine."

As she neared him, her pace quickened, causing her to stumble and fall . . . into him. He enjoyed this moment that her shoulder kissed his chest and his hands wrapped around her. This, plus the scent of lavender from her skin, left him feeling weak in her presence.

She straightened and arrived at the window seat, where she gently placed herself. "Colonel George, my apologies."

A throbbing in his heart. George tried not to stare at her. He realized he was as he found his seat.

Tea steeped in a silver pot embossed with

the seal of the Philipse family, a lion emerging from a coronet, with its tongue sticking out of its mouth. A delicious hint of citrus combined with coconut emerged as his cup was filled three-quarters. The wisps of steam rose and curled in the sunlight coming through the window.

The conversation lulled before it even began.

He watched as she placed a cloth napkin between the porcelain and her hand. The cup was blue and white and depicted a leaping deer.

"Have you seen the family of fawn by the river?" She began with a nervous twitch in her voice.

He motioned a nay with his head.

"I understand Frederick took you on a tour of the manor property."

The lands seemed to go on infinitely. Lord Philipse gave him much of his time after the church service, providing him a tour of the property, which had taken generations of Philipses and nearly a century to amass through purchase agreements with the Iroquois and Ottawa tribes and good standing with the British Empire. Under their proprietorship were businesses of commercial trade and milling. On the estate were located great revolving wheels and milldams for the growing flour industry, as well as the largest of greenhouses. At the family's dock, he was shown where the sloops brought goods from East India for trade. On the empty parcels, young farmers leased acres, benefiting from the fertile soil. George, too, owned a small parcel in Virginia — his mother's land is how he always thought of it — but few options for farming. It was certainly nothing compared to the Philipses'.

"They just arrived this week." A quaver in her voice emerged. "The deer."

"I did have a view of your library." The sheer volume alone impressed him. Without a formal education, he relied on books. "It seems for all of us a knowledge of books is the basis upon which other knowledge is to be built."

And off she went, articulating her feelings about the literary genius of the classic authors. "I look upon their writings as fine art." She told him how she spent a significant part of her time in her library. She conversed without hesitation, much different from her first greeting: "It is my presence to be in your pleasure." A darling beginning.

He admired her lips while watching them move as she conveyed details of Herodotus's legend of the Phoenix. "Out of the ashes. Out of nothing comes life," she told him. He listened carefully to the rhythm of her cadence. While her eyes under lengthy lashes fell to her tea, he found himself taken by her voice, which had a melody to it. "According to one of my favorite playwrights, Joseph Addison, 'Reading is to the mind what exercise is to the body,' and I agree."

Her face expressed such serenity, her composure was of the majestic sort, and yes, her frame was exquisite, but it was her mind that strengthened his affection for her. Education perfects what nature's hand creates. Thus distracted in her precious company, George forgot that tea is hot. He cowered after feeling a burn on his lip, almost spilling the beverage.

"Colonel!" Her eyes opened wide. She reached over, touching his knee. "George!" She shook her head. "Was the tea brewed too hot?"

With her hand upon him, he wasn't sure he remembered what pain felt like. "I am fine."

"I will have another pot made."

"This is fine." The concern she showed for him was quite apart from what he was used to. "Please continue."

She moved her hand back to her teacup.

Her voice had a flutter to it as she began to speak again. "If I may say, it may be your writing that I have found most profound."

"Mine?"

"Your journal . . . *The Journal of Major George Washington.* I have read it several times."

At no time had he thought anyone would read his scrawl. "*You've* read my journal?" He had expected only a quick review by Virginia's Colonial governor. "I did not in the least conceive . . . that it ever would be published, or even have more than a cursory reading."

"It was printed in its entirety in our *New-York Mercury.* And not only published here in New York. An acquaintance of mine in London wrote me that she, too, had read it."

Mary Eliza Philipse read his journal! He was informed in a meeting of the General Assembly that it was published. Now he was learning this was not just in Virginia. In no way was the writing prepared for print. "I can do no less than apologize . . . for the numberless imperfections of it. There intervened but one day . . . for me to prepare and transcribe from the rough minutes I had taken."

"I found no imperfection."

She read it. That was done. How could he even offer an explanation? It was printed without his consent, without even time to correct its flaws. "I had no time to offer it in a more proper form or to correct or amend the diction of old."

"I felt quite anxious for your well-being as I read it." She sat quietly listening, her head tilting at times as he began speaking of the wearying journey down one creek where they were obliged to carry their canoes to get over the shoals.

"We remained in the water half an hour or more."

"I was captivated by your bravery through your travails."

This surprised him, that she would have any interest in the journey to the French commandant. He went on about how the horses grew less able to travel every day, with the cold increasing fast and the roads becoming much worse due to the deep snow. She seemed absorbed by his account. "After completing that journey," he added, "I feel I have a strong enough constitution to survive the most difficult of trials." He never had such a long conversation with a woman about such.

"Had you been educated in skills of survival?"

If only he had had such an opportunity. He preferred not to discuss his lack of education in any area. "I saw that every stratagem that the most fruitful brain could invent was practiced. I can't say that ever in my life I suffered so much anxiety as I did in this affair."

She continued to have queries for him as to what he ate, where he slept. She asked specific details about whether there was a heavy current in the river, whether it was dark, and whether he was afraid in the water. He answered each of her questions honestly.

"And as for you, Miss Mary Eliza Philipse, I would imagine you an esteemed writer."

A dimple on her cheek appeared. "I would be honored to offer an affirmation on that account; however, I have written nothing more than a few lines of poetry."

A dimple only on the right. Whether there was one on the left, he still did not know.

"I would enjoy much satisfaction in hearing these lines."

"It would be my honor to share one with you, George, but from what I see behind you, there is a footman awaiting your presence in the foyer."

The time was a few minutes after five o'clock, and the agreeable interview between the pair had gone on for more than one hour. A coach was awaiting the colonel's presence for a meeting scheduled at King's Arms Tavern.

His heart was succumbing to a tender passion. Could it be the infancy of a courtship? He hoped it so.

George and Beverley approached the front of the two-story building at the southeast corner of Whitehall and Bridge streets. A sign with a lion and a bird battling for the crown was affixed to the heavy door they opened. The great hall released a scented medley of smoke, rye whiskey, and roasted beans.

It sounded as if the place was serving up a meal of high-volumed swearing inside. The noise helped distract George from his thoughts, which were completely engrossed with the interview with the belle. The journal. She read it! Without his knowledge, it was printed. He wrote it for the governor's perusal only. He would be sure that type of thing would never happen again. Every word from this point forward would be fit for print. And even with that, their discourse seemed to move in a pleasurable fashion. He wondered if their time together went too well. Affairs of the heart had not ended well for him up to this point. He recalled what he had come to believe — there is no truth more certain, than that all our enjoyments fall short of our expectations; and to none does it apply with more force, than to the gratification of the passions. He believed this firmly . . . up until now.

"How d'ye," said a white-swelled woman in greeting. She was holding a tray of jumballs shaped into an intricate knot. George's stomach jumped. He was fond of spiced shortbread.

"Mrs. Baron, good day." Beverley led the way.

"I've already filled your bumpers at the far corner, gentlemen."

"The first coffeehouse in the New World, Colonel," Beverley said, turning to him, "right here in our New York Colony, dating to the last century."

In a booth sat Mary's brother, who introduced another Delancey, the sheriff's uncle, Oliver. They exchanged mutual salutations. George took a seat next to Oliver.

"Oliver, I must tell you." Frederick sipped his drink. "The colonel can dance better than the finest of gentlemen."

"You're very kind," replied George. "Trained by your friend Fairfax."

"The good governor?" asked Frederick.

"His nephew, George William Fairfax."

"We had the honor of hosting Governor Fairfax, along with George William and his lovely wife, Sally. They spent a number of merry days with us upon the governor's return from the Indian Council at Albany. Sally and Mary got along swimmingly."

A green velvet privacy curtain enclosed the booth.

"George William?" Oliver put down his drink. "The West Indian boy?"

They looked to George.

Frederick added, "His visage appears to indicate a Creole parentage."

"Yes," George stated. "His grandfather served as chief justice of the Bahamas."

Outside of this, not a drop of serious talk ensued during the "meeting" Frederick asked him to attend. Instead, Mrs. Baron brought in a game board, and they took in a hit at backgammon. Frederick beat Oliver twice, and George won two games against Beverley.

"You see this antique." Frederick pointed to Oliver. "He needs your fashion sense, Colonel. A dandy he is not."

"Do you not favor my frock?" Oliver held up a sleeve.

" 'Tis pitiful with its trolly lolly upon the arms. Just wretched."

"At least it is made of domestics," Beverley pointed out.

George felt the need to say something witty. "I might add that I do not conceive that fine clothes make fine men, any more than fine feathers make fine birds."

" 'Tis true. Take the alarming appearance of the raven," said Frederick. "Yet a bird of valor."

"The raven indeed." Beverley pulled on the bell rope. "Fill up the bumpers!"

Trifling chat continued. George kept in mind the edict from his discipline book: *Drink not too leisurely nor yet too hastily. Before and after drinking, wipe your lips.* A hearty bowl of oysters arrived at the table. Manhattan Island was a seaport with a steady flow of small trade, he was told. The oysters were considered some of the best in the colonies. Another heaping bowl arrived, and then another. *It's unbecoming to stoop much to ones meat, keep your fingers clean and when foul, wipe them on a corner of your table napkin.* He denied himself the pleasure of more than just a few. This was not an occasion for indulging, and certainly not one for slurping oysters from shells. This was an evening to form a proper impression on a family wealthier and more educated. He did not want to appear an unrefined man, especially with the considerable matter still to be discussed.

The night went on without a bit of conversation upon the subject at the forefront of George's mind. 'Twas a meeting that did not satisfy his doubts. Their conversation, yes, was pleasant, however trivial. George wasn't expecting to sleep well this night.

Chapter Ten: A Morning's Light

> The day seems now to dawn upon us, but Clouds and tempests may yet arise to endanger our Bark . . .
>
> — GEORGE WASHINGTON

Now, being the morning afterward, Mary felt anxious. She heard her brother's coach return; it was well into the night, too late to ask about the particulars of the meeting. Her brother and George — what was said? Had he even mentioned her? She was so very eager to find out, but it was only dawn.

"What shall become of me?" Mary spoke the words aloud while alone in her bed-chamber. The Prelude and Fugue No. 2 in C Minor by Bach was playing in her head. Thoughts of the prior afternoon swirled about. She attempted as delicate a walk toward him as she could, wanting to appear genteel. She hoped her footsteps did not echo too loudly as she was often told they did. She even practiced a sashay with Susannah beforehand. “Step softly,” her sister had advised.

Embarrassment filled her mind as she reflected on the moment she tripped on the rug. She rushed, for she knew she needed to take her seat quickly before the tune’s up-tempo returned. Her nerves took over. She stumbled left. Her shoulder hit his chest, which did give her a touch of his solidity. Built by hands divine for certain.

Then the moment lasting too long. Could she think of nothing better to ask about than deer? Why not ask about his military position? His expertise in field command? His home in Virginia? No, instead she brings up deer! A thousand and one times she pictured him. Any sense became ruffled in his presence. Just his physical mass appeared as if it could wrap around her and protect her from the world.

She was overly gregarious about literature. She was sure of it. While often her greatest deficiency was conversation, sometimes without the ability to articulate a syllable, she went on without hesitation with him. He hardly said a word on the subject. He just looked at her with a heavy eyelid in a romantic sort of way. Blue with a touch of gray. She sighed at the memory.

She placed her hands on the ornate wallpaper next to the fireplace. The fire from the birch logs rose to warm her hands. Watching the flame, she let her fingers move along the wall as she imagined what it would be like to place her hands around George and feel his lips on hers. Oh heavens! His lips. The tea was too hot. She should have let it cool before it was poured. She hoped he did not suffer a burn.

The stove plate on the floor at the front of her hearth caught her eye. The engraving, an Old Testament passage with no spaces between letters, cast in relief in a slab of iron, was created long ago to ease her mind when sorrow roused a maelstrom of emotion within:

ICHHABEDENRABENBEFOLENDICHZWERS
DIBD K17C

Today she did not want to give thought to the seventeenth chapter of the Book of Kings and the passage "I have commanded the ravens to feed thee." It reminded her of her broken will and the shrill call of the raven. If it weren't for those birds, she might not have been rescued those years ago — the day Elbert vanished in the river's current. If not for the raven, she would have been left to die, as she should have been. She didn't like ravens.

She stared at the words for a time. Her eyes moved to a cleanly cut piece of birchwood that she reached down to pick up and used her strength to place over each of the letters in the metal. When the letter *I* was still peering out, she looked upon it with disgust. Heat struck her hands as she maneuvered another log to cover the letters on the metal slab completely.

She was tired of rereading these mournful chapters of her life. Tired of being afraid, of crying herself to sleep, of the nightmares. She wanted to think of the mingling of sweetness and gallantry, of generosity combined with charm, of the man who was helping to restore her one heartbeat at a time. George did not look upon her face with pity, as did so many others. It seemed he might know nothing of her past. When his eyes gazed into hers, she felt alive with the hope of a destiny still to be discovered.

With a newfound breath within, Mary walked toward the window. Her feet stopped at the shelf. She checked the position of the newspaper, the one that had printed George's journal. Relief. The paper was neatly placed, with writing away from the cursed.

Glancing out the window, she espied something unexpected. Temperance and François. What a splendorous sight! This was the first time she ever saw Temperance holding a man's hand. She was always so busy in the kitchen, she seemed to have little time for beaux. Temperance smiled widely as she bid him farewell; she looked happy. So happy. Mary was happy for her. Love. Everyone needs more of it in their lives.

Footsteps in perfect even tempo sounded from the stairs. A knock at the door. It was Temperance. "Mr. Angevine has asked me to advise you that five articles of correspondence have arrived for you. Ten more arrived yesterday, one of them an invitation delivered by the sheriff himself, which requires a response. He is a persistent one, that Mr. Delancey."

"Captain Delancey." Mary rolled her eyes. "He's made certain I know of his title." The constant requests from him — she paid no mind to them. "Temperance?"

"Yes, Miss Polly."

Mary desperately wanted to ask her about *son petit ami,* but she refrained. "The banquet was more than any of us could have asked for."

"The evening was my pleasure. The food

that remained was placed in packages, as you suggested, and taken to the church for distribution to the need-filled." Temperance's face had a beautiful glow to it.

"My gratitude for all you've done."

The morning was chilly, requiring Mary to put on a woolen riding coat. Around her waist, the brown fabric fit snugly and fell wide at the hips. She wrapped herself up with a silk scarf. She put on leather gloves and a riding hat. "You are capable of the impossible, Mary Eliza, for you have survived the unthinkable," she murmured, remembering how her father said it with such inspiration. She had promised Papa she would say it each day.

She hurried down the stairs and out to the back porch. The winter air enveloped her in its coolness. The sun was low on a clear horizon. A soft wind blew from the northwest, bringing with it a trace of hay. She practically skipped toward the stables. Riding always made her feel alive. Her breath left a trail a smoke. She could hear Mr. Chew speaking loudly.

"She has a pretty large swelling under her belly."

"In foal, you suppose?" Was that George she could hear with him in the stable?

"I suppose, or occasioned by the buckling of the girths too tight," responded Chew.

George's voice alone made her feel giddy. She regained her composure as she entered.

"Gentlemen, a good day to you both."

"Miss Philipse, good day. Would you kindly take a look at Colonel Washington's horse? I believe her in foal."

Mary was glad of the request, for it kept her from wanting to stare at the commanding presence before her. "May I ask the name of this fine mare of yours?"

For a moment, George seemed incapable of an utterance. After a hesitation, he spoke. "Diamond."

Mary looked at him quizzically.

"Her name. Diamond."

"A lovely name." Mary gently placed her hand on the filly. "Diamond. Shall we place her with the gentle mares on the hill at the north, Mr. Chew?"

"I will see to it. He's named every one of his horses, Miss Polly." Chew pointed to them. "Each of them hath a name."

He names each of his horses, how endearing, she thought.

Mary approached another one of George's horses, a chestnut bay.

"This is Woodfin." George followed her. "A horse that carries the English crown upon his shoulder . . . and my Jack, spotted like a fawn upon the side of his neck. This horse has come a long way after being injured in a fall."

"Oh, the poor creature."

"How did he recover, Colonel?" asked Chew.

George patted the horse. "I followed Gervase Markham's directions as near as I could."

"Markham has the surest ways to cure a horse's malady in the known world," added Chew.

Mary smoothed her hand across its hide. "Which remedy was used to effect a cure, Colonel?"

"I had the horse slung upon canvas and his leg fresh-set — walked him on three legs, with the sound leg tied up very sure with a garget, to require him to put weight on the lame leg. When I let down the lame leg and let it stand on the ground, I heated a little water and clapped it onto the swelling that remained. I then tied up the lame leg again and repeated the same."

"What about the bloodletting, Colonel? Tell her about the bloodletting."

She saw George signal with his hand to Chew to discontinue that conversation.

"Let me introduce you to the rest of the

team." He walked with her to the next horse. "Rock was bred in Pennsylvania. Not a spot of white on his dark brown coating, standing strong and fourteen and a half hands high. Prince is near a twin to Rock. This here is Buck. Crab belongs to Captain Mercer. This fine bright bay is the largest horse of the group and has not been named as of yet."

Mary enjoyed his introductions.

"What do you think of the name Bale?"

"That will suit him just fine with his coloring." Mary replied. "A rather tall horse."

"Fifteen hands high, yes," he responded.

He paid such kind attention to his horses, unlike the sheriff, calling them "specimens." How ludicrous!

"And a remarkably large hind, wouldn't you say?" asserted Chew.

"Mr. Chew tells me not to dare ride with the finest equestrian of the colony."

"And who might that be, Mr. Chew?" she asked coyly.

"I must apologize for telling the colonel of your prowess on horseback."

"Very kind of you, Mr. Chew." Mary added another blanket on the horse before lifting herself up to sit sidesaddle. "You're welcome to join me, George."

Not even a second passed before George

mounted Woodfin. His buff wool riding coat trimmed in a light green silk was quite elegant with its coattails down the back. She quite liked his fashionable boots, black at the bottoms with brown turn-over tops. She also could not help but notice the outline of a coin in his left-hand pocket and his leg's strength through his buff-colored buckskin breeches, which fit like a second skin on him.

The pair moved the horses in a sedate walk out of the stables. 1W was branded on his horse. *W* for Washington, she was certain. 1W — the same as Willoughby, but for a different reason. Her father gifted her this mare. She recalled his words that day: "I have branded her with a one and a *W*, for I have only *one wish* for my Mary Eliza," Papa had said to her. "My wish for you is freedom . . . to let go and allow love to find its way to your heart."

"Would you care to see the deer park?" she blurted out to George. Not again, she thought, after the word was already out of her mouth — deer!

He nodded, not taking his stare off of her.

"Quite easy in hand is your Woodfin," she said to fill the quiet.

"As is your Willoughby."

"I believe in caring for him with tenderness."

"I experienced the tragic loss of a horse in my youth." A sympathetic tone surfaced in his voice. "Now I treat all with a discipline of proper care and a good amount of exercise."

Arriving at the park within minutes, Mary pulled back the reins. They dismounted. Westward, upon a sloping path to the river, the family of deer was before them. "Not a person is allowed near them. Frederick takes fine care of them. Never has one been hunted on our property. They are in their first year. They still carry the light yellowish brown tone."

"And I would imagine the younger they are taken, the easier they are raised." He looked directly into her eyes. "The view adds a romantic and picturesque appearance to the whole."

The use of the word *romantic* impaired her rational thinking.

He began to speak again, thankfully. "And what of the deer distinguishable by the darkness of their color?"

She shook her head to clear her mind. She knew this answer. "From England. Near a dozen have been brought here from different parts of the world. Frederick holds the office of Keeper of the Deer Forests. It's been passed down for generations in our family. He formed our deer park himself, yet he often laments the damage to the gardens."

"At a loss, I would be, in determining whether to give up the shrubs or the deer!"

As she laughed, a ringlet fell to the front of her face. George reached over, placed his fingers upon it, and took time in moving it away from her cheek.

Happy emotions spun around inside her head. She searched for something to say to him. "Would you care for some dirty chocolate, George?"

She watched him cock his head before he answered yes.

He placed his hands around her waist to assist her in mounting Willoughby. Her lips let out a sigh. After he mounted, she prodded her horse into a canter. The two rode to the manor.

George whispered to her after they had dismounted. "I hope you have not forgotten my request."

"What would that be?"

He spoke into her ear. "To hear your lines of verse."

Jitters simmered up inside. She responded

the only way she knew how — by moving quickly past him. She walked to the nearest door. It was the one to the lower level. They entered from the side entrance into the dim cellar, which extended under the southern portion of the manor below the west parlor.

What she noticed caught George's attention with light from a small window shining onto them — columns of ten-shilling and tenpence pieces in neat linear formation, filling the rectangular working tables.

"The counting of toll moneys begins in about an hour from now," she said. "Much work needs to be done, for King's Bridge is the only crossing to the mainland."

George was silent, staring behind the tables at the canvas bags filled with coin piled on top of one another.

She felt the need to explain. "Charity and humility. That is where true worth comes, not from coin."

He took a moment before responding. "One thing is more envied than wealth."

"And what might that be?"

"The circle of an amiable family . . . in a situation free from cares."

His words, "free from cares" — that is how she felt in his presence. She guided him up the stairwell. "If you would, please follow me, George."

"A demand I so ardently wish for."

She tiptoed up the stairs. He copied her manner of walking, which made her chuckle. They quietly made their way to the first floor of the manor.

"If you would kindly find a seat in the parlor. I will be in the kitchen to have our beverage made." Mary hurried to see Temperance, who quickly answered her request. She measured a pint of milk and brought it to a boil with a stick of cinnamon in a chocolate pot. When the liquid was hot, Mary sweetened it with Lisbon sugar and added cocoa pieces. The mixture emitted the most pleasing of scents. She watched Temperance pour this into cups with two handles, one on each side. Mary hoped this might offer more protection for the colonel, as she didn't want to have another burning incident.

To the second floor, Mary scurried to get out of her riding clothes and find a poem. Which could she choose? Most of them harped on sorrow, on gloom. Might there be one? Please let there be one, she thought. One that would be acceptable, maybe one of no measurable importance, of a jovial nature.

Had she even written a poem like that? She shuffled through the papers on her desk. Was there not a moment of merriment in her world she could have made the subject? Each focused on guilt, on regret. He did not need to know the truth about her, not now. If he knew she was cursed, he would certainly run from this place.

Chapter Eleven: Poetry's Intimacy

> I feel the force of her amiable beauties in the recollection of a thousand tender passages . . .
>
> — GEORGE WASHINGTON

George stood by the window, holding his two-handled porcelain cup. Although tempting his nose and tongue, he hadn't touched the dirty chocolate. He focused now on the view across the Hudson to New Jersey. Like stoned fingers, a rock wall rose more than one hundred feet from the ground. What a strong encampment that place would make, he envisioned. War had not come to this place. If it did, troops would be protected by nature's camouflage and by the rushing river. And if units were stationed on this side of the river as well, not an enemy's boat would get north of this town.

The steam rose in a swirl from the surface of his drink, reminding him of the incident with the last hot beverage he drank with her. A bit of a burn lingered on his lip. He did enjoy how her hand felt on his knee. Her touch was gentle and her expression of concern sincere.

Now he could hear Mary Eliza's voice from just outside the entryway. She began to read verse aloud. Her poem? It must be. About a bluebird. She arrived. Her soft pink gown revealed the skin below her neck. She had changed out of her riding clothes. He smiled at the thought. She would look lovely, he fancied, in anything she wore, or didn't wear.

She read from a linen paper with a whimsical tone to her voice.

> Alas! The bluebird to a sill arrives,
> Into his reflection he peered to see whether still alive,
> In his breast, the pit-a-pat of his heart yielded delight,
> For a beauty in the fairest form which had enchanted his sight,
> With an adjustment to his peruke he designed,
> To yield an affirmation if the divine creature was so inclined.

"And that, George, must clearly be the

finest piece of literature you have ever heard."

For an instant, he couldn't decide which was lovelier, the poem or its author. Then her eyelashes fluttered and she curtsied, and he knew.

"The finest, yes, regarding a bird and his peruke." He laughed, which astonished him. It wasn't like him to laugh aloud.

As he laughed, she laughed with him, adding, "Possibly the only one written upon that account."

"Your poem is very acceptable, as it not only displays your genius but exhibits sentiments . . . expressive of the benevolence of your heart."

"In truth, it is pure fiction," she said with a smile so wide it revealed the truth. The left. Yes. One dimple on her right cheek. Another on the left.

A new opportunity presented itself for him to speak eloquently, unlike his morning with her. He wasn't even able to voice a greeting in the stable. Diamond? This was all he could utter to her! A simple "Good day" would have sufficed. He was not going to let another chance go by with the heiress. "Fiction is, to be sure, the very life and soul of poetry — all poets and poetesses have been indulged in the free and indisputable use of it. To oblige you to make such an excellent poem, on such a subject, without any materials but those of simple reality, would be as cruel as the edict of the pharaoh which compelled the children of Israel to manufacture bricks without the necessary ingredients."

"If only I knew a hero who could provide the subject for literary greatness."

He took a sip of the chocolate, careful of the heat touching his lips this time. "Heroes have made poets, and poets heroes." He noticed a blush surface on her cheeks. "You could choose Alexander the Great. He is said to have been enraptured with the poems of Homer."

"If only I had lived in such an age." She picked up the cup with both hands.

"An age proverbial for intellectual refinement and elegance in composition, where the harvest of laurels and bays was wonderfully mingled together."

"We still have great poets in this age who have brought intimacy to their work, as the Countess of Winchilsea does." Mary recited a stanza of her "Letter to the Same Person":

> Love without Poetry's refining Aid
> Is a dull Bargain, and but coarsely made;
> Nor e'er Poetry successful prove,

Or touch the Soul, be when the Sense was
Love.
Oh! Cou'd they both in Absence now
impart
Skill to my Hand, but to describe my
Heart . . .

Savoring the last sip of the beverage, he took her in — all of her, even the trace of bashfulness she seemed to carry about her own beauty. He glanced around briefly, taking in the luster of this place and the sweets of domestic enjoyments. What more could a man ask for than to reside in a pleasing country seat with an enchanter who had regard for him? Many other suitors would revel in the opportunity to be in his place. The affluence of the family. The influence in society. And yet here she was alone with him, reciting poetry.

"I believe it's time to hear your writing, George."

Mary Eliza Philipse — he was enamored of her. No paper was necessary for his poetry. He started to speak. "From your . . ." He stopped himself. Being that he was feeling confident that he had piqued her interest, he rose from his chair and sauntered over to her. She seemed near startled when he placed himself in close proximity to her on the long cushion. His thigh grazed hers. She drew a quick breath and rustled her gown. He removed the cup from her palm and placed it down onto its saucer. Porcelain clinked porcelain.

Shifting his body toward her, he took both of her hands in his and relished the softness of her skin. He'd written the poem long ago, but now was the first time it was fitting to recite to someone:

From your bright sparkling Eyes, I was
  undone;
Rays, you have, more transparent than the
  sun,
Amidst its glory in the rising Day,
None can you equal in your bright arrays;
Constant in your calm and unspotted Mind;
Equal to all, but will to none Prove kind,
So knowing, seldom one so Young, you'l
  Find.
Ah! woe's me, that I should Love and
  conceal,
Long have I wish'd, but never dare reveal,
Even though severely Loves Pains I feel;
Xerxes that great, was't free from Cupids
  Dart,
And all the greatest Heroes, felt the smart.

Her face brightened in this very moment

as a flower emerging from the darkness to bathe in the light. "George, you are a true gentleman."

To be a gentleman, act a gentleman.

Finally.

Affirmation.

CHAPTER TWELVE: THE WINNER'S CUP

. . . I consider storms and victory under the direction of a wise providence . . .

— GEORGE WASHINGTON

New York City

At precisely five minutes after four, tensions ran high. Voices rose into a frantic roar with shouts of elation and worry — "Run!" "Hurry!" "They're coming!" Any vestige of refined manner vanished in the one moment the dirt began to fly and a beat erupted like the thunderous roll of drums. Speed and endurance were the only way to survive the heat — three of them, to be precise.

Just off the riverfront, with a cold breeze leaving a chill, a spectacle never before seen in the colony was unfolding at a sanctuary, not produced for a peace but for a rush.

A six-horse race was under way on Delancey's newly built private track, the first in New York, positioned west of Broadway at Church Farm, near Trinity Church. The track was surrounded by oak fencing. The crowd standing behind it stood at least ten deep.

An unusually large wager was set for today: three hundred pounds. The winner's award was the silver cup, a double-handled presentation vessel with a dome cover and engraving. The race would match Delancey's newest Thoroughbred, Cub, to the rest of the lot, including the most revered of New Jersey's horses, Old Tenor. This was the inaugural race. The announcement was published in the *New-York Gazette:*

> On the 18th of February, the New York Subscription Plate will be run for any Horse, Mare or Gelding, carrying eight Stone Weight, Saddle and Bridle included, the best in three Heats, two Miles in each Heat.

In the crisp air, refined fellows who donned cocked hats and rich greatcoats, as well as common folk attempting correct fashion, completely lost themselves. Mary was surrounded by polite society — as they called themselves — emitting not only a whiff of tobacco but also one of mendacity.

The shouts grew louder as the first lap

was completed in two minutes, the third in just over the same. Out of the fifth, the winner was still in question. Which one would capture the treasured prize?

Mary remained still. She was flanked on every side. She didn't like crowds, but she had no other choice but to come, if she had hopes of finding her hero. For two days since their time together, her head filled entirely with thoughts of him. If George was in the crowd, she'd not yet seen him.

The number of other men attempting to attract Mary's attention was endless, each outdoing the other with their salutations. The poet, Scandal, offered her a rose along with a greeting in rhyme. Another fellow, Daniel Webb, asked Susannah to beg Mary for a moment of her time. The third, Colin Dufresne, got on tiptoe to reach over the crowd to give her an invitation to dine with him. Her reactions to them were pleasant, except to the one with the raised eyebrow, the sheriff. His self-admiration irritated her.

The vision before her was captivating. It was hard to take her eyes off the horses with the extreme slope in their shoulders. They raced in a cluster. The roar of hooves thundered. One mare of strong muscling and significant bone structure launched, capturing the lead.

"Onto victory!" she heard Scandal shout. "Into history!"

"Triumph be yours!" Bernadette Clara Belle, standing by Mary, cried out. When Bernadette lifted her arms to cheer for the Delancey mare, her petticoat, already with a hem inches short of appropriate, rose above her knee. Bernadette never missed an occasion where finery was displayed. Her head was quite comically adorned with a tremendous headdress created of yellow ribbons with vivid red accents that glistened like rubies — Mary surmised they were only colored glass. Oh, and that feather, too, was in her hair, the same one from the ball, Mary assumed.

"Cub's in the lead!" exclaimed Bernadette.

In the lead by a mile, it seemed, the English mare bore the Delancey coat of arms, bright red with a lion and a shield of three spears. As for Old Tenor, he was nowhere.

The shouts grew more intense — "Cub!" "She's coming." "Cub will be victorious!"

Delancey lost all sense of himself as he screeched, "She's mine. All mine! The plate is mine!"

Mary watched as Cub sped with ease to the finish. This was not the end. As onlookers erupted in applause, the animal became startled and took off. The horse bolted through the gate with the rider still on its back.

Bedlam ensued.

She watched the sheriff's usual air of importance dissolve into chaos. He darted from his position, climbed over the oak fencing, and hotfooted it down the course. His hair, always in perfect order, was instead representative of the moment.

Mary bit her lip to avoid a grin. Gentlemen scrambled to the outside field, where the mare galloped in wild circles. For quite a time, Delancey himself was run amok, chasing the tail. The rider jumped off. Scandal practically grabbed the horse a few times before the mare won this game of cat and mouse, leaving them in the dust.

After a few minutes' time, a riderless Cub returned on her own to the track and stopped in the center of it, as if to take a bow and await a bouquet before the guests. The crowd roared.

This was followed by a dreadfully long ceremony, in which the sheriff waxed grandiloquent about his influence on horse racing, "Triumph is clearly in the hands of the just. Earth hath provided us her abundant favor — this has led to the defeat over the bulwarks of the foe. I take the greatest satisfaction in this day, for I have received the most favorable outcome. We have cut down the hand of the spoiler and ruined his rise. We have become heirs to an eternal achievement." His speech finally ended as the sun found its repose, but not before he called himself "Father of the American Turf."

The winning audience made its way to the Horse and Cart Inn. It was near nightfall when Mary and her family arrived after a short walk. Bold red bunting lined the balconies of the second and third floor of the club, while below hundreds of guests stood awaiting entry. This is where the elite converged with alacrity to enjoy handsome entertainment. The Philipses were escorted around the crowd, in through the rear door and up the stairs to the second floor. The inn was owned by the Delanceys. This caused Mary's spirits to rise.

That touch of a kiss lingered upon her hand; George had taken his time in saying farewell. He had been whisked away from her just moments after reciting his poetry. Brother Frederick and the sheriff's father, Lieutenant Governor James Delancey, had invited him to meet the dignitaries of the town. She hoped to again hear those words,

"From your bright sparkling eyes, I was undone," but alas, his belongings were removed from the manor and carried to the Robinson town house on Pearl Street on the island. He'd tour New York with the Delanceys by day was what she was told.

Mary had waited her entire life, not for someone like him, but *him.* In the pages of her mind, she had envisioned his strong chin and broad shoulders — even his voice sounded familiar. When his lids lowered slightly in a most romantic way, she felt as if she had seen that endearing expression before. She was more surprised she hadn't known him than she was by the profound impression he was leaving on her heart.

As the thoughts of him whirled about, a soothing voice spoke to her from behind. "Miss Mary Eliza Philipse. Neither time nor absence can impair the warmth of fondness I feel in your presence." His words left her without any of her own. George turned her around, clutched her bare hand, and lifted it to his lips. The now-familiar tingle shot through her.

In place of a greeting, she settled her hand into his folded elbow, his strength feeling like chiseled rock and savoring of manliness — soap combined perfectly with brawn. Her nose stayed close to him as she escorted him in a slow walk to the balcony overlooking the Hudson, where they could be alone. Twilight's reflection rippled upon the river. Above them twinkled a dome of lights. Her hip leaned against an ornate French wrought-iron railing. "Do you believe" — she shifted her gaze upward — "anything can endure longer than the stars in the sky?"

Before answering, he moved within a space of her. He gently took her chin into his hand. "The chain of sincere love." His lids dipped. "If strong and lasting, it will endure while sun and stars give light."

At this, his face came nearer to hers, so near as to almost touch. Her own eyelids closed as she felt his breath on her lips. The hairs on her arms stood up. She could feel the beating of her heart as the flame grew larger and, in its bright splendor, the sound stronger. Was it a choir she was hearing? Music sounded its rhythm in the fast-approaching moment that Cupid's feathered dart was striking.

The loud booming of drums struck a distracting chord, interrupting her bliss. A band in formation marched directly below the balcony, bringing Mary back into proper position. Musicians on celebratory parade traveled by. Mary became flustered.

George seemed to pay no attention. His

face lifted to the cluster of lights above. His finger pointed to a pattern of stars. "Andromeda."

She looked up at the constellation. "The chained maiden of mythology."

His hand fell on her waist, causing her to stir. "Stars aligned in a perfect sequence."

"As the legend goes, she was saved from death by the bravery of her hero."

He brought her body nearer to him. "She is in perfect view this night."

"Andromeda is displayed in 'The World in Miniature,' I've read. The entire universe is represented in the exhibit. It's made the transatlantic journey from England. It is now here in our New York."

George led her farther away from the door and the noise of the crowd inside. His hand latched on to her waist.

"A transatlantic journey . . . it is one I could never take." She felt comfortable talking with him. "I have a rather delicate makeup when it comes to capacious waters. The only place I have a desire to travel to is Barbados, where my father was born and his grandfather served as governor."

"My brother, Lawrence, and I were graciously received on the island of Barbados."

"Oh? My father would often speak of the rough seas in getting there."

"Rough seas indeed. During the thirty-seven-day passage, we experienced hard squalls of wind and rain, with a fomented sea jostling in heaps. Pretty large swells made the ship roll much and me . . . very sick."

She always pictured in her mind what the trip might be like from beginning to end.

"Upon our departure from Virginia, we found clear and pleasant weather for a sail, with fresh gales of wind, even saw a great many fish, including dolphin."

"A dolphin!" Her palm grabbed hold of the outer part of his arm. "I've never had the pleasure of seeing one." She didn't want to let go.

"But soon, even the seamen confessed that they had never seen such weather before. It was surmised there had been a violent hurricane not far distant."

"How did you make it to the island?"

"We were greatly alarmed with the cry of 'Land' at four o'clock one morning. We quitted our beds with surprise and found the land plainly appearing about three leagues distant. We weighed anchor and arrived in Carlisle Bay."

"That is quite a journey to take. Why, George, did you make such a trip? For trade? Or for repose?"

His eyes shifted down before answering. "We hoped the warm air would benefit my brother's health at the time."

She touched his hand with hers.

"The doctors, they had hoped time in the islands, the fresh air, might bring a cure. The white plague claimed him in the summer of 'fifty-two."

"My deepest condolences for your loss."

"No one entertained a higher opinion of his worth than I."

She wished that year, 1752, never happened. Devastation struck the Philipse family, too, during that summer. Both the father who held her like a treasure and her Margaret were taken from her. "I, too, George, experienced a deepest loss during that same time of that same year. My sister, my Margaret . . ." She tried to hold back tears. "She died of that same terrible disease in the summer of 'fifty-two."

George grabbed hold of her right hand and held it tightly.

"She was so young, so good and just, with a warm heart." She inhaled deeply. "And Lawrence?"

"He was a captain and a well-respected member of the legislature. He left behind a widow, Anne. His death left us both numb."

"George, my sister, she died alone . . . all

alone." The memories rushed in of how she would sing outside Margaret's door and wait for her to clap — one, two, three, four, five, six. "They would not let me near her. They would not let anyone near her. She left this world all alone." She could not speak further, as grief overcame her.

"I understand the pain in bidding adieu to those we love," he said gently.

"It is my fault, George." She had never spoken about this with anyone outside of the family. "I was the first to get the fevers. If only . . . I had stayed away from them. If only . . . I had kept them back."

He wrapped his arms around her.

She leaned her head upon his chest. "The hurt is so deep, I feel I will not be able to take another day without her. I wait for the day when . . . I can let go of the pain."

Melancholy seeped into her spirit. Mary's eyes watered.

Their quiet was a deep quiet.

He kept her in his embrace.

The evening's affair was a protracted one. The longer the evening went on, the more unintelligible sounds from the bumper men reached George and Mary. The aroma of the claret was formidable.

The two of them reentered the gaming

room as Delancey yelled, "To Satan with morality and ethics. Bumpers for all of the guests!"

This was answered by drunken laughter.

"A toast to the possessor of the most valued mare," said Scandal. "Now, take your standing as turf's king with flair."

Delancey bowed with great flamboyance and hollered, "More wine! Bring out the cards! Bring out the dice! The evening is becoming dead. Let's hope for comedy or dread, something of consequence to happen."

Mary could hear the scraping of spurs. Could it be? The man with the raven hair covered in powder seemed to come from nowhere and made his way to the center of the crowd. James Jay's voice was thick with anger. "If you should witness a prized racehorse surrender the cup to a lackey, would you not presume deception by a cheat?"

This caused an eruption from the Delancey brigade.

"Look at this fool, stubborn as a mule!" Scandal mocked him. "Dare you enter uninvited?"

"Leave him be," answered Delancey. "When a man is as drunk as he, how can we expect reason? I pity you, Jay."

"I will not be indifferent to the treatment I have received," shouted James, "by the likes of those who have sold their souls to the king."

"Dr. Jay, you heathen. You've spent too much time with experiments in the dungeon. The work has clouded your mind." Delancey spun a finger around his head.

"Your obsession with the lion disgusts me." James stumbled forward.

"Jay, your obsession with the glass disgusts us all!" Scandal snickered.

"If you have anything, even a suspicion to allege against me, you will candidly declare it, in order that I may vindicate myself to you."

Frederick and Beverley rushed toward Mary.

"The time for departure has come." Frederick took hold of her arm.

"Colonel Washington, we must be leaving with Polly. A carriage for you is awaiting your departure when you are ready."

They did not say another word. Frederick and Beverley flanked Mary on each side, moved her swiftly through the crowd and out the door. Not a good-bye was said between her and George.

Mary could hear the sliding of the spurs as she was helped out the front door and moved swiftly into an awaiting carriage. The face of her nightmares glared out the window watching her every move.

"As goes the mother, so, too, the daughter."

She would never forget his threat.

Chapter Thirteen: A Hundred Eyes

> Silence . . . speaks more Intelligably than the sweetest Eloquence.
>
> — GEORGE WASHINGTON

From the windows above, soothing sunlight flooded the rotunda. Here, clove mingled with spice to fill the air. *Matthiola incana* blooms stood tall in a high metal vase on top of an ornately carved wooden table in the center of the room. The Robinsons' town home on Pearl Street on Manhattan Island was appointed with care throughout.

As each hour passed, uncertainty remained as to whether Mary Eliza Philipse would receive him today. A pain in her head was the explanation, the reason she did not leave her bedchamber this day. She, as well, stayed at the residence. George knew there must have been other reasons. The abrupt departure the evening before yielded questions.

George walked past an extensive array of portraits that hung on walls ornately covered in rich silver and gold fabric coverings. He clasped his hands behind his back. George felt eyes on him, faces in frames judging him as he moved with a steady pace.

Beverly was with him. "The painting of your mother, does it still hang in the entryway?"

"The one by the hand of Captain Middleton?"

Beverley nodded.

"It does." George's late father, Augustine, had commissioned the portrait of her. The artist used subtle tones and feathery strokes on a dark background. The painting caught her likeness, yet it conveyed a softness rarely seen in her. More often, the business of managing the family's small farm weighed on his mother's head. "Middleton is the only artist for whom she sat."

Beverley paused and turned to him. "You missed it, Colonel; the sheriff ran about like a madman at his own race!"

"My absence was on account of a tour reviewing the lands of the Hudson."

"He would have kept you longer if you hadn't insisted on returning." Beverley moved him through the spacious gallery, where a number of paintings of the majestic

Hudson hung. They separated the portraits of those lost from those still alive. "I hear Delancey's aide brought you very near the estuary."

"I saw the strong current of the river up close."

"Very close, from what I understand."

"The pointed fin. Have you seen it yourself?" George asked.

"Only once, and in the distance. The shark was enormous. Did he mention that the creature took a man in the very spot you visited? The fish lurched forth and grabbed a fellow at the leg and brought him below the waves, near the great rocks in the town of Yonkers. The man disappeared, never seen again, taken by the devil himself. And now you have survived the area we call 'Spiting Devil.' "

George pretended to wipe his brow.

Beverley pointed to a trio of portraits as the paintings moved to depictions of the living. "The hand of John Wollaston. Susannah's father commissioned the portraits when the three sisters were in their blooming years — chosen as the artist's first sitters in the Americas. We keep Margaret next to her sisters. Susannah refuses to move her to the other part of the gallery, for she is 'alive in us,' Susannah says. The critics reviewed Polly's painting. 'Nature and we must bless the hand that can such heavenly charms portray and save the beauty of this land from envious obscurity' is what was written of hers."

How glorious Mary Eliza would look painted with the brush of Captain Middleton, George thought. He analyzed Wollaston's portrait further. Her expression displayed something more, something that instantly moved him, mixing admiration with concern. She had laid her heart before him on that balcony.

In her painted expression, he could see genuine and deep sorrow.

Elegance weaved with torment.

Grace intertwined with heartache.

Beauty combined with anguish.

"There is sadness in her eyes," remarked George.

"Polly has suffered through tragic times. A devastating illness took the life of their father and their Margaret. She's felt responsible for their deaths, you know . . . and the others."

Be not Curious to Know the Affairs of Others. This was an edict George followed. Her mother — he still did not know the circumstances of her death.

"She has a brave spirit. The guilt of losing

her mother seems to live in every fiber of her being. The passage across the Hudson River is a precarious one," Beverley explained. "When our Polly was only a child, she tried to save a little boy, the gardener's son. Precocious, he was. The child jumped into the water leading to the Hudson River by the Yonkers manor and Polly ran after him. They tell me she tried with all her might to swim to him, to rescue him. She has never been able to wipe the tragedy from her mind."

"The young boy?"

"His body never surfaced. The night became even more tragic for the family. Lady Joanna Philipse heard her little girl's screams and jumped into the water. It is believed the fine lady swam to her daughter and gave her a push that prevented her end."

George felt a lump in throat. "Such a tragedy for a young girl."

"The Hudson, Colonel, chooses whom it takes. I have heard many stories of that horrific night. If not for the raven, I'm told, our Polly might have died there, too, in the night. Their shrill call from above her nearly breathless body alerted a rescuer to her whereabouts. He found her lying, half-submerged, in tall grasses at the water's edge. And now we will do anything and everything to protect her, to keep her safe."

Now George understood the emptiness he saw in her. A genuine soul untouched by airs and honest about her own limitations. She truly was one of the most exceptional women he'd ever known.

As he took in Beverley's words, George felt a strong need to bring Mary Eliza Philipse into his embrace, to protect her, to surround her mind with peace.

Chapter Fourteen: The World in Miniature

The Mind of Man is fond of Novelty.
— GEORGE WASHINGTON

A faint sound coming from under her chamber door startled her. Mary quieted her breath. She remained still, though her heart pounded. A man's footsteps sounded in the hall. Had she locked the door?

She had kept the covers over her head since her arrival here last night. The bed was her solace, sleep her escape. She didn't want to see anyone today. Her spirit forbade her from rising. It had been a difficult end to the night. Deep feelings buried inside her were roused, leaving her emotionally spent. And seeing that man brought back the anxiety she so desperately wanted to rid herself of.

Papers slid below the oak door. She allowed one eye to peek out from under the quilt. The paper on top appeared to be an advertisement cut from *The New-York Mercury.* Curiosity lifted her from bed. She tiptoed and her bare feet felt the touch of the cool wood below her feet. What she read wiped away her fright and made her mood dance:

> To be seen at the New Exchange, that elaborate and celebrated piece of mechanism, called the Microcosm, of the World in Miniature. Built in the form of a Roman Temple, after twenty-two years close study and application by the late ingenious Mr. Henry Bridges of London. It will be shown every day beginning at ten in the morning.

George. He must have been the one at her door. He, too, slept at the town house of Beverley and Susannah. She hadn't seen him since her departure from the inn.

On a second paper, in the most beautiful hand, with script displaying thin upstrokes and wide downstrokes of loops and curves, was written:

> Mean-time the Song went round; and Dance, and Sport,
> Wisdom, and friendly Talk successive stole
> Their Hours away. While in the rosy Vale

Love breath'd his Infant Sighs, from
Anguish free,
Fragrant with Bliss, and only wept for Joy.

Had George placed heavier pressure on the nib as he wrote the word *Love*? Mary stared at the deeper, larger strokes on that particular word. She closed her eyes. She fell to pieces in his arms the prior evening. He put her back together and helped her see she was not alone in grief. He understood her and her frailty, which she was never comfortable revealing to anyone.

" 'Love breath'd his Infant Sighs,' " she whispered.

She brought the written words closer to her heart. The thought of him looking at her in that tender way made her feel so special, so *loved.* She raced to the door and unlocked it. No one was in the hall when she opened it. She couldn't wait another minute. She made her way to the upper floor. She tapped at the door. "It is I," she said in a quiet voice.

The door swung open and she leapt into the room, falling on her knees in front of her sister with papers still in hand. "He's written me the words of the poet Thomson. 'Love breath'd his Infant Sighs . . .' "

"Truly?" Susannah knelt down next to her.

" 'Love breath'd his Infant Sighs, from Anguish free,/Fragrant with Bliss, and only wept for Joy.' He's written me the words of the poem 'Spring.' Susannah, I am without words over this, over this man. It is not to be believed the impression he is leaving on my heart."

Susannah hugged her. "It may be you who also holds him in gentle sway."

"Susannah, I feel as though I've been restored." Mary felt so much changed in her in such a short time, yet she was more herself than ever before.

As Beverley assisted the sisters in exiting the chaise outside the exhibit hall, statues greeted them. Mary almost became one herself from embarrassment. The merchants appeared frozen in place as she placed her feet, in jewel-embellished shoes, upon the path leading to the exhibit hall. She carried a parasol adorned with feathers to shield her from the sun. That was Susannah's idea. It is the fashion of the day, she insisted.

Mary wore her hair braided, with each braid carried over to the opposite side, and upon her nape a swath of hair hung low in the form of a snood. She chose a costume with a soft hue that reflected her delight. The peach-colored taffeta dress embroidered with tiny gray swirled designs was paired with a white petticoat. Upon the sleeves hung white silk frill. Mary felt flushed, not because of the strangers' glares, but because of the man who was leaving a profound impression on her.

With a pleasant, dignified air, George neared her. "Miss Mary Eliza Philipse, it is an honor to see you this day." He was wearing a most fashionable suit of silvery gray silk. She couldn't tell for sure, but she thought there was a lining in a salmon color. The suit's opulent buttons shimmered in the afternoon light. Their outfits matched, as if they'd purposely coordinated them.

She took in his clean scent. "My deepest gratitude for the invitation, George." She laid her hand upon his offered arm. The feel of him set her insides aflame. They approached the New Exchange, which sat right in the middle of wide Broadway. It was considered the center of commercial importance. The place for the public to rendezvous bore unique architecture. The rectangular enclosed part of it sat high in the air, supported by grand arches. Below them, merchants traded their goods with their carts moving to and fro between the curvatures.

A sprightly, talkative fellow greeted the

four of them near a stairwell to the exhibition house. "Your passage into the World in Miniature!" He handed them highly designed tickets embossed on silver metal. "My name is Mr. Bridges, but my father often called me 'Genius.' "

She found this "genius" amusing, with his hearty greeting and spectacles that enlarged his eyes to double a normal size.

Mr. Bridges practically marched up the outdoor spiral staircase. Mary followed behind him as George's hands held her waist. Glee overtook her as she went around and around. She never climbed like this before, feeling as if life were turning her from the end of one journey to the start of another.

"Welcome to an astronomical phenomena that has traveled the globe," Bridges announced as he opened a grand door. "You join an elite company of those who have stood in its presence, including the royal family of Britain and Sir Isaac Newton, who spent time with my father's creation while checking the mechanisms." His arms spread out wide as he walked to the center of the space. "Ladies and gentlemen, our world in miniature!"

The golden display stood twelve feet high and ran along the walls of the room: an intricate composition of sculpture, paintings, and metalwork — filled with a visual and musical extravaganza — a representation of the known universe. An amazing variety of scenes moved in exact time to several pieces of music.

"Open your ears to hear the harp and the hautbois." Bridges placed his hands behind his oversized ears. "The organ, the spinet, and flageolet combine to produce the music of Signor Corelli and Mr. Handel. Inside the great Microcosm, the mechanisms are carefully constructed to gratify the ear while accompanying each moving scene. The music is coordinated to match with great exactness the vision before you."

On tiny instruments, sculptured Muses positioned in a Roman temple played Mary's favorite aria from *Radamisto* in perfect tempo. "Our song," she whispered to George, " 'Ombra Cara.' " She hardly knew where to fix her eyes. Mostly, she wanted to set them upon George.

The pleasing images were just shy of innumerable. She leaned in for a closer view. Miniature gardens in metal with an orchard of trees and vines in full bloom caught her attention. She imagined sitting with George in such a lively, green, and luxurious place. She thought of him taking her in his arms.

George spoke quietly to her and she felt his lips gently brush her neck. "To sit under your own vine, your own fig tree . . ." She adored how the wisps of his hair tickled her cheek as he spoke. "The enjoyment of peace and freedom combined." Every word he said sounded to her like elegant prose. "I would rather be on my own farm than be emperor of the world."

She settled her hand in the bend of his arm again as they viewed the exhibit and its wonderland. Orpheus played his lyre in the forest. Lilliputian horses pulled a golden chariot fit for a king. A whimsical land emerged with birds of fantastical variety, each moving in harmony to the music being played.

George guided her to the three-dimensional models of the solar system. They watched Jupiter and his four satellites, in exact proportion, completing their proper revolutions.

"George, look!" She pointed. "Andromeda."

" 'But happy they! the happiest of their Kind!/Whom gentle stars unite . . .' "

She recited the next lines of the poem. " '. . . and in one Fate/their Hearts, their Fortunes, and their Beings blend.' James Thomson's 'Spring' is a favorite of mine."

Just as the planets abounded, she felt her heart follow, performing its own dance to the diurnal motion. Together, they studied the next piece of art. Two miniaturized wooden ships sailed closer and closer to each other. "It's been said, 'How vast the sea proves no obstacle when two ships are destined to meet.' " Her eyes met his. They remained here for a few heartbeats.

"Shall I show you the most exceptional part?" announced Mr. Bridges. "Ladies and gentlemen, the inner genius of the World in Miniature." The maker's son unlocked the sides of the exhibits to show the internal mechanisms: wheels of minute size whirling in synchronic time. Each of the scenes' pinions cranked and spun and pumped. "The clockwork of the exhibit is so exact that the orbits complete their mutual transits while following the velocity of ten months' motion in ten minutes. My father spent his life creating this marvelous structure. And when it was finished. exceeding his expectations, he continued making considerable improvements. Twelve hundred wheels and pinions in unison. In harmony."

Mary stood amazed by the work and the word harmony. It felt right — the two of them together — Mary and George. Their thinking, their doing, their being, in sync . . .

in perfect harmony. As they walked toward the exit, her spirit teemed with enthusiasm.

They departed the exhibit and started down the spiral staircase. The aide to Lieutenant Governor Delancey was standing at the bottom with what appeared to be letters in hand. For the first time she could see what she had pictured in her mind; well-defined muscles at the sides of George's face clenched along his jawline.

"Colonel, my apologies for this interruption. I've been requested to deliver these to you with expediency."

George was given two scrolls of correspondence. "If you'll excuse me," he said to Mary and her family. "My attendance on a matter is necessary. I must settle some important business."

Mary's emotions sank. The worried look that appeared on his face distressed her. What is in those letters? she wondered.

Chapter Fifteen: The Defiant One

There is nothing more necessary than good intelligence to frustrate a designing enemy.

— GEORGE WASHINGTON

Insubordination. Or worse. The letter infuriated him. George gave a specific command to Captain Roger Morris; he refused to comply. First, George asked as a fellow aide-de-camp. Then he asked as a colonel. Both times, Morris acted injurious to the cause, denying George access to the journals concerning the military's movement leading up to the Battle of Monongahela.

George would have written the details himself if not for the bloody flux. He had volunteered to serve in the Braddock expedition, yes, to serve king and country, but in truth, he had a selfish motivation, to gain knowledge of the military arts. He was very clear to the parties involved that this was his desire. Yet now he remained with nothing tangible.

He unrolled the letter from Morris to reread it:

Dear Washington
I own, I am at a loss what to say in answer to some particulars in your Letter; & shall only appeal to your Judgment, from what I say.

My orderly Books, being lost I could not gett an authentick, one that was proper, & therefore was obligd from Necessity, to omit, what I would have complyd with, with Pleasure, if I had had it in my Power.

I must now conclude to desire you to forbear your Judgment, till I am convicted by Proof, or very strong Presumption, of what I am sure at present I am innocent of —

I am as I always was Your very well Wisher, & obedt Sert
Roger Morris

George's temper flared. Morris! He remembered how colorfully the Brit sang before sending those men to their deaths. The soldier with the floral boutonniere! George rolled the letter.

Who was in charge — a British officer of lower rank, or a soldier of the Americas of higher standing? A meeting with the commander in chief should answer his questions of whether he had justifiable command over British officers. George needed to deal with the matter immediately. The second letter granted his request to meet with the general in person in Boston to answer the question once and for all.

Chapter Sixteen: He Cannot Tell a Lie

> . . . I hope I shall always possess firmness and virtue enough to maintain (what I consider the most enviable of all titles) the character of an honest man.
>
> — GEORGE WASHINGTON

The coach was conveying them to the Yonkers manor — Mary sat next to Frederick, Susannah nestled close to Beverley.

"About the town with a Southern officer," Frederick said in a teasing manner.

Mary wanted to pay no attention to him.

"The Delanceys tell me there was quite a scene in front of the New Exchange."

She tried to take her mind off her discontent with Frederick's prying by thinking of George. Her feelings for him were becoming inexpressible.

"How is it that you conduct yourself in such manner?" her brother continued. "I appreciate being informed."

A deep sigh came from her lips. "Frederick, the colonel traveled five hundred miles on horseback to be here. The least I could do was accept an invitation from him."

Her brother turned to Susannah and Beverley, "The Delanceys believe him to be phlegmatic in his address."

Susannah sat up straight, with hands folded. "I believe his countenance is marked by caution and watchfulness."

Mary copied her sister's seated position. "The faculty of concealing one's own sentiments is a requisite of a statesman, is it not?"

"It is a common feature in commanders of the military," Susannah backed her.

Beverley affirmed with a nod and added, "He is an honest man. To this, I can attest."

"Are you certain?" asked Frederick.

"If I may offer an example from our childhood, one involving a sorrel beloved by his mother, but of a fierce nature, which resisted any attempt to be reined."

"His mother's horse?" inquired Frederick.

"What is she like?" Susannah leaned on her true. "His mother."

"Compared to my own parents, of her, I was a thirteen times more fearful."

"How else would we expect her to be?" Mary felt the need to defend the woman.

"She is a lady who demands discipline and morality from her children," said Beverley.

"I hear she is a beautiful woman," Mary noted.

"And what of the horse?" prodded Frederick.

"It was believed there was not a person who could ride this furor of an animal. Of course, George was of a different opinion. Upon his request, my brother, John, and I assisted in trapping the animal into a closed space and pushing a bit into its mouth. With that, Washington sprung upon its back and tore off into the fields. The power of George's strength could tame even its grandsires. He held on to the wild steed with all his might. The conflict went on for longer than our comfort could have imagined. We soon regretted taking any part in this enterprise, for the struggle between man and horse became near terrifying as the horse used all of its energy in one forceful effort that resulted in a violent plunge to the ground."

"What of George?" Mary burst out.

"Unharmed and without even a bruise," Beverley told them.

"And the horse?" Mary was completely engrossed in every detail.

"Died right there before us."

The sisters gasped.

"George was devastated," Beverley asserted. "Never again did he treat a horse with less than extreme tenderness and care."

Mary adored how he named each one of his horses. So this was why.

"What tale did you tell to his mother?" Frederick leaned back.

"We planned out several stratagems."

"I would suspect." Frederick folded his arms.

"Though George had little interest in our lie making. At breakfast the next morn, Mrs. Washington asked us if we had seen her favorite steed. When there was no answer, she asked it again. George replied, 'Your sorrel is dead.' "

Mary leaned forward, truly fascinated. Strong and brave and honest. This man was gaining possession of every part of her heart.

"A look of shock appeared upon his mother's face. 'Dead!' she snapped. 'How could this be?' George went on to tell her the whole story, how the horse had been beyond controllable, how he had asked us to aid him, and how in his fight for mastery of the horse, the sorrel fell to the ground in a violent fit and died right there."

Susannah brought her hands to the sides of her cheeks. "And what was the mother's reaction?"

"She turned red as a beet. After a minute's time, she spoke, saying she regretted losing her favorite horse but rejoiced in knowing her son always spoke the truth. My brother and I can attest to this: George Washington cannot tell a lie."

"Hmm. I wonder whether I should test this theory," countered Frederick.

Mary rolled her eyes. The last thing she needed was for Frederick to interrogate George.

Frederick shifted his eyes to look out the window. "It's unfortunate that his military position requires him to journey to Boston."

"George is leaving us?" Mary's heart dropped like a lump of lead. "When?"

He kept his focus outdoors. "The Delanceys tell me the colonel received a letter, requiring him to leave for New England on the twenty-third."

"Of this month?" She felt a queasiness well up.

"Yes, Polly."

"Beverley, is not his birthday the day prior, on the twenty-second?" asked Susannah. "Is this not true, my true?"

"The twenty-second, yes. Well, this is according to the Gregorian calendar. His authentic date of birth, I believe, is on the tenth or the eleventh."

"This calls for a celebration, Frederick." Susannah's eyes lit up. "A ball."

"Another ball?" Frederick turned to look at her. "It would not be appropriate on the heels of the other."

"There must be dancing on his final night, Frederick," chimed Susannah.

"I cannot approve."

"We could invite a select group for a small private affair of kind entertainment without the show of ceremony," Susannah suggested.

Mary tried to hold back the thrill that raced through her, knowing George might be in the manor once more. Would he kiss her hand again? Might she feel his lips upon her own? It was almost too much. She had to get a yes from Frederick. She just had to. She knew just what to say.

"And, Frederick, we could send an invitation to Mrs. Rutgers." Mary knew Frederick had grown fond of the woman. She saw his eyes linger as his dance with Elizabeth ended the night of the ball. "Elizabeth."

Was that redness she saw flash on Frederick's cheeks? She knew an affirmative answer was coming.

"Very well."

Chapter Seventeen: Bread and Butter Ball

Oh Ye Gods why should my Poor
Resistless Heart
Stand to oppose thy might and Power
At Last surrender to cupids feather'd Dart.
— GEORGE WASHINGTON

Yonkers-on-Hudson

For his birthday of his twenty-fourth year, he could think of no better way to mark it than with Mary Eliza Philipse. He would put aside military matters at least for today. So, wearing a brilliant red woolen coat accentuated with a turned-up collar, he looked the part of a man on the precipice of greatness in his red-and-ivory-striped waistcoat, a white silk cravat about his neck. His breeches were ivory, with vertically lined gold buttons down the sides.

George arrived at Philipse Manor just past five o'clock in the afternoon. Each day spent with her he relished. Her ease in conversation. Her intelligence. Her humility. For these and so many other reasons, he was succumbing to love's passion. His fortune, he knew, was not sufficient to maintain her in the manner to which she was accustomed. He needed to be assured his devotion was enjoyed by her. Without such, if feelings are not reciprocated, the heart struggles. He learned this once before and pledged he would never again. The lowland beauty, she tore apart his spirit.

With Mary Eliza, he felt something more. She seemed to truly enjoy being with him, even dancing with him, and hearing his mediocre poetry; he'd never recited a poem to anyone before. His lack of education and his lack of wealth did not seem to matter to her; maybe she didn't know. Either way, he realized he'd never felt this way before about himself. Confident. Accepted. Yes, with her, he felt he was enough. With Mary Eliza Philipse, the dawn shined bright and propitious.

In Mary's bedchamber, the ladies dabbed perfume of lavender-steeped water to her neck just before the dressmaker, Rosie Sherwood, added a sheer white mull fichu with a ruffle to the bodice of Mary's dress — a last-minute request. Mary believed the neckline was too plunging without it.

Music was playing one floor below the bedchamber. Sir Tenoe had made the request of Mary that only joyous songs be played this night. She had agreed. This would be Tenoe's first ball since being declared free. He would also be introducing a new dance to the colony, one that he taught her. "The Waltzen," it was called.

Singers burst into the chorus of Handel's *Messiah.* "Hallelujah, Hallelujah, Hallelujah, Hallelujah." Little Lulu, sitting on a stool, hummed along to the muffled music, not knowing the words of the verses in the least, but "Hallellujah" she sang out perfectly.

The young girl stared at Mary with eyes wide. "Are you's getting married today?" Lulu asked, interrupting her mother's work.

Rosie's eyes peered over pointed spectacles at Mary, the corners of her eyes wrinkled from smiling. "He is a tall, handsome-bodied, manly man, isn't he, Miss Polly?"

"That he is," Mary agreed. A nervous excitement came over her. "And Lulu, today's not the day." Just the thought of a wedding caused Mary to want to spin around with her arms out wide. "When I do get married . . ." She paused. "Well, if I get married, we will dress you up, Lulu, as a princess for the banquet."

Mrs. George Washington. What would that be like? Mary wondered. Euphoria wrapped in bliss, she imagined. Mary never pictured herself a bride before meeting him. He would, of course, have to choose her. That would have to come first. He would have to ask her brother to negotiate a settlement, then ask her to be his. Negotiations! Those took time. She remembered how long it took before Beverley and Susannah signed an agreement. Maybe time a colonel leading a regiment of the South did not have, if he even wanted to propose, if he even wanted her to be his true. But if he did, and if she said, "Yes! Yes! Yes!," well, she would walk down the aisle into the arms of her Prince Charming. Mary was so elated to see George, she felt her heart could jump out of her skin.

George viewed the belle as she walked rather quickly down the staircase to greet him. The fabric of her gown matched the tones of his costume, red-and-white shimmery striped silk. As the light of a sun's ray through the window landed on her, her décolletage was visible to him.

When she reached him, dimples on her left and right cheeks greeted him. He realized, here and now, that the time apart from her had pained him. "Mary Eliza Philipse." He slowly kissed one hand and the other.

She sighed. "The days have been dreadfully long without you."

He followed her through the foyer. She wore her hair up in a style that displayed her smooth neck and shoulders. Her upswept waves wrapped around a floral crown that he was admiring as she turned toward him.

"Do you like it?"

George nodded.

"The *Myosotis.*" Mary lightly touched the small blue flower buds. "Legend states that the wearer of the forget-me-not will never be forgotten."

Forgotten she would never be, he thought.

She smiled with a blush and continued into the parlor, where a fire burned brightly in the hearth. Her aroma lingered as she walked, so redolent of what beauty should smell like.

Frederick approached with a woman standing close by him. "Colonel Washington." Frederick reached over and gave him a firm grip. "Have you been acquainted with Mrs. Elizabeth Rutgers?"

George greeted her politely.

"Would you care for a beverage, Colonel? Ale? Wine?" asked Frederick.

"Wine and bitters, please."

Frederick hesitated. His brows lifted. "Together?"

George didn't think much of his drink choice. He often combined Madeira with lemon juice, nutmeg, and a sprinkle of sugar.

Frederick shrugged his shoulders and turned to a man George recognized from the other night at the banquet, the French chef who had worn a toque. He wore it still.

"François, if you would, wine and bitters for the colonel. For you, Polly, as well?"

She said yes. Both of her hands were wrapped around George's bent elbow.

"Colonel, you bring us a new way of thinking," Frederick acknowledged. "Wine and bitters, interesting."

The drinks were delivered with a stirrer made of a feather with its bottom half cleared.

" 'Tis a peacock's tail?" asked Frederick.

François handed the beverages to George and Mary. "Do you not approve, Lord Philipse?"

"My thanks for the cock tail." George gave the chef a nod.

"A cock tail for me, as well," said Frederick. "And one for Beverley. Beverley, would you care for a cock tail?"

Beverley looked perplexed but nodded in agreement.

After they received the cocktails, Frederick beckoned them and the few other invited guests to gather: "A toast to our guest of honor," declared Frederick. "On this, your birthday of the twenty-fourth year. We wish you success in your endeavors! And now, we shall partake in the games of the evening." Frederick led the group into the drawing room, where tables were set up.

George offered Mary a chair. He couldn't pull his eyes away from her as he watched her frame delicately take a seat by a kindling fire. It appeared her heart was growing attached to him. True devotion. This is what he wished for. In the composition of his own heart, he knew, there lay a great deal of inflammable matter. Dormant. Asleep. Now, with the torch put to it, it might burst into a blaze.

George and Mary were teamed up against Susannah and Beverley. The four of them sat before the walnut gaming table with their hands atop it, settling in for the long haul. The wells were filled with gaming chips.

"It is about time I can take revenge for

the losses of my boyhood." Beverley dealt out fifty-two cards, facedown, each player getting thirteen.

George hadn't played cards with Beverley since their days at Ferry Farm. Friendship with the Robinson brothers, as he saw it, was like a slow-growing plant that withstood the shocks of adversity. George knew well to be courteous to all but intimate with only a few, and to let those few be well tried before you gave them your confidence.

Beverley revealed the trump card — the suit of clubs. "I believe I will have to make up for John's losses as well."

"Your brother is a gentleman for whom I entertain the highest respect and greatest friendship." George noticed Beverley's ante. George was not fond of gambling; moreover, at this table, the stakes were high: Five shillings equaled ten days' military pay.

The card game went on in white-knuckle fashion, with wins for one team and then the other.

Each took a turn in winning a trick by showing the highest card. George had a heart. He won this trick. Mary grabbed George's arm. "Tied! Three tricks for them. Three for us!"

"This must be the tensest game of whist we've ever played, Polly," Susannah exclaimed.

The play went on. Twelve tricks were completed. "Who shall be the grand winner of this measly prize?" quipped Beverley. It came down to the last round.

Measly. Not so for George. He turned the last card faceup. The heart would be the trump card for this round. Play continued. Mary nearly jumped out of her seat with excitement at her card. Victory was theirs. "I've never enjoyed a game of whist as much as this!"

"It seems Providence protects you again, my friend." Beverley reached his hand out to George. They shook hands.

"It is infinitely wise and kind."

The dancing master, Sir Tenoe, entered the parlor. "Let the dancing begin!"

The musicians were playing brilliantly, the sounds echoing through the manor.

George and Mary walked through to the dining room, where the banquet table was set for a royal gathering. George had no appetite for viands, instead choosing just a piece of bread with butter.

"Are you not hungry for supper, George?"

Tonight, he was not, although his nose enjoyed the feast. What he desired most was to take Mary Eliza Philipse into his arms. "I appreciate an evening where music and dancing are the chief entertainment."

"At the least, we can share a bit of bread." Mary broke off a piece of the upper crust from his hand. She reached into George's breast pocket and pulled out his handkerchief, and in it she wrapped the bread. "There is no need for formality" — her brown eyes under raised brows shot him a look — "among intimate acquaintances."

George wanted to plant his lips on hers right then and there.

Mary led him to the foyer, away from the others.

"Be it remembered that pocket handkerchiefs served the purposes of tablecloths and napkins and that no apologies would be made for either." He took a bite of the bread in her hand. "Shall we therefore distinguish this night by the style and title of . . . the Bread and Butter Ball?" He spoke with his mouth full.

"I am fond of both." She twirled to the doorway of the dance floor, motioning for him to follow. "And, of course, fond of one of the guests, as well."

The dancing master called out, "Tonight we introduce to the colony the most graceful of dances: the Waltzen."

"May I have this dance, Mary Eliza Philipse?"

A dimple on the right cheek and one on the left.

All his eyes could see was her. All her eyes could see was him.

His breath touched her lips as their bodies came ever so close. His left hand settled at her waist. His right hand took her left hand into his. The instrumentalists struck the first chords of "Air on the G String." Her body pressed against his. The form of lyrical movement in the dance had her in a dreamy state, and her heart was swaying toward him even further, giving wings to reciprocal endearment.

Following the three-quarter time, they moved continuously on the floor with a whirl that propelled her into constant motion. Their feet moved in three beats in a perpetual flight. It left Mary dizzy, not as much from the turns as from the proximity of her lips to George's neck. She had never known how handsome a gentleman's neck could be. He had a fine one, muscular. She wished she could place her lips upon it, just to confirm her thoughts; she wouldn't dare.

His powderless chestnut hair was pulled back. She was glad of her evening shoes with their raised heels, which brought her lips closer to his. She inhaled him — clean, manful, with a hint of bergamot, combined into one scent. She could never tire of dancing with him.

She couldn't tell how long they had been hand in hand, body against body. With him, time could not be counted in any rational sequence, but melded into one big beautiful moment. They soon found themselves on the outside of the northern doors, still moving to the music of the instrumentalists. Even the coolness of the air did not lower her body's temperature.

Her brother also was there, and he quickly moved toward the two of them. "Colonel Washington, I must ask you this. I've been told you cannot tell a lie." Frederick might have had a glass too many. "This is the truth?"

Mary near leaped in between the two of them. She couldn't believe her brother's audacity.

George answered politely. "I hold the maxim no less applicable to public than to private affairs, that honesty is the best policy."

"Does it not concern you that others may have an unfair advantage, knowing of this attribute?"

"I believe that worry is the interest paid

by those who borrow trouble."

Before Frederick could ask another meaningless question, Mary quickly led George away, rushing him toward the staircase. It must have been her heel that caught a plank on the floor, for suddenly she found her herself tripping and falling *up* the stairs.

"It is the first time I have ever seen a person fall up the stairs!"

She burst into giggles from his remark. Normally, she would have been flustered by her clumsiness. She needn't bother with airs around this man.

George joined her in her mirth. They both laughed to the point where her belly hurt. Mary took his hand in hers and guided him onto the second-level staircase. They soon found themselves up another flight, still laughing, until they were outdoors on the roof balcony of the manor.

The stillness of night would have been glorious for most with the moonlight shining upon a calm river. But the sound of a raven in the distance disrupted her thoughts, making her feel an anxious chill. As the pitch began its descent into her bones, George stepped nearer to her and gently placed her body in front of his and wrapped his arms completely around her.

He brought her close to him, protecting

her. They remained quiet, taking in each other and the view before them.

"What is it that will make you a happy man, George?"

"More evenings like this one." His voice sounded soft in her ear.

She was absorbed by his loving tone and there, in the night, became lost in his arms. In his strength, her fear dissipated. His cheek touched her temple, and she could feel the roughness of his skin. "And what would make you truly happy, Mary Eliza Philipse?" Her name sounded divine when he said it.

She adored him. "Hearing more of your poetry."

"My mediocre poetry?"

"I wouldn't say mediocre, more like poetry on the verge of distinction."

He covered the side of her face in light kisses. "More like on the verge of extinction." His lips found her dimple. "Very well, 'What will make a life truly blessed? . . . A good estate on a healthy soil, not got by vice, nor yet by toil.' "

"Ah. He gifts me with rhymes."

" 'Round a warm fire, a pleasant joke, with chimney ever free from smoke. A strength entire, a sparkling bowl, a quiet wife . . .' "

"A quiet wife — where might you find one?"

" 'A quiet soul, a mind as well as body whole.' "

She sighed.

" 'Prudent simplicity, constant friends, a diet which no art commends.' "

"If an evening like this, 'tis a diet where no eating commences."

He laughed and continued. " 'A merry night without much drinking, a happy thought without much thinking. Each night by quiet sleep made short, a will to be but what thou art.' " His voice sounded more tender. " 'Possessed of these, all else defy, and neither wish nor fear to die.' " He turned her shoulder so that she would now be face-to-face with him. " 'These are things which once possessed will make a life that's truly blessed.' "

Her lower back tingled as his left hand caressed it, his right through her hair, and she let her head fall back. George placed small kisses at her neck as he spoke to her. "The charms of your person, and the beauties of your mind, have a powerful operation."

"George . . ." She turned her face away from him. "I am undeserving of your kind attention to me. There are things you should know about me — scars that live deep within me that I may never erase."

He cupped her face in his hands. "These have endeared you to me."

Her world changed as his lips found hers. The intensity set her thoughts on fire, her heart into a rapture, her body toward a heavenly serenity.

With earnest ardor, his mouth parted her lips, sending delicious shivers down her spine. Love's radiant luster shone ever bright, awakening in her a new passion she had not known was within her.

"How do you affect me so?" she whispered to him.

His cheek brushed against hers. "Everything which partakes of your nature has a claim to my affections."

She treasured this man, everything he stood for, everything he was. In his arms, she let go, until their hearts were beating as one. She remained in her blanket of protection as he took her will and breathed it back to life.

With George in her world, she felt whole.

Chapter Eighteen: Cromwell's Head

> There is a Destiny which has the control of our actions, not to be resisted by the strongest efforts of Human Nature.
>
> — GEORGE WASHINGTON

Boston

If only he had more time with her. Another week. A year. A lifetime. Instead, he left the manor the morning after the tantalizing grip of affection devoured them on the roof's balcony. He might have asked her right then to be his forever . . . if they weren't interrupted.

Now, more than two weeks later, George was spending his final night in Boston. He journeyed here to Massachusetts where there was business to attend to. He also used a few hours to visit a jeweler, one highly recommended, who melted metal into the shape of a ring.

George's journey to meet the commander

in chief of the British forces in North America was only partially successful. George hoped to be granted a royal commission in the British Army, but that was not to be. The general did establish a level of respect for him. British officers had previously refused George's command, claiming that a Virginia officer did not outrank a British officer of lower rank. The commander in chief ordered that that form of disrespect would no longer be acceptable.

Tonight George found himself at the Cromwell's Head Inn, a musty and dusty old place that looked as if it hadn't been tidied up since the turn of the century. On a wall, a whale's jaw opened wide, and on shelves were displayed the trophies of hunts at sea.

George lowered his head when he entered. The ceiling planks hung low. He was also in need of a larger seat. The small stool was hardly big enough for him, nor was the table, which he towered over. Still, he followed his edict: *When you sit down, keep your feet firm and even, without putting one on the other or crossing hem.*

Captains Mercer and Stewart sat at the table with him, leaning over to read his instructions. They traveled with him to the northern colony.

George was writing with his quill. "Blood-warm?"

"Little more than blood-warm, Colonel," advised the inn's owner, Anthony Brackett, a short, stout man with bulging eyes. He offered George and his contingent lodging during their stay in Massachusetts. When they first entered the center of town, Captain Stewart knocked his head right into the tavern's low-hanging swing sign as they walked by it, causing him to need a moment to recover.

"Then put in a quart of yeast," Brackett instructed.

George read the recipe aloud, wanting to double-check his transcibing of it: "To make small beer, take a large sifter full of bran hops to your taste, boil these three hours; strain out thirty gallons into a cooler and put in three gallons of molasses while the beer is scalding hot. Let this stand till it is little more than blood-warm. Put in a quart of yeast. Bottle it the day it is brewed."

"Aye," answered Brackett. "If the weather is very cold, cover it with a blanket and let it work in the cooler twenty-four hours; put it into the cask and leave the bung open till it is almost done working." Brackett placed wooden trenchers of a dark meat and a dish of porridge in front of the men, for what would be their final dinner in the colony.

Stewart and Mercer watched out the window as nearly every person showed respect in front of that low-hanging tavern sign. "Are they bowing to the sign?" Stewart still had an obvious red mark on his forehead.

"I've hung the sign for Cromwell's Head low to force each passerby to make a reverence to our Lord Protector. We pay homage to a man whose design was not dominion. His judges were the traitors. They were the enemies. Oliver Cromwell was a man who refused the title of king."

" 'Tis true, Cromwell's head was put upon a stick?" Mercer prodded him.

"Carried about like a trophy," Brackett grumbled with disgust in his voice as he walked away.

"Was he hero or traitor?" Stewart turned toward George. "Oliver Cromwell. Was he a hero or traitor, Colonel?"

George could have been very clear about his feelings regarding the Lord Protector of the Commonwealth of England, Scotland, and Ireland. It was during the usurpation of Oliver Cromwell in the mid-1600s that George's family had emigrated from one of the northern counties of England, but whether from Lancashire, Yorkshire, or one still more northerly, he did not know precisely. "Hero?" He showed one palm. He turned the other hand over. "Traitor? One's character is rarely drawn until decades, even centuries, after the sphere of action has long come to a conclusion."

George watched as Brackett lumbered to the table with a small sculpted head on a stick and placed it right in the center of the table with a thump. "They should exhume his judges and behead THEM!" Brackett said. "The wretches humiliated the legacy of an honorable man by removing his body from the grave, dragging his corpse through the streets, and taking off his head."

"But what of his body?" Mercer interrupted him.

"His daughter, Mary, removed it from the burial site, protecting it from harm," Brackett replied.

" 'Tis a memorable name, Mary." Mercer looked at George.

The name was memorable indeed; however, George felt a bit of irritation when Mercer uttered it.

Mercer's attention was quickly taken by the belles outside the front window of the tavern. "A man who hopes to retain control of his heart should never venture to the north. The ladies are beyond lovely."

"Magnificent," emphasized Stewart. "Our north country is made of beauties."

"Better than those other ladies we've seen, with their bad air and bad shape, like crooked boards." Mercer continued his diatribe, yet again, contorting his body to show a sloping of the back. "Quite different from the enticing, heaving, throbbing, alluring, exciting, plump breasts common with our northern belles."

Let your recreations be manful not sinful. George was careful in this, and hence, he could hold back no longer. "In forming a connection, many considerations besides the mere gratification of the passions are essential to happiness."

"Aye." Stewart nodded.

Mercer puffed, clearly irritated.

"Do we soon return to New York, Colonel?" asked Stewart.

George had learned the answer from a letter he received from stable master Joseph Chew. In it, Chew wrote on a number of matters. He added a postscript on the back of the letter, stating, "I have this moment a Letter from our Worthy friend B. Robinson. He, Mrs. Robinson, and the agreeable Miss Polly and all his family are Very well."

This was the answer to his request that he

had desired to hear: agreeable.

George reached down to feel the small box from the jeweler in his pocket. “We leave in the morning.”

CHAPTER NINETEEN: A SOLDIER AND A LOVER

. . . know my good friend that no distance can keep anxious lovers long asunder . . .

— GEORGE WASHINGTON

Yonkers-on-Hudson

Mary wished George had stayed longer. Another hour. Another day. Forever. He asked for a return visit. She said she was agreeable to it. Of course she was agreeable to it.

Here on the hills' northern pasture, Mary stood alone, her only company the mare named Diamond and her foal. The horse gave birth while George was away in Boston. Mary bore witness to the miracle. Her tears flowed when the filly emerged after a trying delivery. No matter how many times Mary saw the birthing process in the stable, each was a wondrously emotional event.

Today, in the open air, she watched the foal — a young one experiencing life with a mother to help guide the way, a bonding, an intimacy that would remain for a lifetime. Infancy is a splendid thing, she thought, a masterpiece of the heavens, when is born a destiny that, if allowed to flourish, will see its bestowed graces realized.

Taking in the chorus of robins in the trees, she listened for their whistles proclaiming the approach of the new season. Their melody was leading her into the throes of a wistful embrace. Mary found the harbingers of spring exhilarating. Her mother had been right: This time of year offered great possibility as the day followed a more capacious circuit in the hemisphere; even the shriveled bud began to break through winter's tomb — nature on the threshold of glory. The grass displayed its wee blades. The new shoots upon the weeping cherry tree emerged. Their fragrance wafted on a mellow breeze.

"Each flower must emerge from the darkness to bathe in the light." Mary recalled her mother's words, as well as the emotional inflection she had used to express them. Mama had always sounded as if she were singing. If her voice had been a season, it would have been spring, for there had been such hope in Mama's words.

Mary squinted to see as far as she could.

From this highest point of Yonkers, she could canvass the fine landscapes stretched out before her — valleys and hills and waterways; the Hudson and the rivers to the east of it were in view.

She found the entire picture breathtaking — hope in its inception.

For so long, she refused it entry. She turned hope away. Those times she did try to find a light within her, her spirit blocked this vision, chained it and shut it down. Despair always defeated her, dragging her into its abyss.

Mary found a place to lay her heavy blanket and put her quill to paper:

How came you to this place
Where virtue and vice hide
With ardor in your embrace?
Shall I allow you to be my guide,
Or remain behind the guardian's wall?
Let me succumb to dreams of sweet
  delight.
Into your arms, allow me a fall,
But, alas, a cursed star only lives in the
  night,
And destiny must be allowed to bloom.
For what I am, I may never know,
There was such grief and gloom.
That was long ago.

Today, grant me release from my cry,
On Cupid's wings, let me fly.

If only she had reached for the flower that day. If only . . .

Regret is not a pretty thing.

The sadness of that day and the many other sadnesses that followed remained for so long. She was tired of the torment. She was tired of living in the past.

George, my love. Without him even knowing it, he was showing her the way.

As she peered about, she thought she could see an image of him, moving quickly. She rubbed her eyes to clear her mind's confusion. When she opened them, she saw with clarity. It was George. In the distance, her hero, her charming. George was coming! With the most perfect posture, he rode with exact rhythm to the stride of his Woodfin. She watched him coming closer.

Without caution, she arose, took one step and another. Soon she was allowing her feet to hit whatever ground was beneath them. One foot leaped in front of the other. Her legs were flying free, for she adored how his eyes gazed into hers, how her heart trembled each time he neared her. She loved the way he touched her without even touching her. If joy could be writ upon her chest, it would be inscribed in capitals. Cupid's feathered dart struck her hard. Today she was ready to surrender to sweet dream's delight. Had she felt this way before? Never.

The belle of the North was in flight on love's wings. Mary Eliza Philipse was running to *him.* She was a dream — pleasing, beautiful, captivating, with a hundred pure charms. He longed to bring her into his arms as he watched the morning sun and its majesty of light glimmer in her long waves, which came undone, flowing up and down with her graceful movement. She didn't try to cover herself, though her breasts pressed against the fabric of her dress. As he dismounted and laid his feet upon the fertile ground of her land, he moved to meet her, knowing the season had now come.

Love refused to take pity on her as she reached him. Mary, overpowered by emotions, threw herself into his arms. She laid her head upon his chest. She felt his heartbeat on her temple and listened as he released heavy breaths. "I worried you wouldn't come," she said as she sank into his arms. She never wanted to let go.

He stroked the side of her face. He felt her shiver. He placed his other hand into the back of her hair, feeling silkiness through his fingers. He felt her relax in his arms, soften. "Mary Eliza Philipse, my fond heart overflows with joy to see you." She smiled and her lips trembled. A thrill ran through him as he took in her smell: lavender.

How perfect her name sounded coming from his lips. This left her in ecstasy. She couldn't say a word, for there were no words to express the feelings of her heart. First she felt anxious to greet this man. Then she feared kissing him. Now that she knew she adored him, she was afraid to lose him. She realized that she had fallen for him the first moment her name came from his lips.

Sensing her comfort, he felt at ease to make known his sentiments. "If my expression was equal to the feelings of my heart . . ."

His lips were calling her to where warm kisses play. She shyly turned her face from him, for the intimacy of the moment was too much for her to take in. "How did you find me?"

"Mr. Chew directed me to Diamond and the foal. He tells me of the trials you had to bear in helping to deliver her. How brave of you."

"She is beautiful and bears the most lovely patch of white, shaped as a heart. She hath not a name, George."

"What do you suggest we call her?"

We. What a beautiful sound that word carried. She had never known it to be so glorious until he said it. *We.* "Shall we call her Valentine?"

He brought her close to where her body was against his. "I find that name entirely perfect." He was beginning to feel such a deep attachment to this woman. He wondered if it was the sort of devotion that belonged to a man who loves only once in a lifetime. He prayed it would be so. "My poor heart. How will it stand to oppose thy might and power?"

She cherished his words and the way he said them, sounding like love in perfect rhythm.

He placed his face against hers and began to take in her breath. "And now lies bleeding every hour, for she will not take pity on me." He removed his long red greatcoat and laid it on the ground. He knelt on it and guided her down to him. Both faced each other, their bodies close, near close enough to touch.

"I believe it is you who should take pity on my heart." Her voice was tender.

He wanted to carry a kiss to her and give her assurances of his fond regard. He took both of her hands in his. "I'll sleep among my most inveterate foes and with gladness never wish to wake."

At this very moment, a realization came clear — one that she never imagined, for she never knew romance in real life, always thinking it a matter of fiction that played out in a poem or a song, but now, as she thought of the wonders of what it would be like to share his bed, as her one hand let go of his and her fingers threaded through his loose hair while staring into his blue-with-a-touch-of-gray eyes, as she fought to keep her lips from reaching up to devour his, as she shifted her gaze to her riding dress, which had slipped off her shoulder, as she lifted her dress back in place, and as she watched him move it back off her shoulder, a truth emerged from the deepest depths of her heart: Mary Eliza Philipse was in love with George Washington.

Her cheek grazed his hand and her creamy skin lingered there — the feel of loveliness in the flesh. His adoration grew fierce at her touch. A light wind moved her hair just so. He moved his fingers to the loose strands and put them back in place. She closed her eyes at this. She looked blissful. He spoke to her quietly. " 'Twas perfect love before, but how I do adore." She was completely still, despite the curve of her lips, which ushered in an angelic smile. He placed a kiss upon her dimpled right cheek. Another kiss he laid upon the left dimple. Gently, he kissed every part of her face.

Again and again, softly his lips touched her skin, leaving a sensation each place he lingered, until she dissolved into his tender passion.

Her lips parted to meet his.

Below the brightness of the meridian sun, two breaths became one.

■ ■ ■ ■

Part III
The Deception

■ ■ ■ ■

Chapter Twenty: Friend or Fiend?

> The turning points of lives are not the great moments. The real crises are often concealed in occurrences so trivial in appearance that they pass unobserved.
>
> — GEORGE WASHINGTON

Winchester, Virginia

George paced the floor of the room he rented at Cocke's Tavern. For four pounds a month, he could lay his head amid the clamor of the evening's bumper men playing fives and the odor of bumbo and ale seeping through the walls. In the day, he conducted his business here.

His personal secretary had accompanied him on his return to Virginia. "You know nearly every military man is resolved to serve under the new general and finding every stratagem possible to journey to New York to do so." John Kirkpatrick laid a new scroll flat to transcribe a letter.

George would have liked to do the same — journey to New York. His British superiors turned his requests down. Months passed since the day his treasured one shed tears upon their parting at that place he fondly remembered as Valentine's Hill. His mind filled with thoughts of her, every detail of her, down to the softness of her skin at the nape of her neck. Little time was possible for good-byes. He yearned to be back in that northern colony to visit his lovely. He wished he had something to remember her by. A miniature — wouldn't that be fine — a portrait miniature that he could place in his pocket and carry with him everywhere he went.

His confidant, stable master Joseph Chew, had pledged he would keep the colonel abreast of Mary Eliza's comings and goings. George wished he could have waited on her for days more; however, an order from the British forces required his return to Virginia. The decision was made to build a fort. "Barbarities daily committed by the French and their Indian allies" is how the crisis was described. George was placed in charge of the construction in the "town of Winchester, in the County of Frederick, Be it Enacted, by the authority aforesaid, That the commander in chief of this colony, is hereby impowered and desired to order a fort to be built with all possible dispatch in the aforesaid Town of Winchester, and that his honor do give such orders and instructions for the immediate erecting and garrisoning."

George began the work the day he arrived in Winchester. Now, months into the mission, he knew that just one fort would not be sufficient. This was dangerous territory. The enemy lurked within miles of this place. George proposed a chain of fortifications to be built on the frontiers, in Augusta and Bedford, and one in Hampshire. George also pleaded for additional men as well as additional supplies.

Even more crucial was getting approval to march against the enemy and stop the incursions once and for all. The prospects for this improved: A new British commander arrived in the colonies to replace the prior general, who refused George's request for an offensive maneuver. It was this new commander to whom George now wrote.

"Must we include the full title, Colonel?" Kirkpatrick was seated at a small desk by the window. He dipped his quill in an inkwell and waited.

"It is expected." George's heels made even-tempoed thumps as he walked with his hands clasped behind his back.

" 'The Right Honourable, John, Earl of Loudoun — General and Commander in Chief of all His Majesty's Forces in North America and Governor and Commander in Chief of His Majesty's Most ancient Colony and Dominion of Virginia'?" Kirkpatrick waited for a reply. "I shall add 'the most pretentiously recrementitious holder of titles of Great Britain.' "

George held back a grin as he asked Kirkpatrick to read back what he'd written in a first draft. Kirkpatrick cleared his throat and began, first reading Loudoun's title in its entirety again, with a smirk, followed by the body of the letter:

> We the Officers of the Virginia Regiment beg Leave to congratulate Your Lordship on your safe Arrival in America: And to express the deep Sense We have of His Majesty's great Wisdom and paternal Care for his Colonies in sending your Lordship to their Protection at this critical Juncture.
>
> Full of Hopes that a perfect Union of the Colonies will be brought about by Your Lordship's Wisdom and Authority, and big with Expectations of seeing the

extravagant Insolence of an Insulting Subtle and Inhuman Enemy restrained, and of having it in our Power to take our desired Revenge: We humbly represent to your Lordship, that We were the first Troops in Action on the Continent on Occasion of the present Broils, And that by several Engagements and continual Skirmishes with the Enemy, We have to our Cost acquired a Knowledge of Them, and of their crafty and cruel Practices, which We are ready to testify with the greatest Chearfulness and Resolution whenever We are so happy as to be honoured with the Execution of your Lordship's Commands.

Kirkpatrick drew a breath. "What would you like as the final salutation?" he asked. " 'Your most obedient Servant'?"

George signed most letters that way. "If I could have a moment on that matter."

Kirkpatrick rose from his seat. "Take time, then. Decision making, like coffee, needs a cooling process, as you always say. I'll pour myself a cup of George in the meantime. Would you care for one, Colonel?"

While most Virginians began the day with a mug of ale or beer, Washington favored coffee. "Black, please." *Cup of George.*

George knew he never said that, but just shook his head. Kirkpatrick was indeed a card.

George pondered the various possible endings for the letter to Lord Loudoun. "Obedient servant" didn't seem the most appropriate. Instead, he told Kirkpatrick, " 'In behalf of the Corps, George Washington, Colo.' "

Chapter Twenty-One: Andromeda

. . . to this hour I am held in darkness . . .
— GEORGE WASHINGTON

Yonkers-on-Hudson

The portrait artist placed a bouquet of roses on Mary's lap as she sat in the west parlor with autumn's golden light seeping though the window. "Every daughter is her own kind of flower." She thought of her mama. "What kind of flower am I?" she recalled asking her mother as Mary's nose settled into a bloom to inhale its perfume. "Oh, my Polly, you are a beautiful rose."

Out of all the flowers she could be, did she have to be a rose? The rose is a diabolical bit of nature, Mary had come to realize, a complicated flower — much like the charms of life that entice and betray. The rose's alluring perfume draws one in, only to have sharp thorns puncture the skin.

The lace around her neck made her skin

itch. Mary tried to keep still. She scratched quickly, put her hair back full in front of her, and made sure not to cover the lovely lily of the valley that was affixed to a brooch at the bustline of her gold gown.

Three hours crawled by with the painter stroking the canvas, stepping back, asking Mary to sit still, sit up straight, adjust the roses. He painted for another hour.

Susannah's lips pursed. "Wilting will commence if you have her sit much longer."

Mary wasn't sure if she was speaking of the flowers on the brooch, those in her lap, or maybe Mary herself. "May I see it?"

The painter nodded. Mary rose from her seat. She shook her foot several times, for it had taken a nap. She carried the roses with care. She planned to place them into an arrangement to deliver to Lulu, Rosie's little girl.

Susannah smiled, her full teeth showing as she stared at the canvas. "Captain Middleton. She is breathtaking!"

Mary leaned her head around to view the canvas. Odd. She didn't remember smiling during the sitting, yet he painted dimples on both her right and left cheeks. The dimples had been passed down to her from her mother, her wavy chestnut hair as well. The painting before her displayed a radiant, blushing beauty. She had to look at it twice, for she could hardly believe it was a likeness of her.

Maybe she *was* beautiful? Or — more likely — it was the result of a fine brush in talented hands. She never heard of James Godsell Middleton before. In fact, the only other portrait she knew he painted was of the mother of the man Mary tried not to think about every minute of every day. This was the information, at least, that Susannah learned from her true.

It was George, she believed, who commissioned Middleton. The painter, though, would not confirm the payer's name. "A gift from an admirer" is how he put it. She hoped George would smile, too, when he saw it. The moment when they would be together again filled her thoughts entirely.

She examined the portrait more closely. On her brooch, the painter stroked tiny buds into the shape of the constellation of Andromeda. Mary walked away to hide her giddiness.

Andromeda!

She came back to the painting again to be sure. Yes. Painted specks in the shape of the chained maiden. First the dimples, then the constellation. She was certain the portrait was commissioned by George. And the artist was beginning a portrait miniature from the large painting. He would say only that it was customary to have a miniature made from the same. She wondered if he would deliver that to her George. Six months now passed since she had seen him in the flesh. She would wait for him to return. Theirs was a perfect felicity.

"*The New-York Mercury* has arrived!" Temperance called out to the sisters.

"The wedding announcement is expected to be printed today!" exclaimed an elated Susannah as she received the two publications from Temperance. One of them, she placed to the side. As for the other, she turned the pages until settling on one of them. Susannah read aloud:

> Last Thursday night, Colonel Frederick Philipse, Esq., of Philipsburg, in this Province, was married to Mrs. Elizabeth Rutgers, Widow of the late Anthony Rutgers, Esq., and Daughter of Charles Williams, Esq., Naval Officer for the Port of New York; a very agreeable Lady and possessed of every Virtue and Accomplishment that can adorn her Sex and make the Marriage State truly happy.

"How lovely for them! I wish you would

have danced on that night." Susannah's disappointment with Mary was clear.

Mary danced — one dance — with her brother on his wedding night. She refused to dance with the other men who asked, many of them military officers.

"Just because you dance with someone doesn't mean you are ruining yourself for Colonel Washington, my sister."

"I danced. Did you not see my minuet with our dear brother?"

"It seemed every bachelor was waiting for a chance to waltz with you."

That would not be. The feelings of her heart were unalterably fixed. Mary caught a glimpse of the other newspaper brought into the parlor. The *Virginia Gazette.* How perplexing, she thought. "Who delivered this to the manor?"

Susannah shrugged.

"May I see that other publication?" requested Mary, knowing the colonel who captured her heart commanded the Virginia Regiment.

Susannah carried it over to her. Mary placed down the roses, and took the publication to the light of the window. Nearly the entire front page was taken up by one article:

An effeminate Creature, that spent all his Time in the Company of Women, Feasting, Rioting. Certainly, Censure cannot be silence; nor can the Public receive much Advantage from a Regiment of such dastardly Debauchees.

They employed themselves in nothing but Banquets, Games, Parties of Pleasure and Carousals. Public Rewards were bestowed on those, who gave the most magnificent Entertainments; and even to such Cooks of Genius, as were best skilled in the important Arts of inventing new Refreshments to tickle the Palate.

Mary realized the author was comparing the commander of the Virginia Regiment to the most scurrilous military leaders in history. An assault on George? Her George? How could it be! She couldn't believe what else was written about him: "Sensual Indulgencies were his daily Employ," she read. "Their Country calls; and see! the Hero runs to save her." Save *her*? Could they have been speaking . . . of *her*? Written anonymously, signed L. & V. An anonymous coward! It had to be . . . or someone else. The article continued with a passage from Virgil:

Quis metus, o numquam dolituri, o semper inertes
Tyrrheni, quae tanta animis ignauia venit?
Femina palantis agit, atque haec agmina uertit?
Quo ferrum, quidue haec gerimus tela inrita dextris?
At non in Venerem segnes nocturnaque bella,
Aut, ubi curua choros indixit tibia Bacchi,
Exspectare dapes et plenae pocula mensae —
Hic amor, hoc studium —

She translated the passage in her head as best she could. She moved herself to her bedchamber to be alone. Feelings of dread creeped through her. She looked again at the passage. Mary covered her mouth with her hand to stop a scream and rushed to her shelf for a book with an English translation of the *Aeneid.* After swiftly turning page after page, she found it:

What fear, what cowardice has filled your hearts,
O, sluggish Tuscans, O you, who are never ashamed?
Can a woman drive you to scatter and turn your ranks?

Why bear our hand with useless swords
and spears, steel not made to fight?
But you are not slow to love or for battles
of the night, nor when
the curved pipe proclaims Bacchus' dance.
Wait then for the feast and cups on the
plenteous table,
Your passion, your pleasure is there.

Was she to blame? Others might have taken her attention to him — and his to her — and turned it into salacious gossip. She stepped back from the newspaper and remained still. An esteemed colonel reduced to this with the stroke of an evil pen. Hatred in ink. He must be devastated to have read such an offensive article, she thought.

She knew better than to believe any of it. Not George.

She looked down to see her laced glove stained red. Blood. The sight made her queasy. She tried to shake her head to clear it of its dizzy feeling. A thorn must have punctured her skin. This reaffirmed what she already knew.

A rose has thorns.

Could it be her curse beginning to defeat him? Censure George? She prayed it would not be so. She knew she should have shunned him. That would have kept him protected. The newspaper — she neatly folded it and quickly moved to place it on the shelf of her bookcase above the other, words away from her.

A disturbance overwhelmed her and she felt faint. She dropped her body into a chair. She looked again at the publication to be sure it was in proper position on the shelf — writing away from the cursed.

Right there, she fell down to her knees in prayer:

Please, angels, take up my fight. Protect him. Keep him safe. Please, angels, listen to my prayer. Protect George from the enemy. I've hurt too many. I am the one who deserves to be punished. Don't let him be cursed by the cursed. Please, angels, don't give up on his plight; don't leave him alone, for a rose . . . for a rose has thorns.

Worry, when it got ahold of her, caused her mind to begin playing its tricks. Inner demons, they weaken your faith. They put strange thoughts into your mind. Inner demons don't fight fairly. Like a nightmare, they strike even in waking hours. She was trembling. Think of nothing. Empty your mind, she told herself. Terrifying images would often haunt her when she lost herself in despair. She had gotten glimpses of the frightening pictures in her head throughout her life. Lately, they were darker than ever, clouding her rationality. Drag me. Punish me. Leave me to rot. She should have been the one taken.

A thick white fog rolled toward her, turning dark as it crept over filthy ground. From it, a little hand emerged, reaching for her in desperation. She couldn't get to him. She couldn't save him. A beast with a crooked finger pulled her away, covered her mouth until her throat closed from the dust, her air taken away, plunging her into nothingness.

The night that changed her days was becoming clearer. She was remembering what happened, why she ran outside when her mother said to stay put, why she was always terrified when the man of her nightmares came near her.

She rose from her kneeling place, walked downstairs to the kitchen, grabbed hold of a knife, and entered the darkness of the cellar.

Chapter Twenty-Two: The Invisible Enemy

I hate deception . . .

— GEORGE WASHINGTON

Winchester

George wanted to take the author by the neck. Infuriating! Two thousand words on the front page of the *Virginia Gazette,* each one driving a dagger through his reputation, inch by inch. How dare someone write such lies, and with identity concealed! Who would dare accuse him of such inordinate depravity? Signed anonymous with a pseudonym — L. & V. Washington slammed the paper down onto his desk.

In black and white were printed accusations of drunkenness and profanity in his regiment:

No Profession in the World can secure from Contempt and Indignation a Character made up of Vice and Debauchery; and no Man is obliged to treat such a character as sacred. When raw Novices . . . never used to command or have been found insufficient for the Management of their own private Affairs are honored with Commissions in the Army.

Kirkpatrick charged into the room, holding a copy. "Vain babbling! Worthless — malicious — envious sycophants!" Kirkpatrick became angry in the face and stomped his foot. "Colonel, these assertions are utter nonsense. Insanity. Who dares write such slander?"

Never express anything unbecoming, nor act against the rules moral before your inferiors. George chose civility in Kirkpatrick's presence, although he wanted to utter coarse words against the article's author.

"Ill-natured slander!" asserted Kirkpatrick. "Two, three, four men gathered together to propagate lies and lay them onto paper."

Let your conversation be without malice. George tried to remain calm. He made clear that he wasn't interested in discussing this with Kirkpatrick.

His secretary seemed to get his message and walked toward the doorway. "Remember what Alexander Pope says — 'Envy will merit, as its shade, pursue, but like a shadow, proves the substance true. . . .' "

George also knew what else Pope had written: "Be silent always when you doubt your sense." He read through the article once more. The most scathing denunciation of his ability was printed in the paper.

. . . Soldiers differ; some will shed their *Blood,*
And some drink *Bumbo* — for their Country's Good.
Some in the Field will nobly risque their Lives;
Some Hero like, will *swear,* or play at *Fives.*
Some show themselves the genuine Sons of *Mars:*
Some brave in *Venus'* or *Bacchus'* Wars,
Can show their *lecherous* and *drunken* Scars.

. . . when the Officers give their Men an Example
of all Manner of Debauchery, Vice and Idleness,
When this is the Case, how wretchedly helpless
must a Nation be? What useless Lumber, what an

Encumbrance is the Soldiery.

Men of Virtue and true Courage can have no Heart to enlist, and mingle in such a Crowd. And the few of that Character, that may be among them, are in Danger of catching the general Contagion; of being damped and mortified at the Sight of such Scenes of Vice, Extravagance and Oppression.

The article continued with a final strike at his reputation, with a quote from Shakespeare that the writer used to defame him.

Men's Flesh preserv'd so whole but seldom win.

George's jaw muscles clenched. He could nearly feel his blood getting hot. If there was a person who believed him incapable of command or, more seriously, in need of censure, he wanted to know who it was. No one would endeavor to act more in the interests of the military than George.

Certainly his inexperience had led to some mistakes in his leadership, but his first principle in every move he made in the military was a deep love to serve. He was sensible enough to know that some in his contingent were idle. He was far from exonerating the traits of his officers, but to compare him to a prince who destroyed his empire — this was blasphemy.

A heavy knock at the door of his room at Cocke's Tavern drew his attention. He answered it, still holding the publication, to find the Honorable John Robinson, Beverley's brother. George had asked him to come. He was glad to see him for a number of reasons, one being affirmation, the other a personal favor.

"A vile and ignorant scribbler!"

George needed that confirmation.

"To be aspersed in such a way!" Robinson found himself a seat and grunted before his muttering continued. "To whom shall we give credit for the malicious reflections in that scandalous libel?"

George's pacing was emphatic as he stepped toward the window of the room, hesitated, and turned back. "I do not know."

"I have never heard any man of honor or reputation speak the least disrespectfully of you or censure your conduct in the least."

"I have followed the strictest dictates of honor." George placed himself on a bench near the one window in the room. He opened it with his right hand; he needed some air.

"No man can blame you for showing a proper resentment at it."

"I assure you my conduct will remain honorable so long as I am able to distinguish between good and evil."

"I hope you will allow your ruling passion, the love of your country, to stifle your resentment. At least await the arrival of Loudoun in Virginia."

George glanced around at the four walls of his small room. He had to gain control of his emotions. An utter attack on his character from an anonymous writer! He walked to the hall for a moment's escape from the confines of the space. He called for food and drink for his guest. *Be not angry at table whatever happens and if you have reason to be so, show it not but on a cheerful countenance.* Then he returned for a discussion on the subject that would be dear to the heart of any man. "May we speak on another matter?" George cleared his throat. "The personal one."

Chapter Twenty-Three: Lord Loudoun's Banquet

. . . it is uncertain how far the Enemy may attempt to pursue their Victory.

— GEORGE WASHINGTON

Yonkers-on-Hudson
December 24, 1756

Ten months had gone by since George swept Mary into his arms and she felt, for the first time in her life, whole. Now her eyes welled up. Sitting on a wooden stool feeling distraught, she slouched. The only light came from the window in her painting room in the cellar.

Live or die?

What would be the choice?

Mary begged herself to close the door on what had been, to say good-bye to the dark. She had grown tired of hiding herself away, of losing herself in loneliness. She wanted to finally put an end to the demons, put an end to the memories of that beast, before they put an end to her. She placed her fingers on the knife's hilt and grasped it tightly. A primal anguish screamed out from the base of her soul.

"Die!"

The blade made its incision.

She pictured the powerful imagery in that story she read many times about the legend of the Phoenix. In the myth, the grand bird builds a nest of death and, with a clap of its wings, sets fire to itself, and burns in flames in the midst of an inferno.

Death was not the end, but the beginning.

From the ashes, the Phoenix rises, brilliantly rises. Feathers in the boldest peacock blue, eyes sparkling sapphire, the magical bird takes flight, illuminating the night sky in newfound life, one that is brighter, more radiant than before.

Renewal.

Rebirth.

With the paring knife, she tore into a rose, and into another and another, lashing the pile of flowers before her; they were blood-red, as were her fingers from the nicks of their thorns. The deepest red roses she chopped down to where only the blossom with a short stem survived. The stems with their thorns, she tossed away.

She arranged the roses in a radial fashion

to make a full base in the low Delft vase. Bright blue irises, twenty in total, emerged from the center — tall, reflective of the rise to a new beginning.

She wished she could experience the same.

She heard footsteps.

She put down the knife.

She assumed it was Frederick coming to negotiate her surrender. Her siblings wanted her to attend the banquet hosted by Lord Loudoun. She hadn't been to a gala since George left. Every day, he was in her thoughts. Every day, she waited for word from him. The only letter that arrived was to Beverley, from Beverley's brother, asking whether Frederick would consider negotiation through letters, for Colonel Washington's physical presence was not possible at this time. Mary was elated, for negotiation could lead to nuptials. Frederick balked, saying such was unheard of. "Any such discussion has to be done face-to-face," he told her. She fought him on this, but in the end she relented, for she believed with certainty that George would return for her. He promised he would return to her.

She wiped her eyes as her visitor entered.

Sir Tenoe. He was silent. The first thing she noticed was the scar on his face, which looked even deeper in this light. She cast her eyes to the ground as she tried to regain some type of composure. Blood on her hands. Slits, small ones, covered her fingers.

"Sir Tenoe." She used the fabric of her dress to cover them. "Forgive me. I knew not of your visit." He was hired to serve as dancing master for the night's grand banquet. She was glad of this. It was the only reason she even considered attending. Why he was here left her perplexed. "Was it Frederick who sent for you?" She blew out of her mouth to get the hair away from her eyes. It wasn't like him not to speak. She wondered what it was that he wanted to say. From his long silence, she surmised it wasn't something she wanted to hear.

He reached out to touch the floral garlands that lined the walls of the cellar room and his fingers lingered on the dried petals painted blue. "Each of us has a scar."

That was not what she expected.

"Mine" — he gestured to his face — "mine is on display for everyone to see."

Mary remained quiet as she listened to him.

"This wound, it is who I am."

With her head, Mary motioned for him to take a seat at the empty stool in front of her.

He followed her direction and took to

staring out the window as he spoke. "I had just turned thirteen. I was poor, without a father. The day that left me branded I had scraped food for supper when I saw them — a group of men. They smelled of whiskey; they stumbled, with a little girl in their grip. She was no more than eleven, twelve, no more. I'd never seen her before. They slammed her down to the ground. They hollered things, horrible things, at her. 'Pay no attention, boy. Move on,' they ordered." Tenoe spoke slowly. "Leaving would not be my option." A rhythm of short quick breaths followed. "One of them put his hands over her mouth. Another held her down. I charged into their circle in the alley. 'Release her!' I shouted. I was enraged. I'd never been so angry in my life. I heard them snickering. That little girl's eyes stared at me in fierce desperation." Tenoe's eyes shut tight. "My mother . . . she had faced that same fate; for her, I stayed; for her, I fought. One punch. Then another. I stayed. The six of them, they beat me bloody. I stayed. I fell down. I rose. I stayed. The child got up. She ran. I wouldn't move until that girl was clear out of sight. I saw the broken bottle coming. A man struck me across the face with it. I stayed . . . until that girl was clear out of my sight." Tenoe looked right into Mary's eyes. "I wear this scar with pride."

Tears burst from Mary's eyes.

"Fate put me there that day, just like it puts me here today." He reached out for her hand. She could see him looking at the bloody pricks on her fingers. "Destiny doesn't care that we're wounded. Destiny sees through scars. All that destiny sees is light."

An awkward fifth wheel, that's what Mary felt like in the carriage as Frederick and his new bride made goggle eyes at each other on one side. Beverley, whispering to Susannah, who giggled, sat next to Mary; the three of them were positioned quite close. Beverley was nearly covered in the fabric of their bell-shaped gowns, which spread out wide. Mary looked out of the window past the leafless elm trees, hoping to find a light to guide her destiny. Not a brightness flickered anywhere.

Her brother's periwig took an unexpected bounce as the carriage moved off of the central thoroughfare of Broadway and onto Whitehall Street, where the banquet was to take place on the southernmost point at the tip of Manhattan Island.

Within the walls of the massive fort curtained in stone, inside the fort's residential mansion lived the new general and commander in chief of all His Majesty's Forces in North America, the governor and commander in chief of His Majesty's Most ancient Colony and Dominion of Virginia. Why he had the longest of titles, Mary could only surmise. She wondered, too, why he decided to take up residency in New York rather than in Virginia.

As she stepped from the carriage to the ground, Mary could hear her brother say to Susannah, "Do you not think she should have worn a piece with her gown?"

Her brother was dressed in holiday ostentation from head to toe: a fully woolen greatcoat of a deep purple adorned with velvet trimmings and nearly thirty gold buttons down the front. His chain marking him Keeper of the Deer Forests was on proud display.

Mary didn't answer him. She refused to wear anything fancy to the banquet, especially gems. Rosie made a last moment's choice of a simple gown made of deep green Spitalfields damask, with an added brooch of a yellow flower; the costume was certainly less fancy than the usual wear for such an event. Her hair was wrapped above her head, high, but not high enough to be considered gaudy.

She was here for one person only. She promised Sir Tenoe that she would attend. How could she not? Here she was.

Mary relaxed a bit when she saw two belles approaching her. Cousins Eva and Margaret arrived at the same time. Not just the Van Cortlandts and the Kembles would be in attendance; the Livingstons, the Delanceys, and every other polite family in the colony were expected.

"Have you seen Lord Loudoun's chariot?" Margaret appeared elated to be attending. " 'Tis black and pure gold!" She did look lovely in her bold red gown, her blond ringlets flowing. "I hear he even brought from England his personal *valet de chambre* and *maître d'hôtel.* Groomsmen, coachman, footmen, postilion, as well!"

"We know. We know." Eva stayed close to Mary's side as they walked through the enormous entry door. "And who needs to import nineteen horses? Every one with green velvet housing embroidered with the coat of arms of the Loudoun family. I hear they filled an entire ship."

Mary was glad she was arriving with these ladies. They took her mind off her worries. The crowds would be enormous. She could already smell them.

"What will be the reaction when the British officers see Miss Polly Philipse in attendance?" Eva took Mary by the arm. "Every military man will be wanting to join the regiment of your admirers."

"Eva Van Cortlandt, you are aware I have no desire to meet a man this evening," Mary muttered.

"Her heart is fixed," replied Eva. "Any gentlemen who have demands on our Captain Polly are desired to apply immediately, as we have great reason to imagine the company will soon be broke!"

They placed themselves on either side of her as they entered. Mary took one last breath of fresh, chilled air. As the large doors opened, pine smacked with cinnamon welcomed her.

Everything in view was red. Red flowers were everywhere she looked. Upon pillar stands in every corner were vases filled with forced red blossoms. Long-needled garlands, with cinnamon sticks and red ribbons as decoratives, traveled about the winding stairwell's balustrade in the center foyer. On the doors hung wreaths made from winter's greenery with red-ribboned bows at their tops. The assemblage of redcoats parted to give the belles room to approach the host of the evening.

"Could that be London?" Margaret asked

with burgeoning excitement.

"Loudoun," Eva groaned. "Must be. I can tell by how high his chin is lifted."

The gentleman of high rank seemed to hasten his conversation with the sheriff's father, Lieutenant Governor Delancey, as they neared him. Costumed in bright red velvet with shimmering gold tassels, Loudoun stood high on his heel.

"The Dutch millionaire's family," Mary thought she heard an aide say as the man she assumed to be Lord Loudoun moved from his position to greet her.

"How is it that I may sufficiently thank you, Miss Philipse, for not only your polite acceptance of my invitation but also for the agreeable gift of your flowers?"

"The Philipse family wishes you a splended holiday," she responded in an amiable manner. The floral arrangement of the Phoenix design clearly arrived.

"I am abundantly honored to have your presence at my gala this evening. You are welcome in my humble abode at any hour, always." His voice was higher in pitch than Mary would have thought for a person in his position, his face so pale, it seemed he must have been powdered white. "And may I add all the compliments of the season to you, Miss Philipse." His pure white hand, decorated with a ruby ring, brought her gloved hand up to his lips. He kissed it. She flinched.

The ladies escorted her to the reception line, where the salutations were endless, with one officer after the next awaiting Mary's arrival. Her hands were kissed far too many times.

One colonel hastily licked his palm and smoothed thinning gray hair over his baldness as she drew near. He mumbled a few lines to her, which she forgot to listen to. She did catch his name: Colonel John Stanwix.

Then another colonel, Thomas Hickey, greeted her, followed by a lieutenant colonel, Hugh Mercer.

"Are you a relation of Captain George Mercer?" asked Mary.

"I've been asked the question before," replied Mercer. "My family hails from Scotland, while the other Mercer hails from Virginia. However, as I understand it, I'll be headed there in a week's time and hope to finally meet the captain I am connected to, though in name only."

"Pray be so kind as to present my regards to Captain Mercer . . . and Colonel Washington." Just saying his name sent shivers down her spine. She felt a warmth on her cheeks.

" 'Twould be my pleasure, Miss Philipse. My wish for a merry Christmas to you and your family."

Mary noticed Margaret adjust her hair ringlets as they approached a strapping Englishman with dark eyebrows that stood out against his powdered hair. Thomas Gage was his name.

Eva's face filled with giddy anticipation as they approached the next man. Mary always found him to be an interesting-looking fellow with waved hair that flared like a bell.

"It is he! It's Scandal," whispered Eva.

He spoke to them in rhythmic verse. "Let me sigh, for nothing can be more delightful to the eye, nothing more penetrating to the heart than seeing the glorious women of this colony from whom I'll never desire to part."

After Eva's hand was sufficiently kissed, Mary had to pick her up from a curtsy that lasted longer than necessary.

"I understand congratulations are in order, Mr. Pownall," Mary said to him.

"Lord Loudoun has been gracious to add Secretary Extraordinaire to my title," he bragged.

This greeting was followed by one with Delancey, who was dressed in a showy and gay manner for the evening. Mary tried to move past him quickly or else be caught up in his stare, accompanied by a single lifted eyebrow.

The next officer was quite fashionable, buttoned up, light brown hair combed neatly and tied back, and smelling significantly scrubbed. His nose was large, shifted to the left, and had a serious mark on it. "In this moment, my heart takes flight." He flashed his ivory. He fell to his knees, saying, *"Genista triquetra,"* with an animated expression as he merrily kissed her gloved hand not once but three times.

Mary winced and pulled her hand away. "Sir, please."

He rose and spoke with a British accent. "When a lady possesses every grace and beauty as is possible to attain, do you not believe she should be praised for such a fine choice in flowers?"

Mary's brooch — a yellow flower whose formal Latin name was *Genista triquetra.* The fellow was right. *Genu,* from the Latin word meaning of the knee. She was quite surprised he knew of it, but now she understood his reason for kneeling.

"Your charm alone affects me so." Loudly he made this proclamation. "I do declare, here and now, if you deny me the pleasure of one dance with you this evening, you will send me to the grave."

"Sir, I must present a nay in that regard, for I hardly know you."

"My name is Roger Morris, captain in His Majesty's Army and at the service of the finest belle of the ball."

"It does not become me to bear witness to such public proclamations." Mary hurriedly moved past him and right into Bernadette Clara Belle's towering structure erected at the apex of her head. The entire circle of maidens by Bernadette's side, including Emily Joyce and Elle Cole, was on a parade of pretension, showing off the mountainous monstrosities that called their heads home. If Mary could measure Bernadette's hair, she presumed it would equal a yard high, being that it was buttressed with gauze, ribbons, and that feathered quill again. She had seen garish fashions before, but these heaps might very well take the cakes. She stood in amazement, gazing at the bigness that literally stood up on its own.

"You never afforded me a correspondence in response to my letter to you." Bernadette emphasized the *s* sound in her speech with her usual coquettish tone. For years — it seemed forever — Bernadette had not had a kind word to say to Mary. Now, suddenly, she decided to attempt a connection.

Mary delayed a response, for she was still astonished by how such a pile could remain balanced upon Bernadette's head. The letter, she had never read, assuming it a disingenuous attempt at friendship. She wondered whether Bernadette used the feather on her head to write it. "Yes, while my spirit had a willingness to write, the flesh would not guide my quill," said Mary.

Eva and Margaret faked a smile to Bernadette and moved Mary into the hall. Once they were away from the crowd, Eva began to joke about the military men they met in the reception line.

"I surmise none of these lads has made an impression on our Captain Polly Philipse. Therefore, we shall now determine those killed, wounded, deserted, and discharged from Captain Polly's regiment during this, the Campaign of 1756." Eva pretended to write upon an imaginary scroll. "And what shall we make of that valiant nobleman who bows before his captain?"

"The Morris fellow's forehead was nicely sized," added Margaret. "I believe a sign of distinction."

Mary laughed. She was surprised they didn't comment on his nose.

"Our Earl of Loudoun?"

Mary shook her head.

"Very well. Although I believe he would be interested in mustering occasionally. He did offer you an invite to the mansion . . . at any hour. I shall give, now, the conditions of the others, and if you disagree, please acknowledge." The two of them listened to Eva's silliness. "What of Colonel Stanwix?"

"He nearly looked devastated by Polly's reaction to him."

"What was my reaction to this Stanwix fellow?"

"You hardly noticed him," noted Margaret.

"I didn't hear a word the man said to me."

"I would say wounded and taken by surprise," offered Margaret.

"And what of our sheriff, Captain Delancey?" Eva looked at Mary.

"Outlawed!" Mary couldn't help but offer her assessment of him.

"Tell me where the charmer is on the list." Margaret stared at the officers' line.

"Colonel Gage?" inquired Mary.

"Colonel Gage. Just the name affects me so."

"Let us place him in the regiment of Captain Margaret," suggested Mary.

"There is no doubt he will have you on the dance floor this evening," Eva assured her and turned to look at Mary.

"Pownall?" asked Eva with a glint in her eye. "Or shall we go by his pseudonym, Timothy Scandal. He is a Secretary Extraordinaire, indeed. The finest writer in all of the colonies. He is the scholarly author of the political letters printed in our newspapers. He's proficient in Latin, as well, which clearly I am not, even in the English language."

"Yes, but after seeing your minuet, Eva, he is 'likely to desert' the Captain Polly regiment and for certain join that of Captain Eva."

"I only hope of it. And now we return to the condition of our Captain Roger Morris."

"Discharged," asserted Margaret. "No, no. Wounded."

"Ah, yes, but the one who kneels, it seems, has an adoration for her which runs deep." Eva's lips went crooked as she put on her thinking face. "I will mark him down as 'shot through the heart.' "

Shot through the nose would be more appropriate, thought Mary.

Attention was being drawn to the grand staircase as the Delanceys called for the crowd to enter the foyer.

The lieutenant governor, with his son the

sheriff at his side, made the announcement. "May I introduce our Lord and Victor, John, Earl of Loudoun, our general, our commander in chief over all our forces, regular and provincial, and governor general of Virginia."

"How many titles does one man need?" Eva whispered.

Mary tried to prevent a guffaw from being released from her mouth as Loudoun walked to the center of the room. After polite yet dull applause, he began to drone on about his dominions. He spoke in a patronizing tone.

Before Loudoun uttered his final word, the kneeler approached Mary. "I would be the most crestfallen officer in the world if you should not allow me one dance this night."

The first chord was struck. She saw Sir Tenoe on the floor, leading as dancing master.

Mary found herself with Captain Morris in a moment's time as the crowd moved them to the center of the room. She tried to separate from him; however, he became more emphatic with his requests. "You shall plunge me into a evening of wretchedness! I shall cry aloud as you banish me into a dismal abyss!" exclaimed Morris.

In order to not make the awkward situation worse, especially with the importance of the event for Sir Tenoe, she reluctantly began to move with him, although resisting conversation. His teeth were fully on display. The singer erupted into "Love's but a Frailty of the Mind."

"My first opportunity," Captain Morris practically sang out, "to dance with the one on whom is fixed the chief happiness I wish to enjoy in this world."

At least he wore no hair powder. She felt thankful for that. She caught Sir Tenoe's eye; he nodded his approval.

She kept a distance between herself and the captain as the two of them moved about the dance floor. He had a gaiety to his step. Her eyes kept falling on his pinned flower. She didn't recognize the species. She was curious to ask about it, but to question this fellow might lead to further conversation, which she wanted to avoid.

"If there's delight in love," the singer crooned, " 'tis when I see that heart which others bleed for, bleed for me." The final verse.

Mary decided to speak. "Please, give me leave to acquaint you with the fact that I have no intention of courtship. I am quite content with my present situation." She hastily made her escape; the moment of release was liberating.

It wasn't even a minute's time that passed before a group of little boys grabbed hold of her. "Miss Philipse! Miss Philipse!"

What a pleasant surprise it was to find her young friends at the ball. She recognized the boys one at a time, nodding to each. "Mr. Livingston, Mr. Livingston, Mr. Jay, how do you do this evening?"

Henry Livingston Jr., with cute chubby red cheeks and hair so blond that it could be considered white, darted toward an adjacent parlor with his hand still in hers and sat her down on a bench near the fire. " 'Tis the night before Christmas!" he said.

"Oh, Henry, it certainly is."

"My cousins, Robert and John, have tired of listening to my rhymes."

"Of what subject are you composing? Something that makes you happy?"

"Tonight. Tonight makes me happy, 'Tis the night before Christmas." She could see his mind working hard. "And all through the house," he continued, "nothing was astir. Not even a horse."

"That doesn't rhyme at all," Robert interrupted.

"I find your rhyme thoroughly enjoyable," Mary encouraged Henry.

"I am now eleven years of age, Miss Philipse," announced John.

"Mr. Jay, you just had a birthday?"

"I did."

"And what do you want to be when you grow up?"

"A justice of the peace, just like your father, Miss Philipse." John Jay stood up straighter.

"Me, as well." Robert's posture followed suit.

"A noble profession, sirs. I shall call you by different names from henceforth: the Honorable Robert Livingston, the Honorable John Jay, and the poet Livingston."

"Thank you, Miss Philipse," they chimed in unison.

"Have you seen my brother this evening?" asked John. "He has been looking for you."

A shudder came over her. She turned quickly to look over her shoulder, scanning the room for the beast with the green eyes hard as glass. Her throat went dry as she turned back toward the boys. The day had come. She had to confront him. She had to bring herself out of this darkness. This was the only way. She knew now what had happened that night, the one that marked her life before and her life after. James Jay was responsible. Address him. Find a release from the weight of it, she encouraged herself. There was no other way forward. She thought of how Sir Tenoe fought and fought when evil confronted him. She had to do the same . . . for herself. With that, she got up and straightened her stance. "And I am looking for him as well."

It didn't take long for her to find the subject of her fears. He was standing alone in the corner of a hallway just outside the room where she had been with the boys. Her hands trembled. She clasped them together to stop them from shaking. She remembered the pain of that day so long ago, in the room of the cellar at the manor, as he pulled her hair and wouldn't let go. "You will be my queen, and I your king" had been his words to her. The smell of his hair powder — she could never get his stench out of her. She was just a little girl at the time. She remembered running from him, his spurs sounding as he chased her. She had closed the door to the cellar, holding tightly to the knob. He fought from the other side of the door.

Now she approached him with purpose in her walk, and she pointed her finger into his face. "YOU! It was YOU who caused the nightmare that lives with me every day of my life," Mary cried out to him. She finally found the voice to put an end to his tyranny over her. "You who made me fear the water, fear the dark, fear the unknown. It was you. You tormented me over and over again. I was just a little girl. Then, the day you dragged me into the room in the cellar. Held my face into the floor for so long I could not breathe. I had to run for my life, until I found myself outside, alone on the south porch. You caused me to run. My mother would be alive if not for you. I lost her because of you."

"Oh, my dear Polly, I am deaf to your words, for I hear only a yearning in your voice." James Jay lifted a hand to her face, and with the other, he placed a tight grip about her waist. His hair powder was thick and crusty at his scalp as he grabbed her and pushed her into a darkened room. "You affirmed it, my darling."

It had been dark then, too. So dark. She was scared. Her little arm hurt when he pinched her. She held the doorknob as tightly as she could. Keep him away. He was coming for her. The door pulled open. She tried to close it. He won. He grabbed her and dragged her down the cellar stairs, into the tiny room with the small window. He pushed her down. She covered her eyes. She wanted him to disappear. He yanked her hair back as he held her down into the hard ground and repeated the words to her: "You will be my queen, and I your king." She was too scared to yell. He said it again, then screamed at her, "Affirm it! Affirm it!" His face covered her face. She breathed in his hair powder. She gasped for breath, taking in dust; it covered her tongue and throat. She couldn't yell. "You will be my queen, and I your king. Affirm it!" "Yes," she whispered. He let her go. She ran outside, where Elbert found her, and by the river he picked a flower to make her happy.

Now a fog began to envelop her. Her body shuddered. She struggled to get free. Tears flooded her eyes and shut her throat. Her vision blurred. Her hand fought him, pushing him from her. She fought until she couldn't breathe. His hand was over her face. The darkness won. The drag of his spur upon the floor followed as she felt him lift her up. The shutting of the door was the next sound she heard, until he spoke in a wet whisper close to her face. "Whether it be in life or in death, you are mine and always will be."

Chapter Twenty-Four: Doubtful Spring

I am left like a wanderer in a wilderness.
— GEORGE WASHINGTON

Winchester

The temperature dropped near twenty degrees, leaving the air miserably raw, much like his mood, since he spent the Christmas season in near desolation. His reputation had been damaged by a still-unknown scribbler and his hopes of a holiday in the North dashed. George stood at the edge of a six-foot-wide hole in the ground, glaring into its empty depths. It seemed a lost cause.

"Can't say there will be any likelihood of a spring," Lieutenant Charles Smith said as he placed down an empty bucket. He'd been digging for water for months now. He was one of the few officers who didn't complain over lack of money, lack of clothes, or lack of protection. Smith continued to serve at the fort for another reason: His military status would likely keep him from conviction.

"How many feet?" George designed the well on paper and figured Smith's oversize hands were strong enough to use the hand tool to create holes in the limestone. After all, Smith's fist killed a man with just one punch; the fellow died on the spot.

"The hole is near ninety feet deep." Captain Stewart was overseeing Smith's project.

Not a drop of water in it.

"Fill it with gunpowder and detonate. Continue to one hundred feet," George instructed them.

The only drop came from above. A misty rain fell for days, making everything damp, like his optimism. His mouth was dry.

Not reaching water added to his troubles at this fort. The other more pressing issue was war. Twenty people were killed just twelve miles from the garrison. George sent a detachment to find the savages — without success. How could he secure a frontier of more than 350 miles with minimal manpower? He was using every means in his power, but the effort was in vain.

Even protection of the fort itself was unacceptable. George was in need of twenty-four cannons. Twelve-pounders protected it now, and only a few. As he looked up to the bastions, he knew they were nearly defenseless. An attack with a half-pounder could destroy it and destroy them. Maybe he was capable of an hour's defense. Maybe.

The blank sky was welcoming deep, dark clouds. George headed back to his space inside the partially built fort. Sweeping winds picked up quickly, pushing the rain against the single window of the room. He felt choked by these four walls, so tight, and by his circumstances. On his desk, he rolled out the designs for the fort. Fully constructed, it would include four bastions and barracks for 450 men. But now, even the mission itself he questioned. Why did this place exist other than to keep a colonel and his men trapped in a barren and dangerous frontier with ambiguous orders?

Adding to that frustration, the announcement of the name change a day earlier; it nearly infuriated him to be stationed at Fort *Loudoun.* This Loudoun — this newly appointed governor of Virginia — never responded to George's welcome letter six months prior nor stepped foot in Virginia! How could Loudoun protect a colony when he knew nothing of its defenses or its terrain?

George moved to a small table by the fire

to eat the last of the pickled white plums Mary Eliza had sent to him in a hand-carved trunk with a brass lock. Her gift of preserves, tipsy cakes, and catsup of different flavorings — including mushroom catsup — provided the only enjoyment in the months that passed in winter's cold.

He felt an unease as his fork entered the last slice of plum and he lifted it to his mouth. Over the time away from Mary, he had collected any information he could about her. The assessment presented by Captain Hugh Mercer was more than any man with dignity could take. A banquet was hosted by Loudoun, where officers gawked at the woman who held his heart. "I will wait for you" is what she had said to him. He knew she was true to her word. He placed his elbow upon his desk and let his forehead fall on his hand.

Loudoun! The man who called Virginia his dominion! Throwing banquets was more important to that man. George knew he himself had sacrificed much, risked even more for a position in the military and a chance at a better life not only for him but for the colonists, who ought to have days of peace. He wanted to fight. He wanted to protect. He wanted to save a people! Many of them suffered at the hands of the enemy, and now this!

George took out his quill for a second letter to this Lord Loudoun. It irked him even to write his location — Fort Loudoun. In page after page of rage, George presented his bitterness and frustration like a malcontent. He got to the end:

> . . . if, under all these concomitant Evils I shoud be sickened in a Service that promises so little of a Soldiers reward.
>
> I have long since been satisfied of the impossibility of continueing in this Service without loss of Honour . . .
>
> Althô I have not the Honour to be known to Your Lordship: Yet, Your Lordship's Name was familiar to my Ear, on account of the Important Services performed to His Majesty in other parts of the World — don't think My Lord I am going to flatter. I have exalted Sentiments of Your Lordships Character, and revere Your Rank; yet, mean not this, (coud I believe it acceptable), my nature is honest, and Free from Guile.
>
> We have my Lord, ever since our Defence at the Meadows, and behaviour

under His Excellency General Braddock been tantalized; nay, bid expect most sanguinely, a better Establishment; and have waited in tedious expectation of seeing this accomplished. The Assembly it is true, have, I believe, done every thing in their Power to bring this about, first, by Sollicitting His Honour the Lieutenant Governor to Address His Majesty: and next, addressing His Majesty themselves in favour of their Regiment, what Sucess these Addresses have met with I am yet a stranger to.

In regard to myself, I must beg leave to say, Had His Excellency General Braddock survived his unfortunate Defeat, I should have met with preferment equal to my Wishes: I had His Promise to that purpose, and I believe that Gentleman was too sincere and generous to make unmeaning offers, where none were ask'd.

And now before I sum up the whole, I must beg leave to add — my unwearied endeavours are inadequately rewarded — The Orders I receive are full of ambiguity: I am left like a wanderer in the wilderness, to proceed at hazard — I am answerable for consequences, and blamed, without the privilege of Defence!

He continued on a page more. He exhaled. It was done. He folded the fifteen pages and put them aside. He would read them through before sending them to New York.

Another letter needed to be written. He would return for her, so he had told her before his swift departure when their moment upon Valentine's Hill was interrupted by a cavalry of British officers rushing to present him the memorandum from the assembly requiring his immediate departure on account of a fort needing to be built.

If only he had refused the order and chosen love instead. If only he had reached out for her hand and asked her then to be his and only his for all time. Happiness, moral duty, they should be able to be connected, inseparably connected.

George brought out the gift he'd purchased in Boston, which he so desperately wanted to take to her. He imagined her eyes looking at him in that loving way and how they would react as she opened the box. He then pulled out the last letter he had received from Yonkers. Joseph Chew had kept his pledge to keep George abreast of her situation, "Pretty Miss Polly," wrote Mr. Chew, "is in the same condition and situation as you last saw her." She was waiting for him, just as she promised. George, too, was in the same condition. This frustrated him. He and she should be moving forward, not remaining in stasis.

Chapter Twenty-Five: Genu

But alas! we are not to expect that the path will be strewed with flowers.

— GEORGE WASHINGTON

Yonkers-on-Hudson

Mary didn't want to do what Frederick told her must be done. Her stomach felt sick over it. He was right, but that didn't mean she should be happy about it. She would quickly thank Captain Roger Morris and be done with it. It took her this long to finally agree. Months had gone by since the banquet. Her world had gone silent that night.

It had been Captain Morris who discovered her lying alone in the dark in that room where that scoundrel left her. She had little knowledge of what happened. An image flashed in the back of her mind; she forced the thought into hiding, for she wanted to keep its awfulness from even herself.

She would keep the conversation with the

captain short. More than anything, she wanted the guards assigned to her by Lord Loudoun gone. The protection began after the banquet. They followed her each time she set foot outside, each time she rode on horseback. She wanted to get fresh air alone; instead, she had to deal with officers trailing her. Valentine, the horse born to George's mare, outsped the guards every time. George would be proud. She wrote to him numerous times to keep him abreast of the young horse, which, although small, was still a fine mare. She hoped he received these letters, but how was she to know? He never wrote back, not a word. She understood, for he was a colonel fighting a war. There would be little time, she surmised, for writing letters.

She heard the clip-clop of hooves hitting the cobblestone path leading to the front door of the manor. Through the window to the right of the doorway, she saw the arrival of an ostentatious chariot. It looked as if a sheet of ice covered the exterior, for the black color had an extreme gloss. A golden lion shimmered upon its door. Green velvet housing covered the livery.

Dressed in a yellow suit, the man Eva had taken to calling "Genu," Captain Morris, stepped onto the path. He wasn't particularly tall. He was close to her height if she wore a satin heel. He held something sizable concealed behind his back. The last thing she wanted was a gift from him.

The captain had a spring in his step as he walked to the manor's front door. He appeared to her as a summer's garden in bloom, with embroidered flowers on the fabric of his coat that were large enough to see from a distance.

She planned to answer the door herself. No attendant for this. She needed the greeting to be over before it even started. She moved back from the window as he drew closer. The sound of his heels could be heard near the doorway. A quiet moment followed. Maybe he decided to turn around. She did not hear his heels click again. The lightest tap at the door came next. He must have seen her at the window. How humiliating, she thought. She waited before opening the top portion. If she looked only from the top, this affair would be done with sooner. Otherwise, he would expect to be invited in.

She undid the latch and opened it. Before she could get out the sentence she planned to say to him, he took off his tricorn hat and brought his hand from behind his back to reveal giant-sized flowers — with faces like the sun.

"For you, the *Helianthus verticillatus.*"

An awkward lull followed. She peered out the top of the door but could not see the stems. She undid the latch to open the bottom half. "These flowers are known to grow double this size."

"Where do they come from?"

"They are native to France, Italy, and Spain. There are other species of this genus, as well — of the smaller variety." He pointed to the seeds at the center of the flower. "If planted at the correct time of year, your gardeners will find they can be propagated quite easily, especially in the greenhouse."

"The flower heads appear to be tilting."

"I surmise due to their flexibility . . . or for reasons of kneeling before beauty." With these words, he knelt before her. "Without flowers, you might as well live out of this world." He handed her the bouquet. He stood back up, said a brief farewell, and strolled off.

Mary was left holding a bouquct of sunflowers that carried a scent of musky earthiness. She realized she never thanked him for what he had done. She would hear of it from her brother.

Chapter Twenty-Six: State of Denial

I am become in a manner an exile . . .
— GEORGE WASHINGTON

Fort Loudoun

Dullness ruled. George could do no more than acknowledge its power. The days dragged on. The months dragged on. Fifteen months passed.

He wiped his brow; the heat was sweltering. He smelled of sweat and he didn't like it. He sat at the slant-front desk he recently obtained and opened the prospect door to expose the interior drawers. He did his correspondence here. The desk was plain but neat and not very large — spacious enough to store his papers.

Today he shuffled through the letters he kept aside for personal matters. He tried continually to get leave to make his travels, to take care of the personal business he should have addressed when he was in New

York with Mary Eliza in his arms. Now he was trapped in this lonely place, protecting a frontier with an inadequate force and dealing with skirmishes from a crafty enemy. Left nearly defenseless. Still alive, until the time the savages decided to attack.

He organized the letters from his superiors again. He put those next to the ones he sent; George transcribed every letter he wrote, so that he could review any one of them at a later time.

To Colonel John Stanwix in New York, he had written:

> I should be much obliged, cou'd I obtain your permission to be absent about 10 days to settle some private affairs of very great consequence to me — You may be assured, Sir, I shall make no ungenerous use of your indulgence if my request is granted; and that I shall not quit my post if there is even an appearance of danger.

His commanders denied every such request, writing back to him:

> I hope Col. Washington has not been upon the Cerimony of not going for ten days on his private affairs without my leave, hope he will always take this upon

himself, being well assured of your not being Absent from your Command where your presence is so very necessary . . .

George made additional requests. Each one of them was denied: "yr Absence on that Account from Ld Loudoun must be suspended till our affrs gives a better prospect . . ."

How could the affairs give a better prospect if they never bolstered the number of troops or arms? Instead, he waited in a fort not yet complete for want of moneys and materials. He looked over his letter in response:

I did not purpose when I asked leave, nor ever intended to be answered, but at some favorable time, when the Service could admit of it without any detriment.

Why was it only he was refused personal leave? It seemed every other officer but him had such an opportunity. He again wrote to Stanwix:

I took the liberty in a letter to ask leave to be absent about 12 or 14 days, if circumstances in this quarter would permit; but having heard nothing from you since, I am inclined to address you again on that head.

The response to his request, he reviewed:

> tis more than a fortnight ago that I answer'd your letter when you mention'd its being convenient to your private affairs to attend them . . . in wch letter I express'd my Concern that you should think such a thing necessary to mention to me as I am sure you would not choose to be out of call should the service require your immediate attendance . . .

As he sat, frustrated, he heard a knock at the door. The post rider had mail for him. "Colonel Washington, for you," said the messenger.

George opened the packet and was pleasantly surprised by a letter from Chew. He quickly sat down and opened it. Washington had written him to inquire about the subject so dear to his heart. This was Chew's reply:

> Dear Sir
> I hope the Conclusion of the Summer may bring forth something at Present Every thing look dark & Gloomy. I find no fault with the measures taken and the scripture forbids us to speak Evil of

the Rulers of the Land . . .

as to the Latter part of your Letter what shall I say, I often had the Pleasure of Breakfasting with the Charming Polly, Roger Morris was there

George stopped here for a moment as shock struck him. Roger Morris! It couldn't be.

(dont be startled) but not always, you know him he is a Ladys man, always something to say, the Town talk't of it as a sure & settled Affair.

George slumped back in his seat, devastated to hear such news.

I can't say I think so and that I much doubt it, but assure you had Little Acquaintance with Mr. Morris and only slightly hinted it to Miss Polly; but how can you be Excused to Continue so long . . . I think I should have made a kind of Flying march of it if it had been only to have seen whether the Works were sufficient to withstand a Vigorous Attack, you a Soldier and a Lover. Mind I have been arguing for my own Interest now for had you taken this method then

I should have had the Pleasure of seeing you — my Paper is almost full and I am Convinced you will be heartily tyred in Reading it — however will just add that I intend to set out tomorrow for New York where I will not be wanting to let Miss Polly know the sincere Regard ~~you~~ ~~h~~ a Friend of mine has for her. and I am sure if she had my Eyes to see thro she would Prefer him to all others.

now my Dear Friend I wish you Eternall Happiness and Content and assure you that I am with sincere Esteem Your most Obedt Servt.

Jos Chew

CHAPTER TWENTY-SEVEN: THE GAMES THEY PLAY

> The game, whether well or ill played hitherto, seems now to be verging fast . . .
>
> — GEORGE WASHINGTON

Yonkers-on-Hudson

Mary nearly burst into an uproar. She stormed into Frederick's library. "They stole him!" She shut the door hard, turned to her brother, and waxed impassioned. "Right off the street!" Frederick quickly shifted his eyes to the left. She hadn't realized they were in the company of Beverley. "My apologies, Beverley."

"Polly, I know what you're here to discuss," said Frederick. "I have been told that the dressmaker's husband willingly signed the contract to serve."

"Leaving a tavern at midnight is not a time to sign up for Britain's army. J. E. Sherwood has a wife, a son, and a daughter who is not well. He must be allowed to return home. Rosie is alone."

"I cannot assert myself into every predicament your townspeople find themselves in," her brother declared. "Influence ceases to exist if not used prudently."

"They have nowhere else to turn, Frederick."

"Beverley, what do we know of this situation?"

"Lord Loudoun has assigned a recruiting captain who has lugged many a man right off the street. The colony is a paradise for recruiters. A captain offers ale, flashes gold before their eyes, and can twist a nay into an affirmation from any chub."

"Frederick, please. Mr. Sherwood is a good, hardworking man."

Beverley continued. "Not only here, in the colonies of Maryland and Pennsylvania, they've even signed up indentured servants to enlist, offering them freedom after their service. The same for slaves in the South. Of course, the masters, they see these recruiting officers as thieves. However, those seeking freedom have signed up in plentiful numbers. They've made the best soldiers in America, from what I understand."

"And Frederick?"

"Yes, Polly."

"Rosie fears British soldiers will move into

her home on order of Lord Loudoun. They've taken over homes in New York City."

" 'Tis true," Beverley said. "Loudoun is demanding colonials quarter the troops under the Mutiny Act."

"An Act of England — extended to America?" asked Frederick.

"Aye. Lord Loudoun has used one enacted in Scotland to allow for troops to be housed in private homes. And one separately enacted in England, forcing the allowance of incidentals."

"Thirty companies have arrived in the last month." Frederick's brow furrowed. "I never considered where they would be sheltered."

"And there is no legal redress!" Mary added.

"Calls have been made elsewhere for the Crown to put an end to quartering any man in America — but to no avail. We should negotiate to prevent their use of the manor and of the church. They've turned churches into hospitals elsewhere in the colonies."

"Our St. John's?" Frederick looked anxious. "They would not dare. And the manor?"

For a moment, no one spoke.

Frederick rose from his seat, stepped to

the window, pushed aside the curtain, and peered out. "Polly, I believe now is the time to allow a visit."

"A visit? What does one have to do with the other? The visit already occurred."

"A chance meeting at the entryway will not do. Captain Morris lives in Lord Loudoun's mansion and is an aide to him. How can we ask for help if you still haven't thanked him? This has gone on too long."

"Frederick, a visit is not necessary. Since the last visit, this captain has been near me every time I leave this place."

"And you've spoken not a word to him."

"You say he is one of my two guards now; however, there must be gossip, for he follows too close. He even came inside the manor one morning while I was breakfasting!"

"This captain in His Majesty's Army is a well-respected one. Polly, I expect you to keep your pledge."

"I have not affirmed anything." She turned her back to Frederick.

"One for the other."

Her head ached with a dull throbbing that did not stop its constant beat for the two days since she agreed to a visit from the kneeler. Today Mary was attempting to create a French dessert. Being surrounded by sweetness helped take her mind off of the day's miserable task.

Mary watched as Temperance carefully removed a lovely ring from her finger, a gift from François, and placed it into a box on the shelf above her. It was a posy ring, the kind with a secret inscription hidden inside, that it may touch the skin. She adored the inscription inside Temperance's ring: *Retrouvons-nous à minuit.* Mary knew the translation: "Let us meet at midnight." Mary's eyes shifted to her own hands. There was no posy ring. She couldn't even imagine the feeling of receiving such a ring. Mary often imagined what romance would be like. Find a love that makes you feel free. She believed she had found this in George. And yet she waited still for his return.

"We have not time for silliness, François." Temperance laughed at his serenade over his pot. "Please tell him, Miss Polly." Temperance gave her hands over to a full-force kneading in a bowl of dough.

"*Ma chère petite amie.* I sing to my pot for to awaken the flavors. And I suggest *le pain* you are making will need a half pound of butter."

"More butter! The French style is excessive." Temperance rolled her eyes.

Mary should have been entertaining the guests, but this was, for certain, more enjoyable.

"François," Mary asked, "have the clove gilliflowers been steeping for long enough in the lemon's juice?" Mary wanted to create a perfect marbling effect on the fruit wafers she made from his instruction. François suggested taking the pulp from plums, putting it through a hair sieve, adding three ounces of that to six ounces of fine sugar. Both were heated on the fire until almost boiling. Mary poured the mixture onto glass and let it almost dry.

"Parfait," he said.

With his help, she added the coloring from the steeped cloves, which gently maneuvered through the wafers to add the red effect.

"Miss Polly, we are fond of you in the kitchen, but should you not be attending the garden party?" asked Temperance. "François will take the dessert wafers out to you when they are ready."

Today was the day she was to thank Captain Morris for his gallantry those months ago. "One for the other," as Frederick had put it. This would bring J.E. home to Rosie and Lulu and Jeffrey. Mary had no choice, though it seemed too long after that Christmas Eve banquet. And it wasn't as if she hadn't seen the man. Not only did he follow her as a guard nearly every day, he sent a new species of flower to the manor each morning with a note explaining its origin and a note requesting an interview. Genu. She thought of how Eva got down on her knees as she said the name.

Mary, of course, never responded to Morris. Her heart was fixed. But would George come back for her? Not receiving any word from him was sowing doubt as to whether he would return for her. Sixteen months passed. She reminded herself he was fighting a war.

Mary walked out to see the battledore feathers flying in an utterly confused fashion. Three women — Bernadette Clara Belle, Emily Joyce, and Elle Cole — stood in a circle, playing with the paddles on the velvety lawn near the slope that led to the water.

Before she could reach them, she was stopped by the sprightly captain.

"Miss Philipse, if I may," Captain Morris said. "Might there be a day we could ride together?"

Mary looked at him, hoping silence would imply indifference.

"I could ask the other guard to hold back."

She didn't answer.

"If, in fact, you cared to ride alone, I would be sure to give you that space."

She didn't want him to be kind to her. She wanted to dislike him. But not having the guards would give her a chance to finally ride fast without stopping or riding sidesaddle. It would finally give her freedom. So, she turned to the answer she and Susannah had conjured up for any request from Captain Morris. "Apply to my brother, for he, and only he, will provide you with a response."

He smiled wide and buckled, falling an inch short of having his knees touch the lawn. "Alas, the spark of hopeful attention I so desperately desire!"

"Polly, join us!" called out Bernadette, who was wearing a dress too low at the top for such a game and the same feather in her high hair.

'Twas true that Mary was not fond of these ladies, but she felt thankful now for an excuse to move away from him. She had good reason for inviting the belles.

"And Captain Morris, thank you for your assistance the night of the banquet," she said quickly with a small smile. She walked toward the ladies. She didn't look back.

Play stopped as Mary came into the circle.

"He's handsome, Polly, and magnetic!" Bernadette offered the captain a flirtatious smile and wave. "Don't you agree, Emily?"

Emily gave a wink to the other officers near Morris. "I will need a moment to admire the dapper fellows before us."

"Is it true none of them has presented a ring as of yet?" Elle asked.

Bernadette, Emily, and Elle giggled. Mary was having difficulty masking her distaste.

"If any of these men asked, I would give them my hand," Bernadette said, "immediately."

"Solely your hand?" Emily lifted her bosom higher.

Bernadette shifted her dress lower at the top.

Mary was miffed. "Ladies, would you consider joining hands with a man who does not possess the whole heart?"

Elle appeared surprised by the question. "With any of these men, certainly, except for Captain Morris, of course. He has his eyes on someone else."

"Should not the state of marriage be accepted with only the most honest intentions?" Mary wasn't sure why she was even debating the topic.

"If you find a man willing, you should immediately seize the opportunity, Miss Polly," said Bernadette with a smirk. "Act up quickly to the nuptial vows, especially true for one who is past the age of prudence."

Mary could have fired back a retort. In truth, she knew Bernadette was right.

Mary needed to end the discussion. "Let us play."

With wooden paddles in hand, the four of them, three of them giddy, played the game. Back and forth they went, with one winning, then the other. Bernadette was in a frenzy, trying to hit each feathered birdie. Mary couldn't have cared less who was winning, but Bernadette was playing as if a laurel-wreath crown were at stake. They played in a round-robin style, two against two, then Elle versus Emily, and finally, Bernadette versus Mary. Bernadette's eyes narrowed; her face became stern, more serious than Mary thought it capable. Mary found this quite amusing. The birdie flew back and forth in the air and back again.

The officers began to cheer as the match went on longer than Mary would have expected. Bernadette's hair flew high in the air, left to right. Bernadette was quick, but Mary was strong, so strong that she at last hit the birdie hard, too hard; it went high, so high and far, they had to look up at it.

Hair fanning behind her, Bernadette raced

for the birdie. She was headed for the slope. Mary ran after her, shouting, "No, Bernadette! No!"

She wouldn't listen.

"Please, leave it be!"

She didn't stop.

"You're too close." Mary rushed after her. "Bernadette, no!"

But Bernadette kept going and leaped. Her hair unwound from the mass atop her head. The feather came loose and launched into the air.

"Be careful of the rocks!" Mary yelled.

Bernadette hit the birdie. A shout of triumph emerged from her smiling lips. The grin was quickly wiped away. Her body hit the ground with such force they felt the ground shake. She tumbled and tumbled down the hill. She neared the edge, the one that led to the water, off the stubby cliff.

Mary screamed louder and picked up her pace. "Please, no!"

Her heart screamed out: Mama says it's dangerous.

Chapter Twenty-Eight: Melancholy Things

I shall be anxious till I am relieved from the Suspence I am in . . .

— GEORGE WASHINGTON

Fairfax, Virginia

Sunset's reflection rocked gently on the calm waves of the Potomac River. Some of the happiest times of George's young life had been spent with the Fairfaxes in this very place — Belvoir. The family had given him hope of a firm position in a society otherwise elusive to him.

He was out of Fort Loudoun, where he felt like an exile. He wished his quick visit were taking place under better circumstances. His late brother's widow reached her hand up high, placing the backside of it onto his forehead. "You look pale," Anne Washington said to him. She was wearing all black.

Speak not of melancholy things, and if oth-

ers mention them change if you can the discourse. " 'Tis truly one of the most beautiful seats on the river." The air breathed purer for him here.

They stood on the manicured grounds of the estate. The gardens with tamed bushes in geometric symmetry displayed not a leaf out of place. The property had belonged to Anne's father, Colonel Fairfax, who died the week prior. The service took place the prior afternoon.

The last time George had seen Colonel Fairfax, he made one request of George; it was the same as Lawrence's desire: "Keep the enemy far from Virginia." George wasn't sure he could fulfill their wish — not with an incomplete fort, an insufficient number of officers, and the British commanders remaining mute to George's many requests.

Now George and Anne were joined by her brother, George William, who motioned for a servant to bring closer a tray with wine glasses and a carafe. "Your name was never far from my father's lips, 'George Washington's good health and fortune is the toast at every table,' my father would say." He handed a glass to George. "So now we toast you, Colonel Washington. Glad we are to have you here."

Anne interrupted, "He is not well, brother.

The best drink for him is pure water."

"The best drink for him . . . sister . . . is a red Burgundy."

A rush of chills spread through George's body.

"Are you sick?" Anne asked George.

"Of course he is sick." George William's wife, Sally, approached. She was also wearing black, but with a laced collar that showed skin along the neckline. "When love seizes the heart, separation causes a fever stronger than any medication will cure."

George knew there was truth in her words. He hadn't seen Mary Eliza in a very long time. When he would be able to, he did not know. Every request for an extended leave had been denied. He would need ten days, at the least, to make the journey.

"Drinks, whether water or wine, cannot cure heartache," added Sally. "May we discuss the personal matter at hand?"

"When did Robinson last contact you?" George William took a sip of red.

"Is this an appropriate time for such a discussion?" George did not drink.

"Father would want to see you married, see you happy." Anne turned to the servant and asked for pure water.

"On July tenth. I had thought they had quite forgotten me."

"Have you asked for leave, George?" Anne took the glass of wine from George's hand.

"I have. Multiple times. I've offered to take the time whenever the service could admit without any detriment."

George William took the glass from Anne and gave it back to George. "What was the response?"

"The colonel, John Stanwix, expressed concern that I should think such a thing necessary, that I would choose to be out of call. After additional requests, I was told no orders from him, nor Lord Loudoun, will move me from my present station."

"And any news from New York?" George William asked.

"Just two weeks ago, a friend wrote to tell me Miss Philipse has had a pain in her face."

Sally placed her hand over her heart. "Oh, the heiress waits for her George. Of course she would have a pain in her face. Imagine her longing. Look at you, the handsome and brave colonel of His Majesty's Army."

"The only way to learn the truth is to journey there yourself," George William added. "You must arrive in person. This type of negotiation must be done . . . in person."

Sally motioned to a servant for a quill and paper. "Darling, certain gifts must be presented on such a visit. We must place an order for you with Captain Dick."

George William continued. "There must be conversation with the elders, discussion of your worth, in regard to your estate. Her worth and estate must be discussed. There must be guarantees."

"You shall try again." Anne handed George a glass of water. "It makes no sense to keep you away so long."

George knew differently. Nearly every officer in New York and beyond had his eyes set on Mary Eliza. George was coming to the realization that a scheme must be in the works. A letter from a colonel whom he had served alongside in the Braddock expedition made this clear when he wrote that "a very considerable regular force is now in New York, but what they will be employed in is more, by far, than I can inform you." The letter's author, Colonel Thomas Gage, was working on the hand of heiress Margaret Kemble. George recalled meeting her at the Yonkers manor; she was Mary Eliza's cousin.

"You must try again," Anne said kindly.

"Write this down, darling." Sally waited a moment for her husband to prepare the paper, and began to list the items of necessity:

A Compleat sett fine Image China
2 dozn fine wine glasses Ingravd
Fine Oblong China dishes
Tureen
Two dozen Fine Plates
One dozen ditto soop
1 ps. Huccabuck Towelling
1 ps. 9/4 Irish Sheeting 74 yards
5 10/4 Damask Table Cloths
1 dozn damask Napkins

"This must be sent with the utmost expediency," she added.

"And I will speak privately with Captain Stewart." George William looked up from writing, turned and gave a wave to Stewart, who had journeyed with Washington here. "He and I shall discuss a next step. We shall inform you at the proper time. This must be done."

He motioned for George to drink.

George chose the wine.

Chapter Twenty-Nine: A Weakened State

Hence it follows that love may and therefore that it ought to be under the guidance of reason. For although we cannot avoid first impressions, we may assuredly place them under guard.

— GEORGE WASHINGTON

Yonkers-on-Hudson

Mary's head hit the rocks hard. She sensed a bloody warmth on her skin. Droplets fell, one, then another, until her yellow dress was colored red. She ran after Bernadette, watching her body tumble down the slope. When Mary reached her, she clutched onto Bernadette's arm, but the force of the fall defeated Mary's strength, the downward thrust too great, causing Mary to lose her balance. Bernadette plunged off the rocky edge, taking Mary with her.

The screams and muffled shrieks echoed as if they were coming through a cloud.

Ladies melted into a woeful mass of sorrow. Officers flooded them. Mary remembered how Captain Morris raced over, ripped off the shirt he was wearing, and wrapped it around her head. The men carried a bloodied Bernadette into the manor. They laid the body in the east parlor. The belles pulled twigs from her hair in between their echoing wails.

In the months that followed, not an ounce of joy emerged in Mary's spirit. Guilt clenched her in its wretched grip. That day reminded her of what she already knew: She was the cursed one. The letter, the one Bernadette had written her months ago, well, she finally read it after they buried Bernadette in the dirt:

> Dearest Polly,
> You and I share vast amiable qualities, blooming beauties, highly accomplished with qualities that captivate every man who nears us. What we both don't have is the same, as well — our mothers. This is why I wear her feather in my hair, the same quill she used to write letters to your mother, her dearest friend.

When shall our correspondence finally begin?

'Tis what our mothers would have wanted. My wait has been far too long.

Humbly,
Bernadette Clara

Riding Valentine helped bring some peace to Mary's nerves. The farther she rode, the calmer she became; the air cleared her mind, giving her a chance to breathe. Susannah had urged her to ride, reminded her that she was capable of the impossible, for she had survived the unthinkable.

Today the wind blasted Mary's cheeks as she nudged the mare into a bright trot on this late-October afternoon. She sensed the mare's willingness to pick up her pace, so she let her move into a long, bounding stride. They moved fast, as fast as Valentine's legs would take her. Nearly fifty miles they covered.

She looked to her left and a little behind. He was there: Captain Morris, keeping up no matter how fast Valentine galloped. It had been discussed — a match between the two of them. The captain had met with her brother on a number of occasions; Frederick did discuss these meetings with her, letting her know the captain guaranteed to maintain her high sphere of society and make her more content than any other woman could hope to be.

Riches do not ensure happiness. Of this fact, she was certain.

Her brother tried to convince her that there was much to consider: security of the manor, the church, the milling business, the trade business. Becoming linked with the British in New York would protect their property and protect the townspeople.

The requests for visits from Captain Morris grew constant. Their British counterparts bombarded her brother with stories of George. "Don't be fooled," they told him. "Washington is nothing more than a spendthrift, a debaucher, a gambler. He has no money of his own. No land." Mary already knew his worth. He was brave and strong and on the verge of greatness — that's what she truly believed. He wouldn't be a commander for long, they said, for he had already been censured. Hadn't she read what was written about him? Of course she had. She wouldn't believe it; she couldn't. But for George not to write to her for so long . . . Maybe there was some truth in what they were telling her.

Valentine took her to the grove of quince

trees. This place reminded Mary of happier times. They had spoken about love, planned their lives with their trues — the three sisters, back in childhood, Susannah, Mary, and Margaret. She recalled the moment as she rode near the manor gardens that, at their best, flowered with buds of every color. Hours had been spent together sitting in the grasses, the paths lined with flowers, emitting fragrance that invited summer into each breath. The three young girls would gather a blanket and a basket of cakes to delight in the afternoon's warmth, while listening to the gentle murmurs of the rivulet. Margaret played her mandolin. Susannah sang. Mary attempted to dance to their music.

The afternoon of arias descended into levity as they imagined their future loves. Mary and her younger sister would blush as Susannah serenaded the two with verse from Dryden;

> Love has in store for me one happy minute,
> And She will end my pain who did begin it;
> Then no day void of bliss, or pleasure
> leaving,
> Ages shall slide away without perceiving.

One happy minute.

Maybe that is all that love had in store for her.

Her moment of bliss. Had it already passed? She adored the time she had spent with George. The days she was in his arms, she had felt brave and free. Her thoughts became murky without word from him. Did he even want her? Nineteen months without him had crawled by. Layers of ache found a permanent place in her heart. George, she believed, might be better without her by his side. He had more to do. In him was a bright hope. She had seen it in his eyes.

Captain Morris, astride his white horse, reached her and Valentine. They rode side by side now. Each day brought new pressure on her to find a match; she was beyond the usual matrimonial age. Twenty-seven years old. "Past the age of prudence." Bernadette had been correct. Mary shook her head to get the thoughts of that day out of her mind. The tumble. The muffled screams. The bloody hem of Bernadette's dress dragging in the mud. The cursed one had returned.

Living in the manor with Frederick and his bride? Mary couldn't do that much longer. As for a single woman living in New York alone? Unheard of, her brother told her — unacceptable.

She reluctantly took the visits from the captain, starting with one a week, then two, and now three a week. He assured her that his ambitions were solely felicitous and his views honorable.

The horses slowed by a row of oak trees that had moss drooping lazily from their branches. "If curled properly, 'twould make a tolerable periwig," the captain joked.

She found that amusing. She had become weary.

Mary thought of the letters Captain Morris had sent her. Each came with a new floral bouquet. Most of the notes were silly words of love. She hardly paid any mind to them. Then she read one that made her question how she had become so bitter.

> My Dearest Flower
> Upon my departure from you, I frequently search deep within for the reason why I cannot make you the happiest creature on the Earth, for you give me the greatest delight I can imagine having.
>
> When you announced love was nothing more than a jest, I could hardly think of how to respond. I will therefore try again

to find the way to your heart.

Roger Morris

Captain Morris helped Mary dismount. They arrived back at Philipse Manor.

He fell to his knees before her, clasped his hands together, practically pleading with her. "Miss Polly, suffer me not to be in woebegone want for just one smile, one spark of hope. My adoration for thee cannot be exceeded by another. I feel such deep affection for you. I ask that you offer me one spark of hope."

She said nothing.

"I give you my honesty that if you choose another, I will be undone. My affection is for you and only you."

Her spirit was weak. She reached out and allowed her hand to settle into Captain Morris's.

'Twas true love is nothing more than a jest.

Chapter Thirty: A Night's Ride

> To guard against this evil, let us take a review of the ground upon which we now stand.
>
> — GEORGE WASHINGTON

Staten Island, New York

A light snow fell on the close of a winter evening with a purple-hued sky. The sun was setting not only on the day but on George's spirit. A sharp wind bit his face. The freeze clung to his nose. He charged along frost-heaved roads lined with trees that had lost their dress months ago. Woodfin under him galloped as if knowing the necessity of finding a faster pace. Hooves thundering over the dirt released the sound of steady speed. George bounced his heels back to take further command of the horse. At least the horse bent freely to George's will. If only his life acquiesced with the same ease.

He disembarked from the ferry that brought him from Perth Amboy, New Jersey, to Staten Island, New York, at five in the evening. Nearly fourteen miles still lay ahead of him. He hadn't much time to board the next. York Ferry would take him to Pearl Street by nine in the evening.

He wanted to turn off his thinking and stop his brain from analyzing the evil he surmised had transpired. After leaving Belvoir and returning to Fort Loudoun, he had again asked for leave. George made numerous requests to Colonel Stanwix, even to the governor. The responses were the same as they had been since the beginning:

> I cannot Agree to allow you Leave. You know the Fort is to be finish'd & I fear in Your Absence Little will be done.

The denials swam in his head as he rode faster.

> Surely the Commanding Officer Should not be Absent when daily Alarm'd with the Enemys Intents. I think you are in the wrong to ask it.

He hoped the letter he had written to Beverley had been received.

For a year and ten months, George had

remained trapped. How much longer did he have to wait? He picked up speed. He was traveling solely in the company of his horse. The gifts Sally had ordered for him never arrived. The order for items had been sent in September!

George would rather have not read what Captain Stewart's hand had written months later, from Fort Loudoun — addressed to Colonel John Stanwix. He remembered every word of Stewart's letter, having committed it to memory:

> Sir
> For near Four Months past Colo. Washington has Labour'd under a Bloudy Flux which till of late he did not conceive could be productive of those bad consequences it now too probably will terminate in, at least he would not be prevail'd upon in any Degree to abate the exertion of that steady Zeal for the Interest of the Service he in so emenent a manner has always been remarkable for, however about two weeks ago his Disorder greatly encreas'd and at same time was Seiz'd with Stitches & violent Plueretick Pains under that Complication of Disorders his Strength & viguour diminish'd so fast that in a few days he

was hardly able to Walk and was (by the Docr) at length prevail'd upon to leave this place as change of air & quietness (which he could not possibly enjoy here) was the best chance that remain'd for his Recovery . . .

. . . he expresses much concern for his omission of not giving you previous Notice of the necessity he was under of leaving this place and as he's not in condition to write himself desires me to inform you of the reasons of it which I have now the honr to do . . .

George traveled without stopping.

Chapter Thirty-One: His Visit

. . . our Hearts are fired with Love and Affection . . .

— GEORGE WASHINGTON

Mary's hand trembled as she sat at a highly polished carved desk in the drawing room of Susannah and Beverley's town house on the corner of Broad and Pearl streets, with a quill in her hand. A crowd of esquires whose names she did not care to know glared at her as she fidgeted with the unfurled linen scroll in front of her. Frederick and Beverley stood nearby. She put the quill down a third time without a signature. A lady's maid rushed a glass of water to her. Mary took a sip. Her eyes returned to the document and she carefully read it, as if she hadn't quite understood each line the first or second time through.

This Joint agreement made on this day

between Roger Morris of Yorkshire, England, on the one part and Mary Eliza Philipse of Yonkers, New York, on the Other part, Witnesseth that Whereas there is a Marriage Intended between the said Morris and said Philipse. When said marriage Shall take place and be Consummated, it is the intent of the agreement that said Philipse will maintain all of the property, share in the Philipse family milling and trade business, household furniture, Clothing and Ornamentals brot to the said Morris at the time of their intermarriage.

In Confirmation of the foregoing agreement the parties do hereby bind themselves, and their heirs Executors & administrators to the faithful performance thereof according to their true intent and meaning of said agreement. In Witness whereof the parties have hereunto Set their hands & Seals.

Signed, Sealed & Delivered to each other.

She held her breath and wrote "Mary Eliza Philipse" next to Roger Morris's signature. He had signed it earlier in the day without hesitation. The ante-nuptial contract came with the solemn pledge of accompanying Captain Morris to the altar; the vows would be celebrated at the expiration of one week.

It was done.

She jumped out of the chair and rushed from the room. Overwhelming feelings of confusion, guilt, and fear compounded into such a mixed-up mess, she wanted to not be seen by anyone. She raced up the stairwell, into the bedchamber, shut the door, and fell to the floor.

Was Roger Morris an awful man? No. He was a respectable man of good breeding who never failed to declare his sincerity with the best of intentions. Had he kept his word? He had. He protected the town, kept her family from the awful scenes of war. The order to quarter troops in the Sherwood house was reversed and J.E.'s enlistment voided, allowing Rosie's husband to return home.

Still, Mary shuddered at her answer. Polite society told her that what she was about to do was for the best. George was never coming back for her.

The horse ride from the port to the Robinson town house proved difficult; George could hardly see ahead of him with the heavy fall of snow driving thickly. Still, he kept up his pace, for it had been so long since he heard her speak the words, "You are a true gentleman."

Through the tumult of the winter's night, George could make out the image of a lion on a shiny black-and-gold chariot. He arrived, dismounted, and walked through the white-covered path, leaving his large footprints, each nearly twelve inches in length. The time was late, too late to make a call upon a lady. He knew the rules of civility. It was not good manners to do so. He paused for a moment by the door.

Forget rules, he thought. His lovely had already waited too long.

He removed his riding gloves and knocked at the door. He waited for a long minute. He knocked again. The door was answered by Susannah. He had forgotten how much she resembled Mary Eliza Philipse. He was glad to see her. She, on the other hand, appeared stunned to see him. He had no opportunity to offer a greeting.

"Miss Philipse is indisposed," she blurted out to him. "Please wait here." She walked away with an elegant, straight posture yet scampering footsteps.

So George stood, brushing snow from his tricorn hat as he waited outside the front door. Snow continued to fall on him. The door remained open. He could hear a conversation coming from a room at the end of the hallway. A man in a red coat emerged from it and quickly marched toward him. A messenger, he assumed. George stopped him and peered at a packet in the person's hand. "What are you delivering from this place?"

"They are the nuptial papers, sir," was his answer.

"Nuptial papers?" George's heart sank. "Where are they to be delivered?"

"I've been ordered to take them directly to the residence of our commander in chief, Lord and Victor, John, Earl of Loudoun."

"Polly. Polly. You must rise!" Susannah raced into the bedchamber with her voice breaking as she whispered.

Mary lifted her head from the bed pillow. Her sister looked as if she'd seen a ghost.

"HE . . . is . . . here," Susannah said slowly, deliberately.

"He?"

"Colonel Washington is in our entryway." She ran through the words and threw her hand over her mouth.

Mary shook her head. "It cannot be."

Susannah nodded frantically, with her

hand still over her mouth.

"No! No!"

"Shall I have Beverley —"

"Please no!" Mary climbed out of the quilt. "Do not turn him away!" She looked to the window. It was late, too late for a visit, and the weather treacherous. How did he arrive here? Why today? Why not any other one prior to this? She near couldn't believe it until she peered out the second-floor window.

George.

She could see him walking away on the snow-covered path into the night. He was leaving. Passion told her to throw out caution and papers and pledges. Reason told her to remain in place. What was she to do?

"Oh, for heaven's love, what are you waiting for?" Mary said aloud.

When all is lost, only silence remains. Stilled emptiness surrounded him. He could see only darkness, blank air that even the white of snow could not brighten. George walked alone into a trail of wood smoke, the scent that made known it was warming those who had loves to comfort them.

He was alone. He was used to that.

Why had she chosen that man, the insubordinate one? He was certain their marriage was the subject of the nuptial papers.

In the snow-muffled quiet, he heard a voice, her voice, the voice that had a melody to it. She cried out his name. He turned toward the sound and raised his hand to block the snow from his vision. The ache of missing Mary Eliza Philipse struck like a dagger to the core.

Through the flakes, appearing like diamonds shimmering their luster in the moonlight, *she* was running toward him. Mary Eliza was coming.

Before he could find words to say, his arms opened to envelop her. She leapted onto him. He lifted her from the cold, raw ground and both of his arms wrapped tightly around her, and she pressed her whole body against his. He felt her wholeness melting into his arms as if she and he were one and the same. "Words cannot express —" He held himself from speaking, realizing words would only diminish the intimacy of this moment in time. His face found hers and gently he laid a kiss on her forehead and on her right dimpled cheek and on the left.

Mary could not speak. No letters put together into sounds could explain the deep feelings she had for him. She placed her hands into his snow-covered hair and brought his lips close to hers. She wondered, was it fate that brought him here this night, for the snow blanketed them and the world around them, hiding them from its prying eyes. Just the two of them alone, with not a soul to see their yearning for each other.

George felt her lips just a breath away from his. He touched his nose to hers. He caressed her cheek with his cheek. Their lips nearly touched. Her eyes gently closed.

Quiet surrounded them in an alluring peace. It seemed to Mary that nature was bowing in deference to them. Then a beautiful swoosh emitted a sound. Had it been the wind, or had the world released a sigh? She thought the latter.

No longer able to wait for minds to reason, their lips found heaven.

Enthralled by her, George came to realize a simple truth: She was his; he was hers. What had come before, what would come after mattered not.

Together, they were *one.*

The clarity that revealed itself allowed him to reognize that one knows no place; the two of them could have been anywhere in the universe, together or separate, and he realized one knows no time; they could have been in the past or the future, for one exists not only for the present but for eternity, and through these truths George opened his heart to fall in love, in the middle of a storm, in the middle of a street, in the middle of a night, because with her in his embrace, he felt complete, understood, worthy; with Mary Eliza, he felt free.

Their kiss did not have an end. It endured even when their lips parted. Keeping her protected in his arms, he carefully walked through the cover of freshly fallen snow. One set of prints made an impression upon the cobblestone path as they approached the doorway. He carried her over the threshold. He had her now and he would not allow anything to disturb this time with her. He moved toward the fireplace in the parlor. He approached a settee by the hearth. Its bright hue welcomed them like warm rays of sun. Upon his lap she lay, his hands cradling her head to his chest.

In his arms, with his fingertips smoothing her hair, deep feelings stirred inside of her. Heat flooded through from the tippy top of her head down to her toes. Blue eyes with a hint of gray studied her. She bit her lip to stop herself from panting. Blue eyes gazing at her with such adoration. Why hadn't she waited for him? Every ounce of her being had told her to wait. If only George had written to her — at least a letter expressing his feelings — she would have waited and waited. Her face leaned against his hard chest, the beat of his heart on her skin. The pounding. Even-tempoed. Strong. Her ears became buried in the throbbing of it. If she could have remained here in this position forever, she would have been contented, listening, feeling the beat.

She never asked why there had not been word from him, why he had not returned for her.

Many questions he wanted to ask her. Why hadn't she waited for him? Why hadn't she responded to his letters? He wanted to ask her all of it, but his love was in his arms, and if this was the last time he would be with her, he would not let conversation interrupt. Heat reached every inch of his body. Her tears flowed. She never moved from within his arms.

He held her closer, as if he understood. Maybe it was true. Maybe he was protected. She would keep it that way. Keep him away from the cursed.

He breathed in her breath. He knew from her tears. She didn't have to explain. The enemy had won.

Night turned to dawn.

She had fallen asleep in his arms. The last

small flame was burning out in the hearth. George rose and gently placed his precious onto the sofa and covered her in a quilt. He walked over to the fireplace, placed white birch logs into it, and waited to be assured the glow did not go dark. From his pocket, he removed a small box. He set the gift on the table before her.

He left this place.

Neither a sad ending nor a happy ending would come to pass.

For them, there was no ending.

Chapter Thirty-Two: The Prophecy

I have always considered Marriage as the most interesting event of ones life. The foundation of happiness or misery.

— GEORGE WASHINGTON

Yonkers-on-Hudson

She chose to wear Mama's dress. Mary laid her hands on the simple mull fabric with a color on the verge of ivory. Embroidered flowers decorated the base. The neckline was square. The sleeves came out full, then sat tight at the elbow. She tied her hair simply and placed it behind her shoulders. She wore no crown on her head or decorative around her neck.

Brilliance described everything else around her. Three sleighing parties carried her and her bridal attendants up Albany Road to the manor. Mary resided with her dearest cousin for the days leading up to this one. Bells jingled all the way from Van

Cortlandt Manor. The sun was shining. The weather was brisk, requiring a heavy cape of white satin lined in fur.

Eva sat up close to Mary in the open sleigh. "At any time, my hand will be ready to whisk you away from this." Eva placed her gloved hand atop Mary's.

Mary kept seeing him in the crowd, though it wasn't him; it couldn't be. She glanced at the people moving about and thought she saw George. Auburn hair falling past the shoulders of a tall man standing on a corner with his back to her. The sleigh kept going. The same vision flashed before her eyes. Auburn hair. Tall. It wasn't him. It couldn't be.

What else could she have done on the morning after that night? Run after him? She certainly thought about it. Where would she have gone to find him? He left without saying good-bye, left without even a note of farewell. He didn't want her. She could understand why. But the way she felt falling into a dreamy sleep in his arms, she would never forget, like being wrapped in a cloud of warm sunshine, and, of course, there was the kiss. . . .

Mrs. George Washington. It was not to be.

She wondered how she had come to this

place in life.

"She comes! Here comes the bride!" Loud cheers erupted as the sleigh, with an immensely-sized red ribbon at the front and horses in red velvet furnishings, rushed past the townspeople, who ran toward the street to wave to her. Auburn hair in the crowd. She needed to stop looking.

The bells of St. John's Church chimed. She smiled as she looked to the bell tower. Eric Arthur Angevine pulled the ropes wildly, jumping and waving his arms to her. Mary nearly cried when she saw him. My prayers are answered, she thought. Be the light. Keep George away from the cursed. Keep him protected. Blessed. Yes. She knew she was blessed this day. Why, then, was such heaviness weighing on her heart?

The colony's great social event was planned by Frederick and Susannah. Every leading family would be in attendance, as well as the elite members of the British Army. Her brother and sister thought of everything. Garlands made up of flowers of the Holy Night wrapped around lanterns. White bunting hung from cottage windows. The white blanket of snow at the front path of Philipse Manor was cleared, replaced with crimson-colored carpeting to welcome her and the guests into the manor.

Mary had no role in the preparations for this day, except for one demand: Townspeople would have a seat at the banquet. "Guests, high and low" is how Captain Morris put it when speaking of them. The "low" should be seated at a separate feast, he said. She disapproved of this sort of talk, so he agreed to end it. Everyone would be invited to one space.

A hush fell over the crowd as the sleigh carrying Mary arrived. The only sounds were precious squeaks from the lively Lulu. Her crown of forget-me-nots went crooked on her head as she ran in her tilted way to Mary. Ginger ringlets fell down over her freckled face, covering one of her bright green eyes. She looked as darling as a flower girl could in her tiny gown of crimson velvet.

"Do you like me dress?" She spun around and buried her face into the base of the wedding gown. Mary crouched down to hug her tight and straighten the headdress that was askew.

"Today, Lulu, you look like a princess."

Lulu did her best at a curtsy. "I'm 'posed to walk through the people, but I'm not very good at walking, Miss Polly."

"One step after another. You will get there when you are meant to arrive."

■ ■ ■ ■

The bridal attendants led the way, each appearing exquisite in their deep crimson gowns and white gloves. Lulu followed them into the manor, carrying a basket of sunflower petals that she had been instructed to throw as she walked down the aisle. It seemed she didn't make it a step into the room before darting back outside to Mary with a nervous expression upon her face.

"I forgot what I'm 'posed to do."

Mary got down next to her small friend and spoke to her. "Let a petal land everywhere you take a step. It will show me the way." Mary gently tapped Lulu's nose with her finger and kissed her freckled forehead. "Be brave, little one."

With that, the girl gave her a lopsided curtsy, turned around, stood as tall as her little body would allow, and began to walk into the manor with a drag on the right. She turned to toss single petals at the spots where her steps had been. She started before she entered the front door.

A hand signaled for Mary to enter the foyer. She breathed in and closed her eyes. She took one last fresh breath before stepping inside. She worried the smell of the crowd would cause her usual fainting feeling. Susannah, in a golden gown and with burgundy flowers elegantly placed in her hair, met her at the doorway.

Susannah looked at her with a lovely smile. "You look beautiful, my sister." She handed her a bundle of white, red, and yellow flowers tied with a red satin ribbon. "The stephanotis for good luck. The amaryllis for worth beyond beauty. The goldfields for strength. The ivy for fidelity. These are for you to carry."

"Down the aisle?"

"If your day becomes overwhelming, remember to breathe in the bloom."

"Susannah, thank you. I've been nothing more than a burden to you."

"You are my sister and that's the most special gift of all."

Frederick, who was wearing his jeweled deer badge, offered her his arm. He began his walk. She didn't move. He gave her the most bewildered look.

"I cannot go farther," she said to him.

"Polly, hundreds of the highest-ranking citizens have converged on our home."

'Twas true, the parlor was so full, there wasn't an inch for another person.

"Life brings us many predicaments, Polly —"

"I am stuck."

"Today yours is to get to the front of this aisle."

Mary lifted her dress to reveal her pale blue shoe. "No, truly. I am stuck." The heel was caught between two floorboards. She twisted it several times but failed to find its release.

Frederick called the footmen to assist. They got down to free her shoe, one of them lying on the ground. Mary covered her face in disbelief. They finally yanked hard, and the shoe came free.

The walk continued. The guests were staring. Frederick led her forward. She tried not to look at the crowd, instead breathing in the fragrance of her flowers. Ahead of her, at the front of the aisle, was a maroon canopy emblazoned with the crest of the Philipse family, the gold lion emerging from the coronet. The bridal altar was adorned by a tall arch of deep red and bright yellow flowers.

And there, awaiting her, was Captain Morris. Mary never saw so many teeth before; his mouth was spread out so wide. He was fancifully dressed in a most spirited ensemble. Sparkling golden metallic thread ran in a bright zigzag pattern along the edges of his red wool coat, lace exploding from his arms and neck. Were those golden yellow shoes he was wearing? It looked as if he had grown right out of her bouquet.

The rector of Trinity Church, the Reverend Henry Barclay, officiated the service. "Dearly beloved, we are gathered together here in the sight of God, and in the face of this company, to join together this Man and this Woman in holy Matrimony, which is an honourable estate, instituted of God, signifying unto us the mystical union that is betwixt Christ and his Church: which holy state Christ adorned and beautified with his presence and first miracle that he wrought in Cana of Galilee, and is commended of Saint Paul to be honourable among all men, and therefore is not to be entered into unadvisedly or lightly, to satisfy men's carnal lusts and appetites, like brute beasts that have no understanding; but reverently, discretely, advisedly, soberly, and in the fear of God."

The chill first started in her feet and slowly ran up her body. She watched the minister continue to speak. Fog wrapped its ugly hand around her. The words did not have clarity. She heard the words beasts and fear. All else was fuzzy.

The minister continued: "I require and charge you both, as ye will answer at the dreadful day of judgment when the secrets of all hearts shall be disclosed, that if either of you do know any impediment, why ye may not be lawfully joined together in Matrimony, ye do now confess it."

Mary looked back to the foyer. Was that auburn hair? Hard to tell, since there were so many guards blocking the entryway to the parlor. Besides, she couldn't see clearly. She squinted to get a better view.

"Into this holy estate Mary Eliza Philipse and Roger Morris come now to be joined. If any man can show just cause, why they may not lawfully be joined together, let him speak, or else hereafter forever hold his peace."

She felt all eyes on her at this very moment; even the captain stared at her as if words would escape her mouth. If she wanted to say something, the Reverend Barclay allowed only seconds before moving on.

He turned to the groom. "Wilt thou have this Woman to thy wedded wife, to live together after God's ordinance in the holy estate of Matrimony? Wilt thou love her, comfort her, honour, and keep her in sickness and in health; and, forsaking all others, keep thee only unto her, so long as ye both shall live?"

Morris practically sang out his response, loudly exclaiming, "I will!"

The Reverend Barclay turned to Mary. She looked down.

"Wilt thou have this Man to thy wedded husband, to live together after God's ordinance in the holy estate of Matrimony? Wilt thou love him, comfort him, honour, and keep him in sickness and in health; and, forsaking all others, keep thee only unto him, so long as ye both shall live?"

The fog got thicker. Her head grew hot. She felt as if she might faint right there in front of the hundreds of guests. Darkness enveloped her. Wet darkness. Breathe, child. Breathe. She looked around. Where was he? Where was Captain Garvan when she needed him? He hadn't passed the manor in his sailing ship in longer than she could remember. She needed to escape from this place. She was confused. She glanced over at her brother. With a miffed expression on his face, he appeared as if he was about to scold her. He looked so old and silly with a peruke on his head. She let out a giggle.

"Mary . . ." A voice, she could hear a voice. "Mary, are you well?" Captain Morris whispered.

"I am," she replied.

"O Eternal God," continued the minister,

"Creator and Preserver of all mankind, Giver of all spiritual grace, the Author of everlasting life; Send thy blessing upon these thy servants, this man and this woman, whom we bless in thy Name, that they, living faithfully together, may surely perform and keep the vow and covenant betwixt them made, whereof this Ring given and received is a token and pledge, and may ever remain in perfect love and peace together, and live according to thy laws, through Jesus Christ our Lord. Amen."

He joined their right hands together.

Clouds filled every space between her ears. She breathed in the bloom. Mary noticed a wedding ring on her finger. She wasn't sure how it got there.

"Those whom God hath joined together let no man put asunder."

Temperance and François combined their talents for the grandest of feasts, although Mrs. Roger Morris didn't eat a thing. She remained by her husband's side and greeted every person in the manor, even the "humbler folk," as he called them. She didn't correct him; there would be other times for that. The festivities included fine music and a bit of dancing where people could find the room. The crowd was deep. She couldn't even smell them today, for she held the flowers near her nose the entire night. She was glad everyone was with her, joining in the wedding feast. Eric Arthur, wearing pants tightly cinched about his waist, danced encircled by a group of young belles. J.E. held his glass of ale. Rosie's smile never left her face. Her hair was in a beautiful coiffure for the occasion and she held Lulu's hands to "dance fancy," as the little girl described it. The mother and daughter never looked so pretty and aglow.

Before Mary stepped one foot into the dancing circle in the parlor by the foyer, the top half of the grand front door swung open. A howling gust swished through the room, coating the guests in winter's chill.

The music stopped.

Stillness hovered over the crowd.

Captain Morris raced over to the door to shut it. The wind buffeted him. An echo murmured through the crowd. Startled, Mary froze.

The bottom half of the door flew open, nearly striking him.

"Fear not," the captain yelled over the bold gust of air.

Mary didn't believe it. She knew too well that once a door to darkness is opened, it cannot be closed.

A haunting shadow covered the door.

" 'Tis the devil!" Rosie shrieked.

A large hand stopped the door from closing. A tall man, so tall, with the fur of a fox atop his head, met the ceiling. A grave expression marked his countenance. His face was covered in paint, like a native warrior ready for battle. His hair, black as night, fell long over the scarlet-colored blanket draped around him.

The crowd stared upon this mystery of a man.

The light of the candelabra struck him, casting a long shadow now onto the manor's floor. The man made no movement. His hair lifted with the wind. He didn't speak. His eyes looked straight ahead with an expression on his face that looked as if he would slay any man who came near him. None did.

In a deep, coarse voice, prophecy spoke: "Your possessions shall pass from you when the Eagle shall despoil the Lion of his mane."

CHAPTER THIRTY-THREE: AWAKENING

. . . the World has no business to know the object of my Love . . .

— GEORGE WASHINGTON

Mount Vernon, Virginia

The ink flowed. Word after word poured onto the paper, relieving the burden on George's soul. He wrote what was a simple fact, an obvious one to anyone who knew him intimately. His true feelings were as fervent as ever and not in doubt. His honest confession he laid out to a receiver who would never expose it. He trusted Sally and her husband, George William. They were lifelong friends. They had written to him many times on the subject. Now he responded, first with a letter to George William.

In the other letter, the one to Sally, he released his heart's despair on paper:

’Tis true, I profess myself a Votary to Love — I acknowledge that a Lady is in the Case — and further I confess, that this Lady is known to you.

I feel the force of her amiable beauties in the recollection of a thousand tender passages that I coud wish to obliterate, till I am bid to revive them. — but experience alas! sadly reminds me how Impossible this is. — and evinces an Opinion which I have long entertaind, that there is a Destiny, which has the Sovereign controul of our Actions — not to be resisted by the strongest efforts of Human Nature.

You have drawn me my dear Madam, or rather have I drawn myself, into an honest confession of a Simple Fact — misconstrue not my meaning — ’tis obvious — doubt it not, nor expose it — the World has no business to know the object of my Love, declard in this manner to you — when I want to conceal it — One thing, above all things in this World I wish to know, and only one person of your Acquaintance can solve me that, or guess my meaning. — but adieu to this, till happier times, if I ever shall see them. — the hours at present are melancholy dull. — neither the rugged Toils of War, nor the gentler conflict of A — B — s is in my choice. — I dare believe you are as happy as you say — I wish I was happy also —

George signed his name after a word of closing and neatly folded the letter. As he placed the letters to husband and wife together in the same packet, he became distracted by the thumping of a wagon's wheels as they rumbled over the cobblestone path. He'd been staying at the Mount Vernon estate of his late brother, Lawrence, since leaving New York. Lawrence's widow had found another to love. So here George remained alone in this expanse of a house. He had hoped there'd be someone to share it with. It was not to be.

Thuds coming from the circle in front of the west side of the dwelling house drew him to the window in the first-floor study. He watched as proprietor Captain Dick brought the wagon to a stop. Anger boiled in every vein of George's body at the sight. Dick exited the coach and retrieved a crate. George couldn't believe what he was seeing. Boxes. The fine china arrived, late. Too late.

George exited the study with heaviness in his gait. He stomped into a small hallway, through the richly decorated dining room with its bold green color on the walls, into the central passageway to reach the entry, opened the door, and stood glaring at the man and his box. "I suppose I should not have received them at all!" George's hands clasped behind his back.

The captain's eyebrows shot up to his hairline. "Colonel, my sincerest apology for the delay."

George flew into a fit of rage. So unaccountably indolent is Captain Dick! he thought. "Was it carelessness that prevented their coming to my hand till near six weeks after arrival at port?"

"The vessel with your goods was sent to several different ports, without grant to dock." He set down the crate near George. "We were refused the ability to remove the goods from the vessel, even after being docked one month and a half."

"By whom?"

Captain Dick shrugged as he turned away with quick steps back to retrieve additional crates.

George's jaw muscles clenched. He reached down to carry the merchandise into the house. Captain Dick carried another crate through to the study. They set them down.

"I will be sure to make this up to you on the next journey," Captain Dick said. He thanked George again for his patience and quickly walked out.

Just the sight of these boxes made George angrier. He untied the rope at the top and lifted the lid on one of the crates. He removed what looked like a teapot wrapped tightly in newspaper. He slowly unwrapped it and held the china in one hand, the newsprint in the other.

What was he to do with all these goods now? He set the teapot down delicately upon his desk. He noticed something on the page of the printed paper. The *Virginia Gazette*? Each piece of newspaper print that he removed from the fine china made him more enraged. The china was wrapped in salacious falsities. The very publication that printed lies about him. The very article that defamed him — it covered the teapot!

They condemned him, blasphemed him, claimed debauchery, gambling. He was a spendthrift, a drunkard, it said.

They.

They were responsible.

They were the ones. The article was written by the anonymous L & V. The truth sickened George. It infuriated him. He recalled the words of the messenger as he left with the nuptial papers; he was delivering them to the "commander in chief, Lord and Victor, John, Earl of Loudoun." Lord and Victor. L & V.

Keep him away from Mary Eliza Philipse so another could seize her surrender.

He rushed over to the trunk containing his necessary papers. He pulled out the letters of denial: "yr Absence on that Account from Ld Loudoun must be suspended till our affrs gives a better prospect." Their dastardly behavior kept him trapped, until it was done.

Colonel Stanwix followed the guidance of Lord Loudoun, whose aide was Roger Morris. The writer of the article, likely Loudoun's secretary extraordinaire, Thomas Pownall, he of the ridiculous pseudonyms. George learned of the whole diabolical cast from Hugh Mercer.

George raised his head for guidance. Before him were his brother's eyes. The portrait of Lawrence was the only painting in the study. The only one he needed. George decided right then. He would quit his command. He would retire from all public business. The British took her from him. George would leave his military post to be filled by others who had their endeavors crowned with better success than he.

Back and forth he paced over the creaking floor. George walked into the central passageway, heading toward the double doors on the east side of the house. He opened them with force, catching a cold breeze. Before him was the grand Potomac River. This sight had always made him feel hopeful. Not today. That appearance of glory once in view — that hope — that laudable ambition of serving, and meriting applause, was now no more.

George followed the path through the gardens, down the south lane, and finally arrived at the burial place — Lawrence's tomb.

All is lost, George thought as he shut his eyes. "All is lost."

He placed himself on a half brick wall to the left of the tomb. He gritted his teeth. "We are acting under an evil Geni. For we who view the actions of great men at a distance can only form conjectures agreeable to the small extent of our knowledge — ignorant of the comprehensive schemes intended. The conduct of our leaders is tempered with something — I don't care to give a name." Arising from his seated position, George paced back and forth, feeling heat rising to the muscles in his jaw. "Indeed. I will go further, and say they are d—" He stopped himself from saying the word aloud, "Or something worse."

Yes. It was clear now.

They were the enemy.

Part IV
The Reprisal

Chapter Thirty-Four: Note to Self

. . . woe's me, that I should Love and conceal . . .

— GEORGE WASHINGTON

Harlem Heights, New York
June 1776

Ambrosia and nectar found her nose; the scent reminded her of him. Still, after twenty years, it reminded her of him. She forced the steam away with a quick blow to prevent a burn on her lips. She let a small sip of warmth in.

The curtain in daylight shimmered pink, tinting the portico where she stood. Upon the highest point of Harlem Heights, on the northern end of Manhattan Island, her mansion, with its Tuscan columns from ground to roof, emerged like a white palace squarely in the middle of the land between rivers. From here, they'd be able to see the enemy coming.

With her at the mansion was a guest, a friend, Lasthenia Sherwood.

"My pa told me the tale once — of the giants hollering 'Fee Faw Fum.' " The girl who'd grown into a young woman fidgeted with the delicate handle of the gold-embossed porcelain cup. Big green eyes with short ginger lashes swiveled toward Mary. " 'Ne'er be spooked by them giants,' he told me." She gulped the tea.

Looking past the cornfields and grove of white-blossomed trees, they could see them far in the distance. Like predators about to attack the sheep, the ships of the Royal Navy practically covered the surface of the ocean. A tax on tea — that's what many colonists thought this war was over. Mary was of a different opinion.

Mount Morris was prepared — Mary had seen to it — with large supplies of food, enough to feed an army.

"Would you care for something? You must be hungry, Lulu." Mary worried about her.

Lasthenia shook her head. "I'd best get back to my's reading." Her hair — red and long enough to reach her waist — shifted gently as she turned her slim, small frame back to the foyer's doorway. Her muslin dressed billowed. "I ne'er read 'The Blue

Bird' by myself, up tills now."

Mary let her be. She'd have the kitchen prepare her something anyhow.

Below her, the yanking and pulling had been going on all day. Mary knew the timing was odd, being that the colony lay on the precipice of war, but she couldn't stand the invasive species any longer. Her groundskeepers removed the tendrils that had attached to the walls in thatches and climbed until their dead feet surrounded her; ivy is stubborn like that.

So here, alone on the balcony, Mary remained. She'd gotten used to being alone. She looked out — the Hudson to her right, the Harlem River and East River beyond it, to her left. Colonel Morris had wanted to build on this land because of those views. She bought the estate after they married and after he retired from military life. The land had been advertised in the *New York-Gazette:*

> A Pleasant situated farm on the Road leading to King's Bridge, in the Township of Harlem of York Island, containing about 100 Acres; about 30 Acres of which is Wood Land, a fine Piece of Meadow Ground, and more may easily be made; and commands the finest Prospect in the

whole country; the Land runs from River to River.

They argued before he left — she and her husband. He was gone — escaped to England a year prior. He hailed from Britain, but he hadn't left to fight on behalf of his native land. He departed because he was afraid. He had made this clear to her that last day, erupting into a frantic soliloquy about a crime from long ago. No matter what she did or how she asked, he would not reveal what it was that he had done or to whom.

The argument centered around not that, but Lulu. Lulu was not a low guest! His snobbery irritated Mary. What was she to do? Leave Lulu in the street? No one could understand better the feeling of witnessing the last breaths of your mother and your father. Poor Rosie, dying of heartache after Jeffrey took a bullet to the head while lighting the lantern at Hudson's Hook, fired from a ship in the river, certainly not aimed at him, but hitting him square between the eyes nonetheless. Mary and Lulu planted forget-me-not flowers and Mary renamed the site Jeffrey's Hook in his honor. Lulu's father didn't stay alive for long after that.

Yes, Lulu could stay with her for as much

time as she needed.

Mary did not want war. She was not the only one. Other heads of elite families from the New York Colony were of the same opinion. A letter — an olive branch, a last effort to avert bloodshed — had been drafted and signed by several of those families, pleading with the citizens of England. She had hosted the group at her estate. The Honorable Robert Livingston — the boy who long ago had told Mary he wanted to be a chief justice — had achieved success. Now judge of the Court of General Sessions, he was the letter's author:

> Friends, Countrymen and Brethren!
>
> Give us leave most solemnly to assure you, that we have not yet lost sight of the object we have ever had in view, a reconciliation with you on constitutional principles, and a restoration of that friendly intercourse, which, to the advantage of both, we till lately maintained.
>
> A cloud hangs over your heads and ours; e'er this reaches you, it may probably burst upon us; let us then (before the remembrance of former kindness is

obliterated) once more repeat those appellations which are ever grateful in our ears; let us entreat heaven to avert our ruin, and the destruction that threatens our friends, brethren, and countrymen, on the other side of the Atlantic.

Colonel Morris was furious, not about the letter, but about the gathering. He wrote her from England: "I can easily conceive your disagreeable situation, but I did not imagine you would have thought yourself safer under the protection of the chief justice." In her letter in return, she explained that she'd known Robert since he was a little boy — that he needed a neutral place to meet. This did her no good, nor did the letter. The British responded to the peace offering by calling the signers rebellious.

Spirited by the conviction to independence, common folk across the colonies took up arms against the mother country. Hatred moved from ink to blood. First in Boston. New York was next.

To think! George Washington had gained the position of general to defend the colonists in the War of Independence. She couldn't deny that when he walked into a room, he had a commanding presence — a man of authority, a man guided by Providence, the man who couldn't die. No, there was no one better to command than George.

When she closed her eyes, she could recall the day her world changed on a balcony. "Everything which partakes of your nature has a claim to my affections." His whisper in her ear, she remembered it clearly. But that was long ago, long before he left without saying good-bye. George had married well, an older woman, a wealthy widow with a plantation in Virginia, a lady who didn't dance — at least that was the word from Sir Tenoe. Tenoe often wrote to Mary from there and elsewhere, wherever his travels took him to teach the waltz to children of the privileged.

Now George had arrived here in New York, headquartered at the southern end of the island. She peered out as far as she could see. He was out there somewhere. She could feel him.

Mary walked toward the north wing of the house, treading upon the wide-planked floor, and passed through a narrower hall in order to get to the study. She needed to write a letter of her own. It had been on her mind for quite some time.

She squinted as she entered the study. The cornices and moldings were painted extremely bright, a scarlet red. Colonel Morris had been particular about this color; he had demanded an extremely vivid tone with a hint of orange to match the military uniform he had once worn. He despised the coloring on the wall that Mary had chosen — dull gray, with *Helianthus verticillatus* painted in a lighter shade of gray.

Mary placed herself at the intricately carved mahogany desk that once belonged to her mother. She thought of her every day. Mary began a note to her younger self:

Dearest Mary Eliza Philipse,
I know what you're feeling. Cursed one. Rose with thorns. This is who you are. Open your eyes. Awaken to the realization that you are nothing. Blame yourself for their deaths. Take that in. Feel the guilt. Hate yourself. Find the emptiness that the power of words cannot fix.

Does this make you uncomfortable? I'm glad. Now, go deeper into the abyss, into your darkest days, into your deepest fears, and grab your inner demons and choke them until they stop breathing, because until you destroy the fear, the little hand that reaches out to you from the cold darkness of your nightmares, until you let that go, you will forever be encompassed by fear.

Become nothing.

Like a Phoenix, start again. Be strong like the sharp rocks that don't budge even when waves slam against them time after time. When all is gone, there will only be Mary Eliza left. This is when you will BE.

These years have passed and you still hold on to what should have been. If only. Yes, if only. Release yourself of it. Find life beyond the guardian's wall. The battle cannot be won without faith and belief that there is a destiny in our lives, one that even with the most fervent action against it has control of our actions.

So I ask you in your youth to set your sight to the heavens and ask for assistance. Life has not been fair to you. I know this. The path is a long one that leaves you lost without a direction. Sorrow is painful. Unsettledness is lonely. I know what's it's like to be encompassed by both.

Move your focus to love. Love out loud. Love with no fear. Love the love that is right in front of you. Why have you fallen asleep to him? He is right there, holding you in his embrace. In his arms, you feel whole for the first time in your life — the only time in your life. You believe you have no right to him. The mistakes, the loss left you scattered and frail. Don't hide. Don't be afraid. Cease the battle with your conscience. It has consumed you for so long, for too long. Even when you wish to let it go, it instead holds like mud on a shoe.

Remember the words of your father: "Be the light, Mary Eliza. You are capable of the impossible, for you have survived the unthinkable."

Her hand trembled as it did every time her signature was required. "Mrs. Roger Morris," she wrote.

Chapter Thirty-Five: Hail to the Chief

. . . the wound often irritated and never healed, may at length become incurable.

— GEORGE WASHINGTON

New York City
June 1776

George knew this was best, to send his wife back to Virginia. The journey would carry her far from the toil of what was expected: an invasion on New York. Placing a kiss atop the white bonnet on her head, George thought of the many disagreeable sensations resulting from his command of the troops of the United Provinces of North America: One being, that for her, it was a cutting stroke.

"As life is always uncertain" — he bent down to reach her. Martha was a full foot and two inches shorter than him — "I have asked that a will be drafted."

As he opened the carriage door to let her

inside, she turned and offered a meek smile through narrow lips. "The shades below are far from your reach." Her voice was thin, sounding hardly above the level of a whisper. She adjusted her frilled headgear and used his hand to assist her in climbing in. "Besides, you have entered into an engagement, not to quit the theater of this world before the year 1800." She tapped on his hand with her other. "I rely upon your pledge of no breach of contract on that account."

George married the widow Martha Custis in a simple ceremony, one year after Mary Eliza Philipse changed her name. He met the widow Custis on her plantation in Virginia. He proposed quickly. The couple never had children together. Martha had a son and daughter from a previous marriage. Her first husband had passed away eight months before she met George.

"You may believe me, my dear Patsy," said George to her, "when I assure you, in the most solemn manner, that, so far from seeking this appointment, I have used every endeavor in my power to avoid it — not only from my unwillingness to part with you and the family but from a consciousness of its being a trust too great for my capacity."

His wife was afraid of war. For the short time they were here in New York, he had watched her shudder and shake when she heard the sound of a gun firing. She despised it all, thinking the preparations terrible indeed, she told him privately.

His large hand settled on her knee. "I shall feel no pain from the toil or the danger of the campaign. My unhappiness will flow from the uneasiness I know you will feel being left alone. I beg of you to pass your time as agreeably as possible."

As the horses took her carriage out of his sight, George lingered to scan the lands and the shoreline. The sea power of the enemy waited beyond the river, in the Atlantic, staring back at him. Every day, the two sides were seemingly doing nothing more than observing each other's movements from a mile's distance. Waves on the Hudson River moved turbulently, but not as passionately as what was to come.

His mind considered the great task ahead. The powerful fleet of the naval force of the kingdom threatened. Whether this be a place to rendezvous or to facilitate operations, he did not know. Whether they would go north by land or water, and whether they would pay their compliments to him beforehand, he was uncertain.

Experience taught him that it is easier to

stop an enemy from entering than it is to dislodge him after he's taken possession. For this reason, he ordered his forces to repair to this city with all possible expediency.

Nothing seemed of greater importance.

Protect the Hudson.

Possess the Hudson.

He would do whatever necessary to prevent the mighty British from sailing up the river. Lines of defense would be all he could establish, for he had only a hastily formed navy, made up of just private vessels. And as for George's army, his contingents consisted of undisciplined bands of common folk, volunteers of a motley sort, oftentimes half-starved, half-dressed, and now going up against a behemoth.

A year prior at a meeting in Philadelphia, the dispirited colonies chose George to lead — voted in by a unanimous voice. Representative John Adams, out of Massachusetts, nominated him: "I have but one gentleman in my mind for that important command, and that is a gentleman from Virginia who is among us and very well known to all of us, a gentleman whose skill and experience as an officer, whose independent fortune, great talents and excellent universal character would command the approbation of all America, and unite the cordial exertions of all the colonies better than any other person in the union."

George left the room when he heard this. He had been sitting near the exit. Although the cause of freedom from the oppressor was emblazoned in his heart, he was certain he had neither the expertise nor the skill for such a position.

Destiny was of a different opinion.

A steady gait carried him into a temporary headquarters established in a grand two-floor mansion on a high hill, on the corner of Varick and Vandam streets. The white house with an Ionic portico held columns from floor to roof. It sat on the southern tip of Manhattan Island. A series of meetings awaited him inside.

After he entered, George acknowledged both the British deserter, Sergeant Thomas Hickey Jr., now a personal guard assigned to him, and a young housekeeper tiptoeing in the hall.

"Fair day to you, General," the man said to him with the accent of a Brit who'd spent a bit of time in New York.

In the parlor, George offered proper salutations to a sachem, whose name was

Chief Red Hawk. The native warrior had sought out council with him for some time. He'd traveled from the Great Kanawha River, near the Ohio, to offer support to his army — the same man who claimed to have shot at George multiple times at the Battle of Monongahela. The brutal battle all those years ago had been seared into George's memory.

The chief carried himself as one whose maturity in life could be sensed from the grave manner in which he spoke. "I am a chief and ruler over my tribes. My influence extends to the waters of the great lakes and to the far blue mountains. I have traveled a long and weary path, that I might see the warrior of the great battle."

These were surprising words from a man who was once George's rival on the field of war. The chief never took a seat, standing in upright position, with a slight tilt to his back. "It was on the day when the white man's blood mixed with the streams of our forests that I first beheld this chief." He pointed his whole hand in George's direction. "I called to my young men and said, 'Mark yon tall and daring warrior.' "

George realized this daring warrior he spoke of was himself; he recalled the endless gunfire coming at him from the invisible enemy in the trees.

The chief spoke of his own prowess with weapons and how he never missed his targets. Firing at George proved fruitless, he told him; he had shot at him seventeen times. Not a one spilled his blood.

Seventeen times. George had never known this.

" 'Quick,' I told them. 'Let your aim be certain, and he dies.' Our rifles were leveled, rifles that, but for him, knew not how to miss — 'twas all in vain; a power mightier far than we shielded you from harm."

George recollected the blur of the day, the screams of the dying, and the stink of death. He recalled falling as his horse was shot. He had four holes in his coat. Two bullets hit his hat.

Then the enemy's weapons went silent.

" 'He is not of the redcoat tribe; he hath an Indian's wisdom. He cannot die in battle,' I professed to my warriors." The chief seemed to want to let out what had been hidden inside him for decades. "I am old, and soon shall be gathered to the great council fire of my fathers in the land of shades, but ere I go, there is something bids me speak in the voice of prophecy."

George leaned forward as the chief spoke in a quieter voice.

"Listen! The Great Spirit protects you." His eyes shut. He raised his head high. "It guides your destiny." The chief pointed his finger into George's chest, directly at his heart. "You . . . you will become the chief of nations, and a people yet unborn will hail you as the founder of a mighty empire."

With this, the chief offered his farewell, the allegiance of his tribe, and left.

George did not move from where he was standing for some time as he absorbed the native's prophecy. George fully put his trust in Providence, which preserved him up until this point. In it, he had a great reliance. In the past, it befriended him, protected him, bestowed graces upon him. His beliefs went far back to his childhood, to his mother. She always believed the heavens would shield him from harm.

Bullet holes in his coat and his hat. No wound. He should not have survived. The work of Providence, he thought. George remembered well the battle and the field of red clover and carrying the wounded from that meadow of death.

This cause would yield its protection again. It would have to. It would be the only way to defeat an empire.

George walked with certain stride into the

war room to review his military plan for New York. He picked up a large scroll and unfurled it onto a heavy table at the center of the room. The survey of the Hudson was drawn on a map with detailed diagrams of the planned defenses. The Mount Morris estate sat at the northernmost end of the island, squarely in the middle of the land between rivers — high up on a hill, the highest point in the city, offering views of the waterways. This place, Harlem Heights, was the key to the northern country.

George's desire was to prevent any Brit from marching onto that property. He'd set up batteries south of the mansion's location to prevent forces from moving north by land.

On the water, he planned for a chain across the Hudson to New Jersey's Palisades. George marked the spot with his finger along the shoreline near King's Bridge. Here. At Jeffrey's Hook is where the links would begin on this side of the river.

George studied the other defensive structure on paper; a cheval-de-frise would be sunk in the same spot.

The captain of the New York Artillery Company arrived for a meeting with the general to provide his account of ammunitions and weaponry.

George acknowledged him as he entered. "I must commend you, Captain Hamilton, for the masterly manner of executing your work." George knew of the young man, recently commissioned as a captain, who had led a militia of students from King's College that stole — or, as it had been reported to him, liberated — British cannons at the Battery.

"I thank you, General." Alexander Hamilton was youthful in appearance and replied in a firm voice with a twinge of coarseness to it. His name had become known for another reason. He had authored an essay defending the colonists' rights. Hamilton moved to the maps that George was surveying. "The North River. Aye. If we can get there before them, all will be well." His head cocked to one side as he peered over the defensive strategy.

"The Hudson. If lost, it will be of the most fatal consequence."

"We little imagined it would come to this, General. How ridiculous is their assumption that we are quarreling for the trifling sum of three pence a pound on tea."

"They are practicing such low and dirty tricks that men of sentiment and honor must blush for their villainy. They meant to drive us into what they termed *rebellion,* then stripped us of the rights and privileges of Englishmen. If they were actuated by principles of justice, why did they refuse, indignantly, to accede to the terms which were humbly supplicated before hostilities commenced?"

"Jealousy." Hamilton placed his hands in the pockets of his coat. "Wars oftener proceed from angry and perverse passions than from cool calculations of interest. Jealousy is a source of the greatest evils. Give me the steady, uniform, unshaken security of constitutional freedom; give me the right to be tried by a jury of my own neighbors, and to be taxed by my own representatives only."

George became furious just thinking about what the British had done. "We are now embarked on a tempestuous ocean from whence, perhaps, no friendly harbor is to be found. Arms alone must decide it."

A knock on the door interrupted their meeting. Samuel Fraunces entered, holding glasses of ale. He offered to feed the men during their stay, as they were located just doors from his tavern.

"General Washington, Sam took a hole to the roof of his tavern for us!" exclaimed Hamilton as he clapped Sam on the back.

"The Brits fired a cannonball in retaliation for our liberation of their cannons."

"For the cause of freedom!" Sam cheered as he distributed the ale. He announced food would be served in the dining area.

George found a seat on a wide tapestried chair at a polished mahogany table. Roasted turkey wafted in the air. Hunger set in. The day had been too busy to make time for food until this hour. The dish of meat looked appetizing, but George's teeth had been giving him trouble in the form of a shooting pain through his gums. He settled on starting with the side portion of peas on his dinner plate.

George forked a few of them. He lifted them to his mouth.

The young housekeeper, whom he greeted in the hall earlier, ran toward him with her face appearing alarmed. "Poison! Poison!" she shrieked. "The peas is poisoned!"

Chapter Thirty-Six: A Traitor Among Us

. . . guard against the impostures of pretended patriotism . . .

— GEORGE WASHINGTON

Yonkers-on-Hudson
July 1776

Lulu, all freckled innocence and pure cream skin, sat up straight on a cushioned bench. She appeared quite graceful in an ivory floral gown that Mary had made for her. An unexpected picture, considering her choice of language: "Dastardly maggot of a fella. Mum woulda spit on him as he hung from the gallows." She feigned expectorating from her lips.

Mary would have her act more in accordance with her place in high society now; however, in truth she agreed with such an action, and about Rosie — yes, she would have spit on him.

Lulu continued reading aloud, albeit

slowly, pronouncing each syllable, from the *New-York Gazette:*

> In the forenoon was executed in the field, near the Bowry Lane (in the presence of near twenty thousand spectators) soldier Thomas Hickey, belonging to his Excellency General Washington's guards, for mutiny and conspiracy; being one of those who formed and was soon to have put in execution, that horrid plot of assassination.

Mary let out a deep breath. The Hickey plot — it could have killed him, she thought.

"Peas! I ne'er liked those bum vegetables anyhows." Lulu turned the page to continue her pronouncing; Mary had her do this each day to improve her reading. She was advancing quickly, as she worked through the sounds of each word:

> This day the CONTINENTAL CONGRESS declared the UNITED COLONIES FREE and INDEPENDENT STATES.

"What's it mean?" asked Lulu.

"Why, it means that freedom . . . true freedom is soon to come."

"To your birthday!" exclaimed Susannah,

raising a glass in a toast as she entered the east parlor. A footman carried in a tray with three drinks, each glass with the family's engraved silver medal seal — a lion emerging from a coronet.

"Must we still celebrate when reaching my stage in life?" replied Mary, picking up a glass of Madeira and handing one to Lulu.

"Sluice your gob," Lulu said loudly.

Susannah looked dumbfounded.

Mary laughed.

Lulu gulped. "I woulda chosen calibogus if it was me choosin'."

"You drink rum, girl?" asked a perplexed-looking Susannah.

"Who else will be joining us?" Mary asked this question coyly, knowing full well whom they planned to introduce to Lulu.

Susannah looked at Mary with a gleam in her eye as a strapping young fellow walked through the doorway. "Lulu Sherwood, may I introduce you to Nathaniel Gist."

"Is he a beard splitter?" whispered Lulu to Mary.

"No, he is not a ladies' man," Mary quietly responded. "He's a gentleman. We wouldn't introduce you to him if we didn't think so."

"May I stay in this spot? Youse know I don't walk so good."

"Lulu, you can do whatever you like. But please know, no one is perfect."

The rugged dark-haired lad came closer. The Philipse family had offered him a place to stay just northeast of the manor, at one of their outer cottages. Mary approved of him. He was just as Mary had pictured his father, Christopher Gist, the frontiersman who had charged into enemy territory with George all those years ago. She had read about their journey many times in the newspaper that she still kept on the shelf in her bedchamber at Philipse Manor, its writing away from her, always away from her.

The four of them sat and toasted Mary's day. After a few minutes, the sisters gave Lulu and Nathaniel privacy as the siblings moved to the dining room of the manor.

"She appears a child." Susannah glanced back at her as they walked away.

"Hard to believe, but Lasthenia is an adult now. She's asked to be treated as such, yet I, too, still see her as that little girl with crooked pigtails."

Mary was drawn to an appetizing scent as she entered the dining room. Temperance approached. Except for the faint fine lines around her eyes, she hadn't aged a bit in all these years. She wore her hair the same way as she always had, placed neatly into a bun. "*Mes filles* helped with the icing." Temperance smiled as she spoke.

Mary looked over the chef's shoulder to see her twin girls peeking out from behind the door. They were neatly dressed, with their hair pinned back perfectly in buns, replicas of their mother. "We've made your favorite, a great cake with almonds," added Temperance.

"I thank you, and please offer my gratitude to François. The table setting is spectacular."

The table looked glorious, set with a blue-and-white porcelain setting and white flowers. The chairs were wrapped in wide white satin ribbon. The decorated cake sat at the center. The darling setup was in stark contrast to the ugliness of the conversation.

Beverley, Frederick, and Elizabeth were already seated.

"James Jay is the author of it." Beverley sipped his tea.

Just the sound of his name made Mary feel anxious as she took her seat.

"He calls himself a patriot. Nonsense!" Frederick picked up a French biscuit. Elizabeth quickly called over her lady's maid to butter it for him. "Dr. Jay has no such power." Frederick shifted in his seat, for his corpulence was greater than the chair could accommodate.

"If he becomes a member of the New York Senate, he will," added Beverley with a grunt.

"The honorable Philip Livingston is in charge. He would never allow that man to become a member." Frederick ate the biscuit in one bite.

"Robert the elder?" Susannah took her seat, as did Mary.

"Yes, my true," replied Beverley.

"What is that man the author of?" Mary needed to know. Nervousness welled up inside her.

"It means nothing, even if the law were to pass." Frederick spoke with his mouth full.

"Rumor is that an act of attainder is being proposed by Dr. Jay to the new legislature formed by a group of colonists."

"An attainder?" Mary launched out of her chair. "An attainder! Like Fontainebleau?"

They gave her a bewildered look.

"The Edict of Fontainebleau." Mary raised her hands as she stared at Frederick.

Frederick shrugged. "One has nothing to do with the other."

Mary moved about the room. "James threatened this long ago." She paced back and forth. "Under Fontainebleau, the Jay family property was confiscated, their possessions taken, and the family condemned to death if caught in the province. Father told us the story. This is why they arrived here from France . . . with nothing." Mary had always known the beast would return to take revenge. "Do we not believe he would do the same to *us*?"

"Our great-grandfather was kind enough to adopt Jay's grandmother into this family. That should have been enough. She had no rights to the manor." Frederick's lips pursed as he spoke in disgust. A crumb clung to his cheek.

"Where does the senior Jay stand on this?" asked Beverley.

"James was disowned by his father years ago." Frederick nodded as Elizabeth handed him a piece of cake. "Mr. Jay even cut his scoundrel son from the will."

"His brother?" Beverley inquired.

"The Honorable John Jay is a man of justice," replied Frederick. "He would disown his brother, too, if this should come to pass."

"Why would they attaint us, my true?" Susannah sat with a straight posture, as if a board were behind her.

"They've asked the head of every elite family to sign a pledge in person to be considered a friend to the American cause," Beverley replied glumly. "The declaration for independence has now been signed by the colonies."

"Whichever side James is on, find this family on the opposite." Frederick forked into the dessert. "What is Roger's opinion on the matter?"

"Roger?" Mary was confused.

He motioned for her to sit. "Yes, your espoused."

She placed herself back onto the velvet-cushioned, hand-carved chair. "He's written me saying we have only to pray to God to put an end to the unhappy and unnatural situation of affairs. He dreads the miseries that will befall both countries."

Elizabeth had additional pieces of cake cut.

"What of the other families?" asked Frederick.

"The Van Cortlandts have signed the colonists' pledge," Beverley said.

Elizabeth handed a plate with a cut of cake to Mary, who accepted it from her.

"Eva's husband has not signed it, though." Mary couldn't even think about eating.

Susannah sipped tea gracefully. "How is her life on Long Island?"

This is not a time for light talk, Mary

thought. "She's written me that all is fine," she replied anxiously.

"The Kembles have signed, staunchly loyal to the Crown," said Beverley.

"I ponder whether Margaret's enjoying life in Boston with Thomas Gage," remarked Susannah.

More polite remarks, thought Mary. "Margaret's allegiance is torn," she said.

"Oh!" exclaimed her sister.

"She's written me that she prays her husband will not be the instrument that sacrifices countrymen's lives. He is general of the British forces, Susannah."

"The Gage wedding was a lovely wedding," Susannah said.

"The Delanceys?" Beverley asked of Frederick.

"Sheriff James sailed to England six months ago. Oliver and his family remain; he is considering forming his own brigade to protect his property. He has no faith in either side."

"Brother, if we don't formally choose a side, each will believe we support the other," said Susannah.

The prophecy from the night of her nuptials kept repeating in Mary's head. *Your possessions shall pass from you when the Eagle shall despoil the Lion of his mane. Your possessions shall pass from you when the Eagle shall despoil the Lion of his mane.* She had never forgotten it. "An attainder is without judicial process, correct?" asked Mary as she once again began to get up from her chair. Frederick placed his hand on her shoulder to keep her put.

"If passed, those attainted would be declared guilty. You are correct, Polly, and with no judicial process allowed." Beverley had a nervous twitch now in his voice. "Anyone attainted and caught would suffer death."

"And what if the act of attainder finds its way to a vote?" Susannah's eyebrows surged upward.

"We will defend ourselves at trial." Frederick eyes began to close in readiness of a nap.

"Would anyone care for more tea?" Elizabeth chimed in, appearing anxious.

"Unfortunately, Frederick, there would be no trial. Enemies of the state are convicted without proof," said Beverley, "without a chance to defend. If attainted, we would be banished, our lands confiscated, all of our lands, including those in your name." He glanced at Mary and then at his wife. "As well as yours, my true."

"It cannot be!" Susannah cried out in horror.

Mary let it settle in. She knew all along vengeance would find her. "We would be condemned to death as traitors."

"They wouldn't dare!" shouted Susannah.

"Condemned to death, Susannah, if they get to us" — Mary tried to calm a shaky breath — "they could capture and kill us."

"Nonsense! Traitors?" The color drained from her sister's face. She looked as if she would faint right there at the table.

The stench of hair powder attacked Mary's nose. A sick feeling began to swirl in her stomach. "James Jay has no fortune of his own." There was not a touch of powder in anyone's hair in the room. She could still smell it. She felt nearly overpowered by it, like a fog rolling in. She took a deep breath to find composure and asked the question that jolted her back into focus. "That man is distressed of money. Is it beyond the realm of possibility that he could gain commission in a forfeiture sale of our confiscated land?"

"Absurdity — that's what this is. Philip would never allow it." Frederick grunted. "The Honorable Philip Livingston would have to die first."

CHAPTER THIRTY-SEVEN: CHEVAL-DE-FRISE

. . . it must be known, that we are at all times ready for war.

— GEORGE WASHINGTON

Harlem Heights

If it weren't wartime, this would make a charming picture. From the river's edge, just south of Spiting Devil, George peered across the Hudson at the grandeur of the steep precipice — the Palisades. A slight breeze carried with it a breath of lavender; it reminded him of her. Still, after all these years, it reminded him of her.

Mount Morris, as some called it, had fields blanketed in wildflowers stretching all the way from the Hudson River to the east end of the island. Upon the highest ground, beyond the cornfields, sat the mansion that belonged to her . . . and the insubordinate one — the man who had taken off for England when George was named general.

George appeared as a commander should, wearing a blue coat equipped with a rise-and-fall collar, breeches, and underdress in matching buff: That shade, buff, was the same as the uniform for his soldiers. George decided on hunting shirts for the men; no dress would be cheaper, or more convenient. He also remembered the look on the French commandant's face when he, Gist, and his crew of a motley sort arrived in enemy territory in no more than hunter's garb. Even George's expert marksmen would be dressed in such garb. As he looked at them gathered in front of him, he knew it was the right decision. Surprise the enemy. Besides, there was no money for anything more.

General Washington spoke before his men. "The hour is fast approaching, on which the honor and success of this army, and the safety of our bleeding country, depend." He spoke loudly, firmly, clearly. "Let it never be said, that in a day of action, you turned your backs on the foe — let the enemy no longer triumph — They brand you with ignominious epithets — Will you patiently endure that reproach? Will you suffer the wounds given to your Country to go unrevenged? Every motive that can touch the human breast calls us to the most vigorous exertions — Our dearest rights — our dearest friends — our own lives — honor — glory, and even shame, urge us to the fight — And, my fellow soldiers! when an opportunity presents, be firm, be brave, show yourselves men, and victory is yours!" His soldiers applauded him.

Today George would begin to fortify this property. He believed these grounds about King's Bridge well calculated for a defense. Obstructions placed from one side of the river to the other would prevent a British incursion. These would stop the enemy's movement north from Manhattan Island. He would have his troops prepared to defend with a minute's warning. Lookouts would be established at the highest points of Harlem Heights. Every regiment posted in this place, from Morris's house to camp, needed to be furnished with guards to prevent any surprises. George's entire army had pushed northward after the British landed their ships on the southern tip and after they tried to kill him.

His forces would be ready. He would be ready.

A man George considered a fast friend to the colonies approached and spoke to him. "This, General Washington, I guarantee, will stop the enemy from entering Hudson's

River. I call this a marine cheval-de-frise." Inventor and master ironworker Robert Erskine had developed defenses never before seen. One of them was an enormous medieval-style defensive weapon with a steel center frame and long iron spikes projecting outward. It was moving closer to them, carried on a flat cart with wheels, sluggishly led by eight horses. "The consequence of a ship's running against it must either be that she will stake upon it or overset it, in which case the other horns will rise and take her in the bottom, and either overset her or go through her; or else she must break it with her weight, thereby rendering her unfit for further service."

George assigned nearly a hundred men to assist in its launch. He had only eighteen hundred soldiers at his disposal in this place. "Let it be sunk in the darkness," he told Erskine.

George presumed the British would make several attempts at an attack. Their troops lay encamped about two miles south. Their weaponry was being transported from Long Island, he had learned. The signs were clear: They would make an attack soon. By land. By water. He had to put the forces in the best defensive position that time and circumstance would allow.

"As for the chain?" asked George.

"The chain is being completed — twelve hundred links of iron to allow it to reach seventeen hundred feet in length. It will be installed here at Jeffrey's Hook."

"It is of the utmost importance that the greatest diligence should be used to complete and render the defense effectual," added George.

"Aye. Our Benedict Arnold has offered assurance he will oversee the installation of the second chain north in the Highlands, at the shoreline of the Beverley Robinson estate."

George heard Beverley built a fine estate on Susannah's property in the Highlands along the Hudson River. Robinson not only allowed for the installation but also offered residency to Arnold or any other commander, including George.

"And the turtle is complete, General. We needed seven hundred pounds of lead."

"The submersible? And it is operational?"

"Aye, General. The device is completed with a brass oar for rowing forward and backward. It will be sunk by letting in water via a spring near the bottom. It's watertight, General. It will make its attempt below the water upon the British warship *Eagle*. Explosives will be affixed to the sides of the ship and provide enough time to allow for the officers' escape."

Putting his spyglass to his eye, George looked south. What to do with the southern tip of Manhattan Island still remained a question. Till of late, he had no doubt about defending it, but the British had infiltrated with thousands more troops than he could take down. He had to move his soldiers from that place. Now he wondered whether the enemy should have rights to its comforts and conveniences. Could he go so far as to make their encampment useless? Possibly level it, if necessary? Burn it down? Destroy the southern tip? Yes, he believed that was the only way. He would leave the matter to Congress to decide.

The enemy, he feared, planned to enclose his army. If the British filled southern Manhattan Island and obtained control of King's Bridge to the north of his present location, his armed forces would be trapped in the middle, then cut to pieces.

Brigadier General Hugh Mercer rode up to him. He'd become a close confidant of George's over the twenty years they had known each other. George needed to discuss another location with him.

"Mercer, as I look to the west," George

viewed the Palisades across the Hudson, "it appears to me of the utmost importance to have a strong encampment at the post on the Jersey side of the North River, opposite our post. I think it advisable that you detach such a force from Amboy."

"Certainly, General," Mercer responded. "I will see to it. And General, there is news on the subject of government." His Scottish accent was detectable. "The honorable Philip Livingston —"

"Yes?"

"He is dead, General. Fainted from a dizzy spell in chambers. He died right there on his desk. There is word that the medical doctor, James Jay, will replace him as a representative of the Southern District in the New York Senate."

A crushing sound interrupted their discussion, for the massively long cart rolling the cheval flattened a large wooden post on the property. The engraved marker with the words *Mount Morris* was flattened below its wheels. As the cart moved past it, splintered pieces lay on the ground, any trace of the words obliterated.

CHAPTER THIRTY-EIGHT: BY ORDER OF GEORGE WASHINGTON

. . . I have nothing further to add, except a Wish, that the measures I have taken to dissipate a Storm, which had gathered so suddenly & unexpectedly, may be acceptable . . .

— GEORGE WASHINGTON

Harlem Heights

"Philip Livingston would have to die first," her brother had said. He was right. There was no telling what Senator James Jay would do to her and to her family.

Standing on the balcony of her mansion, she believed she was shielded from him, for now. She watched the military men pitching tents on her property. The general must be there among them, she thought. She searched as carefully as she could for auburn hair. She wondered what he looked like after all these years.

"He's a tall, handsome-bodied, manly

man," said Lulu as she arrived, carrying a rolled paper. "Just like Mum always said."

"Are you certain?"

"About my mum?"

"Well, no, that is what she always said. Are you for certain it was General George Washington?" Saying his name gave her a slight tingle.

" 'Twas him. But I was a wee girl last I seen 'im. Looked like the same to me."

She remembered that day when Lulu, such a sweet little child, standing at her mother's side, talked about the tale of the bluebird before Mary's first encounter with her charming.

Lulu handed her the packet she was holding. "I invited him, just like you asked. His cub asked me to bring this to you."

"His aide?"

"Sort of a dumplin' kind of fella — a bit of a short, thick man. Hugh Mercer was the name."

Hugh Mercer? Mary wondered if it could be the man she greeted long ago at that forsaken banquet on Christmas Eve. She had heard a Mercer was in New York. "Well, thank you, Lulu. You are very kind to do that for me."

"After all you's did for me? I'm forevers in your debt."

Mary smiled as she opened the correspondence. She immediately recognized the hand in which it was written — its slim upstrokes and larger downstrokes, made up of elegant loops and curves:

By order of George Washington:

Whereas a Bombardment and Attack upon the City of New York by our cruel and inveterate Enemy, may be hourly expected: And as there are great Numbers of Women, Children, and infirm Persons, yet remaining in the City, whose Continuance will rather be prejudicial than advantageous to the Army, and their Persons exposed to great Danger and Hazard: I Do therefore recommend it to all such Persons, as they value their own safety and Preservation, to remove with all expedition, out of the said Town, at this critical Period — trusting, that with the Blessing of Heaven upon the American Arms, they may soon return to it in perfect Security. And I do enjoin and require, all the Officers and Soldiers in the Army, under my Command, to forward and assist such Persons in their Compliance with this Recommendation.

A bombardment? An attack south of her mansion in the city could certainly leave one of her most prized possessions damaged or destroyed. She needed to depart at once to retrieve it from her town home on the southern tip of the island on Stone Street. She quickly made her way out of the mansion and toward the coach. She got in the driver's seat with her fine mare, Valentine, in front of her.

Chapter Thirty-Nine: Mary's Mansion

. . . evils of this nature work their own cure; tho' the remedy comes slower . . .

— GEORGE WASHINGTON

Mount Washington

He made a headquarters of Mary's Mansion. From here on the widow's walk, George could look out to monitor the movements of his forces. The massive estate in Harlem Heights offered a perfect view of each of the waterways around the island of New York City as well as the woods and fields. From the southern tip to this place, only one road was large enough for an army's wagons to travel. For the British, no other way was possible by land. They would have to pass through here to get to points north. George ordered impediments along the route. "Fell trees across the roads. Dig deep pits," he ordered his men. "Have it broken up and destroyed in such a manner as to render it utterly impassable."

Other defensive maneuvers were under way. The cheval was sunk into the Hudson. On land, the troops positioned themselves properly in preparation for an attack. The building of a fort at Jeffrey's Hook was under way.

Still, at this point, George's fear of failure exceeded his expectations of success. Nearly thirty thousand men made up the British lines. Add to that, they were fighting troops regularly trained, superior in arms and with battle experience. His were men who dragged themselves out of domestic life, not used to living encamped, inexperienced in arms, and without confidence. Would they be frightened by their own shadows when confronted? George believed it possible.

His numbers were insufficient. Even if he collected his divided army from Long Island, Governors Island, Powles Hook, Red Hook, and Horn's Hook into one body, it would still be wholly inferior against the enemy.

The months leading up to this point had been a failure militarily. The night before, the attack on the Royal Navy, underwater with the submersible, had failed to sink the *Eagle*.

At the battle across from the river on Long

Island, the British had outflanked his men. He would have lost Brooklyn, too, if the dense fog hadn't rolled in during a night-time retreat across the river. In great secrecy, they evacuated on any seagoing vessels they could find. Most were just rowboats. They were slow and small, but Providence sent a wind. They tarried until every last man crossed the East River. George left the fires burning and moved thousands of troops in silence across the water through the fog.

George turned to the doorway and moved to a gray-walled study with its moldings painted in a red as bold as the color of the British uniforms. George took a seat at the desk to write to Congress. He needed to tell them that the power of words could not even describe the impossible task before him. His army, as he looked at it, was broken. George began composing a letter to the president of Congress, John Hancock, in the forenoon.

> We are now encamped with the Main body of the Army on the Heights of Harlem, where I should hope the Enemy would meet with a defeat in case of an Attack, If the Generality of our Troops would behave with tolerable bravery, but experience to my extreme affliction has

convinced me that this is rather to be wished for than expected; However I trust, that there are many who will act like men, and shew themselves worthy of the blessings of Freedom. I have sent out some reconoitring parties to gain Intelligence If possible of the disposition of the Enemy and shall inform Congress of every material event by the earliest Opportunity.

A voice cried out from the hall: "Redcoats! Redcoats in the fields!"

George rushed out to the portico and looked through his spyglass. The British were advancing northward. George hurried to mount his stallion.

He found his colonels and ordered them to take 150 of the Rangers to investigate. He headed to the advanced posts, moving straight toward the enemy. He needed to assess the situation properly. For about two miles he rode, from the northernmost end of the camp to the southernmost. They had arrived. Thousands of them. The enemy was before him in large bodies of troops, moving from the southern tip to Harlem Heights. How this event would end, only God knew. The bullets whistled through the air.

Exchanges of gunfire erupted between the

British advance parties and the detachment that George sent out to investigate. A colonel raced up to him on horseback. "The advance party is in a skirmish, General. There's more of the enemy concealed."

One brigade was in a confused, disorderly jumble. His greatest fears of defeat were being realized. "Good God, have I got such troops as those!" shouted George. Men with no experience, no expertise, no willingness to take orders made up his ranks. George threw his hat to the ground in a furor. "Are these the men with which I am to defend America!"

George felt the ground shake below him.

"The redcoats are in hot pursuit, moving northward!" yelled a colonel.

That's when George heard them, the pounding of hooves. The enemy rushed downhill. This was followed by bugle calls — a quick series of pulsating double notes. The British were playing "Gone Away." The fox has left its refuge. The hunt is on. A mocking gesture to George.

George ordered a contingent from the New England regiments, volunteers who'd been farmers up until now, to face the enemy with him. They set out bravely, heroically. He wanted to draw the whole of the British units into the open field, cut them off from hiding in the extremity of the wooded areas. A feint attack at the front forced them out. He ordered another contingent to take to the trees. To George's surprise, the plan was working. The gunfire of his sharpshooters from nature's camouflage was easily hitting its targets. The British were falling in huge numbers.

Their forces wanted to entrap him. He entrapped them with a horseshoe offensive.

He ordered three companies of riflemen from Virginia to get to the rear of the enemy's lines. A larger force of additional Rangers reinforced by riflemen, this one led by Captain Hamilton, moved to the left. Another contingent took the right.

The enemy was trapped.

"Take the cornfield!" the general ordered.

His crew of a motley sort was winning.

Yes, the hunt *is* on.

Chapter Forty: Burn It Down

> Tho this place is under a cloud at present, I have no doubt but that it will Phoenix like again rise into consequence out of its own ashes —
>
> — GEORGE WASHINGTON

New York City

The little hand reached out to her. Mary grabbed it tightly, so tightly that she was nearly amazed at her strength. No mud spotted her shoes; Elbert's were polished to a shine. "There's no mud, Elbert." The boy smiled wide. The dirt could not touch them. The child's feet were above the ground. No way could he slip. No way could he fall into the river. The two of them turned their eyes to the water, so clear and glorious and blue. She could see all the way to the bottom. Across the still surface moved a reflection of black birds, ravens flying high, soaring, away from her, far away, even past the guardian's wall. Elbert's sparkling eyes turned back to her; they were aglow like an angel's before her.

A loud pounding distracted her. Mary wanted to get back to Elbert. The knocking grew heavier, more intense. "Please, let me go back to him," she whispered. Something was burning. She coughed to clear her throat. She jumped from her bed, awakened from her deep slumber by fire. She slipped on shoes, rushed out of her bedchamber with whatever gown she had on, and raced down the stairwell. Someone was knocking. She answered the door.

A stunned face looked back at her. "I saw a coach at your front." The soldier spoke to her calmly but with intensity. "Why are you here, madame?"

"It is my home."

"The city's on fire. We've been ordered to take you out of here."

"By whom?"

"Please, madame, we must go!"

Before leaving, Mary raced back into the parlor, grabbed a painting off the wall, wrapped it in a table covering, and left.

The scorching air smacked her in the face. The burning odor seeped into her nose. Her eyes stung. She shielded them with one hand. With the other, she clutched the covered canvas. She placed the painting in the coach and tried to climb on Valentine while covering her mouth to stop the taste of ash. The soldier told her to enter, that he would be her driver.

She refused this. He made way for her.

"An officer will lead you out."

"Your name?"

He jumped on a horse, headed in a southern direction. "Nathan Hale," he replied from a distance.

Her mare charged ahead, veering around the hellfire. The mighty inferno swallowed the homes across the road. Smoke poured out onto Stone Street. The wind carried flames toward her. The odor of charred wood was everywhere. On each road she passed, another home quartering British troops burned to ash.

As she rode on Broadway toward the northern end of Manhattan Island, the heat was intense. She watched as the British soldiers tried to put down the flames with Newsham engines. She'd seen them operate before — how they streamed water nearly 150 feet. This time, they appeared dry. No fire bells sounded. Not a fireman could be found anywhere.

Valentine never galloped this fast before. She looked back and saw the city behind her glowing orange, engulfed in flames.

She rode her way out of the ruins.

Hatred, indeed, moved to blood in New York. Was it the work of human hands? George must have known. The timing of his order. The broken engines. No firemen anywhere. How could he allow this to happen? Burn a city down. What kind of man would do such a thing! Yes, maybe they were right about him. How dare he! Burn it to the ground, she thought. She knew where he was. She would find him and speak her mind! "Make way!" She'd charge in. She wouldn't pay his guards any mind. "Where's the general?" She wouldn't wait for an answer. She'd demand his attention. "I have been disillusioned all these years by an idea of a man. Now I know what has been in my mind is distant from reality. You retreat and you burn!" He would return only a cold stare. "How do you not feel a deep sense of sympathy for a city that is now in ruins? Fire burned a third of this metropolis down! Who is responsible for this?"

"Providence — or some good honest fellow," he would say, "has done more for us than we were disposed to do for ourselves."

"And you will let this go without justice served!"

"Had I been left to the dictates of my own

judgment, New York should have been laid in ashes before I quitted it!"

"It's been burned to the ground!"

"Ah, yes, a new town is fast rising out of the ashes of the old."

She pulled the reins to stop Valentine where the road was blocked by a cluster of cannon. Ominous clouds rolled closer and looked ready to burst their storm upon her. A man in a hunting shirt and tricorn hat approached.

"By order of the general, the road to Mount Washington is not passable for a coach's travel. You must turn the other way," he commanded her.

"Mount Washington?"

"Yes, ma'am."

Had he changed the name of the estate from Mount Morris to Mount Washington? she wondered. "And where is this general, so that I may make a request personally?"

"Ma'am, he is in the mansion on Mount Washington. I'm ordering you to turn the other way."

"Mount Washington! This is my property! You turn the other way." She had never been so angry. "Let me through!"

Another man interceded. "Wait, please, madame." Both rushed to speak to another officer, who appeared to be of a higher rank.

For a time she waited and watched. Dark clouds that appeared ready to release their burden cast a shadow over Harlem Heights. Mount Washington? Is there no other land in all of the colonies he could have named his? Mount Washington. Revenge? Could it be? Questions swirled through her mind. She had sent him an invitation for tea, only.

In front of her, soldiers piled logs into stacks. A fort? Were they building a fort on her estate? Here? Yes, she would have plenty to say to him. She couldn't wait to see the general. He named her property Mount Washington! Now he was building a fort on it.

A soldier of higher rank approached her. "Oh." He stopped in his tracks. "Mary Eliza Philipse, my apologies."

"Mrs. Roger Morris," she said, correcting him.

"My name is Captain Hamilton. I will see to it that you are escorted safely to your home."

"I thank you, Captain Hamilton." She wanted to say more, but instead, she stayed quiet. She knew he was there — George.

She rode as fast as she could, trying to race past her escort; however, obstructions lay in the way. Trees. Deep pits. The road to her home was completely destroyed. She needed to follow the captain. She had no other choice. Thunder sounded. Drops, light ones, fell on her. She would tell the general her mind today!

She dismounted outside the portico of her mansion. Captain Hamilton was there to receive her horse. Six soldiers guarded the entrance. Mary grabbed the painting from the coach, adjusted the covering, and moved toward them with a quick step, shielding the canvas from the wetness. She was seething.

Inhaling a deep breath, Mary readied herself to fight for entrance into her own house.

Those guarding the entrance made way for her, greeting her kindly. No one stopped her. She found Lulu standing in the foyer; she helped her with the painting, which was almost bigger than Lulu.

"It near knocked me straight over."

"What did?"

"Shot right through the roof! Those redcoats!" hollered Lulu. "The cannonball. It came straight through the house. Left a hole right in the ceiling."

"A cannonball? You are all right, Lulu?"

"I told them the redcoats were comin'. I

saw them, 'cause I was standin' on the porch. They went straight out and stopped those coats from getting here, but the reds — they fired and fired and fired. Anyhows, it's in the basement — the cannonball — and they's covered the hole with wood and things."

"Thank God you are all right."

"We's won. The British went running from this place. We's won. Soldiers told me we brought them good luck. The general had his men protect me."

"General Washington?"

"Yes, the manly man."

"Where will I find him?"

Lulu pointed to the stairwell.

Mary swallowed hard and suddenly felt nervous. "I'll take the painting upstairs. We leave soon for Yonkers, Lulu. It's not safe for us to stay much longer." Mary checked her heart with her hand to be assured it hadn't leapt from her body. It was pounding hard now.

She climbed the steps to the second floor ever so slowly. A sensation ran from the very top of her head down to her toes. She expected a war meeting and loud, boisterous officers to be shouting orders at one another. Instead, only steady raindrops hitting the window made noise. The door to her study was partially open. She'd store the painting here. She walked in quickly.

She nearly lost her breath. General George Washington was seated right there in front of her, alone at her desk near the window. His hair, now cinnamon mixed with salt, fell carelessly over his broad shoulders. She scanned down his loose ivory linen shirt; it was tucked into his breeches, fitting snugly. His calves looked like tree trunks relative to the chair's slender wooden legs. Black shoes with gold buckles covered his large feet. Her eyes rose then to his sizable hands. It somehow felt so intimate, knowing her hands had been on the same wooden surface his now touched.

His writing hand stopped. He calmly placed down the quill and raised his head from the paper.

She got her mind to stay focused and willed away her desire. "You have taken on a Goliath." She spoke quietly.

Slowly, his face, with those familiar strong features, turned toward her. His eyes opened wide. He made no other move.

"Have you lost your mind? A fight against an empire?" As the words came out of her mouth, she didn't believe them herself. Only one man could defeat the British forces, and he was sitting right in front of her.

He was silent.

The pounding in her chest beat faster, in harmony with the drops outside the window, falling harder.

His immense frame lifted from the chair — a tall, handsome-bodied, manly man.

"All that is dear is at stake." His voice was gentle and sincere as he spoke.

A deep shooting pain in her core emerged; the ache that had been buried so long finally found the power to be felt.

"The spirit of freedom beat too high in me. The British nation deprived us of the most sacred and invaluable privileges . . . *justice . . . truth* . . . And to execute their scheme . . ." He paused. A hint of hardness took over his tone. "Nothing else would satisfy a tyrant and his diabolical ministry."

"And *you* will single-handedly force the English from the continent?" Indignation emerged in her voice.

His teeth clenched. She could tell from the muscles appearing at his jawline. He took a moment. She heard him exhale. Then he spoke. "Listen well to what I tell you and let it sink deep into your heart. We have punished the English and made them sorry for all the wicked things they had in their hearts to do. We have sworn to take vengeance on our enemies. We were determined to shake off all connections with a state so unjust, and unnatural."

She had to turn her face away from him. The two of them were standing feet apart, yet she could feel him as if he were pressed up against her.

"There can be no doubt that success will crown our efforts, if we firmly and resolutely determine to conquer . . . or to *die*!" His voice was firm.

Death, no, not death. Please. Not death, her mind yelled out. "To die?" Tears begged to be shed, but she turned them away. "To die?" She stared straight into him.

"I'll die on my feet before I'll live on my knees! I am a *warrior*!"

She recalled the daily prayers she said for him: Keep him alive. Angels, protect him. Don't let the curse find its way to him. Save him from me. Here he was in the flesh before her. Strong. Alive. Should she run the other way? Should she run as fast as she could into his arms? Something inside begged her: Love out loud. Love with no fear. Love the love that is right in front of you.

The storm intensified now, becoming furious. A rumble of thunder sounded.

She could sense him analyzing her. The painting gave her a moment to think. She clumsily tried to keep it from falling over, but she couldn't seem to calm the quivering of her hands. The covering fell away. She steadied the portrait finally, leaning it against a wall. She could say nothing. She feared her face flushed crimson, for the heat rushed to her cheeks. To think how the years passed, and still she felt the same for him.

George moved his gaze to the painting. He took his time with it. His eyelids lowered in a most romantic way. His mouth tilted into a half smile.

What lay hidden in the shadows of her soul now surfaced. "At what cost?" Honesty poured out of her. "At what cost, not to you, but to *me.* I've spent my life pained that I lost your heart. I've hardly been able to bear it." She could hold back her tears no longer. "Still now, decades later, I'm hardly able to bear it. Now you tell me that you are willing to give *your life*! And General Washington, I tell you, nothing else would satisfy 'a tyrant and his diabolical ministry' more than that."

He approached her, walking ever so slowly. "George." His shirt buttons, two of them, were open at his neck. It could have been seconds, but each step felt like an eternity.

With his fingers, he moved his long hair back, away from his face.

"George." She spoke in hushed tone, with her tears trailing. "For me, losing you entirely, that I could not endure."

He was a step away from her now. He reached over and moved a wet wave of hair to behind her shoulder, his hand touching her cheek as he did so. She caught a glimpse of his sun-burnished, exposed forearm. He smelled of soap mixed with brawn, perfectly combined. She recalled his words to her so long ago: " 'Twas perfect love before, but how I do adore." Had she said this aloud? She hoped it was not so.

All she could see was him.

All he could see was her.

The woman who still appeared the belle of the North was before him. The woman who had fallen asleep in his arms those years ago. The shadows of age had not reached her. Her warm, sweet breath fanned the skin on his arm. The blush on her cheeks tugged at his heart. She still smelled the same: lavender. Her damp hair fell free. Her dark eyes shone love, true love, the same as before. The thoughts of Mary Eliza, and the desire for her, were never quenched.

Everything about her was the same as before, everything except for her choice of clothing. As she peered down at herself, in only a nightdress, with moistened fabric from the rain clinging to her skin, a panicked look appeared on her face. Her beautifully arched eyebrows rose high. She stepped back from him and shook her head. An embarrassed tilt appeared on her mouth. Mary turned and walked away from him, toward the door.

The sound of thunder pierced the room. George turned toward the window. Lightning flashed. When he turned back, her eyes with those slightly tilted eyelashes were staring at him, scanning every inch of him. Her hand touched the doorknob.

Alone with George. She had waited so long for this moment. Envisioned what he would look like. What he would feel like. Every detail of him she had stored in her mind. Nothing had changed. The same hero of the South was before her. Their years apart mattered not. Nothing felt so right as this. She never let go of her affection for him, never let go of the kiss that had no end. Even now, she felt a oneness between them. His caress upon the nape of her neck — she wanted to experience it again. His lips placing soft kisses on her cheeks, his strength lifting her from the ground. She wanted more. More of him. More of them.

She closed the door.

They remained gazing at each other. It was long ago that he had come to realize a simple truth — she was his and he was hers. Then a soft smile appeared on her face — one dimple on the right, one on the left. He watched her turn the key to lock the door.

"The world can never know," she whispered wistfully.

Mary Eliza returned to him.

Chapter Forty-One: The Heart of Neutral Ground

You know the value of secrecy in an expedition circumstanced like this.

— GEORGE WASHINGTON

Valentine's Hill, Yonkers

Never could George remember a time in his life when he was in such a divided state. The war moved George to Yonkers. George made his headquarters on Valentine's Hill, on the northern pasture of the Philipse property, where he once enjoyed time with Mary Eliza under a meridian sun.

George stood atop this highest point of town. From here, he viewed Philipse Manor; she was there, safe. He would keep it that way, order his men to safeguard this property, consider it the heart of neutral ground.

Earlier this day, George traveled with Blueskin along the main roads leading here to make an inspection of them. He ordered they be lined with stone fences. The adjacent fields needed to be divided off with stone as well. He had good reason. Narrow paths would make it impossible for British wagons of ammunition and artillery to pass or would at least slow their pace. He remembered how all those years ago General Braddock had leveled every molehill to allow his wagons to pass. George surmised the British would do the same now — make the roads proper for travel.

Every other route, he entrenched with a line of camps and ordered troops to slaughter any redcoat who passed.

The preceding days proved chaotic. Enemies don't succumb easily. On the Hudson River, the unthinkable transpired nights before. In the waters off Philipse Manor, four British warships, including the *Phoenix* and the *Rose,* fired their cannons. George ordered vessels, including one sloop of a hundred tons, the other packed with combustibles, a small craft, and two galleys, to face them — nowhere near the immensity of their warships. It was the best he had. The forces grappled for hours. Conflagration laid waste to two of the Royal Navy's warships. One sank. The other disentangled itself. The warships retreated. The British dropped down the river, headed for New York Harbor.

Without any true warships of their own, the American forces proved victorious in this battle, one of the first solely aquatic engagements of the war, here off Mary's property in Yonkers. His first victory on land, that, too, took place on her property in Harlem Heights. It was as if the finger of Providence had a hand in both, blinding the eyes of the enemy. The British were closing in fast. A few days would determine the course of this war. What became abundantly clear to him was that this contest would not be easy nor swift. How long the duration, he did not know.

Now George gripped the hilt of his brother's sword. What the British had done to him, to them, to the colonies, this needed to be rectified. How could a man of virtue hesitate in the least in making the choice to lead this fight? He was more determined than ever to end their hold.

What he did know for certain was that he was up against an empire whose resources were nothing short of inexhaustible, a force whose fleets covered the ocean's waters. Soldiers who had harvested laurels across the globe were his opponents. What did he have?

No preparation.

No money.

Not nearly enough men or supplies.

What he did have was the resolve to win.

Here on Valentine's Hill, with a sunrise emitting bold colors of hope, George removed Lawrence's sword from its sheath. Untrodden ground was beneath his feet. Destiny was calling him to a greater purpose. Where it would take him, he was not certain.

George placed a knee to the ground and prayed aloud. "The Lord God of Gods, the Lord God of Gods, He Knoweth, and Israel. He shall know; if it be in rebellion, or if in transgression against the Lord, save us not this day."

George rose with an unconquerable spirit. Revolution was calling him. He stood ready to fulfill the high destinies that Heaven appeared to have intended for him, and for all of America.

Freedom was in his grasp.

Chapter Forty-Two: Let Freedom Ring

. . . truth will ultimately prevail where pains is taken to bring it to light.

— GEORGE WASHINGTON

Hudson River

Cry out. Throw yourself into the water. Shed a tear.

Nothing.

Mary just stood there unsteadily, letting herself be rocked by the currents. Her pale fingertips grasped the side of the sailing vessel. She felt the worn, dry wood scraping against her hands. Leaning over the rail, she took a hesitant breath of sea air. Her body did not violently protest as she supposed it would. You fear the water, she thought. On this morning, she stared straight down into the dark vastness, watching a single wave as it rose and as it fell.

Along the shoreline of what was her home, the autumn tones of the leaves looked like a necklace of gold, curving up and down rolling hills. She never viewed the land like this before, by boat. The property carried farther than the eye could see. She wondered whether she had explored every acre. Nevermore could she place her feet upon the fresh, tender grasses that tickled her toes or put her nose into the fragrant, curved petals that effloresced her hope.

The days passed now. George moved north of Yonkers. He hadn't left without a promise. "Not a battle scar will this place see," his aide told her. "It will remain the heart of neutral ground."

Mary escaped alone when the ship's horn blew — one long sound, followed by two in quicker succession. She knew the day had come. Her entire family scrambled for their lives, not because of the war, but because of the beast. She would not dare name him. She would not give him the dignity. Beverley and Susannah rushed to their estate in the Highlands, where Benedict Arnold was encamped, and pledged to protect them; Beverley planned to start his own regiment, made up of indentured servants and slaves. Sir Tenoe would return to New York to join and wrote Mary that he'd have *Liberty to Slaves!* embroidered on the uniforms. Frederick would soon be headed east toward

Long Island. Temperance and François vowed they would care for the manor as best they could, believing firmly the Philipse family would return. Lulu stayed with Nathaniel Gist, who gave his word that he would keep her safe inside the Sherwood house. This disappointed Mary; however, she had no time to convince Lulu otherwise. Men, radicals, were coming for Mary, coming for the traitors.

The Act of Attainder would not remain in place, the general's aide told her. A captain in George's army, Alexander Hamilton, already spoke out against the New York legislation, which with one vote charged, tried, and convicted her and her family of treason, without proof. Maybe this law, the harshest ever passed in any colony, would one day be reversed.

Or maybe all was lost.

She might have stayed a day or so longer, if not for George's letter to the family. One simple, cordial line was written to her. She interpreted this as his signal to her to make an immediate escape. If they found her in the colony, the attainder ordered that she be put to death. But leaving this place, how could she leave, leave her mother? Mary remained by the Hudson for this very reason. In the waves is where she left her.

In the same waves, she was leaving her again.

Before her, sunset's reflection of oranges and pinks set the river on fire. The flames lobbed to and fro.

What would her father think of everything that had happened? She couldn't imagine he would have ever let this come to pass. "Be the light, Mary Eliza," he had told her. Papa, I tried my best. My best wasn't good enough, she thought. Every day, she recited the pledge she promised him she would say: "You are capable of the impossible, for you have survived the unthinkable." Maybe Papa was wrong.

She saw the legal notices, stating judicial recourse was forbidden. Everything would be confiscated — the manors, the land, the mills, the bridge, the barns. Auctioned off to the highest bidder, and just like that, all these would vanish from their hands. The confiscations began with the animals. The sheep fetched thirty-one shillings each. Mary, with her head covered by her cape, nearly ran onto the stage to protest when they were accepting only three shillings for poor Valentine. She was weak and old, yes, but a good horse, solid in physique and gentle in temperament. Mary always felt safe with Valentine, just as she had in the embrace of the one who had given her the mare.

Wind moved the *Gabriel,* faster, farther.

She felt too heartbroken to think further about Valentine or her valentine today. She would put those out of her mind. She closed her eyes, hoping the darkness would wash away the treacherous label forced upon her.

"Traitor! Traitor!"

The words repeated in her head. What had she done wrong?

Nothing.

Take her home. Take her property. Take every last one of her possessions. With everything gone, maybe she could finally let go.

Nothing.

That is what she was. No longer an heiress. No longer a landowner. No longer the belle of the colony. She was nothing. During her entire life, she had always tried to hide from it, shoo it away, ignore it, fight it. None of that mattered; fate is foreordained.

Forget.

She wanted to tear pages out of her memory and watch them sink in the depths of the river.

A sudden breeze sent a chill through her. The hairs on her arms stood up. She was cold. Captain Garvan rushed over to her.

Such kindness from a man who knew she could offer him no compensation. Here he was saving her again. In the decades she had known him, he had never asked anything from her.

Another man never asked for anything but her love. The moments with him she treasured. Would she have to forget even George? How could she not cherish the tender passions that rendered her whole in his arms? No, these pages of her life she would remember and protect. They would not see the river's floor, nor would the world discover what she desperately wanted to conceal. Not today. Centuries should pass without the truth's being revealed.

What she wanted now was in her trunk. She refused to leave the item behind. The captain helped her over to the chest crafted from the land's robust oaks. He had wrapped the trunk in canvas and secured it with rope to be sure no harm would come to it. Trying to keep her balance, she knelt down next to it, watching him unravel the protective covering. She undid the silver latch.

She opened it and removed the quilt with frayed edges that lay inside. Mary had kept this safe for decades. The captain smiled. He remembered. He wrapped her in the blanket of blue flowers when he rescued her as a little girl.

Taking the blanket from her, he opened it wide and waited to embrace her in it.

About to close the trunk, curiosity begged her to look deeper. Below were her beloved things: her mother's psalmbook and the diadem with her mother's face in ivory, which Mary had quickly wrapped in silk. Beneath that was the wooden box Frederick handed to her moments before she made her escape. She hadn't had time to examine the contents. Within it she expected there to be currency. Instead, she found a pile of folded papers. Dozens of letters. She carefully removed one. As she straightened the folds, she recognized the writing immediately. The script displayed thin upstrokes and wide downstrokes of loops and curves.

Her mind began to race.

Papers from George. They were dated 1756. Had they been written then and never delivered to her? She watched as her deep breath dissipated in the air. Had he held these from her — Frederick? She worked her brain hard, trying to remember the details. Mary recalled the heartache as she had waited for George to return, without any word, not a note, that he was alive, that he would return. Negotiations had to be done in person; she remembered her brother remaining firm on this, clearly firm on this. Then Captain Morris, playing guard, staying close. They had deceived her. They had defamed George, vilified him. They had kept them apart so that another could possess her. The truth was clear now. She wanted to turn the boat around and release a fury on her brother. She wanted to race after George and tell him . . . tell him the truth of what had happened! And what? Stop a revolution?

Mary's eyes fell to the writing before her. He'd written the lines from Thomson's "Spring":

'Tis Love creates their Melody, and all
This Waste of Music is the Voice of Love;
That even to Birds, and Beasts, the tender
Arts
Of pleasing teaches. . . .

But now the feather'd Youth their former
Bounds,
Ardent, disdain; and, weighing oft their
Wings,
Demand the free Possession of the
Sky. . . .

On Ground

Alighted, bolder up again they lead,
Farther and farther on, the lengthening
Flight;
Till vanish'd every Fear, and every Power
Rouz'd into Life and Action, light in Air
Th' acquitted Parents see their soaring
Race,
And once rejoicing never know them more.

Her eyes opened to see them — ravens soaring above. They were flying away, past the Palisades, beyond the earth formation that she had always considered her protector — the guardian's wall.

A power greater than her took control. She had to accept this. Accept everything.

George. He had more to do. Providence, she was sure, had him marked for a great purpose.

Garvan got down next to her. "Breathe, Mary. Breathe." He covered her in the quilt.

The sun's rays shone brightly on the water ahead. She watched them, the birds, taking possession of the sky, flying far into the light, flying free. This was her chance, maybe for the first time. Yes, the first time. When you are nothing . . . this is when you will be like a Phoenix rising from the ashes. A new beginning.

They called her traitor. She'd refuse the title.

They showed her hatred. She'd find love.

They took everything, leaving her not even a pence in her pocket, but she knew that no being can be poor who is rich in spirit.

Underneath the papers was something more. A smaller box, decorated as a gift. Her fingers fumbled with it. This must have been from him. As she lifted the lid, her breath stopped. Inside was the softest of velvet bags tied at the top with a satin string. Carefully, with a trembling hand, she undid the bow. One hand cradled the bag; two fingers reached within. She removed a posy ring. She brought it into the light. Her eyes focused closely to read the inscription along the interior rim. The hidden message came through with clarity — words that touched her deeply. She reread the line as the weight that had held her down for so long, for too long, finally released her.

She realized her truth and finally knew who she really was. She was *Mary Eliza,* and she was enough.

As long as there was breath on her lips, she decided right then, she would live.

In her hands, destiny was etched into metal: *Where there is love, there is freedom.*

ACKNOWLEGMENTS

First and foremost, I would like to thank the power of curiosity, for this is what propelled me to search, physically and digitally, through dusty basements and attics, as well as storage units in libraries, museums, historic sites, and churches. Words cannot express my gratitude to the lovers of history who for centuries have kept the records. Through these thousands of documents, this story emerged. Special thanks to the University of Virginia for the comprehensive collection of the Papers of George Washington, the Library of Congress, the New York Public Library, the New-York Historical Society, George Washington's Mount Vernon, Harvard University's Houghton Library, the Huntington Library, the Morris-Jumel Mansion, the Philipse Manor Hall State Historic Site, the Costume Institute at the Metropolitan Museum of Art, from which fashion throughout the manuscript was drawn, Yonkers City Hall, the Sherwood House Museum, St. John's Episcopal Church, the Historic Hudson Valley, the Boston Public Library, the Fraunces Tavern Museum, Jeffrey's Hook Lighthouse, the Hudson River Museum, Old Dutch Church, St. Joseph's Seminary, the Van Cortland Manor House Museum, and countless others.

Boundless thank-yous to my wise and brilliant editor, Elizabeth Beier. If not for you and publisher extraordinaire Steve Cohen, this story may have never made it into ink. To the whole team at St. Martin's Press — Paul Hochman, Michelle Cashman, Leah Johanson, Clare Maurer, Meg Drislane, Donna Sinisgalli Noetzel, Kerri Resnick, Jennifer Donovan, Carol Edwards, Carly Sommerstein, and Laura Starrett — my gratitude. Over the years, numerous individuals have had a profound impact on my career, most especially my longtime agent and dear friend, Sandy Montag. Thanks also to Peter Dunn, David Friend, Tony Petitti, and Janine Rose.

My sanity might have been lost somewhere between the first and second page if not for my family. To my husband, Michael, if not for your inauguration as mayor of Yonkers, New York, this story may never have been discovered. Thank you for believing in me, encouraging me, and motivating me. It's meant the world to me. To my writing and research assistants, otherwise known as my children, Michael, Alexandra, and Christopher, you are our everything. To the great bunch of relatives who read and read and offered suggestions and propped me up, and even found the title for this novel over Sunday dinner, my gratitude to the Calvi family, the Spano family, the Ragone family, and the Circosta family — thank you for your suggestions, your research, and your patience. I adored our readings by the bay and our laughs over wine and cheese.

To my dear friends Alexandrea Denis and Andrea Smyth, your joy is infectious — thank you for joining with me on this adventure and helping to bring this story to life. To the many, many others, including Josyane Colwell, Danielle Parker, Dana Tyler, Nancy Montag, and Michael Downs, thank you from the bottom of my heart.

To all of you in my hometown of Yonkers, New York, I am forever in your debt.

RESOURCES

Custis, George Washington Parke, 1781–1857. *Recollections and Private Memoirs of Washington.* New York: Derby & Jackson, 1860.

Flick, Alexander Clarence, 1869–1942. *Loyalism in New York During the American Revolution.* New York: Columbia University Press, 1901.

Glasse, Hannah, 1708–1770. *The Art of Cookery Made Plain and Easy.* London: Prospect Books, 1983.

Grose, Francis, 1731?–1791. *A Classical Dictionary of the Vulgar Tongue.* London: S. Hooper, 1785.

Hall, Edward Hagaman, 1858–1936. *Philipse Manor Hall at Yonkers, N.Y.: The Site, the Building and Its Occupants.* New York: American Scenic and Historic Preservation Society, 1912.

Irving, Washington, 1783–1859. *The Life of*

Washington. New York: John W. Lovell, 1855.

Jefferys, Charles W. (Charles William), 1869–1951, Gerhard Richard Lomer, and Allen Johnson. *The Chronicles of America Series.* Roosevelt, ed. New Haven: Yale University Press, 1919.

L. & V., "The Virginia-Centinel. No. X." *The Maryland Gazette,* November, 25, 1756: 1. Print.

Manuscripts and Archives Division, The New York Public Library. "George Washington notebook as a Virginia colonel," The New York Public Library Digital Collections. 1757. http://digitalcollections.nypl.org/items/18d75990-8319-0132-56d7-58d385a7bbd0.

———. "Lawrence Washington letter to unknown person," The New York Public Library Digital Collections. 1749. http://digitalcollections.nypl.org/items/f13a2b90-e23d-0133-0b0f-00505686a51c.

Morris, Rogers. Letters to Mary Philipse Morris, 1775–1777, Morris Jumel Archives, New York.

Pargellis, Stanley McCrory, 1898–1968. *Lord Loudoun in North America.* New Haven, Conn.: Yale University Press, 1933.

Parkman, Francis, 1788–1852. *Montcalm and Wolfe.* Boston: Little, Brown and

Company, 1884.
Sargent, Winthrop, 1825–1870. *The History of an Expedition Against Fort Du Quesne, In 1755: Under Major-General Edward Braddock.* Philadelphia: For the Historical Society of Pennsylvania, 1856.
Sparks, Jared, 1789–1866. *The Life of George Washington.* New York: Miller, Orton & Mulligan, 1856.
Timothy Scandal Adjutant, "A Return of the State of Capt. Polly Philips's Dependant Compny, with the Kill'd, Wounded, Deserted, and Discharg'd &c, during the Campaigns 1756 & 1756 (sic)," December 25, 1756, LO 6475, Huntington Library, San Marino, California.
Washington, George, 1732–1799. *The Journal of Major George Washington: Sent by the Hon. Robert Dinwiddie to the Commandant of the French Forces in Ohio.* New York: Reprinted for J. Sabin, 1865.
———. *The Writings of George Washington from the Original Manuscript Sources, 1745–1799.* Washington, D.C.: U.S. Government Printing Office, 193144.
———. *The Writings of George Washington: Being His Correspondence, Addresses, Messages, and Other Papers, Official and Private.* Boston: Little, Brown, 1858.

———. *Washington's Rules of Civility and Decent Behavior in Company and Conversation: A Paper Found Among the Early Writings of George Washington. Copied from the Original with Literal Exactness.* Washington, D.C.: W. H. Morrison, 1888.

———. George Washington Papers, Series 1, Exercise Books, Diaries, and Surveys -99, Subseries 1A, Exercise Books -1747: School Copy Book, Volume 1. 1745. Manuscript/Mixed Material. Retrieved from the Library of Congress, www.loc.gov/item/mgw1a.002/.

———. A.L.s.to [Sally Cary Fairfax]; Camp at Fort Cumberland, 12 Sep 1758., 1758. Susan Dwight Bliss autograph collection, MS Fr 167 (57). Houghton Library, Harvard College Library.

Washington, George, and William W. Abbot. *The Papers of George Washington, Colonial Series,* vol. 1–10. Charlottesville: University Press of Virginia, 1993.

Watson, John F., 1779–1860. *Annals of Philadelphia and Pennsylvania, in the Olden Time: Being a Collection of Memoirs, Anecdotes, and Incidents of the City and Its Inhabitants, and of the . . . Inland Part of Pennsylvania from the Days of the Founders,* 2d ed. Philadelphia: Penington, 1844–1843.

Whipple, Wayne, 1856–1942. *The Story of Young George Washington.* Philadelphia: H. Altemus, Co., 1918.
Wilson, Woodrow. "Colonel Washington." *Harper's New Monthly Magazine,* no. 550, March 1896.

FURTHER READING

Aulnoy, Madame d', 1650 or 1651–1705. *The Fairy Tales of Madame D'Aulnoy.* New ed., with additional illustrations. London: Lawrence and Bullen, 1898.

Chaucer, Geoffrey, d. 1400. *The Complete Works of Geoffrey Chaucer.* Oxford [Oxfordshire]: Clarendon Press, 1894–1900.

Dryden, John, 1631–1700. *The Poems of John Dryden.* London: Oxford University Press, 1935.

Hemstreet, Charles, b. 1866. *The Story of Manhattan.* New York: Charles Scribner's Sons, 1901.

Hoyle, Edmond, 1672–1769. *A Short Treatise on the Game of Whist: Containing the Laws of the Game, and Also Some Rules . . . Bath.* For W. Webster, 1743.

Johnson, Samuel, 1709–1784. *A Dictionary of the English Language: In Which the Words Are Deduced from Their Originals, and Illustrated in Their Different Significations by Examples from the Best Writers, to Which Are Prefixed, a History of the Language, and an English Grammar.* London: Printed by W. Strahan, 1755.

Jones, Thomas, 1731–1792. *History of New York During the Revolutionary War: And of the Leading Events in the Other Colonies at That Period.* New York: Printed for the New-York Historical Society, 1879.

Kirkwood, Agnes E. *Church and Sunday-school Work in Yonkers: Its Origin and Progress.* New York: G. L. Shearer, 1889.

La Chapelle, Vincent. *Le Cuisinier Moderne: Qui Apprend à Donner Toutes Sortes De Repas, en Gras & En Maigre, D'une Manière Plus Délicate Que Ce Qui en a été écrit Jusqu'à Présent: Divisé en Cinq Volumes, avec de Nouveaux Modéles de Vaiselle, & des Desseins de Table dans Le Grand Goût D'aujourd'hui, Gravez en Taille-douce,* 2d ed., rev., corr. & augm. La Haye: V. La Chapelle, 1742.

Markham, Gervase, 1568?–1637. *Markham's Master-piece Revived: Containing All Knowledge Belonging to the Smith, Farrier, or Horseleach, Touching the Curing All Diseases in Horses.* London: Printed for John Wright and Thomas Passinger (12th print-

ing), 1681.
Morris, Richard. *Flora Conspicua.* London: Printed for Longman, Rees, Orme, Brown and Green, 1826.
Tomlinson, Kellom, 1690–1753. *The Art of Dancing explained by reading and figures whereby the manner of performing the steps is made easy by a new and familiar method.* London: Printed for the author, 1735.
Thomson, James, 1700–1748. *The Seasons: A Poem.* Boston: Crosby and Nichols, 1862.
Winchilsea, Anne (Kingsmill) Finch, countess of, 1661–1720. [from old catalog]. *The Poems of Anne, Countess of Winchilsea.* Chicago: University of Chicago Press, 1903.

ABOUT THE AUTHOR

Mary Calvi spent years wondering about the heiress who lived in the grand manor in her hometown of Yonkers, New York. Curiosity propelled her to do her own research. This novel is based on what she uncovered. Calvi is a nine-time New York Emmy award-winning journalist at WCBS-TV. She serves as a New York television anchor and reporter. Mary is also First Lady of the city of Yonkers where she serves as a member of the board of Hudson River Museum. This is her first novel.

The employees of Thorndike Press hope you have enjoyed this Large Print book. All our Thorndike, Wheeler, and Kennebec Large Print titles are designed for easy reading, and all our books are made to last. Other Thorndike Press Large Print books are available at your library, through selected bookstores, or directly from us.

For information about titles, please call:
(800) 223-1244

or visit our website at:
gale.com/thorndike

To share your comments, please write:
Publisher
Thorndike Press
10 Water St., Suite 310
Waterville, ME 04901